The Reclamation Project

By

Ruth Marie Davis

AmErica House
Baltimore

2001 by Ruth Marie Davis.
All rights reserved. No part of this book may be reproduced in any form without written permission from the publishers, except by a reviewer who may quote brief passages in a review to be printed in a newspaper or magazine.

First printing

ISBN: 1–58851–292–4
PUBLISHED BY AMERICA HOUSE BOOK PUBLISHERS
www.publishamerica.com
Baltimore

Printed in the United States of America

Dedication

This work is dedicated to my father, Ralph,
who taught me that my dreams are only
realities that have yet to happen.

Thank you Daddy,
for proving that while any man can be a father,
it takes a really special man to be a Dad.
You will always be my greatest hero.

I would also like to dedicate this book
to the veterans of the United States of
America, for their many sacrifices in
the pursuit of freedom and justice, and
to those who lost their lives in the attack
on the World Trade Center. May we
ever remain one nation under God.

Acknowledgements

A very special "Thank You" to Mr. John Dunne of Voyage Magazine in the United Kingdom for his continued support, guidance and inspiration, and to Priscilla Welch of Priscilla's Photography in Yuba City, CA., for snapping my photos on literally 'a moment's notice.' Also, to Larry Landis for the laptop without which this book would never have been written, and last but certainly not least, to my big fat cat Trenton, who laid by my side as I wrote and winked at me often.

The Reclamation Project

PROLOGUE

Tutankhamun stood just behind the creature, a smug, yet somehow uncertain smirk on his unusually puffy face. At first, Lindsey thought he had darkened his lower lids with kohl, but then realized that his eye sockets were just horribly dark underneath...as though he were ill.

From behind the sickly, smirking Tut stepped yet another creature, nearly identical to the one who now stood only inches from Lindsey's face, forcing her gaze upon him as his glassy eyes blinked side to side like that of a lizard.

Opening her mouth to scream, Lindsey was horrified when no sound came forth. The slanted gaze and hideous countenance consumed her as she stood before the man–creature. His bluish–green skin covered in small, barely definable scales glinted in the muted glow of the room behind him.

With sweat rolling down her temples, and blood drying on her legs and knees, Lindsey tried desperately to tear her riveted gaze from the yellow eyes of this demon whose stare seemed to be rendering her body incapable of obeying the commands of her mind.

"So like the sons and daughters of man," hissed the creature slowly, his 'S's lingering long after the words had been spoken. "When in the face of fear, your first instinct is to pull away and run, instead of standing and fighting for your own puny lives...."

She couldn't breathe; she had lost her baby and would die here at the hands of this hideous creature. Too weak to defend herself against the attack, Lindsey went limp and submitted to her own death.

Chapter One

June 7, 2250

Glen Steiner spun around in his chair, the disbelief, mingled with pure excitement, still visible on his aquiline features. His vintage glasses had slipped down to the base of his slim nose, causing his bushy black eyebrows to stand out even starker against his pale skin.

"Do you know what this means Kevin!" Glen's excitement was almost palpable, "Have you got any idea what technological advancements are in the making here?"

Kevin grinned at Glen's childlike exuberance, although his own pulse had been pounding at the speed of light since they'd received the news. He opened his mouth to speak just before Glen cut him off.

"Why Kevin?" he asked. "Why all of the sudden, out of nowhere…." His voice trailed off mid-sentence and his eyes took on a glazed, almost maniacal light. Pushing his wandering, black framed glasses back up the bridge of his nose, he let out a low whistle.

Kevin no more had the answer to that question than Glen did. His sandy blond brows drew together as he squinted in the never–bright–enough, artificial light of the lab, giving him the temporary appearance of being much older than his thirty–seven years. This was beyond anything he'd ever thought possible, but there it was, the authorization…signed, sealed and delivered as the old cliché went, right from President Albanion's desk. The first female president of the United States was making quite the name for herself. His blue eyes met Glen's brown ones, and unsaid words were spoken between them. History was being made and they were right there on the ground floor.

Before their respective noses, was the document granting them the legal right to conduct human cloning experiments…years and years of experiments that had begun back in the 1990's with Dolly the sheep were about to come to fruition. This was truly a scientist's dream in the making. Of course, there were many who would not accept the fact that their work would be perfectly legal; it was the morality of these experiments that had been questioned by the churches, among several other organizations and individuals. Still, how could the world and its inhabitants turn away from such technology? How could they ever expect to progress, ever achieve such invaluable knowledge without experimentation?

Glen's mind was on overload. He had been working and conducting experiments in microbiology, gene splicing and cloning since graduation and that was a good number of years ago. He remembered in his college days, learning about the DNA samples taken from some Egyptian mummies back in 1999…over two hundred and fifty years ago. Finally, finally, the chance to clone a human being.

Why in the world this authorization had come with the explicit instruction that the first, legal humanoid cloning attempts were to be conducted on ancient Egyptian mummies, was beyond anything he or Kevin could either one begin to comprehend. Theirs was not to know why, but to do. Who could second guess the mind set of the government anyway?

Kevin broke Glen's train of thought, "God, I wonder what old Howard Carter and Lord Carnavon would think about this!"

"Hell, Kev," replied Glen, his glasses making their usual slow descent down the bridge of his nose, "I'm not even sure what I think about this. I'm not entirely certain I can think at all right now."

"Yeah, I know what you mean, my friend." Kevin felt as frazzled as Glen looked, "It's like your mind is spinning a mile a minute, attempting to focus on a million different aspects of this thing, and not quite latching on to any of it. Hell, just the initial steps will be fascinating beyond words. Can you imagine watching these people grow up and mature into adulthood?" Kevin spoke as much to himself as he did to Glen.

"They certainly were adamant in the meeting about us being sworn to secrecy. Of course, that's not something I have to worry about." Glen shook his head and sighed, "I hardly leave this place anymore. I probably couldn't find my way back to my apartment if I tried to."

Kevin knew Glen well enough, especially after having worked in such close proximity to him for the past ten years. He knew Glen virtually lived at the lab, although he wasn't quite sure if it was because Glen was so dedicated to his work, or if it simply boiled down to the fact that he didn't have much to go home to. Kevin, on the other hand, always made it a point to enjoy at least one day a weekend…workload permitting. He'd invited Glen to dozens of social gatherings and excursions, but Glen seldom ever accepted his overtures of friendship outside the lab. 'Hell,' he thought, 'what's wrong with asking again, the worst Glen could do is render his usual declination.'

"Well Glen," grinned Kevin, "we're going to have a lot of work ahead of us. What do you say we go have a drink to celebrate?" He saw the vaguest interest flash across Glen's face, only to be quickly replaced by a slow shake of his head. That momentary flash encouraged Kevin, "Come on Glen, its Friday night. You work twenty hours a day and sleep in the staff lounge as it is. Once we start this new project we probably won't either one see the light of day for quite some time."

Glen glanced toward the paperwork and myriad of specimens on his desk awaiting his attention, and Kevin, knowing what Glen would say next, cut him off before he had the chance, "Don't bother telling me you have too much work to do. You know as well as I do that you can't think past your own eyes right now. I say we go out for a couple of drinks, unwind a bit, and rest up over the weekend. We'll be launching into utter madness first thing Monday morning."

Glen ran his fingers through his still more black than gray hair and rose with a sigh, reaching for his street jacket, which was hanging in its usual place; haphazardly over the back of his chair. He traded it for his lab coat and threw Kevin a rare grin, his glasses finally having reached the very tip of his nose. "You're a convincing man Kevin, and to be honest, I don't have the strength to either resist or argue." Glen shook his head slowly, he supposed there wasn't anything wrong with taking a break or having a drink …and at that moment, he needed both.

Glen walked across the room to the floor safe and tucked the authorization letter safely inside until it could be copied and disbursed throughout the necessary channels. Almost all the equipment had been readied in advance, even though they hadn't really believed there was a snowball's chance in hell of the authorization actually coming through. It wouldn't be long before they were underway and history would be made.

"Come on Glen, it's already late…let's get a move on." Kevin's Cheshire–cat grin belayed the tone of his words. "Let's go take in some action."

Glen smiled to himself. The 'action' he preferred wasn't quite the same as what Kevin would be looking for, but he supposed he could do with some down time just the same. Glen had never really been able to figure Kevin out. This tall, blond scientist, who at thirty–seven years old was an equal in knowledge to scientists more than twice his age, with twice as much experience. It was well known that Kevin had graduated from medical school at the age of twenty–four and had gone on to pursue doctorates in molecular biology and forensic anthropology.

It was also rumored that Kevin Sanders was gay. He never seemed to pay attention to any of the female employees at IBAT, above and beyond the professional, working relationships…and IBAT, the common abbreviation for the Institute of Biotechnology and Advanced Technogenetics, employed some very attractive female assistants, couriers and clerks.

Glen and Kevin had met four years previously when Kevin had accepted a position, and transferred to California from the firms' sister corporation in Florida. Kevin certainly did not look like most scientists…at least not like any Glen had ever met. In fact, he looked more like someone you might see in a movie, or modeling the newest designer wear. His slightly curly, sandy bond hair was cut a bit longer than any of his male colleagues and his body suggested that he worked out at least semi–regularly. There wasn't much exercise to be gleaned from working in the genetics lab. Kevin's skin tone was also a bit darker than the predominantly pale countenances of the other staff members. It seemed that he managed to entertain a bit more sun exposure in his life than most of his counterparts. Since air quality was far too poor to be outside for more than an hour or two, Glen could only assume that Kevin utilized the 'Sun Center,' a huge building with the simulated warming rays of the sun, and a man–made ocean, complete with waves and sand.

In any event, there certainly was no wife, or any children waiting at home for Glen. His work, simply speaking, was his life. He knew though, that Kevin Sanders wasn't gay. He knew it the minute their eyes had met. He would have recognized that. In truth, he had found himself secretly hoping that he would…he didn't. Kevin was as 'straight' as they came…he was just too serious about his work to make goo–goo eyes at any of the female employees.

The doors to Kevin's sporty Centurian slid open with a barely audible 'whoosh,' and they settled comfortably in the semi–prone, body–molding seats. The ultra feminine voice of the control center greeted Kevin with a welcome that was nothing less than flirtatious.

"Where do you wish me to take you to Kevin?" purred the computer.

"Sal's place please," replied Kevin cheerfully.

A gentle whine indicated the pulse–injection units were activated, and the vehicle left the ground ever so gently, before making a smooth ascent.

"Was that good for you Kevin?" teased the computer.

"It's always like the first time with you Babe," Kevin joked in return.

"Crimany Kevin, what the hell do they program into these new models?" asked Glen truly amazed that he was so out of touch with the times.

"Anything you want my good man, anything you want."

The two men relaxed in companionable silence, but it wasn't long before Glen's mind returned to the new project. Why the government had specifically chosen the mummies of King Tutankhamun and his wife, Princess Ankhesenamun was just as bizarre a decision as he could imagine. Why not Albert Einstein, Ben Franklin or Abraham Lincoln? It just didn't make sense…a fascinating concept though, without question.

Of course, no clone would have any memories of a previous existence. They would be copies, duplicates, but only of the flesh, not of mind or soul…nothing more. These would be human beings cloned with the DNA from the mummified corpses of a long dead boy–king and his princess–wife…they wouldn't know anything more about their lives in Egypt than what they could be taught. He wondered though, what their minds would be like, if they would learn at the same pace as a birth person.

The clones would certainly look the same as the people had when they'd lived, but as history had relied solely upon ancient drawings and exaggerated sarcophagus depictions, the thought of actually gazing on the honest–to–God countenances of the real King Tutankhamun and the Princess Ankhesenamun was almost beyond imagining. What would the boy–king look like? And his wife…they hadn't known until they received the missive from Washington that the authorization had included the cloning of two mummies. Princess Ankhesenamun was purported to have been a great beauty in her time. Of course, Glen was no Egyptologist, but he knew that the daughter of the legendary beauty, Nefertiti would have to be at least passably pretty by any standards.

Glen thought of his handsome colleague and smiled to himself; if the clone of the princess grew as fast as they anticipated, she'd reach maturity, take one look at Kevin, and pledge him her undying love for the next four hundred years. This thought brought to mind yet another one, and Glen broke their mutual silence.

"I wonder who this world renowned Egyptologist they're sending in will be," he half–stated, half–questioned.

Kevin chuckled slightly, "Probably some old relic of a guy about as ancient as the mummies themselves."

Glen hadn't even realized they'd touched down until the door gently slid open in response to Kevin's voice command, and he found himself almost blinded by the bright lights and colorful crowd gathered around the establishment.

'Sal's' was apparently quite the 'hot spot.' A valet appeared seemingly from nowhere to park the Centurian, and the two men had barely exited the vehicle when the shiny, black craft lifted slowly from the ground, before ascending directly to the floating garage atop the building.

Glen followed Kevin past the crowd milling about outside the building. Most of the women seemed to be dressed in iridescent, body–forming ensembles of varying colors. Their clothing appeared to have been constructed of some sort of clear, rubbery substance, that emanated a luminescent glow all its own. Glen was unaccustomed to this 'mod' group, and had clearly been around the white lab coat crowd at work far too long. He resolved to try and get out more often.

Once inside, Glen's first impression of 'Sal's was that it seemed more of a large, upscale pub than a plain bar or lounge. The establishment boasted a heavily accented Italian motif, which continued into the spacious Italian restaurant in the rear. He remembered Kevin saying that he ate there a good deal on his day's off…whenever he didn't just decide to throw a nutriment pack in the re–hydrator. Kevin also told him that to the best of his knowledge, no one had ever seen or met the owner, 'Sal' directly.

It was by a sheer stroke of luck that the two men found bar stools to sit on; which was only due to the fact that a couple had just risen and were walking away from the stools as Glen and Kevin approached the neon glow of the bar.

The tables were packed, and there was virtually standing room only, but everyone around them seemed to be having a good time and the overall mood was pleasant. A laser light show flashed in time to the strains of 'Seal,' singing 'Kissed by a Rose.' That one was a real oldie but goodie, and one of Glen's favorites. It was obvious that the mysterious 'Sal' was a collector of all things Italian, except for his current choice of music.

There were antique machine guns and Tommy guns from the Italian gangster era, and a crumbling, gangster–style hat with a sign below that read, 'Once owned by Al Capone.' A special corner was reserved for a collection of replicas of the Leaning Tower of Pisa…which had leaned a little too far and toppled to the ground back in 2014. To top off the aggregation, a seemingly ancient zoot suit, that looked as though it was in danger of turning to dust at any given moment, hung above the bar. All of the displays were encased in protective glass covers and placed high up on the walls…they had to be virtually priceless.

"Gee Kev, do you come here often just to wind down? This place really isn't too bad." Glen observed that several gentlemen were glancing his way and found himself returning an occasional smile or two. Still, he didn't want Kevin to notice. In spite of the fact that they were halfway through the twenty–third century, the world at large seemed to have regressed rapidly with respect to Gay Right's Issues; a fact that secretly tore at Glen's insides. Although gay marriages had been legal only a century earlier; the changing of time brought about the gradual change of laws, until homosexuality had ultimately become a crime punishable by imprisonment.

In a way, Glen had managed to convince himself that it was all for the better; he didn't have the time to devote to a relationship with anyone…especially not now; not with this entire project ahead of him.

It was then that Glen realized Kevin had not answered his question of a few moments earlier, and turned his full attention to his friend and coworker. Kevin appeared to be a million miles away.

"Hey Kev," chuckled Glen, "thought we weren't going to dwell on the project."

Kevin didn't make a sound, and Glen realized that the pretty female bartender was also trying to get his attention.

"What can I get for you gentlemen?" asked the pretty blond.

No response.

Kevin's head was turned slightly to the left, away from Glen, his eyes focused on something, or someone, that Glen could not see from his present position.

"Excuse me Sir." Again, the bartender queried Kevin, beginning to sound a bit irritated, and causing Glen to become quite curious as to what had Kevin so transfixed.

"Uh, oh, I'm sorry," Kevin suddenly came out of his self imposed trance and afforded the young woman a winning smile, showing perfectly even, white teeth. The bartender actually blushed…all vestiges of irritation gone from her round face. Glen never ceased to be amazed at the impression Kevin made on the ladies, in spite of the fact that he did nothing to encourage them. Even the ones at the lab who thought he was gay went out of their way to brush by him in the hallway, or sit near him in the lunchroom.

"Do forgive me Pretty Lady," Kevin's smile broadened into a full fledged grin. "How about a couple Lunar Lights to start us off?" The bartender's pulse visibly pounded in her neck, as she turned away with a sigh.

"Well, well, Kev," intoned Glen with a smile; "this is certainly a side of you I've never seen before. I had no idea that our own Dr. Sanders was such a charmer."

"I'm not at work my friend," returned Kevin, "work is work and play is play, and I feel like playing tonight. I'm a scientist…I'm not dead." As Kevin spoke, he flashed his eyes to the left and nodded his head briefly. Glen leaned forward and peered around his friend, following his eyes to a very attractive brunette sitting four stools to Kevin's left. She was talking to a dark haired woman seated to her right, whose head partially obstructed Glen's view.

"Ah, I see what has you so captivated there Mister Kevin," laughed Glen, "she's a pretty one indeed. Maybe you should try talking to her, eh?"

"Well maybe I just will my good man. Watch and learn." Kevin rose from the stool, and placed his credit chip on the bar to cover the drinks that were arriving at that very moment.

The bartender looked slightly perplexed and a good deal disappointed as Kevin walked away. She set the luminescent drinks on the bar top and took the small, octagon chip lying next to them without a word. She dropped it into the slot of the credit–calculator she wore on a belt around her waist. In a second, it popped back out a slot in the side of the unit and with a last glance in Kevin's direction she tossed the chip back on the bar top and walked away.

Glen followed Kevin's progress and saw that he had made his way to the lady in question, 'Ah,' he thought, 'the confidence of youth mixed with good looks…I should be so lucky.' He glanced down at the glowing concoction in his glass, and reasoned that he could probably find his way through a dark room with it. He sipped the aqua colored liquid slowly and it warmed up in his mouth, yet felt cool going down his throat when he swallowed. The flavor was very unique, almost like a mixture of flowers and honey with a bit of a bite. All in all, the velvety texture and sweet taste were quite pleasant.

"Ah, one of my favorite drinks," the voice on his right broke into his enjoyment of this newly discovered taste sensation, and Glen looked up to see who it belonged to. He found that the nondescript woman who had been occupying that seat had left, and in her place sat a very friendly looking, middle aged man with a well trimmed mustache, olive skin and a slender build. It was the man's eyes that caught Glen's immediate attention. There was something in their amber depths that reached out to him. Returning the newcomer's smile, Glen introduced himself and extended his right hand in greeting.

"Yes, it is very nice to meet you," the stranger replied, "I am Geovanni Basalori, but my friends call me Sal…and this is my establishment."

"Good evening," Kevin nodded slightly, before fastening his gaze on the younger of the two women. "I was wondering if I might have the unequaled privilege of buying you two lovely ladies a drink?" Kevin played the grin out to its absolute fullest. The object of his attentions turned slowly in her chair and gave him a penetrating look.

"Do I know you sir?" questioned the chestnut haired beauty. Her incredibly light blue eyes met Kevin's green ones, and he found himself almost drawn into their depths. "Excuse me Sir," repeated the young woman, "do I know you?"

It wasn't easy, but Kevin shook it off. Staring into this woman's eyes was like being pulled into the vortex of a tractor beam.

"Well no, ummmph," Kevin cleared his throat, suddenly feeling like a high school boy on prom night. He hadn't even glanced at this woman's dark haired companion. He simply couldn't take his eyes off the vision in front of him, "Um, I'm really sorry," he apologized, "I just saw you sitting down here, noticed how incredibly attractive you are, and thought maybe you'd allow me to buy you a drink."

"Is this a come–on or what?" she asked, her eyes all but boring into his soul.

Kevin stuttered, dumfounded. This had never happened to him before. He was normally an incredibly articulate person, and didn't quite know how to react to this unexpected reception. Before he could even form the words of a reply, the brunette tossed several strands of her spiraled mane over her shoulder, and leveled him a steady look.

'My God,' he thought, 'she's got the most beautiful eyes I've ever seen on a human being in my life.'

"Am I supposed to fall off my bar stool now and genuflect to you?" Kevin downgraded from senior prom to eighth–grade prom. "Perhaps I should just throw myself in your arms and beg you to take me to your place." Her friend chuckled, but he still didn't remove his gaze from this woman's eyes. "Or maybe I should just jump on your body and have my way with you right now," she continued, "why prolong the inevitable, eh?" Her expression was stoic, her tone facetious, but her eyes held the barest hint of a teasing glimmer.

Kevin straightened to his full six–foot–four–inch height, and glanced slyly at this obviously intelligent, clearly articulate young woman, realizing as he did so, that he had seriously underestimated her character. She obviously wasn't mindless, and probably couldn't be intimidated on a bet. Not that he'd ever want to intimidate her, it was just his guess that it couldn't be done. Kevin saw her in a new light, beyond the startling beauty of her eyes…which were quite difficult to get passed.

"I could have asked if Heaven knew it was missing an angel?" he joked, hoping to catch another glimmer of a smile from her…however brief. He extended his right hand in a formal greeting, "Okay, can we start over?" I'm Kevin Sanders, Doctor Kevin Sanders." There was a momentary look of surprise across her heart shaped face, but it was gone just as fast as it had appeared, and was replaced by a rather puzzled look.

Kevin couldn't help feeling just a bit smug. So, she was impressed to learn that he was a doctor. It seemed that having those little alphabets after his name, hard earned as they were, definitely had their perks outside the workplace, as well as within it. She'd certainly take him up on his offer of a drink now.

Reluctantly, or perhaps a bit shyly, the beautiful young woman extended her hand in return greeting, and a small shock wave ran up Kevin's arm when their fingers touched.

"It's nice to meet you Doctor Sanders," he noticed that she accented the title a bit more than was necessary, "Lindsey Larimer is my name, and this is my mother, Olivia."

For the first time, Kevin took in the woman sitting to his right as he stood facing her daughter, 'Well, I've certainly made a mess of this,' he thought to himself, as he extended his hand to the attractive woman in her early fifties. "Your mother you say," he grinned, "I thought perhaps she was your sister...there is a definite resemblance."

Olivia grinned in obvious disbelief, "I wouldn't have guessed that you had thought anything of the sort, since this is the first moment you've actually laid eyes on my face." Her friendly smile indicated that she found the entire situation quite humorous. Her daughter didn't seem to fully share in her humor.

"You are quite the sliver–tongued devil aren't you Dr. Sanders?" purred Lindsey, "but we can afford to pay for our own drinks. Have a nice evening, Dr. Sanders." Again, the heavier accent on the title. Lindsey turned back around in her chair and without a pause, returned to the conversation she'd been having with her mother, before Kevin had made his less than successful appearance.

"So," Glen grinned, "did you get her link code?" The look on his face told Kevin he knew the meeting had not gone well.

"Well, not exactly," was Kevin's thoughtful retort, "but she did say something about jumping my body and having her way with me."

The questioning lift of Glen's left eyebrow relayed that he didn't believe a word of it.

"No, seriously, she really did." Kevin's lowered head gave further credence to Glen's disbelief. His mortification knew no bounds.

Glen hardly recognized his apartment. There were many times he simply fell to sleep on the air–lounge in the lab break room. There was always someone willing to make a food run, or a delivery service to bring it right to them, not to mention the numerous re–hydration units for those who weren't sick and tired of nutriment packs.

Tossing himself down on the air–sofa, Glen found his thoughts returning to the personable 'Sal.' Sal had shared with him the fact that he preferred to remain anonymous to his customers, allowing him to watch his place from the patron's point of view. Of course, the staff knew who he was, but it was apparently one of the best kept secrets around.

Why Sal had chosen to reveal his identity to Glen seemed to have surprised them both, and Glen found it a most welcome and pleasant surprise. Sal had regaled Glen with several comical anecdotes about the restaurant business, and discussed the numerous Italian artifacts he had collected over the years. The two had exchanged link codes, but Glen didn't know if he'd ever hear from Sal again, or if he would have the time to devote to making any type of connection. Still, he had to admit he'd found himself quite drawn to this deeply interesting individual.

"Television," he commanded of the empty room, "channel 316." The words had no sooner left his mouth, when the far wall of his living room split and separated in the center, revealing a small pedestal, above which a holographic image came to life. The Science Channel blared out a documentary on the new city being constructed on the ocean floor near Florida, with an expected completion date of only one month away.

'This is truly a new era,' thought Glen, his eyes fastened on the crystal clear hologram. A beautiful glass–domed, fully self–contained city, complete with a ten–by–ten privacy fenced back yard was being featured. The narrator announced that for an additional five million credits, one could enjoy a back yard nearly twice that large, but many of the dwellings and businesses within had been purchased shortly after construction began some ten years ago.

Glen could only imagine how awesome it would be to own a dwelling with a grass yard. Those were his last thoughts before he slipped into the arms of Morpheus.

The flat roof of Kevin's garage parted as the sleek, black Centurian descended and landed gently on the aluminum floor. The roof closed and the lights came on as the door to his vehicle slid open and he stepped out.

Walking a few steps to the entry portal, he went through it and placed the palm of his hand on the flat, tile surface, located just to the right of another sliding door. The door opened with a swish and he found himself staring into the darkness. "Lights," he almost barked. The kitchen was immediately aglow with light from several lumi–bulb fixtures.

He walked across the small room to the nutriment cabinet and scanned the meager selection within. Rummaging through its contents revealed only five nutriment cubes; of which two contained pizza; two with a chicken, rice and gravy entree, and one containing roast beef with potatoes and peas. He chose the roast beef and placed the palm sized cube into the re–hydrator that was built into the wall, next to the nutriment cabinet. "Heat," he commanded. In six seconds the door opened and there before him was a steaming hot meal…partially synthetic though it might be.

Kevin didn't know what was taking the damned re–hydrator so long to process the packages…he'd have to have it looked at. A man could starve to death in the time it took that thing to prepare a meal. He'd also have to do some shopping in the morning. There were slim pickings here and he had to get through the entire weekend.

Placing his hot meal on the floating table in front of his air sofa, Kevin commanded the television to select an 'oldie but goodie' movie. The computer in his living unit was programmed with the same voice and pseudo–personality as the one in his vehicle. He was in no mood for purring, feminine voices and made that clear to the computer immediately. It selected a re-mastered movie made in 1999, entitled, 'The Mummy,' with Brendan Fraser and Rachel Weisz. The holographic figures of the actors took form as soon as the movie began. 'There's irony for you,' he thought, as he began to shovel steaming mouthfuls of roast beef with gravy into his hungry body…'irony indeed.'

Lindsey and her mother had giggled like schoolgirls all the way back to Lindsey's newly leased condominium. They had taken an air–cab, since Lindsey wasn't familiar with her new surroundings just yet, but her mother's presence beside her alleviated the feeling of being alone in this fast paced city. She had to admit the evening had been somewhat of a comic relief for her. Having just relocated to a new city to be a part of a new and fascinating scientific breakthrough had been a bit nerve wracking. The antics of the very good looking young doctor as he had attempted to introduce himself, had been quite humorous, and Lindsey had to admit to herself that she almost felt bad for her less than cordial treatment of the poor man…almost. She was pleased that her mother had closed up her own home in Colorado, and agreed to accompany her and stay on for a couple of months until she had at least partially acclimated to her new surroundings. The loss of her beloved father only a few short years ago had taken a toll on both mother and daughter, and they had decided that the time away would do them both some good.

Since her father's death, Lindsey and her mother had grown closer than they had ever been before. While Lindsey had always been the apple of her father's eye, and he had all but worshipped his little blue eyed angel, Olivia had often taken somewhat of a backseat in her daughter's affections. She never minded though, for she knew that Lindsey's love of all things Egyptian had been manifest since her earliest memory, and her passion, drive and intense quest for more knowledge, endeared the girl to her father so that they became nearly inseparable early on. Their beautiful daughter had taken the place of the son her husband would never have.

Olivia's one wish had been to give her husband more children, but after a cure for cancer had been discovered in 2201, followed by a cure for AIDS in 2205, the world's population had nearly doubled in the span of five years. It was then that a national law was enacted, allowing only one child per family…any subsequent pregnancies were medically terminated by statute. Only those women who already had more than one child, or were pregnant at the time the Population Enforcement Act was implemented, were not affected. Lindsey's energy and vigor however, had been equal to that of several children, so her parents never felt that they had really missed anything.

Now, back in her daughter's room in the elevated condominium, Olivia sat next to Lindsey on her soft, warm airbed, and laughed about the young doctor at 'Sal's' having so terribly botched his introduction earlier. She knew that he had also piqued her daughter's interest with his just–this–side–of–arrogant attitude. Lindsey's father had made a similar introduction to his wife many years ago and Olivia shared that introduction to her daughter as they sat and talked companionably together.

Lowell would have been so proud to know that his daughter had been chosen to work on this new, top–secret project at IBAT. Olivia thought of her tall, handsome husband, and missed him with the part of her heart that had been reserved for him and him alone. She knew that her husband had been so proud of their daughter while he'd lived that he couldn't possibly have extended his pride any further. It didn't stop her from wishing he were there to share in the moment. She remembered Lowell kissing her goodbye, as he left to give a presentation on the Library of Knowledge at the university. Olivia had offered to let him take her transport, as his had started making a strange sound upon activation.

"You worry too much, Olivia," he said with a smile. "I'll drop her off to be serviced after the presentation, and link to you so you can swing by and pick me up."

Olivia kissed her husband again before the door folded down on his transport and the vehicle ascended, and disappeared from view.

The mid–air explosion had torn her husband's body to pieces. She would never forget that hot August day in 2240, only two months after Lowell and Lindsey had discovered the hidden library. If only she had insisted that he take her transport. If only…but the Lord had simply decided he wanted Lowell Lindsey home; and home he had taken him.

Kevin awoke early the next morning, the temperature of his floating air bed was down a little low, and he made the necessary voice command to increase it a couple of degrees. He lay there for another moment and then stumbled across his room, cursing as he stubbed his toe on one of his shoes he'd left lying on the floor. Kevin had never been much of a morning person.

He knew a cleansing would make him feel much better, and running his hands through his tousled mane, he made his way to the cleansing chamber that adjoined the sleeping room. Once ensconced in the clear, circular, tube, Kevin verbalized his wish to be thoroughly cleansed. The warm, pleasantly scented mist surrounded him, invigorating and reviving.

After completing the three minute cleansing process and donning his clothes, Kevin made his way back out to the garage and entered his vehicle. Although his body felt tingly and clean, the cleansing had done little to improve his disposition, and he still felt the residuals of being so thoroughly shunned the night before.

"Good morning Kevin," sounded the soft, feminine voice, "where to so early on a Saturday morning?"

"Take me to the nutriment center," was his curt reply.

"Still smarting from the rejection Kevin?" replied the ultra soft reply.

"Take me to the nutriment center in silence," Kevin responded, "you're not supposed to be listening in on my private conversations."

"It was rather difficult not to, the way you carried on about it to Glen when we drove him home."

"I said I wanted to transport in silence, did I not?" His irritation was upgrading to an all out bad mood.

"As you wish."

The roof of the garage opened and the craft lifted slowly upward and then off at a ninety-degree angle.

Fortunately, Kevin noted that there weren't many shoppers as he hovered into the grocery store. At his command, the top of his Centurian retracted so that he could clearly see all the items on the shelves. The aisles were wide enough for two crafts to hover side-by-side, as the patrons voiced their selections from those offered. Kevin was busily making his choices when he noticed a young woman on the rearview screen of his control panel. He looked again just to be sure. It was none other than Lindsey; the woman he'd met at Sal's the night before.

Kevin smiled to himself, and wondered if perhaps she'd seen him en route, and decided to follow him. Some women were like that, he reasoned…they would profess no interest initially, and then end up chasing a guy around. He wouldn't imagine Lindsey to be the type, but it sure seemed like quite the coincidence to him. Well, he'd made the first move, and it was up to her to make the next one. He continued selecting items and watching the rear–view panel. The beautiful woman in the translucent, compact 'Orbitor' didn't seem to be looking in his direction at all. Perhaps she was playing hard to get.

Twenty minutes later, having made many more selections than he had intended, Kevin found himself hovering in the check–out line. It was then, he noticed the 'Orbitor' ascending and turning about, as though going back for a forgotten item, 'She probably doesn't want me to know she's following me,' he thought to himself as he placed his credit–chip into the pay–slot. In less than five seconds, his purchases were lowered into his car and he hovered out the exit doors. The Orbitor was nowhere to be seen.

Chapter Two

Kevin's Centurian set down gently in the parking area of Glen's apartment, some three hundred feet above ground level. The building, like many of its counterparts, was nestled atop a pillar–like appendage, allowing the entire complex to be raised or lowered, depending on weather and air quality. Kevin made a mental note to check into the possibility of relocating to such a dwelling. He liked the privacy of living in a single–dwelling unit, but on the days that the air quality was particularly bad, he didn't have the option of raising his home to escape it.

Kevin hadn't made it three feet from his vehicle, when he saw Glen enter the garage area and walk toward him. He wondered if Glen was as excited about this being Monday morning as he was. Monday's were certainly never exciting for Kevin, but he found himself quite looking forward to getting started on their new project. The look on Glen's face as he strode up to the Centurian answered Kevin's question. Glen looked like a kid with a new toy he couldn't wait to play with.

It was just about dawn as Kevin's vehicle merged into the commuter lane of the already crowded 'skyway.' What should have been a glorious pink and yellow sunrise, was unfortunately, more of a light, gray–brown halo around the hazy orb of the sun. It seemed that the twinkling city below them was in for another poor air-quality day.

"By the way Glen," smiled Kevin, "I thought I'd tell you the young lady we met at Sal's Friday night followed me through the nutriment center on Saturday?"

Glen experienced a momentary pang at just the mention of 'Sals.' The more he had thought of Sal over the weekend, the more he had found himself reflecting on the compromised quality of life he had been delegated to.

Glen wanted to talk about his meeting with Sal; wanted to tell Kevin how attracted he'd been to the engaging, intelligent and captivating Italian restaurateur. Forcing his mind away from the subject of Sal, he replied to Kevin's question, "Followed you around the nutriment center did she?" He smiled and adopted a teasing tone, "Are you sure it was her?"

"No two women could look like that...it was her all right," was Kevin's smug reply.

"Did she say anything to you, wave, acknowledge your presence?" queried Glen, trying to conceal a lopsided grin, and silently thankful for having something else to occupy his thoughts.

"Well, not exactly," replied Kevin, slinking down a bit lower in his seat, "I don't think she wanted me to know she was following me."

Glen's less than believable, "Oh, I see," only served to embarrass Kevin further.

The Centurian set down smoothly in the employee parking area, and the two men exited, making their way to the transport–walk that would convey them effortlessly to the entry door of the lab division.

IBAT was a top security installation, and the measures taken to maintain that security required the utilization of the most advanced identification system available. In order to gain entry, Kevin and Glen went through the process of placing their respective right hands over the identification panel for initial recognition, and then peered into the retinal–indicator, speaking their names aloud as they did so, to complete the procedure.

The heavy, metal doors opened to allow their entrance to the purification room. The familiar rush of air and enveloping sweet smell of disinfectant indicated that their bodies were now completely free of any harmful bacteria. The finalization of the purification process prompted the voice–activation system. Both men stated their individual identification numbers, and a second set of doors opened to allow their entry into the hub of the lab division, itself.

The CEO of IBAT, Professor Garreth St. Germaine, immediately singled out the two scientists when they entered the colossal facility. Hundreds of lab technicians were already busily embroiled in their scheduled tasks, yet there was paradoxical quietness, broken intermittently by the hum of an instrument or the sound of liquids being poured.

Professor St. Germaine struck an impressing figure. Taller than Kevin, and a good deal meatier, this man looked like a small mountain in a white lab coat. He extended his hand in greeting and addressed Kevin and Glen in his familiar British accent

"'Ello, and good morning gentlemen," he beamed. The slight gap in his front teeth leant an almost boyish appearance to his otherwise rather stern looking countenance. "This is an exciting day fine sirs, is it not!" His excitement was contagious, and both Kevin and Glen grinned back in unison, as they exchanged greetings.

"I'd like you two to join me in the council room if you'd be so kind," said Professor St. Germaine, as he turned and led them down one of the hallways that ran from the circular main lab to the private offices and meeting rooms.

The CEO chatted pleasantly as the two men followed him along the corridor, until he stopped before a polished aluminum door and placed his hand over the identifier–panel. The door slid aside, and the three men entered the room and took seats at the clear, circular table that nearly filled the entire conference area. Several other IBAT staff members had arrived ahead of them and had already been seated, awaiting the commencement of what was certainly going to be a very momentous meeting.

"This is going to be quite the interesting adventure indeed," announced Professor St. Germaine, with his ever present, gap–toothed grin. He was literally rubbing his huge hands together in anticipation.

Both Kevin and Glen nodded in acknowledgment. The entire staff at IBAT was composed of only those individuals who were exceptional in their chosen fields. This new project, being one hundred percent government financed, was a definite indicator that they would have anything and everything required for its success at their disposal.

A moment later, the metal door slid aside and several more engineers, technicians and specialists entered the room; the hum of their voices breaking the comparative silence. Once everyone had taken their respective seats and the chairs were all full, Professor St. Germaine stood and greeted the group at large, "Firstly, I'd like to say that I couldn't be more pleased about this project, and I'm sure you all share my feelings." Professor St. Germaine folded his massive hands in front of him, "I am most secure in the knowledge that we have not only the finest equipment at our disposal for this project, but the finest minds as well."

"Here, here!" echoed several of the individuals present.

"Well, ladies and gentlemen," continued the CEO, "today marks the beginning of a history changing, technological breakthrough that until now, we could only dream about. I know that telling you all how lucky we are to be involved in this project is an understatement at best." His words elicited chuckles from several members of the assemblage, before Professor St. Germaine continued speaking," As you all know, the next few weeks will be critical. I realize that many of you have families at home, but it will be necessary for all of you to remain here at IBAT for at least one full month." The subsequent groans from several individuals elicited smiles from others. Professor St. Germaine chuckled, "This is why you get paid the big credits folks!" Another round of chuckling followed this rejoinder, "In any event, I'd like for you to all meet our newest colleague, who comes to us from Cairo, Egypt, where she's been studying and performing research for the past few years." Professor St. Germaine indicated someone seated several chairs to his left, and the beautiful woman with chestnut hair and light blue eyes pushed back her chair and stood up. Glen choked and Kevin's body threatened to turn to gel and slide off his chair onto the floor.

"I am sure you are all familiar with the name of the late Dr. Lowell Larimer," continued Professor St. Germaine, as he resumed his introduction of the young woman who now had all eyes upon her. "Of course, I am referring to the world–renowned archeologist who discovered the Great Library of Knowledge in the Giza Plateau of Egypt just ten years ago."

The appreciative nods and murmurs confirmed that all were indeed familiar with the name of the famous Dr. Larimer. "Well, I am pleased to inform you all that we are fortunate enough to have Dr. Larimer's daughter, who is also an excellent Paleontologist and Egyptologist in her own right, on staff here at IBAT for the duration of our new project." Professor St. Germaine nodded toward Lindsey, "So with that, I shall leave her to make her personal introduction." The CEO took his seat to the rousing applause of the now fascinated group.

If there had ever been a time in his life that Kevin felt smaller, more insignificant, or shallower than he felt at that moment, he couldn't remember it.

"Good morning," acknowledged the pretty young woman, her eyes singling out Kevin as she spoke, "my name is Lindsey Larimer, Doctor Lindsey Larimer." Kevin squirmed like a six–year–old in church, being singled out by the pastor for ill behavior. "I am pleased to have been chosen to work on The Reclamation Project."

Kevin was scarcely listening to the young woman's introduction. Even in a lab coat, she was one of the most stunning women he had ever seen. Her soft, melodic voice entranced him, the movement of her lips as she spoke nearly took his breath away, and the thought of his actions the night before humiliated him beyond words. He hoped she hadn't noticed him wince.

"As I'm sure you all know from the media coverage surrounding my father's discovery, I was with him the day the seal was broken on the doors to the ancient library, which was found hidden beneath the Great Pyramid of Giza." The gathering of professionals was clearly enthralled at this firsthand recounting of a truly great moment in history.

Lindsey's fingertips rested on the edge of the table as she addressed her new colleagues, and Kevin couldn't help noticing how pretty her hands were; how her long tapered fingers ended in well–shaped, well–manicured fingernails. He also noticed that she wore no jewelry…more specifically, no wedding ring.

'Get over it, for the Love of God!' thought Kevin, chastising himself for his errant, wandering mind. He didn't quite know why in the hell just the mere sight of Lindsey had such an effect on him. This project was of extreme importance, and he couldn't afford to allow his mind to wander off whenever he laid eyes on this woman. Had there been one day, one incident in his life he could change, it would have been his ridiculous, self–righteous introduction of himself a few nights ago. Who could have known?

"I assure you there is no way to describe how it felt to be twenty–five years old, not long out of graduate school, and standing on the threshold of one of the most important and long sought after discoveries in the world." Lindsey's smile was dazzling, and her eyes were bright with the remembrance of that hot day in July, as she relived it to the assemblage in the meeting room.

She had accompanied her father and his entourage of assistants to further explore a recently excavated area near the base of the Sphinx.

For many centuries, archeologists had been attempting to prove the existence of the fabled library; a library that was purported to contain the answers to the questions man had asked about his own existence, since the beginning of time immortal. Legend had it that even the answers to how the pyramids had actually been built, and more important, why they had been built were contained in these ancient scrolls of wisdom…if they existed. Her father believed in the existence of this library, and because he believed, Lindsey believed too.

It was common knowledge that several archeologists had found a room under the sphinx back in the year 2000, and had even televised their finding, so sure were they that they had been about to find the ancient library. Unfortunately, their search yielded no more than a few previously undiscovered passages and chambers before the project was abandoned. She wondered how the world would have changed had the library been found then, wondered how much different life might be now.

Several weeks earlier, her fathers' workers had discovered a discolored area just below the sand line of the Sphinx. Lindsey had been taking a nap in her small, temporary dwelling nearby, when her father had linked to her and asked her to join him to excavate further. He had simply refused to continue until his daughter was at his side. Ultimately, the workers unearthed a long ago sealed entrance into the Sphinx itself that had apparently been overlooked by the archeologists of the twenty-first century.

There within, was found a rather strange area on one of the walls in the massive room, an area that appeared to be of a slightly different color, but only under the beam of one specific type of artificial light. After several failed attempts, the workers realized that no matter how hard they tried, their lasers would not penetrate the material. Finally, her father had ordered that the workers cut around the impenetrable surface, and was immediately rewarded when a yawning passageway appeared on the other side.

Lowell and his daughter had led the research team through the seemingly endless corridor, descending further and further downward, until Lindsey was certain they were about to visit the very bowels of earth. After what seemed like a half day of walking, the weary group came upon a stone stairwell, its massive steps ascended sharply upward, and in the general direction of the Great Pyramid of Giza.

It was then that Lowell began to sense his lifelong dream, his ceaseless quest, was finally going to come to fruition; he was about to discover what others had sworn never existed. At that moment, Lowell Larimer realized that he and his daughter stood quite literally at the threshhold of the greatest historical discovery imaginable; the unearthing of a legacy older than recorded time.

Breathing a great sigh, and holding his daughter close, Lowell savored the moment…a moment so divine he found himself overcome with emotion…with a feeling of reverence that comes from experiencing a deep, affective, religious experience.

When their lengthy climb finally ended with a landing, followed by twelve perfectly cut, massive stone steps that led upward to a stone platform and a solid wall, the explorers felt as though they had all been the brunt of a horrible, ancient joke. Lindsey's father, not about to give in to defeat, set his men to work with their high powered lasers in an attempt to cut through the thick, rock wall. It was at the base of that wall, on the large stone platform, that eleven of his best workers began the painstaking chore before them, while Lindsey, her father and several of the remaining workers waited below with bated breath.

Surveying the walls around her, Lindsey wondered at the fact that whatever hieroglyphics had once been inscribed on the wall, had long since been chiseled off and removed entirely.

After what seemed like an interminable amount of time had passed, Lindsey's father made his way slowly up the steps to the highest platform, where his workers continued their efforts with very little success.

What happened next, was one of the most fascinating and yet horrifying experiences of Lindsey's life. Her father had reached the top stair and had no sooner stepped onto the stone platform, than the entire thing gave a groan and disappeared below, leaving a gaping chasm where the platform had just been.

Lindsey's scream reverberated off the walls in the enclosed stairwell, giving it an almost unearthly quality, as the sound pierced the ensuing silence like the cry of a banshee. Everything happened in a rush, as the workers below ran up the remaining steps to where the topmost platform had stood only moments before. Lindsey reached the top first. She was horrified at what she was afraid she would see, but she had to look, had to know what had happened to her beloved father. The sight that greeted her was one she would go to her grave remembering.

There, about twelve feet below her, stood her father and the eleven workers staring in awe and wonder at each other, and the ancient door that stood before them, bearing a seal such as they had never seen before. As though feeling his daughter's horrified gaze, her father raised his head and met her eyes, "This is it, Little Miss Lindsey…we are here!"

It didn't take but a few moments for full understanding of what had just happened to dawn. Clearly, the platform worked much like a scale–type elevator. It simply required the weight of twelve people to lower itself to the library entrance. Accordingly, fewer people on the platform should raise it.

It was at that point, that Dr. Lowell Larimer refused to proceed any further without his daughter at his side. Ordering the crew to lower a rope, he firmly secured it to one of the workers standing closest to him, and ordered that the worker be pulled up to the surface. As the man's booted feet left the platform with the first pull of the rope, the platform itself began to rise. When the rope was allowed too much slack and his feet touched the stone floor, the platform again began to descend immediately. Finally, the workers above were ordered to pull him up as swiftly as possible, and it was then that the platform ascended fully.

Lindsey's father took her hand, and with full and complete trust, she replaced the man who had been lifted from the platform. As soon as both of her feet had touched the stone floor, it lowered back down again so that she stood facing the sealed door with her father.

The breaking of the seal and subsequent entry into the fabled Great Library of Knowledge was the culmination of not only an intense, lifelong passion and exhaustive quest, but the strengthening of an already intense bond between father and daughter.

The vast array of tablets and scrolls were a sight beyond anything either Lindsey or her father could have imagined. The library was adorned with hundreds of ornately carved statues of Egyptian gods. The intricate, lifelike, features of Ra, Anubis, Horus, Isis, Osiris, and a score of others stared back at the wide-eyed group of explorers. Solid gold figurines glinted in the artificial light cast by the first people to see them in several thousand years, but even these priceless artifacts paled in comparison to the walls of the circular room.

From the floor to the ceiling of this ancient library that had become scarcely more than a legend, the walls were entirely covered with thin, inlaid strips of pure gold. Every inch of each golden tile was engraved from top to bottom with hieroglyphs. The fact that their location devices placed them directly under the Great Pyramid of Egypt was a revelation in itself, and they knew without any hesitation, that this was without a doubt, the depository for the wisdom of the ages.

Goosebumps stood out on Lindsey's flesh at the memory, but she did not waver as she continued to address the assemblage at the table before her. "Of course," she went on, "the deciphering and interpretation of the tablets and scrolls is a very long and involved process, and many top-notch professionals in hieroglyphics and hieratics have been working night and day on doing just that. There's truly no telling how many more years it will take to complete such an undertaking, and I know that everyone is waiting with bated breath for the outcome."

Lindsey's eyes once again scanned the faces of her colleagues, touching briefly on Kevin's somewhat intense, green eyed gaze. She wasn't quite certain why this man's presence unsettled her so. She could feel his eyes boring into her when she spoke, even when she wasn't looking at him, and suddenly found she was experiencing a slight twinge of nervousness.

Having spoken at many lectures over the past several years,

Lindsey managed to continue speaking without skipping a beat. "In truth, although I know that this project has something to do with the information found in the Library of Knowledge, I am at as much of a loss as anyone as to why the governments involved have chosen to clone the mummies of King Tutankhamen and the Princess Ankhesenamun. I do know however, that I have been contracted to teach them of their Egyptian roots and heritage, as well as to research and evaluate their development at its various stages."

Lindsey smiled broadly before continuing, "I find it a little more than ironic that I should find myself in a position to teach King Tut his own native language," again the group chuckled in acknowledgment. "From what I have gleaned thus far, it seems that the information contained in the library was meant to be used by all of mankind. Both the Egyptian government, who of course had to agree to the experiments we are about to conduct, and the United States government, who is financing and overseeing the work, feel that there is a great deal of extremely valuable information in the writings we've found. Both governments agree that there is information to be reclaimed, and that it will somehow require the cloning of these particular individuals. Thus, they have decided to refer to our work on this undertaking as 'The Reclamation Project.'" Clearly, Lindsey had the full attention of all present.

"I must admit," she continued, "I have precious little knowledge of cloning, other than history telling us that the first human cloning experiments started in Great Britain back in the year 2000. It seems that the British government put those experiments to an abrupt halt, as the US government did a few years later. In any event, I would like to say that I am looking forward to working with all of you and to the experiences ahead." Lindsey nodded her head in closing and returned to her chair.

"Here, here!" piped up Glen, and several others echoed his exclamation. Glen glanced at the stoic figure of Kevin seated on his right, and wondered to himself just how much his friend had actually heard of what the lovely young doctor had been saying. He knew Kevin wanted to disappear into thin air and couldn't help grinning at the irony of it all.

Kevin turned just in time to catch Glen's look, and elbowed his friend lightly in the ribs, affording him a friendly glower, 'God, am I really that transparent?' he mused with a shake of his head.

Professor St. Germaine thanked Lindsey profusely and again expounded on how absolutely overjoyed he was to have her on staff, "Does anyone have any questions for Dr. Larimer before we adjourn this meeting?" he offered.

Lindsey was immediately flooded with a tide of questions. It seemed that everyone at the meeting table had a question of some sort, and Lindsey chose to answer them as briefly, yet concisely as possible.

"Dr. Larimer," began one of the female physicists, as Lindsey nodded her head in the older woman's direction, "very little is known about the legendary King Tut, for example; to the best of my knowledge no one has ever determined his exact cause of death. In your work with your father, have you ever found any solid information about why he died at such a young age?"

It seemed that everyone in the room simultaneously held their breath awaiting this knowledgeable young woman's reply.

"I wish I could share some startling revelation with you," she smiled, "but unfortunately, even with all the technology available to us today, no one has ever been able to make any definite determinations. It seems that the illustrious Howard Carter, who was responsible for the initial discovery of King Tutankhamun, was in such a hurry to search out the jewels concealed in the mummy's wrappings, he didn't concern himself with the possibility of contaminating the young king's remains." Lindsey paused and shook her head slightly before continuing, "In the late twentieth and early twenty-first centuries, when the utilization of DNA identification was still quite new and not yet fully understood, more tests were conducted on several Egyptian mummies, including that of King Tut. Unfortunately, the methods were still quite crude, and the scientists of that day unknowingly contaminated the remains further. So, while I understand it is strongly believed that there is enough uncontaminated DNA left in the mummy to successfully clone, there has been an insufficient amount remaining for anyone to make an exact determination as to how he died. The most accepted hypothesis to date is that he was likely killed due to the occipital region of his skull being penetrated with a hunting arrow or similar instrument. There remains the possibility that the young king could have been murdered."

"Maybe we can ask him soon!" Joked one of the Biologists seated near Kevin. This was met with a good deal of laughter from Professor St. Germaine, as well as several others in the room.

Kevin was again drawn to Lindsey's incredible smile, 'A smile that could brighten up an entire room,' he thought to himself, and felt a stab of near jealousy when he realized that her smile seemed to grace everyone in the room except for him. He wanted her to look at him and smile that way, "Dr. Larimer," he began, not quite knowing what he would even ask her. It turned out to be the first thing that popped into his mind, "Do you really suppose the young man will be able to tell us how he died?" he asked with a sheepish grin.

Lindsey leveled him with nothing less than a glare, "I study Egyptian relics and fossils, as well as the ancient Egyptian culture and way of life, Dr. Sanders, I do not recreate or duplicate them."

She looked at him the way a mother might look down at an errant child, "I would think you would be much more qualified to answer that question than I would." Her attention was immediately drawn to the next question, elicited by Professor St. Germaine himself, and Kevin was left feeling about twelve years old. Even Glen was beginning to wonder what had happened to his normally well spoken, extremely intelligent, young friend.

"Dr. Larimer," asked the jovial Professor St. Germaine, "as we all know, history has taught that King Tut's young wife disappeared sometime after he died. Please forgive my ignorance of history if I am incorrect, but this of course, is not something we have ever felt the need to know in our line of work here at IBAT."

"Don't apologize Professor St. Germaine," Lindsey answered, again favoring someone besides Kevin with her winning smile, "that is a very valid question." She couldn't help noticing out of the corner of her eye, that Kevin slunk down a bit further in his chair, "Until about eight years ago, Princess Ankhesenamun's mummy had not been found." Her conspiratorial tone had everyone in the room leaning a little further forward in his or her chairs, so as not to miss a word Lindsey was saying. "In truth, although it is incredibly hard for anyone to believe, the princess's mummy was discovered in the Takla Makan Desert of China in 2242."

Everyone in the room began to ask questions at the same time, so that it was impossible for Lindsey to pick out or respond to any one question in the cacophony of voices.

"Hold on, hold on," Professor St. Germaine held his hands out in front of him and chuckled deeply, "let's not overwhelm Dr. Larimer on her first day. I think we should allow her to finish her narrative before we bombard her with questions," he grinned.

Lindsey smiled thankfully at the good natured Professor and continued, "I realize you would think that a discovery of such magnitude would have been announced to the world and written into the history books." The nods of everyone at the table confirmed their agreement, "One must remember though," she continued, "that there has never been a time in history when an artifact or relic was discovered, that there weren't disagreements among the specialists as to its authenticity or origin. This holds true with the mummy of Ankhesenamun. While there were some that swore this was the mummy of the young princess, others swore it could not possibly be her." She noted that everyone in the room was looking at her with an imploring, 'and'….

"It must also be remembered," she resumed, "that the ancient Egyptians often changed their own names, or began to use a variation of their given names. For example, history has shown that Ankhesenamun was the third daughter of Pharaoh Akhenaten and Queen Nefertiti, and at birth, her name was—

A–N–K–H–E–S–E–N–P–A–A–T–E–N," she spelled out the letters individually, "but the young princess later changed her name to Ankhes–en–amun, which broken down and translated means, 'She lives, or Ankhes.'" Lindsey pronounced the Egyptian word with a throaty emphasis and perfect accent, and continued, "With the second syllable 'en,' meaning 'for,' and 'amun' which means exactly what it is, the name of the Egyptian Sun God, also referred to as 'Ra,' or 'Amun Ra'. In short," she concluded, "the princess changed her name to 'She lives for the god Amun,' which wasn't uncommon when an ancient Egyptian converted to another religion, or wished to show the depth of his belief."

The assemblage nodded in understanding, as Lindsey continued her explanation, "It seems that the mummy in the Takla Makan Desert was found with an amulet bearing the hieroglyphic symbols for Ankhesenamun's name, but on the other side were engraved symbols that translated into 'Amun Ra lives for Ankhesenamun.'" Lindsey's eyebrows lifted questioningly as she explained, "Such an inscription would amount to nothing less than blasphemy in that time, and there are those who believe this is why her remains were found so far from Egypt, and why she was not mummified in the Egyptian tradition. The matter of the mummy's true identity was strongly questioned by many authorities, which argued that there were no acknowledged historical events that would place Ankhesenamun in China at any time. Shortly after my father discovered the ancient library however, the true Queen Nefertiti's sarcophagus was located."

"But I thought Queen Nefertiti's sarcophagus had been found centuries ago," interrupted one of the chemical engineers that had remained relatively quiet until that point.

"Yes," Lindsey conceded, "so did the rest of the world, that is of course, until the real queen's mummy was discovered, and her DNA was compared to that of the mummy thought to be Princess Ankhesenamun, providing indisputable evidence of the young princess's identity."

"Then who was it that they thought was in Queen Nefertiti's tomb initially?" asked the quizzical engineer.

"It turned out to be none other than Akhenaten and Nefertiti's daughter, Meritaten, who it seems had married her father and bore him a child while he was still married to her mother, the Queen Nefertiti."

The simultaneous gasp from everyone in the room sounded almost like a vacuum, and Lindsey couldn't help but smile, although why she found herself looking directly into Kevin's green eyes as she did so, she didn't know. He smiled back and she felt incredibly warm, but continued her explanation, while hoping no one had noticed the interaction

"The fact that Akhenaten married his daughters and had children by them is certainly not agreeable by our standards, but apparently occurred quite frequently in ancient Egypt. Perhaps

Queen Nefertiti displeased her husband in some way, or fell out of grace with the people she helped rule," Lindsey went on, "but it is now known that the cartouche meant for the Queen, was actually used for her daughter, Meritaten. We also know that Queen Nefertiti appears in the mourning scenes in Pharaoh Akhenaten's tomb, which confirms the fact that she outlived him. That ruled out the Pharaoh himself as having been responsible for the placement of Nefertiti's mummy."

"Dr. Larimer," asked the older, female physicist that had addressed her earlier, "if the Pharaoh was in the habit of marrying his daughters, had he not married his daughter Ankhesenamun prior to her marrying King Tut?"

"Excellent question," smiled Lindsey, and then she laughed as she added, "you've been paying attention." She was immediately rewarded with a friendly smile from the older woman, and Kevin couldn't help noting that already, Lindsey was by far the most admired woman in the room…by both her male, and female colleagues.

"Our Pharaoh Akhenaten didn't spare his third daughter either. It seems he married her when she was only eleven years old, and at the age of twelve, the Princess Ankhesenamun gave birth to a new princess, who she named Ankhesenpaaten Tasherit, the child sired by her own father. It seems though, that the child died quite young." Several members of the group looked alternately disgusted and nauseous, but still hung on to every word as Lindsey cleared her throat and continued, "It seemed that not long after King Tut's future wife married her father, her sister, Meritaten had married the Pharaoh Smenkhkare." Again, she pronounced these ancient names eloquently and with a flawless Egyptian accent. "Is everyone sufficiently confused yet?" joked Lindsey, before furthering her explanation, "We know that upon Meritaten's death, the marriage of Ankhesenamun and her father was apparently dissolved. According to custom, she immediately married her sister's newly widowed husband, Smenkhkare. That marriage was of an even shorter duration than the one to her father, as Pharaoh Smenkhkare died in 1333 BC, not long after the wedding and was succeeded by his eight-year-old brother, Tutankhamen. That is when Ankhesenamun married the boy king, making him her third husband and all of this by the time she was only thirteen years of age. So that is how she became the wife of one of Egypt's most famous pharaohs."

"Well, Dr. Larimer," interjected Professor St. Germaine, "thank you once again for sharing your knowledge of this subject." His smile and nod left no doubt that his accolade was most sincere. "Unfortunately," he went on, "our presence is required to get this project off the ground, so we'll have to adjourn this meeting now. I am pleased to announce however, that Dr. Larimer has graciously offered to give a brief lecture for those staff members directly involved with The Reclamation Project." A short, but genuine round of applause followed this announcement before he continued. "As most of you already know, we've been planning a special dinner gathering in the Lecture Hall, which has been turned into the 'Starlight Room' for this evening." He winked and favored his audience with an ear–to–ear grin, "So that everyone will have at least a fair understanding of the individuals we'll be cloning. I'm quite sure after a long day's work, a nice dinner and presentation will be most welcome."

The assemblage voiced their unanimous agreement with this executive decision, and began pushing back their chairs and thanking Lindsey individually, before filing out of the room. Kevin and Glen both stood up with the others and made their way toward the attractive young doctor, who was shaking hands and trying to sort out the names of her new colleagues as they passed by her. Kevin was almost afraid to say anything at all as he neared the beautiful woman with the blue eyes and reddish-brown hair, after all, everything he'd said to her thus far had resulted in his own deep embarrassment.

As with everyone else present, Glen found himself fascinated with this woman's incredible knowledge and the wealth of information she brought with her. He couldn't resist asking a question of his own; one that he knew most of the gentlemen in the room would be interested in hearing the answer to. "Dr. Larimer," he asked, as he introduced himself and returned her handshake, "wasn't the Queen Nefertiti supposed to be one of the greatest beauties of all time?" His eyes twinkled as he asked his question, and Lindsey found herself quite inexplicably drawn to the likable man.

"Yes," she responded with a broad smile, "even the name Nefertiti means the beautiful one comes."

Kevin, standing slightly behind and to the left of Glen, couldn't take his eyes off Lindsey's mouth as her lips moved in response to Glen's query. He searched his mind for a question that would elicit a smile from her just for him.

"So in answer to your next question, Dr. Steiner is it…?" asked Lindsey, as she looked to Glen for confirmation, and received a nod of his head in response, "it is by all means reasonable to believe that her daughter, Princess Ankhesenamun was quite beautiful as well." Lindsey accentuated her last words with a friendly wink, and received a gracious 'thank you' from the somewhat timid Glen.

It was at that moment that Kevin's mouth chose to open of its own accord. To his immense mortification, and quite before he realized it, he'd looked directly into Lindsey's clear, blue eyes and stated that there was no way the young wife of King Tut could possibly have been any lovelier than Lindsey, herself. From Glen's point of view, it was difficult to determine which one of the two turned the reddest.

Back in the relative privacy of the lab research room, both Kevin and Glen slipped into fresh lab coats, and Glen noticed for the first time, the memorandum on his desk inviting all specialists involved in The Reclamation Project to attend the combination dinner/seminar, featuring Dr. Lindsey Larimer. Kevin, peeking over Glen's shoulder to see what had captured his friends' attention, saw the flyer and Lindsey's name seemed to jump off the page at him.

"I guess they must have circulated this over the weekend," said Glen, pushing his glasses back up to meet his eyes, "they sure didn't waste any time once the authorization was finalized."

"I don't know why it is," groaned Kevin, running his hands through his blonde hair, "but every time I get near that woman, I turn into a blithering idiot."

Glen grinned in acknowledgment, "I can't argue that point with you Kev," was his laughing reply.

"Let's get busy," responded Kevin, sounding every bit the recalcitrant schoolboy. "We've got a boat load of work to do."

Fortunately, since many of the staff members at IBAT spent days at a time without leaving the facility, most of them had street wear, as well as some formal wear in their respective onsite, private rooms. For those who did not, the IBAT center offered a shopping mall on the seventh floor for the convenience of their employees who wished to shop in their spare time, without leaving the premises.

For the most part, their first day of direct involvement with The Reclamation Project kept the workers busy until well after six o'clock that evening, and by the time dinner was served to the one–hundred and thirty–five individuals who attended, they were all more than ready for some down time.

Kevin and Glen found themselves sitting one tier above Professor St. Germaine's table, which also boasted the remainder of the IBAT Board of Directors, and Dr. Lindsey Larimer, the featured guest speaker. Kevin couldn't take his eyes off of the beautiful woman, smiling so charmingly, so at ease with the top brass of this world–renowned institution. Her dress clung to her body like a second skin, and the luminescent glow of the material as she moved, appeared as the rings of Saturn slowly encircling her midriff.

Lindsey glanced up from laughing at one of Professor St. Germaine's witticisms, and her eyes met Kevin's directly. She smiled, not sure exactly why, and then returned to the conversation she'd been actively participating in, as the assemblage enjoyed the sumptuous meal set before them.

An hour later, when Lindsey was formally introduced to an eager and appreciative audience, and began her presentation, she captured the attention of every individual present with her first few sentences. For those who had not attended the meeting that morning, she recounted her experiences with her father, including the opening of the Great Library of Knowledge, and the parentage and history of the Princess Ankhesenamun. She went on to fascinate the attentive listeners with a brief history of King Tut's short life, including the fact that his true father was none other than the Pharaoh Akhenaten, who had apparently had yet another wife tucked neatly away. This actually made King Tut the half–brother of his wife, Ankhesenamun! The crowd was both captivated and mortified by this information, and Lindsey could scarcely keep up with the succession of questions that followed.

Throughout the verbal presentation, Kevin found himself incapable of removing his eyes from the captivating vision on the floating platform, facing the audience. Her ability to hold a crowd enthralled was obvious…her ability to keep him enthralled was quite disturbing.

Shortly after eleven o'clock that evening, Lindsey had finished answering the last question, and returned to her table, to the resounding applause of everyone in attendance. As people were preparing to return to their designated sleeping areas for the night, Kevin noticed that Professor St. Germaine was doing everything in his power to catch his attention. Upon realizing that they were being summoned, Kevin alerted Glen and the two men made their way down to the table where the object of Kevin's total focus and attention sat primly.

Professor St. Germaine shook Kevin and Glen's hands in turn. Then in a hushed tone, announced that he had received a message from Washington, DC. "It seems the famed professor's who the government commissioned to decipher and interpret the scrolls and tablets from the Great Library of Knowledge, have expressed a personal wish to meet with the three of you as soon as possible."

"The three of us?" echoed Glen, with a look of dumbfounded astonishment.

"You can't be serious," exclaimed Lindsey, quite taken aback by this information. "Do you mean that Professors' Farrier and McRae actually want to speak with us in person?" Her excitement was palpable, and when Professor St. Germaine nodded his head in affirmation, Lindsey's hand flew to her heart, and she thought for a moment she might faint.

"But why would these gentlemen want to see Glen and I?" queried Kevin, "I've never even heard of them, and I'm certain they haven't heard of us." Clearly, Kevin was as confused as Lindsey was excited.

"Why, you're our main forensic anthropology expert, Dr.

Sanders. Not to mention your background in molecular biology," replied the smiling Professor St. Germaine, "and of course, Glen is our primary biological anthropologist on this project." His whispered words sounded most conspiratorial, "Apparently the learned professors feel that there is information they would like to share with you, or glean from you, who knows? Anyway," he continued, "arrangements are being made for the three of you to join them tomorrow and spend a day or two going over specific information. I've sent a message back to them advising that you will all three be there posthaste, but your work here is crucial to the success of this project, so we cannot spare you for any more than a day or two. In your absence, the work here will continue as planned. Naturally, upon your return, you will immediately rejoin the work in progress on The Reclamation Project."

Lindsey sucked in her breath, feeling almost the same as she had when she'd first entered the gold–plated room of the Great Library of Knowledge. Rising from her chair was almost a challenge, and she thought for a moment that her knees might buckle out from under her, "I've heard," she interjected, "that the professors' are tucked away in some undisclosed, secret place while they review and examine the scrolls and tablets."

"They certainly are," laughed Professor St. Germaine, "and I'm sure the three of you will thoroughly enjoy the surroundings."

Lindsey and Kevin exchanged questioning glances, but it was a moment before either of them pulled their eyes away.

"I'll…I'll have to notify my mother that I'll be leaving town for, ah, a few days," stammered Lindsey, "thank you Professor St. Germaine, thank you." She wanted to say more, much more. This man had just opened yet another door for her, first by contacting her directly to offer her a position at IBAT, and now by allowing her time off to meet with two world renown scholars, who were nothing less than geniuses in their respective fields. Unfortunately, Lindsey was still too awestruck to mumble more than a numbed, "Goodnight Gentlemen," as she turned and joined the last of the audience members leaving the auditorium.

Chapter Three

The transport pod lifted silently and effortlessly from the helio–port atop the IBAT rooftop, and with the exception of the pilot, the occupants within found themselves in varying stages of nervousness.

Lindsey was the last to enter the vehicle, and sat down next to Glen. As the passenger seats faced one another, she found herself staring once again into Kevin's slate green eyes. She made a brief, mental note of the fact that his eyes seemed to change shades of green periodically, and wondered if he'd had iris–enhancement implants.

Lindsey was nervous on several levels. Had she not been so rude to this man seated across from her when he'd attempted to introduce himself the first time, they might be laughing and joking together even now in anticipation of this rare and exciting opportunity they were about to embark upon. Instead, she had chosen to stick her nose in the air and adopt a haughty exterior that had rendered the man incapable of coherent speech. It was her own fault she sat there now feeling like an outsider among two old friends.

Staring out the virtual–monitor that had long since taken the place of smoked glass or acrylic portals, Lindsey watched the rooftop of IBAT grow smaller as the craft continued its upward ascent. The view was so startlingly clear, it looked as though she could reach outside the vehicle and feel the air rushing by. The thought occurred to her that, were she capable of doing so, she'd have stuck her head out instead…much like the now extinct Ostrich had once stuck its head in the sand.

Glen's glasses had again made their way to the very tip of his nose, as he watched the virtual–panel and noted with relief that their ascent had been most uneventful. He pushed the black frames back into place with the tip of his index finger, vowing to check into some of those implants everyone else had. He knew his glasses were obsolete, but so was his way of thinking…at least comparatively speaking. Glen was quite behind the times, perhaps due to his being cooped up in one lab or another for most of his adult life. Hell, just piloting his old clunker of a Chevrolet Corvette made him nervous, in spite of the fact that it was unable to reach an altitude above thirty miles. He'd purchased it new over twenty years ago, right after the holo–monitors had replaced glass and acrylic windows in all transport vehicles, homes and businesses. The continued decline of air quality dictated that one could not spend too much time breathing outdoor air for fear of lung damage. Still, Glen's fear of extreme heights was not alleviated one bit by the replacement of windows.

He glanced over at Lindsey's profile and noted that she too was avidly watching the monitors. Glen smiled to himself…one could just about cut the sexual tension between this woman and Kevin with a laser. He thought of the doe–eyed Sal, and wondered if the other man had thought of him since their meeting the other night. When this project was over, he'd call the handsome Italian and perhaps meet him somewhere for dinner. He just couldn't continue to allow the world to pass him by…not to mention happiness, but realized at the same time that he'd have to be incredibly cautious. At this point, he just ardently wished his two companions would find a way to break the ice.

Kevin watched Lindsey and Glen pretending to be fascinated with the passing scenery through the virtual–monitors. He felt that if he didn't say something soon to redeem himself in the eyes of this beautiful young woman, they would spend the rest of their time on the project staring at monitors and never speaking. He wanted to start over, to pretend the other night never happened; wanted to say something witty and enthralling, and make her laugh with delight. He couldn't even think of what to say or where to start, and cleared his throat, "Ah, Doctor Larimer," he stammered, "I, uh, I want to sort of…."

Glen simply couldn't sit through another episode of 'Mr. Stutters meets the pretty lady doctor.' Kevin needed to be rescued, and soon, "I think what Dr. Sanders is trying to say to you Dr. Larimer, is that he wishes to apologize for his lack of protocol the other evening, and would like to present his introduction anew."

Kevin sat staring at the dark haired man seated across from him, the one whose glasses were once again working their way down the bridge of his nose, and wondered how in the world Glen could be so damned calm when he couldn't. He also wondered how it was that Glen knew precisely what he had been about to say. He looked sheepishly at the auburn haired beauty through his eyelashes, and noticed that the corners of her mouth were beginning to turn up. And then she laughed…and his heart resumed beating.

"Thank you Dr. Steiner," she offered, "I was beginning to get the feeling of being in a tomb all by myself."

Her laugh was contagious, and both Kevin and Glen found themselves laughing good–naturedly along with her. It was just what they had needed to lighten the atmosphere.

Kevin finally found his voice, and with a nod to Glen in acknowledgment of his verbal accomplishment, offered Lindsey a more refined introduction. "Dr. Larimer," he grinned, "might I say that your name and reputation precede you, and that mere words cannot begin to express how pleased and privileged I am by the rare opportunity to work at your side."

Lindsey laughed again in acceptance of his exaggerated greeting, and extended her hand in a gesture of friendship. "Please, Dr. Sanders," she returned, "since we're all three going to be working in very close proximity for some time to come, I think it would be much nicer if we simply addressed one another by our given names." She winked at him playfully as she released her small hand from his much larger one. "Please, call me Lindsey."

Kevin hadn't failed to catch the fact that she had again heavily accented his title, "That's great then," he grinned, "from now on I'll expect you to address me as Kevin." His emphasis on his name elicited yet another quick smile, and he had the feeling that this was going to be a really great experience.

They were on their way to meet with two world–renowned men that had been chosen above all other global scholars to transcribe and interpret the most precious and highly regarded of the scrolls and tablets. They were making what was, for all practical purposes, a clandestine journey to an undisclosed location, to share and receive information of which the rest of the world wasn't even aware. The stunning woman across from him was smiling, her even, white teeth, lending to the picture perfect beauty of her face. What was there not to be happy about?

Not to be outdone, Glen turned to Lindsey, and looking at her over the rim of his ever–sliding glasses, informed her that she could call him Glen, not 'Glen.' He used Kevin's hard pronunciation of his first name.

With the ambiance much improved, the conversation turned to that of the trip at hand, and Kevin and Glen found that they both had questions to present to the pretty Egyptologist sharing their company.

"You know, we were both quite fascinated with your presentation last night, Lindsey," offered Glen, as Kevin nodded his confirmation. "Our work at IBAT doesn't require too much knowledge of Egyptian artifacts, much less Egyptian mummies, but I have to admit that I find myself rather captivated by the whole concept."

Lindsey smiled in agreement, "I've often wondered if I'd still have my passion for Egypt, even if I'd been born to someone other than a world famous archeologist." Her smile was momentarily clouded and a distant look crossed her heart shaped face.

"I would imagine so," answered Glen thoughtfully, "I've always felt that anything we are born with a passion for in this life, is probably something we've carried over from a previous one."

"My father used to say something like that," smiled Lindsey. "It seems like I was drawn to Egypt since the day I was born. I spent half my life in classrooms, and the other half on my knees examining the artifacts my father found and translating the hieroglyphs on them."

"While we're on the subject Lindsey," Kevin broke in, "you said something in your seminar about the information in the library disclosing why the pyramids were built. I'd always heard they were burial chambers for the pharaohs, doesn't anyone know for sure?"

She liked the way her name sounded when he said it. It seemed that when most people addressed her by her first name, it sounded like they were calling her 'Lin–seed.' Kevin spoke it clearly, and she found herself wanting to hear him say it again. "That's a question almost as old as the pyramids themselves, Kevin," she answered. She could have no idea that he felt precisely the same way when she said his name.

"But I never really thought of a pyramid as a tomb," responded Kevin, genuinely interested in what this incredibly beautiful professional had to say, "I've always thought they had something to do with astronomy or some such thing."

"Again, Kevin," she answered, with slight shake of her head, "no one really knows for sure. It seems that some writings indicate a belief that the pyramids were constructed to carry the souls of selected or enlightened pharaohs directly to a higher, spiritual realm in the stars. Sort of like a launching pad for the souls of the dead kings. There were also small, perfectly symmetrical shafts cut from the inside out of the pyramids, since the Egyptian Pharaohs believed their souls could shoot through the openings and join with Osiris in the constellations. Yet other writings do speak of certain astrological connections, such as the tracking of the solstices and equinoxes…you know the Egyptian culture was the first to draw a zodiac. And they did believe that the constellation Orion represented Osiris, their god of the dead. In ancient times, the word Cairo meant Mars, so it seems that while the ancient Egyptians certainly had a very strong affinity with the cosmos, it's all still pure conjecture.

It's odd when you think of it, that the Egyptians wrote about everything from tapestry, to farming, to vital statistics, but never wrote one word about the actual purpose for the pyramids, much less how they could construct something back then that we aren't capable of duplicating today. You never know guys," she said in a purposely mysterious voice, "maybe we'll find out the truth of the matter once and for all. Think about it, the Great Pyramid is one of the oldest dated structures on the planet. From what we have gleaned, it was built by the Pharaoh Khufu, around 2650 BC, who fancied himself to be the incarnation of the Sun God Ra, but even that information could be way off target. Finding out the truth to their real purpose would be quite a revelation indeed."

"That Khufu fellow had quite a high opinion of himself, didn't he?" joked Kevin.

"It would seem so," was Lindsey's amused reply. "But Khufu managed to construct his pyramid which such precision, that not only is it in perfect alignment with Orion's Belt, but it was also placed dead in the middle of the earth's center."

"How exactly do you mean in the middle of the earth?" Broke in Glen, every bit as curious to hear the answers to these mysterious questions as Kevin was.

"Well, I'll try to render a simple explanation," answered Lindsey. "If you were to divide the earth's land mass into equal quarters, the north–south axis being the longest land meridian, and the east–west axis being the longest land parallel, there would obviously only be one place that these longest land lines of the terrestrial earth could cross. That is precisely where the great pyramid sits, right smack dab in the center of gravity of the continents."

Lindsey couldn't help noticing that Kevin and Glen were both leaning forward in their seats, as though hanging on to every word. "Another very important aspect of the pyramids," she continued, "is the fact that each side is oriented with one of the cardinal points of the compass…you know, north, south, east and west. The horizontal cross section of the pyramid is square at any level, with a maximum error between side lengths of an unbelievable less than one–point–zero percent. The Egyptians were a highly advanced people for their time, and even had electric batteries fashioned from clay jars that held vinegar and generated electric power. They needed lights you know, to work deep inside the pyramids. "

Both Kevin and Glen were in awe not only at the knowledge that an ancient civilization had built something so incredibly precise, but also with the fact that Lindsey's mind was like a computer grain when it came to any information on Egypt.

Kevin had no doubt whatsoever that he could stand listening to Lindsey speak for the next couple millennium. It wasn't difficult to think of questions to ask her, since there was a good deal about the subject of the Egyptian Pyramids and culture that interested him greatly. "I've always found it strange that there are no references to the pyramids in the bible," supplied Kevin, "I mean if they're the oldest structures on earth, wouldn't you think something would have been written about them in the bible somewhere?"

Glen answered before Lindsey had a chance to. "There is one that I know of," he offered, "In the book of Isaiah, chapter nineteen…I believe it's verse nineteen that says, 'In that day shall there be an alter to the Lord in the midst of the land of Egypt, and a pillar at the border thereof.'"

"Why Glen," remarked Kevin, his eyebrows lifted in surprise, "you truly do amaze me sometimes." Clearly, his words were spoken in all sincerity.

"Well," I wouldn't get too excited about it Kevin, "it's not like I can ramble off a bible full of verses by memory, although I did attend church quite often as a child." His smile gave way to the fact that his mother had insisted on those lengthy Sunday sermons. "Even so, that's the only verse I'm familiar with that could be attributed to the pyramids. You would think there would be many more references wouldn't you?"

"You never know," answered Kevin, without taking his eyes off Lindsey, "maybe that's something we'll all be finding out about very soon."

A chill ran through Lindsey's entire body and she shivered slightly. This kind of an attraction could be dangerous when they had to focus all their attention on the project at hand.

"So Lindsey," began Glen, "what do you suppose is the connection with these scrolls and the mummies of King Tut and Anksn...."

"Ankhesenamun," clarified Lindsey, as she clearly enunciated the name. "Actually, Glen, if you remember to say something that sounds like an–ox–on–a–moon, and run it together when you say it, you'll be close enough."

Glen repeated the name a few times, as she had said it, and found that it rolled off his tongue much easier.

"And to answer your question," she continued, "I am at somewhat of a loss to explain the connection." She paused and settled her eyes on Kevin's throat, since she couldn't fully concentrate on anything when she looked directly into his eyes. She was sitting in too close a proximity to Glen to crane her neck when she spoke to him, "I can say that in some way I understand the interest in King Tut, since he was buried in Egypt, but Princess Ankhesenamun was found in a Chinese desert. I can't imagine what role she would play in any of this."

"You're right," Kevin's baritone voice cut in, that was something that he'd wondered about since Lindsey had given her first, brief presentation on Monday morning. He'd been rather surprised that no one had asked her to elaborate on that fact, even at the dinner presentation, "What was the widow of our illustrious King Tut doing so far from Egypt when she died?"

"I was wondering when someone would ask me that," she returned with a quirk of one perfectly arched eyebrow, "unfortunately, it's yet another question that no one has an answer for. The fact that she was found so recently is quite strange in itself," continued Lindsey, "it seems that some archeologists uncovered several mummies in the Takla Makan Desert back in the nineteen–seventies and eighties, but they had not been mummified at all in the same way as the Egyptian mummies. That's not even the amazing part," her look was genuinely conspiratorial, and again, Kevin and Glen hung on to every word, "the amazing part," she continued, "is that all the mummies they found were Caucasian."

"Are we talking about ancient mummies here?" questioned Glen; "Caucasians have resided in China for hundreds of years." His glasses were halfway down the bridge of his nose so that Lindsey couldn't see his eyes if she'd have tried to. Her focus remained predominantly on Kevin's neck.

"Actually Glen, we're talking about some incredibly ancient mummies. The ones found in the seventies and eighties had already been dead and buried for over four–thousand years, which is certainly far earlier than history would have placed any Caucasians, anywhere in or near China."

"Amazing!" replied Kevin, "how do you imagine they got there? And more importantly, what were they doing there?" His quest for knowledge was genuine.

"I'm afraid every new archeological find usually brings with it more questions than answers," smiled Lindsey in return.

"What do you think they might have been doing there?" queried Glen, and then before she could form a response, "and did they live by themselves or with the Chinese?"

"Well, in response to your second question," she intoned, "although the group that was found seemed to live primarily in their own familial unit, there was some evidence that at least one of the men had married a Chinese woman. There was also evidence of some trading having gone on between the Caucasians and the

Chinese. As to how they got there, the majority seemed to believe that they had followed herds from the steppes of Eastern Europe and settled in one of the oases scattered throughout the huge desert at that time."

"And what do you think?" asked Kevin softly, almost huskily.

Lindsey felt her heart skip a beat or two before answering, "I really can't imagine anyone following sheep that far and then just arbitrarily settling at the first oasis they come to. It's something I've thought about often though, something my father and I used to discuss." She swallowed the rising lump in her throat at the mention of her dad, and then remembered something else that had fascinated her about the 'Desert Mummies of Takla Makan,' "You want to know something even more bizarre?" she asked, her conspiratorial tone resurfacing. The simultaneous "What!" uttered by both Kevin and Glen made her giggle before continuing, "the mummies of the Caucasian people indicated that some of them were so tall as to be considered giants. What's more, many of them bore the scars of surgeries. It seems that breathing in the desert sand and smoke inhalation from their cooking fires combined to cause massive lung problems. Most of the surgery scars seemed to have been the residuals of lung surgery."

"Apparently," smiled Glen wistfully, "bad air quality is nothing new."

"Giants, you say," exclaimed Kevin, "what constituted giants in those days?"

"Well," Lindsey answered, "it seems that the first male mummies discovered were around six–feet tall, which compared to the indigenous Chinese, must have been quite tall indeed. Even some of the women were as tall as five–feet eight to ten inches. It was the mummies that were found near the grave of Ankhesenamun that were considered the real giants."

"How tall were they?" asked Kevin, his brow wrinkling slightly as he pondered the information Lindsey had been sharing.

"Several of the men were seven–feet tall, and a couple of them were nearly eight–feet tall when the archeologists measured their mummies. Most of the women found nearby were over six–feet tall, with the exception of Princess Ankhesenamun, who although tall for her time, was nowhere near six–feet."

"And these mummies were the ones found near the princess?" pondered Glen aloud.

"Yes," responded Lindsey, "the ones discovered most recently, which is strange, because they were found less than half a mile away from the first mummies that had been discovered in the Takla Makan Desert. They were also the only mummies buried with amulets and medallions imparting homage to the ancient, Egyptian sun god, Ra. Of course," she interjected with a sly smile, "their amulets weren't considered blasphemous, as was the one worn by the princess when her mummy was discovered."

It was then that Glen glanced up at the virtual–panel and noticed their helio–pod was about to land. Both Lindsey and Kevin followed his gaze and realized they'd been talking for the entire fifteen minute trip.

Their exit from the craft revealed that they had no clue where their journey had taken them. Although they were clearly outside, the air quality was substantially better here than it had been in the city. The sky above seemed much bluer, what little they saw of it, and the globe-shaped buildings that rose up around them were reflective, revealing nothing of their contents or inhabitants. In seconds, a hover–transport arrived, and several uniformed men herded them inside. Their dark uniforms bore emblems that the trio did not recognize.

"This is quite the clandestine adventure, isn't it," exclaimed Glen, wiggling his eyebrows for effect, when he realized the holo–monitors in this ride weren't turned on.

"I guess they really don't want us to know where we're going," echoed Kevin, as he settled in comfortably next to Lindsey. In truth, he had made it a point to do so, when he realized that this second craft also had two seats that faced each other.

"Notice that this is a programmed vehicle…no pilot," pointed out Lindsey, in the dim, bluish green light of the transport interior. "I guess they figure you can't tell anyone else where you've been, if you don't know yourself."

Kevin found himself hoping it was a long ride to wherever they were going. He felt Lindsey's nearness most comfortable indeed, and the close proximity in which they sat made it almost feel like they were out on a weekend date…a chaperoned weekend date.

His enjoyment of their present situation was short lived. Much to his dismay, the transport pod came to a complete stop and the door retracted, affording them a glimpse of a world they could only have imagined.

"Where are we?" questioned Lindsey in a near whisper, as she stepped out of the vehicle onto a glossy, turquoise landing.

Glen and Kevin were both too stunned for speech, as they disembarked and joined Lindsey on the marbled platform.

Not one of the three knew where they were, but they clearly weren't anywhere they'd ever been before. Several hundred feet above their heads, they saw that the sky had been replaced by what appeared to be a massive, translucent dome that stretched as far as their eyes could see in either direction. An enormous blue whale glided effortlessly by above the dome, its massive tail fanning the water in an aquatic ballet. The litheness with which this prehistoric, monolithic mammal carried itself through its liquid world seemed in direct opposition to its gargantuan dimensions.

Lindsey couldn't help saying a silent 'thank you' to the Oceanographic Preservation Alliance for Life, or OPAL, that had stopped the slaughter of these beautiful mammals entirely, before, like the buffalo, and so many other species, they became extinct entirely.

From their position on the raised landing platform, the mystical city within the dome was every bit as magnificent as the rare glimpse of the graceful blue whale had been. There were several levels of what appeared to be dwellings, some at ground level, some atop clear, round pillars, and some that looked to be multiple-occupant or apartment dwellings. What was the most breathtaking was the fact that the entire city seemed to light itself. There was no apparent single source of light, but the marbled turquoise streets, as well as the multi-colored dwellings, seemed to glow with a light of their own.

They were still stunned speechless, and hadn't been able to do more than stare at their new surroundings…and each other, when a barely audible hum sounded from under the platform and they felt themselves being lowered.

They were met at ground level by an older and very distinguished looking gentlemen wearing long, white robes and holding a fat, black cat in his left arm. The small, pointed goatee on his chin matched the short, white hair on his head, and Glen thought the man resembled a Shakespearean actor.

"Hello, hello!" He greeted them in a jovial voice that belayed his years, "You must be the young doctors from IBAT" he reasoned, offering them his free hand in greeting. "And you," he beamed, singling out Lindsey as she stood somewhat behind her companions, "you can only be the lovely Dr. Lindsey Larimer."

Kevin and Glen stepped aside, allowing the white haired man with his well trimmed, matching beard, to greet the young woman whom he obviously highly regarded. His eyes were alight with admiration and curiosity as he studied the classic beauty of the face before him.

Kevin elbowed Glen in the ribs and whispered quietly, "If this guy introduces himself as Captain Nemo, I'm outta here."

"Captain Nemo I'm not." The gentlemen grinned broadly. Apparently, his hearing was quite acute. He gently stroked the cat in his arms, and looked at Lindsey as he spoke, "I'll have to apologize for not having introduced myself right away. Please understand that I have been quite looking forward to meeting the three of you. My name is Farrier, Trenton Farrier, but you kids can call me Trent," he said with a wink, "never did care much for formalities."

Glen liked the man already. He hadn't been referred to as a 'kid' for several decades now. There was a friendliness that emanated from their host, and his eyes were honest and sincere. Glen had always felt that the eyes were the mirrors of the soul, and that old souls could forever recognize other old souls.

"Professor Farrier," murmured Lindsey, as full recognition dawned, "you're the Professor Farrier?" Her excitement was quite obvious, and Kevin and Glen were left to look at one another and shrug. Somewhere in the back of his mind, Glen felt that this man's name should mean something to him, but couldn't quite make an association. It didn't take long for him to reach enlightenment.

Lindsey looked to each of her companions in turn, "Kevin, Glen, this is Professor Farrier, world famous Theologian and

Philosopher," she introduced the older man ceremoniously.

It was then that Glen remembered having heard this famous professor's name from his youth when he had attended a summer seminary. Even that many years ago, this highly acclaimed writer and speaker's teachings and philosophies were known to invite both praise, and criticism for his outspoken and liberal views. He seemed to remember though, that the professor was past middle age back then. The guy had to be a good deal older than he looked.

"Please," said Professor Farrier, continuing to stroke the feline's back as the animal purred contentedly, blissfully unaware of anything going on around him, "call me Trent, there's certainly no need for formalities here." His pleasant voice and friendly demeanor put his three guests at ease, as he motioned for them to follow his lead.

Kevin placed his hand on the small of Lindsey's back and she found that she liked the way it felt when he touched her. She smiled up at him as they followed the man in his floor length robes several yards to the left, and then stepped onto a transport walkway that was barely discernible from the floor of the city itself.

Slowly, the foursome was carried along down what appeared to be the main street of this sprawling, domed, underwater city. From their new ground level position, the dwellings seemed even more magical than before, and appeared as though they were constructed of a sea–shell–like material. Some of these buildings were in warm shades of coral, some in varying hues of gray and blue, and yet others that looked like they might have been carved from a single, huge pearl.

As the four passed slowly by the structures, Trent did his best to explain why their location had to be kept secret. "As you must know," his focus was on Lindsey, "your father's discovery of the Great Library of Knowledge was highly publicized news in both Egypt and the United States." Lindsey's nod affirmed that she was well aware of the media coverage surrounding their historical find. "Since anyone familiar with the legend knows that the information contained in the library is powerful knowledge indeed, there would no doubt be many seeking to attain such wisdom for other than the good of mankind. It is imperative that the scrolls and tablets remain in our possession until the deciphering and interpretations are complete. There is no telling what could happen if the information was misused or misunderstood."

Lindsey, of all people, knew the importance of the information contained in those ancient writings, and of the far reaching consequences should such information be stolen, "You have our absolute assurance, Prof…Trent," Lindsey offered sincerely, "that we'll speak to no one outside of those who already know at IBAT."

Kevin and Glen affirmed their agreement, and waited for the older man to continue his monologue, as the transport–walk carried them along.

While Kevin's eyes were still predominantly on Lindsey, Glen found himself overwhelmed by the beauty of this fantasy world. He couldn't help noticing that most of the dwellings were divided by what appeared to be alabaster fences, affording something of what must be the private back yard he'd heard about on the news. Above them, the city seemed to rise in layers, and an intricately designed system of transparent, tube–like tunnels, indicated that a fast and effective mode of inter–city transportation had been devised.

Periodically, they would pass by an ornamental fountain with clear, clean water bubbling up through transparent hoses, and then pouring forth from large shells that seemed to be floating independently above the crystalline pools. All around them, the magnificent ocean embraced the dome, enveloping them in an aquamarine wonderland.

"In any event," chuckled Trent, "I'm sure by now you've deduced you're in an underwater city." The three nodded in unison, and their guide continued, "Well, this is the finished project; the prototype you might say." He waved his right arm, indicating the elaborate architecture of the buildings, "of course, the public has been lead to believe it will be quite some time yet before it's fully completed, though more than half of the units have already been purchased outright; sight unseen."

"I can certainly see why," answered Lindsey, hardly able to take her eyes from the sheer beauty and dream–like quality of their surroundings. She noted with delight as they neared the center of the city, that there was even a town square. Several shops with everything from apparel to gourmet foods dotted the coral colored sidewalks, and a large entertainment gallery dominated the majority of one entire block. Lindsey continued to take in the sights, fully aware of Kevin's presence so near to her, as Trent continued speaking.

"The City is quite complete as you can see," explained their guide, "except that the US and Egyptian governments have uh, rather borrowed the use of it until such time as our work is complete." He smiled conspiratorially before continuing, "In truth, none of this would exist were it not for the information we've gleaned from the scrolls. The exact instructions for creating this very structure were written thousands of years ago by none other than the Atlantians themselves."

Lindsey sucked in her breath and turned to look at Kevin. Neither of them said a word, but both were struck with the realization that if something like this could be constructed within a ten year span based on the information in the scrolls, there was no telling what else they were about to learn.

"The powers that be," continued Trent, "seemed to think it was a much safer place for us to work, and arranged to move in a select group of individuals who were already in the process of deciphering and translating the documents from the library. Only six months ago, the remainder of that team completed their portion of the work on the scrolls and tablets, leaving only Professor McRae and myself here to finish putting everything together and render our final reports."

Kevin looked thoughtful, "I can understand your wanting to see Lindsey," he broke in, "she was after all, one of the first people on the planet to step into the Great Library when it was discovered. Her knowledge of Egyptian culture and writings would certainly be an asset to anyone." He looked at Lindsey and she smiled her thanks at the indirect compliment, "but," he continued, "I don't understand why you wanted to see Glen and I. Our work is strictly limited to Biological and Forensic Anthropology."

"Ah, yes," replied Trent, "I understand you two are rather heading up the team, so to speak, with the actual cloning process. In truth, it was quite difficult persuading the CEO of IBAT to let either one of you go the day after the project got underway. You might say we're really good negotiators." Trent's intelligent gray eyes twinkled, "I might add, Gentlemen, that your backgrounds are both very impressive. Professor Farrier and myself were made privy to your work history files before we sent for you."

Kevin and Glen exchanged questioning glances.

"To answer your question Kevin," Trent clearly preferred addressing others, and being addressed, on a first name bases, "my partner and I agreed that since the two of you are so directly involved with this project, there are certain very important aspects of it you should be aware of as well. Here, we disembark the transport," he finished, without skipping a beat.

Trent stepped off the moving walkway and the three visitors followed him as he made his way toward one of the large, luminescent structures and once there, peeked into a recognition scanner.

The door slid open and the older man bade them enter as he disappeared over the threshold. The inside of the home was every bit as beautiful as the outside, and Lindsey held her breath for a moment, as she surveyed the unique and luxuriant interior.

Kevin and Glen were clearly as taken aback by the sheer splendor of the fashionable, up–scale home as Lindsey.

The twenty–first century reproduction furnishings were like something out of a catalog of antiques. Against one wall was a couch, an actual sofa, not a neo–foam–floating bench, or an air couch that could be felt but not seen…this was honest–to–God furniture. An overstuffed armchair, and simulated wood coffee table, made the trio feel like they had stepped back in time, and Lindsey wasn't sure that she ever wanted to leave.

"It is quite lovely isn't it?" stated Trent, as though he had read her mind, "Thad and I were both extremely pleased with the government's choice of housing." His smile leant no doubt that his pleasure at having been moved to such an aesthetically pleasing environment was highly understated. "I think, my dear Lindsey, that you will find the cleansing room most agreeable."

The lift of her eyebrow and her questioning look, prompted Trent to laugh out loud, before leading her down a short hallway, and then opening a door and standing back for her to enter. There on the left, at the top of three steps, was a bathtub…a real, just–like–

grandma–used–to–talk–about, bathtub, and Lindsey was beside herself with sheer joy at being able to see one first–hand. She had never experienced a form of bathing aside from the cleaning–tube, and there was no water involved.

"Perhaps you'd like to indulge yourself in a nice, hot bath later this evening?" offered Trent with a gentle smile.

Lindsey thought she might cry, and blinked back the tears forming behind her eyes, as she stared longingly at the inviting vessel. She tried to imagine what it would feel like to sink down and immerse one's entire body in hot water. Water bathing seemed almost decadent, what with the demand for the liquid having far outweighed the supply, since Lindsey could remember.

History taught that man had to implement ocean–water–processing plants in the year 2169, due to the waste and abuse of that precious commodity by their fore-bearers. While the plants successfully processed a sufficient supply of potable water to provide civilization with the life sustaining liquid, it also produced mountains of salt that were becoming more and more difficult to dispose of, and the Utah Salt Flats had long since become the Utah Salt Mountains. No matter…there certainly wasn't enough of the life giving necessity to be wasted on frivolities like bathing.

Trent stood in the arched doorway smiling at her, the way her father had done when he'd presented her with a gift and then basked in her excitement and appreciation.

"Oh Trent," Lindsey said slowly, "Trent, there are no words with which to thank you," she lifted her arm in the direction of the seashell shaped bathing tub, "but water is far too valuable to waste on such things."

Trent tilted his head back and laughed openly. With his feline charge still tucked securely within the confines of his left arm, he reached out with his right hand and patted Lindsey's back in a father–like gesture. "You are a charming young woman, Little Miss Lindsey, but you needn't worry, this city was built over a fresh water stream that runs under the ocean floor. That was the primary reason for this particular location having been chosen. The supply is such that what is not required to sustain this city will be routed elsewhere."

Lindsey did not hear his last statement, what had caught her attention was his having just referred to her as 'Little Miss Lindsey.' She searched her mind, and raised her hand to her forehead in concentration.

"Are you all right my dear?" asked Trent, slightly alarmed.

"I've been called that before," Lindsey looked deeply into the friendly face of her host, "Little Miss Lindsey. It was a pet name that my father called me when I was little. But someone else called me that once too, when I was very young."

"Ah," replied Trent, "then your memory is quite good, quite good indeed. I didn't say anything when we met a bit ago, because I was sure you were too young to remember, but I did make your acquaintance on one other occasion." He smiled again and scratched his pointy eared pet on its head; "you couldn't have been more than four–years–old at the time. Your father attended a seminar I spoke at in Canada, and had brought you along. I remember at the time, thinking it quite odd indeed that anyone would bring such a small child to a lecture on the Rosetta Stone. Throughout the very lengthy presentation, I vividly remember how still you sat there in the front row with your father. You seemed to listen to every word that had been said with a rapt attention that one seldom sees in adults, much less small children. I don't mind telling you, I was quite impressed."

Trent grinned broadly as he remembered the little brown haired girl with the huge blue eyes. He'd thought then that she looked like a little angel, and seeing her now didn't change his original assessment one bit. "There was a replica of the stone on display," he continued, "and when the seminar was over, the guests were invited to inspect the inscriptions firsthand. I watched you get up and take your father's hand, fairly pulling him along through the crowd, until you had reached the replica stone. Then to everyone's complete amazement, you actually read from the stone and verbally translated some of the writings into English. I heard your father praise you then, and refer to you as, 'Little Miss Lindsey.' Afterward, your father approached me and introduced himself, and his special little girl," he favored her with another broad smile, "you addressed me then as Mister Professor Farrier, and I, in turn, called you 'Little Miss Lindsey,' which elicited a most charming giggle from you.

That was the one and only day in my entire life that I almost regretted my self–imposed celibacy. I imagined then what it would be like to have a child of my own, and wondered if I'd chosen the wrong path for myself."

"No," replied Lindsey, "the work you have done is legendary. There is no question that you chose the right path, look what you have accomplished in your life. But, you're not a priest are you?" she paused, "could you not have a family and continue your work as well?"

"I'm afraid that would not be possible, Lindsey," responded Trent almost wistfully, "my work occupies virtually every waking moment of my life. It wouldn't be fair to a have a wife or a child that I couldn't spend any quality time with, not fair at all."

"I understand," said Lindsey knowingly, "my father used to apologize to me constantly for being away so much. I think he felt quite guilty, especially when I was very young, for not being around more. You know though," she smiled with the memory, "I never really minded, because what time we did have together was so incredible, so full of love and happiness, that it made up for all those days and nights he wasn't there. Of course, as soon as I was big enough to go with him, we neither one saw much of my mother."

"Well then, Little Miss Lindsey," Trent smiled, "now that we have all the pleasantries out of the way, let me introduce you to my friend and colleague, Professor McRae. He has been looking forward to meeting you, and I'm afraid I shall incur his wrath if I don't present you immediately."

Lindsey smiled, suddenly feeling a bit like 'Alice in Wonderland,' "I'm right behind you, Trent," she said softly.

"And I, you," was his cryptic reply.

Chapter Four

Kevin and Glen were no longer in the living area when Lindsey and Trent returned. Their voices however, indicated that they were somewhere outside and behind the dwelling. Trent led her across the main room and out through a sliding glass panel in the far wall. There, between the house and two alabaster walls that formed the fence, was a back yard from which sprouted real, live grass and ended at the outer edge of the translucent dome itself.

The ocean teamed with sea life and Lindsey found that she didn't know which drew her interest more intently, the literal 'ocean view,' or the grass yard on which she stood. Her perusal of these fascinating new surroundings was momentarily broken when she felt something brush against her leg.

Trent had stepped up behind her, "It seems our mascot has quite taken to you."

"He's very discriminating, you know," sounded another voice.

Lindsey turned to see who was speaking and realized as she did so that it could only be the esteemed Professor McRae. His large belly quivered with his mirth, and his eyes virtually twinkled. "He won't go to just anyone you know."

Looking fondly down at the beautiful, young Egyptologist, Trent smiled and introduced their furry friend. "Little Miss Lindsey, Kevin, Glen," he nodded at Lindsey's companions, seated comfortably behind her, "forgive me for once again forgetting my manners, I'd like to introduce you to our third partner." His wink belied the somberness of his exaggerated introduction; "this is Deuteronomy." As if in acknowledgment of his name, the cat meowed soulfully, and Lindsey felt compelled to lift the animal and nuzzle his head under her chin.

Kevin found himself wondering if Lindsey would favor him with such treatment were he to meow.

Lindsey continued to stroke the feline as her attention was drawn to a school of dolphin's not forty feet from where she stood, their playful eyes and smiling snouts brought a look of pure enjoyment to the young woman's face.

"It's breathtaking isn't it?" broke in Trent, "a most serene place to work and study."

"It's truly the most extraordinary place I have ever seen," replied Lindsey in all sincerity.

"It's beauty pales beside you, Dr. Larimer," the resonant sound of the unfamiliar voice brought Lindsey back to the purpose of their visit, and she turned to formally greet the highly acclaimed Hieroglyphics and Hieratics expert, Professor Thaddeus McRae.

Professor McRae was a rotund man, no taller than Lindsey herself, with a long, gray ponytail and a beard that had probably not seen a trim since it began its initial journey down his chin many, many decades ago.

Lindsey shook his hand and greeted him with a genuine smile. Her father had spoken very highly of Professor McRae indeed, and his name had been mentioned many times in postgraduate School, as his being a man far beyond his time in both insight and wisdom.

"Well how do you like that, Trent? The first beautiful woman I've seen in ten years, and you introduce the cat to her first…and look at the treatment he's getting!" The man's eyes were alight with good humor, and Lindsey knew that not only were these great men, they were good men as well.

Two large desks had been set up on either side of the alabaster fence and it was obvious that the famed scholars preferred accomplishing the majority of their work in the back yard. It certainly wasn't difficult to see why.

"We are so very pleased that the three of you were able to join us," exclaimed Professor McRae, as Lindsey sat in the chair on Kevin's right, facing Trent's desk. "I've already had the pleasure of meeting Kevin and Glen, and incidentally," he paused, "like Trent, I prefer to interact on a first name basis, so please feel free to call me Thad."

The black cat had settled in comfortably on Lindsey's lap, and gave a soft, playful meow, before tucking his paws under his chin and preparing to nap.

"I think he wants you to know," offered Thad, with a lopsided grin and a nod toward the feline in her lap, "that he prefers being called 'Dude.'"

After having been offered refreshments, their hosts took on more serious personas, and the trio braced themselves to hear at least a portion of what information the scholars had gleaned from the Library of Knowledge.

"We certainly have no wish to alarm any of you," began Trent, "but we are very close to being finished with the work we began shortly after your father's discovery of the ancient library." His eyes rested on Lindsey as he spoke, "through our work, and the work of many others, we have uncovered revelations so startling as to be almost inconceivable."

"The information contained in that library," interjected Thad, "could literally change life on earth not only as we have come to know it, but also as we have been taught to understand it."

Trent leaned forward in his chair, "And what's more," he added, "these documents confirm with absolute certainty, the very existence of God himself."

Lindsey's eyes met Kevin's, and Glen's glasses almost fell completely off the end of his nose. It was a moment before any of them could even breathe.

For the next four hours, Lindsey, Kevin and Glen sat spellbound as their hosts recounted much of what had been gleaned from the ancient writings contained in the numerous stones and tablets.

The professors, in turn, spoke of documents found in the library that predated civilization itself. Records immortalized on scrolls and tablets that had withstood thousands of years, and still appeared to have only been manufactured recently. The quality of the paper scrolls was far superior to any that could be made in the present, and was composed with materials that our scientists had yet to identify. The inscriptions were not hieroglyphics or hieratics, but rather, some form of numerical, coded histories and prophecies, that had taken a horde of mathematicians and as many analysts and physicists to even partially decipher.

"If these records are to be believed," stated Trent, "and there's certainly no reason why we shouldn't believe them, given their confirmed authenticity, "God himself did in fact create this planet just as the Holy Bible tells us, complete with Adam, Eve, and the garden of Eden. I'm afraid the atheists of the world are in for quite an awakening once this information becomes public."

"Of course," interjected Thad, "we seriously doubt that the government will reveal all the information contained in the library," he smiled almost sadly, "they will pick and choose what information to reveal, and what not to. The human race has always been quite under–informed, for what the government considers 'the greater good of mankind,'" he shook his head thoughtfully, "so very sad, very sad indeed."

"Well," commented Kevin, as he ran his hands through his ever–tousled hair, "I guess this pretty much destroys the 'big bang' theory."

The older professors looked at one another knowingly. "There was a lot of 'banging' going on, Son, but not as our scientists had interpreted it," smiled Trent.

Three quizzical faces stared intently at the bearers of this information, awaiting further explanation. Outside the dome, the school of dolphins continued to frolic and dive playfully all but unnoticed by the five inhabitants of the Underwater City.

"As any good Christian believes," began Thad, his long gray beard resting against his robe–ensconced, rotund belly, "God created all the heavens and the earth, God being an indefinable, all–powerful entity. The heavens consisted of an infinite number of planets, stars, and moons, broken down into universes and galaxies. According to the ancient writings, all the planets in our solar system alone were not only capable of sustaining life as we know it, but were in fact, inhabited by many races of beings. "Of course," he continued, "this only confirms what the majority of our civilization has believed from the beginning of time."

"Quite so," responded Trent, "but it seems that much of what is written in the bible should be taken even more literally and in a much broader perspective than ever before imagined. We must also bear in mind that the earth itself is a very new planet in the relative scheme of things. That is," he clarified, "with regard to human inhabitation. One must also remember that it took God seven days to create an inhabitable planet, but according to the documents we've studied, one day in God's time is many millennium in our own time.

Many things apparently transpired along the way." He glanced across the lush expanse of grass between himself and his longtime friend and partner, "I believe perhaps I should let Thad explain further, since he's the Theologian, and can undoubtedly shed much more light on the details than I can."

Thad stroked his bushy beard thoughtfully, and noted with a smile that Dude had fallen asleep quite peacefully in the lap of the young woman. "Well," he began, "it is important to remember that God has legions of angels in his service, and the bible makes very frequent reference to this fact. These angels are identified on nine separate levels, or choirs, as spoken of in Catholic theology, those levels being the Cherubim, Seraphim, Thrones, Domination's, Virtues, Powers, the Principalities, the Archangels and the angels, though not necessarily in that order. We can only assume that he is referring to these angelical beings in the book of Genesis by the usage of the words 'us', and 'our.' Firstly," he continued, as his audience sat captivated before him, "we must note that the first two paragraphs of Genesis tell us that in the beginning God created the heaven and the earth, and that the earth was without form and void. It goes on to say that darkness was upon the face of the earth and the deep. God then created the day and the night, and divided the waters from the waters. This chapter goes on to tell us in verse twenty, that after the fourth day, he commanded that the waters bring forth abundantly the moving creature that hath life, and the following verses through the twenty–fifth describe the bringing forth of fowl, cattle and all creeping things. Clearly, there was every manner of beast roaming the earth, and I would imagine that included the great beasts such as the dinosaurs. I realize," he paused, "that this is nothing you don't already know, but what transpires from that point is where we believe the angels themselves were directly involved. Not to turn this into a Sunday school lesson," he smiled, "but we must look to the very next verse in Genesis to fully understand. I shall quote directly, he stated before continuing. "'And God said, Let us make man in our image, after our likeness; and let them have dominion over the fish of the sea, and over the fowl of the air, and over the cattle, and over all the earth, and over every creeping thing that creepeth upon the earth.'" He finished his quote and refilled his lungs with air, "The scripture goes on to say, 'So God created man in his own image in the image of God created he him; male and female created he them.' It goes to follow that if God had not yet created man himself, the us and our could only be referring to his angels."

Glen thoughtfully lulled this information over. He had read the bible in its entirety before adulthood, but had never really given any thought to the actual word usage.

"Remember," continued Thad, "these things all took place in chapter one of the book of Genesis, with no mention of either Adam or Eve until the second chapter, when he specifically placed them not in a garden in Eden, but a garden eastward of Eden. Therefore, it would appear that the land of Eden was already an established domain when Adam and Eve were created, and that the first humans God had created and placed on earth had continued to populate the earth as the Lord had bade them to do."

Kevin sat back in his chair and gave a low whistle. "That would certainly account for Adam and Eve's offspring finding wives, since that would have been quite difficult to do if their parents were the first and only people God placed on the earth."

"Quite so, quite so," agreed Thad, "and according to some of the writings we have been able to decipher, there was quite a span of time that passed between the first human beings on earth and the arrival of Adam and Eve. Enough time that several very different cultures had begun to evolve."

The yard was awash with the luminescent glow of the fence walls and house, combined with the natural movement of the ocean outside the dome, to cast a mystical, aquamarine light that seemed otherworldly, but not at all unpleasant.

Lindsey listened with the same rapt attention she had displayed as a child when she was hearing something that interested her greatly. She knew that the professors had revealed but a small amount of the knowledge contained in the scrolls and tablets, and waited patiently for them to continue. Her patience did not go unrewarded.

"Of course," said Thad thoughtfully; "these are very small revelations in comparison to our other discoveries, which include the fact that there was a great deal of information left out of the bible completely. This is laid out very clearly in the scrolls taken from the Great Library, and for one thing, the 'war in heaven' that is yet to come, written about by the apostle John, in chapter twelve of the book of Revelation is not the only 'angelic war' at all.

The lost pages of the bible describe a war that took place in the heavens shortly before God created Adam, and indicates that there was certainly humanoid life of some sort on this planet much, much earlier than anyone would have guessed. The earth was almost completely destroyed, along with most of the other planets in our solar system. The documents we have examined confirm that Satan, who was in fact, one of God's most favored angels, began to question God's authority and display jealousy toward many of the other angels. There was a war in heaven, a celestial war, and Satan and his followers were thrown to earth. Thus, the devil, who was referred to in the book of Genesis as the serpent, was there to tempt the fair Eve in the garden."

This seemed to strike a chord with Glen, and balancing his elbows on his knees, he addressed Thad from over the rim of his glasses. "I remember questioning a verse from Genesis when I just a kid," he explained, "it was something that God said about replenishing the earth, yet Adam and Eve had not yet been created. My Sunday school teacher glazed over my question without ever really answering it," he finished.

"You have an excellent memory Glen," smiled Thad in response, "and the scripture you're referring to is Genesis, chapter one, verses twenty–seven and twenty–eight. This passage speaks of God creating both man and woman, prior to any mention of either Adam or Eve. Verse twenty–eight states specifically; 'And God blessed them, and God said unto them, be fruitful, and multiply, and replenish the earth, and subdue it…' The usage of the word 'replenish' is certainly indicative of the fact that humans existed here long before the creation of Adam and Eve."

"And what about the other planets, Thad?" asked Kevin, "if the earth was sustaining life that many eons ago, what about the other planets, were they inhabited as well?"

"Absolutely," was Thad's immediate reply, "the writings reveal that all of the planets in our solar system were fully inhabited at one time by beings that we would certainly consider far superior in knowledge to our race of today.

It seems that the war in heaven was precisely that however, a war of such a magnitude, we could not even fathom its extent, and was fought with weapons and ammunition we couldn't begin to imagine."

Thad paused, and for a moment, it was as quiet as a tomb, until Trent picked up where Thad had left off, "These beings that resided on Venus, Mars, Saturn, Jupiter, and even on Mercury, were a most highly advanced humanoid life-form…they were God's own angels. As the war raged on, one by one the surface of the planets these angels inhabited were pelted with weaponry, to the extent that they were unable to sustain life any longer. Satan was thrown down to the earth with his minions, but the angels who had dwelt in our solar system, no longer had their great cities to return to. It seems that while the earth took quite a pounding, it fared far better than any of the other planets, and while many of the Angels went on to other galaxy's, other solar systems to settle, many of them came to dwell right here on earth. The writings are unclear as to whether the angels occupied the earth prior to this celestial battle, or if it was dwelt upon by a human race much like our own."

"Apparently, though," interrupted Thad, "they found the dinosaurs entirely to bothersome and herded them from their fiery chariots, or space crafts if you will, into pits and caverns, ridding the earth of them entirely."

"Absolutely," agreed Trent. "Do remember that God had already begun to replenish the earth by that time, so there were human beings on the planet who were alternately afraid of, and drawn to these new 'gods' that had come from the heavens. Bear in mind that these were not the Archangels, and did not communicate with God directly, but rather, through the Archangels who themselves spoke with the Holy Spirit."

Lindsey fought the urge to scoot her chair closer to Kevin's. Faced with the absolute knowledge of what had occurred in the very beginning of time, she almost felt in need of more support than her chair could afford her.

"This is where the writings on the tablets become very specific," continued Thad. "The inscriptions tell of the Uranians, or the angels from the planet Uranus, settling in an area that they christened 'New Uranus.'" This apparently translates to Atlantis; thereby lending credence to the myth of an advanced civilization that flew around in space–ships long before any form of air transportation was known to have been invented."

Kevin flushed uncomfortably at the remembrance of his earlier comment about Captain Nemo. When he looked up, Trent was grinning at him broadly, as though he had read the younger man's thoughts.

"It seems too," continued Thad, "that there was yet another planet in our solar system that is referred to as Neberu, but all that remains of that planet now is an asteroid belt beyond Mars. The Martians and Annuaki, who had inhabited the planet Neberu prior to its total annihilation, were sort of a 'sister race' you might say, and had constructed mammoth pyramids on both Mars and Neberu. Those of the Martians and Annuaki that chose to relocate to earth after the cosmic battle, settled in and around Egypt, and in keeping with their way of life and cultural traditions, erected pyramids here on earth." Thad looked directly at Lindsey as he spoke his last sentence, realizing that it would have a greater impact on an Egyptologist. He was correct in his assumption. Lindsey's eyes were shining as brightly as the stars themselves as she soaked in this information.

"And what of the others?" she asked Thad quietly, "what of the angels that had lived on Jupiter and Mercury?"

"Some of them came here and settled as well, though their planets were not as heavily populated, so their numbers were much fewer," he responded. "Oddly enough, the Mercurians, or Cherubim's as they called themselves, were a race of very tiny people, while the Annuaki from Neberu, were a race of giants averaging seven to nine feet tall. Unfortunately, Satan and his minions, referred to as the Utukki in that time, were still free to roam the earth and wreak whatever havoc they could. Satan managed to sway many of the giant Annuaki over to his side, and you will note that the bible speaks of giants in Samuel, Chronicles, Numbers, Deuteronomy and Genesis to name a few. Although a few of the giants are heralded for their good deeds, more often than not, they are portrayed as evil; the giant Goliath being a classic example."

Kevin cleared his throat, "So, did these angels actually mate with the humans God had placed on earth?" he asked, all the while looking directly at Lindsey.

"Angels have no sex," Glen responded, "they are neither male or female."

"Well, you're partly right, Glen," answered Thad, "the Archangels are neither male or female, but many of the angels below that divine sect were in fact considered human, although certainly much, much higher on the evolutionary and spiritual ladder. Again, I hate to sit and quote the bible, but to answer your question more specifically, Genesis, chapter six, verse one speaks of the men beginning to multiply on the face of the earth, and daughters being born to them. This refers to the men that God created prior to Adam and Eve. The second verse goes on to state, and I quote, 'That the sons of God saw the daughters of men that they were fair; and they took them wives of all which they chose.'"

"I remember that verse," interjected Glen, "it always rather confused me, but in light of this information, it makes perfect since. Doesn't the next verse speak about the giants taking wives as well?"

"Ah," sighed Thad, "I see you know your bible." His smile indicated that he was impressed with this. "In fact, it states in chapter six in the book of Genesis, that there were giants in the earth in those days, and also after that; when the sons of God came in unto the daughters of men, and they bore children to them. It says that 'the same became mighty men which were of old, men of renown.' You will note here that the giants are also referred to as sons of God, and not by the term men."

The man's knowledge of the bible was legendary, and his ability to quote verse and script astounded his visitors, "If you stop and think about it," interjected Thad, "there are still to this day, people who grow to be seven and eight feet tall. Just as there are people who never achieve a height above a few feet. It seems clear that the descendants of these angels, or highly evolved celestial beings still walk the earth today. Sadly, those descendants of the daughters of man and the Utukki, or the followers of Lucifer, also walk among us. I am sure they have long been the Adolph Hitler's and Jack–the–Rippers of the world. Fortunately," he went on, "there are still many truly decent and charitable people who descended from the righteous angels; those whose allegiance and loyalty to God remained steadfast."

"Probably not as many as there could have been," offered Trent, "it seems that after these beings married the women of earth, beget several generations, and fully settled in, they had begun to enjoy the pleasures of the flesh a little too much, and their hearts were no longer pure. This is, of course, why God instructed Noah, who was pure of heart, to construct the ark and escape the ensuing flood."

"Most certainly," confirmed Thad, "of course, a great number of the angels that had settled here after the cosmic battle, were not happy residing on earth, and had since returned to the heavens to relocate elsewhere. Most of those who remained, and had interstellar transportation, fled the earth, and returned in the aftermath of the flood, when the earth had once again been fully restored.

The Atlantians however, who it seems were originally from the planet Uranus, returned to find that their city was in utter ruin. Their great Atlantis, which had been powered entirely by high–energy crystals, had sunk deep into the ocean, their power source with it. According to the scrolls, Atlantis sunk dead center in the area we call The Bermuda Triangle."

"Well that certainly explains the ships and air–transports that have been disappearing in the area for the past several hundred years," commented Kevin.

"Yes, yes indeed," agreed Trent.

It was then that Thad rose to his feet, "I think we've overloaded these young people enough for now Trent. I'm afraid we would be terrible hosts indeed if we didn't offer our guests some lunch now."

In truth, the three visitors were more than ready to take a break from this recounting of time before time. There was so much to think about, so much to dissect and digest.

Thad rose and followed his friend through the back door and into the living room, motioning their guests to follow.

Deuteronomy's pointed little ears perked up, and with a yawn and a stretch, he jumped down from the comfort of Lindsey's lap, and trotted dutifully after his masters.

Glen, whose stomach was more than ready to be fed, wasted no time, as he jumped out of his chair and fairly sprinted the few steps to the back door.

Kevin and Lindsey both stood in unison, but neither of them moved to follow the other three men into the house.

For a moment there was an awkward silence between them, as they stood facing one another in their domed paradise.

"I'm afraid the longer we stay, the harder it's going to be to leave," said Lindsey, glancing alternately from the lush greenness of the grass under her small, booted feet, to the ocean wonderland just beyond the confines of the dome. She looked up to see that Kevin was watching her intently, and the penetrating look in his emerald eyes sent a chill through her.

"Why don't we take a closer look at the ocean view," he smiled, as he again placed his large hand on the small of her back and led her to the far end of the yard, which met with the edge of the dome itself.

The dolphins had since moved on, but the view was still quite breath taking, and in spite of the fact that their protective bubble was several feet thick, they could see beyond it as though it wasn't there at all.

The romantic atmosphere wasn't lost on either one of them, and Lindsey was fully aware that Kevin had purposely not removed his hand from her back when they'd reached the end of the yard. Lindsey pointed to a mantaray gliding effortlessly along the sandy ocean floor, "They're often referred to as the devilfish you know," she pointed out, "although I think they're quite graceful and pleasant to look at."

"There are many things down here that are graceful and pleasant to look at," replied Kevin, the look in his eyes attesting to the double meaning of his words.

Lindsey's heart quickened its pace, and she felt a flush begin in the pit of her stomach and move upward. Her usual self assured, confident demeanor seemed to desert her entirely, and she suddenly felt quite self-conscience. Attempting to regain her inner composure, she offered him the most charming smile she could muster, "If you're not careful Doctor Sanders," she said, unable to fully meet his eyes, "you might lead me to believe that you're flirting with me."

"That depends, Doctor Larimer," he said, looking quite serious, "on your definition of flirting."

"My definition?" she asked, "What does my definition have to do with it?" her nervousness intensified when his gaze did not falter.

"Do you consider flirting to be a serious undertaking, or a passing verbal fling?" There was a twinkle of amusement in his eyes as he awaited her response.

Lindsey wondered where her store of snappy repartee had vanished to, and suddenly felt quite verbally challenged, "I don't know exactly," was her rather lame reply, "I guess I've never given the thought much consideration."

"Not much consideration," he parroted, "meaning you have given it some consideration?" His eyes crinkled at the corners.

"You're teasing me," she accused with a smile.

"Guilty," he replied, "but only on the last couple sentences. I meant what I said about the graceful and pleasant to look at part." He searched her eyes, trying to read what she was thinking in their clear, blue depths.

"Kevin," she said, turning slightly, and placing her palm on his chest, "you're making me feel some very unprofessional feelings right now, and I'm not sure if that's right or not given our current circumstances." His nearness was beginning to overwhelm her, and she found that her hand did not want to obey her mind's command to remove itself from the muscular firmness of his chest.

Kevin raised his arm from its resting place near her waist, and enfolded her hand in his own, without lowering either. "By our current circumstances," he responded, his eyes taking in the curve of her softly rounded lips, "do you mean being a couple of miles under the surface of the ocean in an enchanted, romantic city?"

"You know Kevin Sanders," responded Lindsey, trying to muster an admonishing tone, "that was not what I meant."

"No?"

"No," she replied, unable to keep a straight face, "we're working together Kevin," she said more seriously, "we can't allow anything to cloud our judgment or interfere with our work on this project."

"You're very convincing Larimer," his addressing her by her last name elicited yet another grin from the blue eyed beauty, "but not convincing enough I'm afraid, because I think we're perfectly capable of handling both."

"Both?"

"Yes, both," his green eyes bored into her quite intensely, "I think we can handle lending our full concentration to the project and to each other. Don't you?"

"But we hardly know each other Kevin," she responded rather weakly, "we just met a couple of days ago."

"Don't remind me," he winced, remembering his moronic introduction at Sal's, "but seriously Lindsey, I'd like very much for us to get to know each other better, a great deal better."

Lindsey's mind was searching for an appropriate response when the back door of the house opened and Trent appeared, "Lunch is ready if you two are hungry," he offered, a smile playing at the corners of his lips at witnessing the intimacy between the couple. He hadn't missed the fact that Kevin was holding Lindsey's hand close to his chest, and made no move to release it when Trent had unintentionally intruded.

The luncheon spread before them was unbelievably sumptuous, and Lindsey noted with excitement that the repast included real, fresh vegetables, succulent lobster tails, and an abundance of fresh fruit. Even Deuteronomy had his own little saucer filled with choice bits of lobster meat, and ate greedily from his kitty-plate on the floor. Lindsey closed her eyes and savored the flavor and texture of the meal. Real food, as opposed to the synthetically generated nutriment packs most people were accustomed to, was quite a delicacy indeed, and rarely seen outside of extremely expensive restaurants.

Thad and Trent explained in turn, that the city sustained a very large greenhouse, capable of meeting the needs of an entire city. Of course, while fully operational, the city was unpopulated, and the restaurants above ground purchased any of the food not eaten by the two professors.

"By the way," offered Thad, "you may have noticed when Trent brought you here, that there is a community entertainment center in the town square."

"Oh, I did see that," commented Lindsey, "of course, all the shops and businesses were closed."

"Ah, so they are," winked Trent in return, "but having them opened is a simple matter that requires nothing more than a link to the control center above."

"You mean," inquired Kevin, "that all you have to do is ask and you can enter the closed buildings?"

"Absolutely," was Trent's hearty reply, "as it happens, Thad and I thought perhaps you young people might enjoy spending a few hours at the entertainment–center later this evening after supper."

"After supper?" echoed Lindsey, "You mean you wish to eat again later?" She looked down at her plate, piled high with food, and couldn't imagine eating yet another meal.

When the remnants of their meal had been cleaned from the table, the five returned to the luxury of the back yard, and sipped drinks as the professors once again picked up the conversation they'd had began earlier.

It didn't take long for the now fat–bellied cat to meander out and settle himself in Trent's lap, delicately licking his furry little paws and gingerly washing away the vestiges of his most agreeable meal.

Lindsey smiled at the softly purring feline as he finished grooming himself and settled comfortably in preparation of his digestive nap. She could have sworn the cat winked at her just before he closed his eyes to sleep.

Again, Kevin seated on Lindsey's right, watched her profile through his lashes. Her delicate, yet firm chin, high cheek bones and aristocratic nose reminded him of a perfectly sculpted statue. Her skin was flawless, her eyelashes full and dark, and it would take an act of God alone to keep him running his hands through that thick mass of auburn hair, at the first possible opportunity.

As though sensing that Kevin was watching her, Lindsey turned slightly toward him and graced him with an angelic smile, before turning her attention back toward the two professors, settled comfortably side–by–side in chairs just across from her.

Kevin was left wishing ardently that he had something, anything to place over his lap, before his interest in Lindsey became glaringly apparent to everyone else.

"I hate to launch right into work after such a wonderful repast with such charming company," began Thad, his girth fully filling the comfortably large chair he sat in, "but there are some questions we must ask you directly, Lindsey." His smile warmed her as he settled his jovial eyes upon her.

"What is it that you need to know?" she asked.

"Well," began Thad, crossing his arms over his rotund belly, the long, full sleeves of his robe fanning about at his sides." Before you found the elevator that led to the door of the Great Library of Knowledge, had you noticed any hieroglyphs…any at all on the walls in the outer corridor?"

"To be honest," Lindsey responded, "before we entered the library, all I had noticed of the walls in the corridor is that most all of the hieroglyphs has been chiseled away. There must have been many, many inscriptions there at one time, but they had long since been removed, and what was left of the painted hieroglyphs amounted to nothing more than a bit of color here and there. It almost seemed as though the paintings had been sand blasted away. Later," she continued," my father and I returned to the outer corridor and looked closer at the walls. We found only one small inscription still remaining at the foot of the steps that led to the scale–elevator."

Both Trent and Thad leaned forward in their chairs as though not to miss a word of what she was about to say.

"It was just a series of ancient Egyptian numbers," she supplied, "the symbol for the number twelve written three times. Of course, later we realized that the number twelve was not only the number of steps that led to the elevator, but also the number of people required to stand atop it before it would work."

"Well," said Thad, again rubbing his bushy, white beard. "It seems that the number twelve does play a significant role indeed." He looked at his friend thoughtfully and the two men exchanged understanding glances.

Lindsey looked at the be-robed men, a questioning look on her face.

Trent smiled, "We have reviewed the holographs you took inside the library. I'm sure you noticed that there were many ancient Egyptian numbers etched into the gold covering of the walls amongst the hieroglyphs and hieratics."

"Yes," Lindsey responded, "we never understood their significance though."

"That's why we were part of the team hired to decipher all those writings," smiled Thad, "and while it has taken many years to do so, we believe we have a fairly good understanding of what those numbers meant."

Glen found himself thoroughly fascinated with the recounting of this information. His work had never before crossed such enthralling boundaries as these, and he felt drawn in by it all, wanting to catch every word, every detail. He inched his glasses back up his nose and sat back in anticipation.

"It seems," began Thad, "that for the first time in the history of the world, we have discovered biblical references intermingled with hieroglyphs and hieratics."

"Biblical references?" questioned Lindsey, her brows lifting in amazement.

"Yes," supplied Thad, as he reached into the folds of his gown and withdrew a computer slide-tablet. He pressed the corner, and the dim, green glow indicated the tablet had been turned on. Depressing the opposite corner between his fingers, he rummaged through the pages contained in the tablet until he came to the one he sought. "It seems that the numbers found in the library are biblical scriptures that all contain direct references to the number twelve." Thad looked thoughtful for a moment before continuing, "They reference the twelve tribes of Israel, the twelve stones set up in the midst of Jordan, the twelve hours in a day referred to in the book of John, twelve stars in Revelation and references to the tree of life, which bore twelve manner of fruits."

The two older men clearly had the full attention of their guests. "Now, you say," said Thad thoughtfully, "that there were a series of the number twelve still remaining on the walls in the outer corridor."

"Yes," confirmed Lindsey, "three twelve's, side by side."

Trent and Thad looked at one another thoughtfully. "Twelve, twelve, twelve," repeated Thad, "perhaps the twelfth book, twelfth chapter, twelfth verse?"

Trent nodded, "And that would be?" he asked.

"Second Kings being the twelfth book of the Old Testament," Thad said almost to him self, "I believe it's the twelfth chapter." He closed his eyes as though concentrating very hard. "Yes, that would be the verse that speaks of masons and hewers of stone buying timber to repair the breaches of the house of the Lord, if my memory serves me correctly."

His ability to quote and recall scripture on command was astounding, and did not fail to impress Lindsey and her companions.

"I'm not sure I understand," broke in Kevin, "what do stones and timbers have to do with the pyramid?"

"That's a very good question indeed," responded Trent, "and one that brings us to the reason we sent for the three of you."

Three sets of eyebrows shot up in question.

"You see," began Trent by way of explanation, "it seems that the pyramid was designed for a much greater purpose than charting the passing of time, or studying the stars. Its primary purpose was interstellar transportation."

The sudden intake of breath by all three of their visitors confirmed the fact that the two older men had their full attention.

"To clarify that particular passage found in second Kings," offered Thad, "was to let he who found the library know that the pyramid could be repaired and used again for the purpose it was constructed to serve."

"You mean to say," said Lindsey, both hands firmly planted on the arms of her chair, as though she were about to jump out of it, "that the ancient Egyptians traveled to other planets?" Her shock at hearing such a revelation was clearly apparent on her astonished face.

"Not exactly," supplied Thad, as he looked again to his friend as though for confirmation of what he was saying, "it seems that the ancient Egyptians weren't allowed, or able to use the pyramid for traveling themselves, but rather, to call upon, or greet visitors from other worlds."

Glen's glasses were once again at the very tip of his nose, his mouth agape, "For the love of God!" he exclaimed, "You mean they really beamed about like in all those old 'Star Trek' movies, a couple hundred years ago?"

"In essence," replied Trent, "yes."

Chapter Five

Their hosts had spent several more hours going over information they'd gleaned from the scrolls and comparing it with the holographs and the information Lindsey had provided from her first–hand accounting. Their revelations about the Egyptian sun god, Ra, having been one of the 'angels' to first land in Egypt, was most startling to hear indeed. It seemed that the writings in the library, the ones written in numeric codes, described a descendent of a Seraphim angel named Emmesharra that had come from the sky in a brightly glowing spacecraft at the site where the Great Pyramid was later built. Naturally, the people living in the land at that time, looked upon their celestial arrival as a god, and called him, Ra, or Amun Ra, meaning simply god of the sun, and thus, the sun god Ra was born.

It was easier to understand why so many of the great pharaohs had referred to themselves as Sons of Ra, since they were undoubtedly descendants of Emmesharra himself. It was almost chilling when faced with the realization that so much of what both Christianity and history had taught up to that point was now in question. On the other hand, it lifted Lindsey's spirits immensely when Thad had read to them from the pages of his computer–slide tablet, on which he'd stored duplicates of the writings found in the library. What he had read was the most awe inspiring revelation of all, the fact that Jesus Christ was in fact the son of the one true God, and was crucified for the sins of the masses, just as the bible described. Although Lindsey's faith had always been strong, these words sent her heart and mind literally soaring.

The entertainment center was magnificent. Trent and Thad had decided to remain behind, having already visited the center many times over the years, when their workload had become so extreme that they needed some time away from it.

Glen had wasted no time in making a bee line for the science and history center located at the far end of the building, leaving Kevin and Lindsey alone to seek out their choice of entertainment.

Kevin took Lindsey's hand, and together they walked the length of the aisles between the rides. Their heads were still swimming from the multitude of information the professor's had shared with them, and they welcomed this unexpected diversion.

It seemed that every virtual-reality ride ever invented was in evidence, and the couple found it almost impossible to decide which one to experience first. The fact that there were no lines to wait through was a definite added bonus.

"How about this one?" Kevin's question brought Lindsey out of its deep reverie, and she looked up to see they'd stopped in front of the roller-coaster ride.

"This looks wonderful!" she exclaimed, "I've never been on a roller-coaster ride before."

"Well, now is your chance," Kevin grinned, as he opened the door to the ride and bade Lindsey to enter. There were six rows of seats in the enclosed, cigar shaped ride, and the pair headed for the seats in the very front.

"This is great, Linds," mused Kevin, "front row seats on every ride." His grin was contagious, and Lindsey almost felt like she was walking on air. They both needed this time to collect their respective thoughts and just enjoy the entertainment offered.

No sooner had they taken their seats, when the screen before them came to life, and they saw themselves at the top of a twentieth century roller-coaster, beginning their spiraling, high-speed descent.

Lindsey felt the wind on her face, her hair blew out behind her and the seat lurched forward. She found herself holding on for dear life. Down they flew at top speed, both certain their stomachs were still back at the top of the virtual ride. They were jolted from side to side; bumping shoulders more than once, as they tilted, turned and looped along until the ride finally ended and the screen went blank. Lindsey was still laughing so hard she had to wipe tears from her eyes, before taking Kevin's arm and following him out the exit door.

It was forty-five minutes, and ten rides later, as they were exiting the Lunar-Scape, that Kevin had departed first and was standing at the bottom of the steps, his hand extended to offer her assistance. Lindsey took his hand and stepped down the last stair, but Kevin did not move back. Instead, he stood there, only inches from her, staring down into her eyes.

"I can't believe any of this Linds," he began, using the newly invented nickname, "I could never have imagined being a part of this in my wildest dreams. But it's you that I find the most interesting, the most fascinating and the most captivating."

Her heart skipped a beat as she stood looking into his eyes, searching her mind for a reply. Before she could form one however, Kevin put his arms around her and pulled her even closer against him. He stared for a long moment at her full lips and could no longer resist the temptation.

When their mouths touched, they were both caught up in feelings unlike either of them had ever experienced before. As Kevin deepened the kiss, and penetrated Lindsey's mouth with his tongue, the proverbial fireworks went off for both of them.

It was at that moment that Glen came walking around the corner, having seen and experienced all there was in the science and history section. When he was met with the sight of Kevin and Lindsey embraced in such a passionate kiss, he spun around on his heels and headed back in the direction he had come. He felt very much like a third wheel, and did not want to intrude. He was happy that his friend Kevin finally got his wish to get closer to Lindsey, but he had to admit to just a tinge of envy. He would certainly never begrudge anyone their happiness; it just seemed like he was forever congratulating everyone else on their good fortune when they would announce their engagement or wedding. While he truly meant it, each one of the congratulations left him feeling just a little more alone, a little emptier. He said a silent prayer to a God he now knew existed beyond question, that he would find someone to love and to love him.

When the lengthy kiss ended, the embrace did not. Kevin and Lindsey could only stand and stare into one another's eyes. They were both almost shaken with the intensity of their feelings, and each knew that this was only the beginning of something that was predestined.

For the next hour, the couple enjoyed as many of the rides as time would permit, touching each other often, sharing more kisses and laughing like children.

It was then that Lindsey thought of Glen, and feeling a bit guilty for having been so self-absorbed, encouraged Kevin to seek out their friend. They found him fully engrossed in an individual, virtually-reality experience that allowed one to fight starships in deep space. The thin film-like band around his head covered his eyes so that he could see nothing but the virtual outer space and the oncoming enemy starships. His hands worked furiously, pressing the laser-launching buttons on the invisible control panel before him.

Lindsey and Kevin were hard put not to laugh, as Glen's face alternately contorted in deep concentration or grinned at his victories. This was definitely a side of his friend Kevin had never seen before. He wondered if he had looked as silly when he had played the game earlier. It was fortunate that Lindsey had played the same game in the next open booth, so couldn't have witnessed his idiocy for herself.

When his session had ended, Glen removed the band strip from his head and placed it on the ring where it had been hanging when he arrived. He looked at Kevin, totally unaware of the entertainment his own actions had provided a few moments earlier.

"You two have a good time?" He asked, reserving a sly smile.

"A most excellent time indeed Glen," replied Lindsey with a beaming smile of her own. "I could really get used to living in this city and enjoying all these great things." She waved her arms out, indicating all the rides and amusements.

"It's certainly been one of the best nights of my life," interjected Kevin, as he looked directly into Lindsey's crystal blue eyes. His meaning was most clear, which elicited yet another broad grin from the woman before him.

"Unfortunately," Glen reminded, "we need to get back and call it a night. Trent and Thad said they wanted to get an early start tomorrow on filling us in on the rest of the information they have for us, and I for one can't wait to hear it."

Once outside, the three stepped onto the moving walkway in the direction of the professors' beautiful big house with the large yard and 'ocean view.' Lindsey stood between her two companions as they glided effortlessly along, enjoying the luminescent glow of the various shops and businesses along the way.

Clearly, the city was being made ready for full inhabitation to take place. As they passed an apparel shop called 'Back to the Past,' Lindsey did a double take to make sure she actually saw what she thought she'd seen. In the window was the most beautiful creation she had ever beheld. Of course her knowledge of twentieth–century apparel was limited to pictures in history books, and the few remaining remnants of what had once been clothing from that time period…but those were now on display in the new Smithsonian Institute. Lindsey knew that the white gown in the window, with its low neckline and thin straps would be stunning in any era.

She didn't take her eyes off the flowing, floor length evening gown with the fitted waist and tiny, sparkling gemstones, until the transport–walk had carried them past the shop, and the dress was out of view. As much as Lindsey would intensely love to own such a creation, she certainly wouldn't have a place in the world to wear a replica twentieth–century costume.

As they neared the professors' home, Lindsey remembered Thad's offer from earlier that day, "Did I tell you that Thad offered to let me take a bath tonight?" she asked the two in general.

"We saw the big tub in the cleansing room that looked like a huge seashell," responded Glen, "I wondered if they actually filled it with water and bathe in it like in the olden days, but can't imagine anyone wasting so much valuable water. I never did get around to asking."

It was then that Lindsey explained what Thad had told her about the city being built on a fresh water stream, located shortly before construction began, and that the water not needed to supply the city itself, was routed to cities above the surface.

"Did you know that every dwelling in this entire city, over three–thousand in all, according to Thad, has a bathtub or a cleansing tube with running water?" she asked Kevin.

"They used to call those showers, I think," supplied Glen.

"Well, in any event," breathed Lindsey, "I am looking very forward indeed to soaking in that nice hot water for as long as Thad and Trent will let me."

"With the way they've taken to you, Little Miss Lindsey,"

smiled Kevin, having addressed her the way he'd heard Thad do earlier, "I imagine they'd let you sleep there all night." He lowered his tone to a whisper and added, "Do you think two people could fit in that tub?" His twinkling eyes reflected his mirth and he received a gentle elbow in the ribs for his effort.

Glen chuckled; apparently having overheard the question meant for Lindsey alone.

There were three bedrooms, and Lindsey was slightly dismayed to learn that Trent and Thad would be sleeping in the living room, allowing their three guests to enjoy the sleeping chambers, with their twentieth–century replica beds, complete with what used to be called comforters…they looked comfortable indeed. Still, it didn't seem right to Lindsey, but Trent and Thad were insistent.

Their guests were delighted to learn that their bags had arrived before they had, and had already been placed in the appropriate bedchambers. To Lindsey's delight, there was also a large, fluffy robe much like her great–great grandmother might have worn. She rubbed the robe on her face, enjoying its softness against her skin, as she made her way to the cleansing room in excited anticipation of her first real bath.

Lindsey put first one foot, and then the other into the comfortably hot water. For a few moments, she just stood in the deep tub, the water reaching a few inches above her knees, and reveled in the silky softness of the pure, clear, precious liquid.

When at last, she submerged her body completely, it occurred to her that sleeping in the velvety softness of this wonderful pool might not be such a bad idea. She thought of Kevin, and a devilish grin played on her face…it would be quite lovely indeed to share this experience with him. Of course, she'd never do such a thing…certainly not after having known him for just a few short days and sharing a few kisses, but still, it wouldn't hurt to fantasize just a bit.

Lindsey sank as deeply into the water as she could without submerging her face, and remembered the feel of Kevin's lips…the nearness of him. So much was happening in her life…so much, so fast. She worried that having a romantic relationship with Kevin might interfere with her ability to fully concentrate on the work before her, but at this point, she couldn't imagine not having such a relationship.

Kevin lay in the extremely comfortable bed in what was normally Thad's room. He wished fervently that he had a bed like this one at home. He couldn't imagine who it was that decided a coverless airbed was an advancement in comfort. It seemed that progress left a good deal to be desired. Even in the midst of such comfort, Kevin knew he wasn't going to sleep any time soon. He simply couldn't stop thinking about Lindsey, and his mind's eye recanted their time together at the entertainment center, the feel of her in his arms, the smell of her hair, and the emotions that came over him when he had kissed her.

Kevin Sanders had kissed many women in his time, many women indeed, but he honestly couldn't remember ever feeling like this about any one of them. The longest relationship he'd had to date had lasted just short of two years. Either he'd simply tired of the relationship, or the woman couldn't tolerate his long hours at the lab. For whatever reason, he just hadn't found the right woman, at least not until now. He realized he hadn't known Lindsey long enough to get down on bended knee and pledge his undying love, but he certainly wouldn't mind taking her home to meet his parents. She was pretty much everything he'd ever imagined wanting in a woman…or in a wife for that matter.

It seemed that marriage had never been on the top of Kevin's priority list. In truth, it wasn't even a subject he thought about…not at least, until his mother would link to him and remind him that he wasn't getting any younger. She was apparently more than ready to be a grandmother. Even then, he thought about it only until their link was terminated. It just felt different with Lindsey. There was something unique and special about her. She was quite possibly the most intelligent, well bred and alluring woman he'd ever met, the type that would make a husband want to hurry home from work and not look at anyone else on the way. 'My God,' he thought, 'I'm crossing over.'

Glen didn't want to leave the confines of the heavenly bed ever again. He'd never felt such splendid softness and comfort in all his life. The pillow under his head was covered with a linen–type case that smelled as fresh and clean as a cleansing tube. He rolled from side to side in the big bed, reveling in the sheer luxury of the satiny covers…if only he didn't have to enjoy it alone. He thought of Sal, and looked at the linking device on the simulated wood nightstand next to the bed. He didn't have Sal's link number with him, and for a moment, he thought of checking the directory to see if it was listed. That thought had no sooner occurred to him than Glen reasoned to himself that he was technically on work status, and it simply wouldn't be ethical.

Turning away from the nightstand, he forced his mind away from the handsome Italian Restaurateur, and thought over all the things Trent and Thad had shared with them earlier. It was so much to assimilate so very much information to take in, and such a short time to do it. As soon as they returned to IBAT, they would undoubtedly be overwhelmed by the massive amount of work ahead, and with all this newfound knowledge to take with him, he wasn't entirely sure his brain wouldn't explode somewhere along the way.

Glen was damned curious to know what else the good professors had to tell them, he knew they were holding something back. He and Kevin were there for a reason…and so far, that reason had yet to be disclosed. He hoped they would find out soon, though he had to admit to himself that given the information they'd recently been privy to, he was almost frightened at what they might hear. Those were his last thoughts before he fell into a dreamless sleep.

Morning in the city under the sea differed only slightly from the night. Settled as it was, on the ocean floor, the sunlight that reached it was very diffused and subtle.

Lindsey had found it most difficult to force herself to rise from the comfort of the soft, warm bed. Her hour long bath the night before had been a luxury she would never forget, and had relaxed her to the point that by the time her head hit the fluffy, overstuffed pillow, she was asleep instantly.

Now, sitting once again on the grass covered lawn between Glen and Kevin, Lindsey found herself, much like her counterparts, wide eyed in anticipation of what Trent and Thad had to tell them next. They didn't have long to wait.

After bidding their guests a good morning, Trent settled himself in his chair with the ever present Deuteronomy languishing on his lap. "Well," he said with a smile, "I guess you young people want to know the real reason we sent for you. You certainly deserve to be told," he stroked Dude's head between his pointed little ears, "but first Lindsey," he said, directing his attention to their pretty, female guest, "there is another question we have for you."

As they so often did, Thad picked up the conversation; "The holographs taken inside the Library of Knowledge show a single stand or table in the center of the room. There were no holographs however, depicting the top of the table or stand. Do you remember exactly what it looked like?"

Lindsey searched her mind; again taking herself back to that day her father had made his magnificent discovery. In her mind's eye, she pictured the golden interior lined with the now famous scrolls and tablets, and the waist–high table that stood in the very center of the room. It was empty, there was nothing on it but several centuries of thick dust, and she relayed that information to the professors.

"What did the surface of the table actually look like?" asked Trent, "how was it shaped?"

Again Lindsey formed a mental picture of the round surfaced table. "It was covered in the same sheets of gold as the walls were," she relayed, "and there was a small, circular indentation in the very center, as though there had been something there at one time, but it had long since been removed. We almost didn't see it at first, because again, the table was entirely covered with a thick layer of dust, and the indentation in the center had been filled in by it. I remember my father blowing the dust off the top, making it visible. We wondered if the table had been designed to hold something with a round base, or if the indentation had at one time held a precious gem or something of value that had since been removed."

Trent and Thad again exchanged a familiar, knowing look, and then turned their attention back to their guests.

"Another thing, if you will," said Trent, and without disturbing the sleeping Deuteronomy, removed the computer–slide tablet from the folds of his robes, "can you explain these dark areas here, here and here?" He had pinched the corner of the tablet until he found the correct page, and then held the thin screen so that Lindsey could see it. The slide tablet revealed a three–dimensional view of the library, one taken by her father's photographer who was always in attendance when something of value or interest had been found and required cataloging. She studied the darker areas on the golden walls Trent indicated.

"Yes, I remember them," she answered, "they were round holes cut out of the gold panels high up on the wall, at intervals of approximately five to six feet. We thought it strange at the time that from outside, facing the entrance door, we hadn't seen a hole above it. My father went back through the door to look again, but the ceiling at the entrance wasn't nearly as high as the ceiling in the library, so the hole on that side of the room was not visible from without."

It was impossible for her to remember that day and not think of her beloved father, the look on his face when he'd first gone down on the scale–elevator and she had run to the edge calling down to him. There had been no fear on his face…only the exuberant look of having accomplished something truly great.

Thad's voice broke into her thoughts, "How large was the round table in the center of the library, Lindsey? Was it very large, and what of the circular indentation in the middle, what size was it?"

"Whoa," chuckled Trent, "give the girl a moment to collect her thoughts before you bombard her with questions."

"Forgive me, Lindsey," apologized Thad, "I'm afraid I do get ahead of myself sometimes."

"No," she offered, "I don't mind, and I know how important this is to you." Her father's memory was still painfully vivid, but she managed a smile before continuing. "The table top itself was quite large, I'd say about like this," she held her arms out in front of her, indicating a large, circular shape, with a circumference of approximately four to five feet, "and the circular indentation was about so big." This time, she used her hands instead of her arms, indicating a circle about four inches in diameter. "There's something else," she added, "my father and I didn't notice at first, but as we were leaving through the only door, we noticed that it appeared to have been sealed from the inside as well, with some sort of a clay–like substance. My father was the first to notice that there were pieces of the clay on the floor inside the library. Since there was no other way out, except through the door in which we had entered, we wondered how anyone could have placed a seal on the door from the inside."

"Um, hum," responded Thad, with a slight nod of his head, "I believe it is as we thought Trent." He looked at his colleague thoughtfully as he crossed his thick legs at the ankles.

Glen felt like he was the only person that didn't understand what was being said. He pushed his glasses back up to eye level with his index finger, and hoped that their benefactors would elaborate sometime soon.

Kevin looked intently at the woman on his left. He pictured her, as she must have looked that day, entering the long forgotten room with her father and his workers. He thought how beautiful she must have been framed by all that gold; what must have been going through her mind at being a part of such a discovery. He hadn't known her then, but somehow felt quite proud of this intelligent, beautiful doctor sitting next to him. She was speaking to the professors again, and he watched her mouth move with her words, taking in her beautiful profile as he did so.

"Does this have a significant meaning?" she asked, "I mean the table and the circular holes in the walls?"

"We believe so," nodded Thad, "as we explained yesterday, we have learned a great deal from the archives in the library, but there were just a few holes that needed to be filled in. No pun intended," he grinned, "but we felt you could help us."

"And you have," put in Trent with a nod.

"You see," began Thad, "it seems that the documents from the library, specifically the ones that looked so new, were actually written by these extra–terrestrial beings that visited this earth thousands of years ago. As we told you yesterday, many of these beings were descended directly from the angels, or the advanced terrestrial race, and had been visiting the earth and its inhabitants throughout the ages."

"Apparently," added Trent, "they had experienced on their planets, many of the same problems we've had on earth. Over-usage of the planets resources for one thing," he continued, "it seems that many of their writings were left here to assist us in finding other useful resources. This city for one," he said, spreading his arms to indicate their surroundings," as we told you yesterday, was fully constructed from those writings and drawings. There was also information on harnessing frozen water crystals from outside the earth's atmosphere, which is something the United States government has been working on since the deciphering of the documents first got underway. The ability to locate other water sources, like the one this city is built upon was also included in those documents. Not to mention plans and information on constructing spacecraft capable of traveling farther and faster than all the scientists and physicists on earth would have ever imagined. Naturally, such things will take years to perfect and achieve, but the work has already commenced on those projects as well."

Glen, Lindsey and Kevin looked to one another in turn, their faces clearly displaying their unabashed awe at what Trent had just shared with them. This of course, was nothing, compared to what they were about to hear.

"Those writings," commenced Thad, "also explained how to place the inhabitants of such a spacecraft as Trent mentioned, into a cryogenic hyper–sleep of sorts, allowing the body to withstand traveling light years away without growing old and dying before reaching the intended destination."

"We also understand something that has baffled mankind since the beginning of time," offered Trent, "how the pyramids themselves were built and the fact that they may well have also been constructed to be used as a weapon if necessary."

Three mouths dropped open and three sets of eyes grew wide in anticipation of what was about to come.

"It has long been conjectured upon," Trent continued, "that the Egyptians had a little help from their extra–terrestrial friends, and thanks to you and your father, Lindsey, we now know this to be an absolute fact. We've learned," he continued, "that the Annuaki, or the inhabitants of Mars and its no–longer–existent sister planet, Neberu," he clarified, "were directly responsible for the pyramids built on earth. We have viewed drawings from the library, depicting disc–shaped spacecraft far more advanced than anything we are capable of creating. Apparently, the Annuaki race were the first to perfect the ability to travel through the space–time continuum without the necessity of a craft.

You may remember that astronomers in the twentieth century were able to see the one remaining pyramid on Mars. The last Annuaki off the planet when the celestial war was being fought probably left through that structure, as I imagine they did after they sealed the library door from the inside. Much like those old 'Star Trek' episodes you mentioned yesterday, Glen," announced Trent with a broad grin, "I believe the phrase they used was actually something like, 'Beam me up, Scottie,' if I'm not mistaken."

Glen threw back his head and laughed unabashedly… certainly something Kevin had never seen before in all the years that he'd known his friend. "I haven't met half a dozen people in my life familiar with those old shows," Glen said, removing his glasses to wipe the tears of mirth from his eyes, "I can't believe that you've seen them."

"'Trekkis' never die," was Trent's deadpan response.

Glen practically howled with another fit of laughter and Kevin was left wondering who this guy was and what had happened to his friend. He'd never seen Glen so genuinely amused, and watching him almost slide out of his chair in fits of hysterical laughter, brought a wide grin to his own face.

The others were not unaffected by Glen's reaction, and within seconds they were all laughing just watching Glen. It was a few moments before the normally reserved scientist composed himself and returned his glasses to their rightful place.

"It seems we have two old movie buffs in our midst," chuckled Thad, "but yes, that is the basic concept. You see," he continued, as the last of the chuckling around him faded away, "according to some of the old charts we've studied, it seems that the earth's surface is rather one huge, round, geographical grid of sorts. In some areas within that grid, the ground itself is highly electromagnetic. The ability to harness and channel such energy could provide an unimaginable power source.

You've all heard of the Ark of the Covenant I assume," he asked the trio, and continued at their simultaneous nods, "the ark in and of itself was quite a power source, and we now know that it acted as a flux–capacitor. The construction of such an ark has been common knowledge for a number of years now, and as a matter of fact, the bible itself provides explicit instructions on how to build one in chapter twenty–five of the book of Exodus.

The bible also tells us of course, that the ark was constructed for the purpose of housing and protecting the Ten Commandments God gave to Moses. Bear in mind as well that Moses was himself a master alchemist, and unquestionably had all the elements needed to construct the ark. The wood used certainly had effective insulating properties, and lead or copper plates inside would act as positive and negative terminals. If properly constructed, it would be able to store and release an electrical charge of devastating magnitude. Were someone without the proper knowledge to try to open it, or even touch it, they would be electrocuted with such a force that their flesh would melt from their bones."

"Does the ark have some significance in relation to the pyramids?" asked Glen.

"Quite possibly," responded Thad, "we believe that the ark may at one time have been used as an actual power source in the pyramids for the interstellar travelers to come and go between their own planets and earth. The Great Pyramid of Giza is built right over the center of one of the most highly concentrated energy fields on earth. Using the ark as a conductor makes perfect sense, only the ark was later removed." He shook his head slightly, "We really don't know if it was in place in the pyramid before or after it was housed in Solomon's Temple."

"There was something in the hieroglyphs engraved into the gold on the walls about the 'container of truth within the container of knowledge,'" supplied Lindsey. "There was also something on the opposite wall about the 'sun disk that could open the heavens with a mortal key.'"

"Precisely!" exclaimed Trent, "which brings us to the reason you're here. It seems," he explained, "that the Library of Knowledge was not lost per se, but rather, taken away. The celestial beings that supplied the knowledge found within, discovered that as time went on, the pharaohs became less reverent toward them. These kings of Egypt began to misuse and abuse their positions as sons of the Gods, proclaiming to have been bestowed certain powers to which they had not been granted in reality.

Several pharaohs, King Tut included, attempted to transport themselves using the power of the pyramid, and this angered the Annuaki. We believe it was then that the ark was taken out of the pyramid, and the room once used solely for interstellar travel was transformed into a library. This allowed the celestial visitors to come at go at will, but only during the periods of the equinox and solstices, which greatly reduced their visits, unless they came by spacecraft which took much longer." He continued to stroke Deuteronomy, who had by now awakened from his nap and was grooming himself with his small, pink tongue again.

"Apparently," broke in Thad, his arms crossed as was his custom, over the rotund girth of his middle, "there were some exceptions."

"Exceptions?" questioned Lindsey.

"Yes," supplied Thad, "apparently there were a chosen few individuals that were given a key of sorts allowing them to supply the needed energy for their other-worldly friends to beam down without waiting for the solstice or equinox." He winked at Glen when he used the term beam, and Glen chuckled deep in his throat.

"Do you have any idea who these chosen people were?" queried Kevin, feeling that he might already know the answer.

"We do believe that at least one of those people was none other than the Princess Ankhesenamun. There is a good possibility that Tutankhamun had a key as well."

Being ready for the response did little to alleviate his apprehension. Kevin had the feeling they were about to become involved in something far more intense than they had originally imagined. "And this is why the Egyptian governments and US chose their mummies in particular to clone," he half stated, half questioned.

"Exactly," answered Thad, "we are relatively certain that the mortal key mentioned in the hieroglyphic inscriptions in the library refer to a human being, a particular human being," he clarified, "one who was given an amulet by these celestial benefactors. If what we believe is true, "he continued, directing his gaze at Lindsey, "then the amulet worn by Princess Ankhesenamun when her mummy was found, may well be able to provide the necessary energy to power the pyramid itself. Perhaps placing it in the indentation at the top of the table in the library is what its original purpose was."

"But the government has the amulet in their possession don't they?" asked Glen, his glasses for once, actually over his eyes where they belonged, "Why don't they use it and see if it works?"

"Oh, yes, they have the amulet," supplied Thad, "but we have only recently come to understand that the amulet itself may be the power source. We have not yet shared this hypothesis with the government officials. They were made privy to the deciphered documents some time ago, that speak of the necessity of a mortal or human key to unlock the power of the pyramid."

"And this is where we come in?" asked Kevin.

"Yes," answered Thad, "the decision to begin cloning came from the government just after they had read our deciphering with regard to the use of a mortal key. Of course, Thad and I have no knowledge of, or experience with the cloning process and what to expect of it. We need you to explain everything you can."

"We believe there could be a great deal of danger associated with this project," cut in Trent, "and naturally, we're quite concerned."

Kevin and Glen alternately took turns explaining the technicalities of the process, the fact that a chemical agent invented only fifty or so years earlier, could accelerate the process, resulting in the clones attaining the age of puberty within a matter of months. The process had to be constantly monitored though, for any signs of hyper–acceleration that could cause the subject to grow old and die within a few years' time. Glen further enlightened the professors to the fact that other advancements in the field of cloning abolished the necessity of a donor gene, thereby resulting in exact genetic duplicates.

"It's important to remember," interjected Glen, "that these cloned humans will be exact duplicates on the outside, but they won't have any memories of who they once were, since we'll be cloning them, and not bringing the actual people themselves back to life. All they will know of who they once were is what they are taught."

"Hmm," said Trent, stroking his pointed, white beard as he digested this information, "are you absolutely certain of this Glen?" he asked.

"Well, yes," answered Glen, "of course we've never cloned a human being before, but everything we know about the process tells us that they will have no past–life memories or recollections."

"Perhaps it is the mere presence of the Pharaoh Tutankhamun and the Princess Ankhesenamun that is required," replied Trent thoughtfully. "If their participation is required above and beyond that, and they have no memory of what to do, the entire project might amount to nothing."

"Still in all," added Thad, "the scrolls warned of dire repercussions if the power of the pyramid is misused in any way by those not chosen by the celestial hosts. Think about it," he continued, "it was closed up and hidden away from the world, and the hieroglyphs removed from the walls in the outer chambers. It certainly doesn't sound like the Annuaki wanted the pyramid to be used at all once they sealed off the entrance."

"The US and Egyptian governments don't seem to be too worried about these repercussions written about in the scrolls," offered Trent, "but then, their reasons might be understandable in light of certain heretofore undisclosed events."

Lindsey shuddered visibly, her face taking on a worried frown.

"Forgive us My Dear," apologized Thad, "we had no intention of frightening you, but this is certainly something we felt the three of you should be aware of, and there is more information we need to share with you that is of the utmost importance...."

"Perhaps Thad," said Trent, as he addressed his barrel–chested colleague, "this information could wait until after lunch?" For a moment, it appeared to Lindsey as though Thad had an almost pleading look on his face, but it was quickly replaced by a friendly smile, and she was left wondering if they might be better off not knowing what this additional information was.

Chapter Six

It was nearly two o'clock in the afternoon when the five had finished yet another sumptuous lunch; Deuteronomy once again enjoying his own little bowl of broasted swordfish, shell fish meat, and tender, cooked shrimp.

After their midday meal, the group returned to the back yard, and settled themselves into their waiting chairs. Lindsey's eyes scanned the edges of the dome, settling on the playful porpoises that had returned, and seemed as curious about the massive clear bubble and its inhabitants, as she was about them.

"Well," began Thad, as he slapped both of his meaty hands on his thighs, "I guess there is no way to cushion what we have to tell you, so we might as well just say it directly. You tell them Trent."

"Your thoughtfulness is overwhelming my good friend," said Trent in mock facetiousness, "but one of us has to, so it might as well be me." He turned to his three guests, concern and curiosity showing plainly on their faces, "As you probably know my friends, diplomatic negotiations have not been going well between the Untied States and China." Glen, Lindsey and Kevin all nodded that they were aware of this, "What concerns the US the most right now, is the fact that in the event of war, it is highly likely that Russia will ally with China against us. The fact that the population in both of those countries are nearly triple that of the US, makes the likelihood of the US winning that war, even with the full cooperation of our allies, quite a slim possibility indeed."

Although Glen, Kevin and Lindsey were all aware that there had been some strain on the relationship between the US and China, neither of them had any inkling that war might be a consequence. The three looked at one another in turn, and then back to Trent.

"You may remember that I mentioned earlier, the fact that we know the pyramids were not only constructed for inter–stellar travel, but to be used as a weapon as well. Well, it is fortunate indeed that Egypt is so strongly allied with The United States. It seems that both governmental entities are of the opinion that if they can learn how to harness and utilize such power, there wouldn't be a country, or countries on this planet we could not defend ourselves against. Of course," he added, "this information will not be released to the public at any time." The look of understanding dawned on the faces of his audience; "The US will pursue this knowledge with all due haste, and with every tool available to them, whatever the cost. They feel that if war is imminent, the pyramid is the only hope we have of victory against such a powerful force."

Lindsey had rather hoped to stay on in the city for just a while longer, after the professors had completed their briefing, but the last of the information they had shared had rather put a damper on her mood. She could see that it had the same effect on Glen and Kevin, but tried not to allow this upsetting revelation to consume her.

Perhaps this would work. Perhaps she, Glen, Kevin, and the other professors, doctors and scientists at IBAT would succeed in their work and assist the government in seeing this plan to fruition. Lindsey had to believe that…needed to believe it, in order to allow her some peace of mind. It was certainly no wonder that the US government was on a mission to reclaim this lost information. It was fortunate that Egypt and the US were on friendly terms, as the help of the Egyptian government was clearly a necessity.

It was shortly after five o'clock in the afternoon that the trio had finished packing their belongings for the return trip. Lindsey had almost hoped to spend another night and enjoy another bath, but knew that they were expected back at IBAT first thing in the morning. They would need to return to their own homes and try to get a good night's sleep beforehand.

"We know your vehicles are still at IBAT, since you came directly here from the lab," spoke Trent, "so have made arrangements for each of you to be taken directly to your homes, and then picked up in the morning and taken to work."

"Sounds like you've thought of everything," smiled Glen. As much as he truly enjoyed this aquatic world they had shared with the older professors, he was very pleased that he would be able to return home for the evening. His mind was on overload from all that their hosts had shared with them, but like Lindsey, he was determined not to dwell on the matter, and to simply do everything in his power to make The Reclamation Project a success.

Once the remote vehicle that transported individuals directly from the surface to the Underwater City, had ascended and settled on dry land, the three were picked up in aero–van provided for them via the professors. Glen was the first to be dropped off at his apartment complex. He bid his co–workers a good evening and then made his way to his dwelling unit, as the van ascended from the parking area and hovered out of sight. Glen found his steps quickening as he reached his front door. Perhaps he simply needed to get back to familiar surroundings before the shroud of gloom that seemed to have settled over him would dissipate.

Inside the spacious transport–van, Kevin and Lindsey found themselves alone again, as the driver was shielded from them by a divider, and could only communicate with his passengers via an intercom device. Before Glen had exited the vehicle, the three had traveled in companionable silence; each lost in their own thoughts. Now, looking down at Lindsey from his seat next to her, Kevin knew he had to do something to lighten her mood, he didn't like seeing her brow wrinkling in concern. Kevin put his arm around his captivating companion, "You know, Dr. Larimer," he said in a husky voice, "I don't even have your link number."

"Nor I yours," she responded, summoning a smile.

"Oh mother!" exclaimed Lindsey, as she entered the front door of her condominium. "I just can't tell you what an indescribable time I've had." She smiled brightly, forcing herself to again squelch the upsetting knowledge she had so recently acquired. Her smile lit up her face, and Olivia rose to greet her daughter from her place on the air–sofa, where she had been experimenting with nail colors in her newly purchased fingernail 'fabri–color' unit. She was pleased to see her daughter looking well and happy, and putting her arms around her offspring in a motherly greeting, she found herself curious at Lindsey's exuberance. "I thought you've been working, Honey. When you linked with me the other day, you said you were being sent somewhere by IBAT to further research."

"Oh, I did, Mom," explained Lindsey, "and we did work of

course, but," she paused staring dreamily past her mother's face, "I just had such a wonderful time doing it."

"Do you supposed I'm too old to go to work at IBAT?" questioned her mother jokingly, with a lift of her eyebrows. "If your job is that much fun, I could certainly consider applying for a position."

Lindsey giggled, and put her arm around her mothers still slim waist, "Come to my room with me while I put my things away and I'll tell you all about it."

Once in her bedroom, Lindsey pressed the panel on the wall and heard the familiar rush of air rise up from the floor. She tossed her silvery, light–weight clothing satchel on her bed, and then fell on top of the concentrated air stream; her arms spread out at her sides.

"So," inquired Olivia airily, as she laid down on the opposite side of the fully transparent bed and smiled warmly into her daughter's eyes, "where did you go?"

"Oh, I'm sorry Mom," Lindsey answered, "I can't tell you that. You don't know how much I wish I could, but I can't."

"Well, what kind of work did you do, Dear?" questioned her curious mother.

"I'm afraid I can't tell you that either," replied Lindsey.

"Well, who were you with?" continued Olivia, but before Lindsey could form the words of her reply, answered the question herself, "I know, you can't tell me, right?"

Lindsey turned her face to the side and stared intently at this wonderful woman, who had married the most wonderful man, and had been such an awesome caring, loving and devoted mother. She wanted to tell her everything, wanted to describe the beauty and romance of the underwater city, to tell her about the wonderful professors they had met and talked to, about the beautiful gray whale they had seen, and the playful dolphins. She could share none of those things without giving away the underwater city that Trent and Thad had been sequestered in for so many years, and at this time, that was still considered very sensitive information.

"Oh, Mom, I'm sorry I...." Lindsey began to apologize. Right now, she wouldn't allow herself to think about any of the frightening possibilities Trent and Thad had warned of with regard to the Reclamation Project, and she certainly couldn't share any of that information with her mother. She vowed to remain light-hearted, and to focus on her happiness for the moment.

"I understand, Sweetheart," smiled her mother. "I realize the importance of security in your work. Can you at least tell me why you look so darned happy?" Olivia smiled, reaching over to brush a few stray wisps of auburn hair from around her daughters still beaming face; "Did you get a credit increase already?"

"No," giggled Lindsey, turning on her side to face her mother, "I didn't get a credit increase." She couldn't help noticing how much they resembled one another, and aside from the fact that her mother's hair was several shades darker, the telltale red highlights were ever present nonetheless. That and a twenty–year age difference were almost all that separated the two women physically.

Lindsey's mind busily sifted through her experiences of the last couple days, in an effort to differentiate the classified information from the non–classified. "I can tell you this," Lindsey said, conspiratorially. Olivia's eyes grew large and her eyebrows rose like two perfectly manicured wings in anticipation, "I took a real, water bath."

"No!" her mother's mouth fell open in absolute disbelief, "you're joking, you didn't take a freshwater bath, did you?"

Lindsey laughed aloud at the incredulous look on her mother's face. "I truly did, Mother, in a deep bathing tub, with hot water all the way up to my neck. I even stuck my head under the water and washed my hair with a foaming, liquid cleanser that came from a dispenser on the wall."

Olivia knew that many people still took real water baths, but only those with unlimited wealth, who could afford to have bathing tubs constructed and installed in their homes, and pay for the water to fill them as well. It seemed unheard of, and such a waste of the life giving, natural resource. "This is part of your job, Lindsey, to take baths?"

Her mother's question elicited yet another bout of laughter, "No, Mom," she answered, wiping a tear from the corner of her eye, "it was in the evening, after we'd completed our work for the day, and I was offered a hot bath before bed. Oh, Mother," she sighed, "It was the most wonderful experience imaginable." She thought for a moment, and then added, "No, the second most wonderful experience imaginable."

"Uh, oh," chided Olivia, as she gave her daughter a knowing look, "Lindsey Marie Larimer, if I didn't know for a fact that you were working the last couple of days, I'd almost swear you were in love."

"Does it show that much?"

"Aha!" Olivia fairly shrieked, "You are, you really are!" The older woman's eyes were sparkling with excitement. There was nothing more in the world that she wanted to see than her daughter's happiness. She'd watch Lindsey grow up to be so very much like her father.

Lowell had been such a passionate and dedicated man, but those qualities were extended outside the work that had consumed so much of his life, and shared equally with his wife and daughter as well. Lindsey had that same passion and dedication that had made her so highly successful in her own field, but Olivia also wanted to see her daughter have a family of her own one day. So far, Lindsey had been too wrapped up in her work to even make time for dating. "Oh, Sweetheart," said Olivia, feeling tears of happiness begin to prickle behind her eyes, "I've never seen you in love before," she sniffled and patted Lindsey's arm affectionately, "can you at least tell me who it is?"

"You've already met him," Lindsey grinned, as she gently teased her anticipative mother.

"Oh, don't you dare make me guess, Lindsey Marie," exclaimed Olivia, all the while, her mind whirling with the faces of the people she'd met since her arrival in California. A few taxi drivers, the airlift operator in the lobby, and a few faces she couldn't clearly remember from the night her daughter took her out for a drink. It dawned on her then, "Not that incredibly handsome young doctor that tried to introduce himself to you at Sal's?"

Lindsey grinned and nodded her assent, "Kevin Sanders," she confirmed.

"You mean Doctor Sanders, right?" Her mother smiled playfully, as she repeated the name the way Lindsey had at the lounge that evening.

"Okay," chuckled her mildly embarrassed daughter, "there's no need to tease me, I've already apologized to Kevin for being mean to him."

"He works with you then?" asked Olivia.

"Yes, and he was also sent out on the same field job, so we got to know each other along the way, and I just can't believe I misjudged him at first. He's such a wonderful man."

"And definitely not at all hard on the eyes." They both laughed out loud, until the masculine voice of Lindsey's computer control-center interrupted their revelry.

"Parcel delivery for Dr. Lindsey Larimer in five, four, three, two, one. Package arrival complete."

"Who in the world would be sending me a package?" questioned Lindsey, more to herself than her mother, as the two women rose from the bed, and walked out into the living area.

"Maybe your young man sent you a gift," supplied her mother.

"I don't see how he could have," returned Lindsey over her shoulder, as she made her way to the delivery portal next to her wall-mounted link-pad. "I gave him my link number, but didn't think to give him my address."

Sliding the panel aside, Lindsey reached into the delivery cubicle and withdrew a carefully wrapped package, with no return address, then returned to her bedroom with the parcel in her arms, and her mother close behind.

She wasted no time in tearing open the wrapping, and then with her hands on her cheeks and her eyes wide, Lindsey stood back in stunned disbelief, staring down at the shimmering white, twentieth-century replica gown. "I don't believe it!" she exclaimed, "it's the dress I saw in the shop window. Oh, mother, it's a replica dress," she explained, as she lifted the frothy, iridescent material and held it close to her body. When the fabric was turned, and the light hit it, the white gown almost came alive with a changing array of pink, green and gold hues that played across its surface.

"Oh, Honey," breathed her mother, "I've never seen anything so beautiful in all my life."

"There's a small slide-tablet," said Lindsey curiously, as she reached down to retrieve the previously unseen article. She turned to the link–port on the wall next to her bed, touched the panel, and inserted the slide–tablet into the opening in its side. The screen lit up, and Lindsey realized, to her amazement that it was an audio note from Kevin. She pressed the panel again, and the computer played the message aloud, with Kevin's voice coming through perfectly. It was as though he was right there next to her, and Lindsey felt a small chill go through her.

"Hello Lindsey," the message began, "I hope you don't think I'm being presumptuous, but I couldn't help noticing how those pretty blue eyes of yours were so drawn to this dress when you saw it in the window. I enlisted Thad's assistance in finding out who the storeowner was and we were able to link to him and offer to purchase the gown. It seems though," he chuckled, "that the shop owner only makes one of each replica gown. I guess the idea is for the customers to pick one they like and then have it custom made to their size. Of course we had no choice," he chuckled again, "but to go directly to the shop and remove this one from the display window. I, uh," he stumbled before continuing, "I had no idea what size you wear, although I would have guessed size perfect," he added jokingly, "and I would have sent it myself, but I didn't have your address. It was fortunate that the professors had the information in their files, and offered to send this to you on my behalf. Anyway, I hope it fits, and I'll be home all evening if you'd like to link."

A series of tones indicated that the message replay was complete. Lindsey turned to her mother, "I can't believe he did this, Mom, it's the most wonderful gift I've ever received."

"Well," returned her mother with a smile, "I'm not going to ask what the 'field work' you were doing entailed, but apparently, there was time for bathing and window shopping." She laughed pleasantly, before adding, "I'd call him and thank him if I were you." She turned and left the room when Lindsey reached toward the link–port.

Glen had been lost deep in thought since they had left the Underwater City. His mind whirled with all the information Trent and Thad had shared with them. He was nervous, and almost wished he hadn't been made privy to such disturbing news as the professors had bestowed on him. He didn't like what he'd heard and felt that the government itself was dabbling with things that might be well beyond their ability to control. Nonetheless, he was already involved, and his position at IBAT did not allow him the luxury of picking and choosing what projects to take part in.

"You have two link messages," sounded the simulated masculine voice of his home–control computer center. Glen seldom received any links from anyone, his self–dedication to his job, not allowing him the opportunity to make any real friends outside the lab.

Reaching almost hesitantly toward the green–hued glow of the illuminated link–panel, he found himself swallowing against the nervous lump forming in the back of his throat. Glen's fingertip had no sooner touched the panel than the screen came to life and Sal's handsome face appeared before him. He noted with some interest that Sal seemed to have been sitting at a desk when he'd left the link–message and several rows of books, the old fashioned paper books, not the modern slide–tablets or book–chips, lined shelves directly behind him, indicating that he was perhaps a collector.

"Hello Glen," said Sal with a beaming smile, "it's Sunday afternoon, and I was wondering if you might like to join me for dinner this evening. You know," he paused and presented another grin, his even, white teeth contrasting nicely against his olive–colored skin," I've been thinking a lot about you since last Friday night." He cast his eyes downward almost shyly, "I've been hoping maybe we could get to know each other a little better. So, link to me when you hear this. I'll look forward to talking to you soon." Sal flashed another smile and reached forward to press the control panel, the screen went blank and then flashed on again to relay the second message. Again it was Sal, only this time he didn't seem quite as jovial.

"Hi Glen. It's Monday morning," he began, "listen, uh," he continued, "I've been thinking, and I really want to apologize if my last link transmission seemed a bit forward. I didn't mean to sound presumptuous, so I'll certainly understand if I don't hear from you. Take care though, and have a good day." Sal ended the transmission, and Glen found himself feeling a trifle dejected. He hadn't told Sal last Friday night that he would be out of town, of course, at the time, he hadn't known. Even when he virtually lived at IBAT, he could access the few home links he received from his office in the evenings when he was on his own time. He just hadn't been able to check them in the past several days. Sal hadn't heard back from him, and so naturally assumed that perhaps Glen wasn't interested in furthering the friendship they had struck up the night they met.

'Geovanni Basalori.' Glen said the name to himself. Even Sal's true name sounded attractive. He pressed the reply area on the panel and the computer instantly connected to Sal's linking–device. After a moment, Sal's face appeared on the screen before him.

"Glen!" he exclaimed, before Glen had even said 'hello.' "How nice to see you, I almost didn't expect to." His smile was most disarming.

"Forgive me," Glen apologized, "I've been out of town and only just returned." He lifted the small suitcase up so that Sal could see it, as though to emphasize the truth of his words, "Or I would have returned your first link right away."

Sal afforded Glen a beaming smile that left him with a rather nervous, fluttering feeling in the pit of his stomach. "Well, I'm glad you did return my link," his dark eyes crinkled at the corners when he smiled, which seemed to be often, and Glen drew in his breath at the sheer good looks of this Latin man.

"I was hoping I'd return to a message from you," said Glen, some of his shyness beginning to fade as he looked into Sal's eyes when he spoke. "And I would very much like to take you up on your dinner offer, I just don't know when I'll have any time off. We're starting a project at work that could well keep me sequestered away for several weeks."

"Not a problem," answered Sal, "I'm just pleased that you linked to me."

It was a full forty–five minutes later before Glen said his 'good–byes' to Sal and terminated the link. He needed to unpack, use the cleansing tube and try to get to bed early in preparation for the busy day he knew he would face on the morrow. He rather doubted he would be able to go right to sleep. He imagined he would spend half the night remembering those liquid brown eyes.

The lab was bustling with activity when Glen, Lindsey and Kevin returned to IBAT on Wednesday morning. All preliminary work had been completed, and The Reclamation Project was well underway. The mummies of King Tutankhamun and Princess Ankhesenamun had been brought in the previous Monday morning, just after the trio had left for their meeting with Professor Farrier and McRae. Their wrappings had been removed, and DNA extracted from their corpses, but the mummies themselves would remain at IBAT until such a time as their clones were deemed suitably stable.

Glen was glad his workload hit him like a ton of bricks when he was finally returned to his regular duties at the lab. Of course, now he had several additional responsibilities to carry out with regard to the project, and didn't realize until late in the evening that he hadn't eaten one bite since the afternoon before. His stomach reminded his mouth of its neglect, but darkness had long–since fallen before he found time to set his work aside and head for the temporary dining area IBAT had implemented in their absence. Crews of eighty or so people worked directly on the project around–the–clock, making the new cafeteria area off the lab a necessity.

Now, sitting at one of the smaller acrylic tables in the makeshift cafeteria, he slowly ate the simulated chicken and vegetable dinner. He could certainly tell the difference between the chewy, almost rubbery, synthetic chicken, and the real food Trent and Thad had treated them to.

Glen's mind wandered back to the words Thad had shared with them on their last day in the Ocean City, and shuddered. Determining once again not to allow himself to dwell on all the worst case scenarios his mind conjured forth, he routed his thoughts back to the memory of Sal's smile and laughter when they had talked the evening before. He needed the distraction, and his need for it existed on more than one level.

Kevin had not seen Lindsey since they had linked the night before. For some reason, he had assumed that the aero–van would pick all three of them up together that morning, instead of individually. He missed Lindsey terribly and almost had to shake himself out of it in order to lend his full concentration to the work before him. He knew that Glen's work at this juncture involved a complete and separate aspect of the cloning process, and that Lindsey's involvement might not bring her anywhere near him for several days. He hoped he could get through it without seeing her, talking to her.

Kevin remembered the conversation they'd had the night before when she had received the package and linked to him to tell him how elated she was. She'd been so happy that her eyes were ringed with unshed tears. That replica gown had cost him almost a week's credits, but when he saw the joy on Lindsey's face, he'd have happily paid every credit he'd ever earned. He had it bad, and he couldn't deny it; not even to himself. He was doing something he had never truly done before. Kevin Sanders was falling in love.

Lindsey's first day at the lab was most interesting and pleasant indeed. She missed Kevin so intensely she could hardly stop thinking about him, but still managed to perform the duties of her new position. Those duties had not been fully defined to her until her return to IBAT Tuesday morning. It was then she learned that for the first few months, her job would consist of advising and overseeing the authenticity of replica garb being created by a slew of seamstresses IBAT had brought in for that specific purpose.

Although Lindsey had no knowledge whatsoever of the cloning process from a scientific stand point, she had been told that the particular process being utilized would cause the king and his princess to grow rapidly, requiring clothing of every manner from childhood to adolescence.

Professor St. Germaine had explained to her that the cloned humans would be raised fully Egyptian. They would dress Egyptian and be taught Egyptian culture, language, mannerisms and customs, but they would not yet be told that they had once been royalty or that they were not birth–humans. He explained that she had been hand chosen for this project not just because of her direct relationship to the discovery of The Library Of Knowledge, but also because of her indepth knowledge of Egyptian language, customs and textiles, including period raiment.

Lindsey found her new position quite interesting, and enjoyed the many hours spent pouring over slide–tablets of Egyptian styles, colors and fabrics. The seamstresses had been chosen for their knowledge of period costuming, and many of them had worked on projects that included the reconstruction of clothing from earlier periods, found on the corpses of peoples who had died thousands of years before.

It was a great job; the prevailing wage credits being paid by the government for her work on the project was more than she would have ever expected to make doing any job. Of course, she found herself working both night and day, so the credits were certainly well earned.

She just missed Kevin so incredibly, and as the weeks turned into months with time for only an occasional link, Lindsey became certain that she was fully and completely in love. Apparently, the old adage, 'absence makes the heart grow fonder' was quite true indeed.

Lindsey missed her mother a great deal too, and wondered how she'd been spending her days. Of course, Olivia loved to read, and Lindsey had brought along her vast collection of mystery novels…Hopefully, her mom had put them to good use.

Since The Reclamation Project was both top–secret, and high priority, all lines of communication with the outside world were restricted to emergency contacts only. Not only could Lindsey not link to her mother, but also the doctors and other employees of IBAT were precluded from leaving their designated work areas, and could link to one another for only limited periods of time.

The last briefing just prior to the project getting fully underway advised all staff members that until such a time as the cloning process was complete and the clones thriving, the communication restrictions would be strongly enforced. The executive committee had apparently felt this dictate was necessary to insure both security and total concentration to the work at hand.

Although IBAT did provide small but comfortable 'studio–type' apartments for their staff, they were very small, very sparse and very lonely in the evenings.

Independence Day came and went, but the work at IBAT didn't even slow down. The fourth of July had long been one of

Lindsey's favorite holidays, but with the exception of a few decorations put up by some of the employees, there was nothing to mark the day as special, and the work continued without so much as a pause.

On a Thursday afternoon, nearly eight weeks after Lindsey had begun her work at IBAT; she finally saw the object of her constant thoughts. She'd been sitting with her back to the door with one of the seamstresses, going over a particularly difficult design, consisting of sewing tiny metal coins to very sheer fabric. The door opened with a slight 'whoosh,' but it opened and closed quite often, as supplies were brought in and finished garments were taken away, so she had not turned. It wasn't until she realized that all work had stopped, and that she no longer had the attention of the woman she'd been speaking to so intently, that she looked up.

Kevin's smile almost made Lindsey's knees buckle when she saw him, and she had to grab at the corner of the nearby table to keep from stumbling. His large, well shaped hand steadied her as she righted herself and afforded him the brightest smile he'd ever seen…a smile that almost took his breath away.

"Good news," he grinned, "all restrictions were just lifted a few minutes ago."

Lindsey was elated. She couldn't think of any news that could possibly make her happier. She would finally get to see Kevin again and spend time with him and her mother. Her smile spoke a thousand words, and it was all Kevin could do not to take her in his arms and kiss her until she was out of breath. He knew however, that all eyes were on them, and spoke to Lindsey in a low tone. "I went straight to Professor St. Germaine when I heard the news," he told her, noting that every woman in the room was listening intently, though somehow he didn't care. "I asked him if we could have tomorrow night and the weekend off work for some much needed R and R." His smile was so disarming; Lindsey could not remove her eyes from his face as he spoke.

"We?" she asked questioningly.

"Yes, we," he returned, "as in you and I."

"And?" she said hopefully.

"And he said yes!" exclaimed Kevin, with his familiar broad

grin. "As a matter of fact, he's agreed to let most all the key support members have the weekend off. Of course," he winked, "they don't concern me."

"Oh, Kevin," Lindsey had to stop herself from throwing her arms around this wonderful, handsome and thoughtful man. She too, noticed the curious and envious glances of the other women, and stepped back an inch or two.

"I thought maybe you'd like to go out with me tomorrow night and spend Saturday and Sunday together," intoned Kevin huskily. "And I'd really like to see you in your new gown."

"There is nothing I would like better," smiled Lindsey, almost shyly. She knew it would be all she could do to get through the next day. Her first date alone with Kevin was a most unexpected and yet incredibly pleasant turn of events.

Glen was quite surprised when Professor St. Germaine had announced all communication restrictions had been lifted, and several individuals, including Glen himself, could have the weekend off. He really wanted to spend some time with Sal if at all possible. He hoped Sal hadn't given up on him, or didn't already have plans for the weekend. That would be his luck.

As soon as he left IBAT on Friday evening, he went straight home and directly to the link–port to contact his new Italian friend.

Sal had been delighted when Glen had linked to him. "You know, that dinner offer is still open," volunteered Sal, "I have a greenhouse, and can have some beef sent over from the restaurant if you'd like a real, home–cooked meal at my place." he offered.

The arrangements had been made, and Glen's heart skipped a beat or two. This was the happiest and most light–headed he'd felt in quite some time.

He'd certainly had no idea that Sal was quite so successful. Granted, his restaurant clearly did an excellent business from what Glen had seen on his one visit, but anyone who owned their own hot–house was obviously quite well to do. Of course, while Glen had certainly never judged anyone on how much or how little they possessed, it was impressive nonetheless. "I would love to have dinner at your place Sal," he smiled, "I can be there in an hour or so if you give me your address."

Glen headed directly for the cleansing chamber. He wanted to look his best when he met Sal in person again. With all this expensive, real food people were feeding him lately, he'd have to join Kevin in the gym, or take the synthetic body–sculpting pills that were becoming so popular.

"I like this one," Olivia suggested, as she pressed the selection panel on the Coif–Configurator in Lindsey's grooming area, a small room located just off the cleansing chamber, and previewed the selection. "Don't you think your hair would look better if you wear it up with the gown?"

"Oh, Mother, I do like that one!" exclaimed Lindsey, "definitely up," she agreed. "But let's set the program to leave just a few strands down at the nape," she suggested, pressing the appropriate settings on the selection panel, "and maybe have them wavy," another press of the softly glowing panel produced the desired effect on the screen. "Like that!" she finished.

Lindsey sat down as her mother adjusted the coned–shaped aperture next to the wall unit over her head, covering her face, and pressed the illuminated panel again. The 'whoosh' sound indicated that the instrument was activated, and the ends of Lindsey's hair were pulled up into the vacuum of the hood. A minute later, the computer announced that Lindsey's new hair configuration was complete, and her mother lifted the arm of the aperture from her daughter's head.

Lindsey stared at her image reflected back to her on the computer screen, displaying how she looked in the new style. She was pleased with her appearance, and sincerely hoped that Kevin would be as well.

The sun was touching the horizon when Kevin arrived to collect his date. Olivia greeted him at the door and invited him inside, just as Lindsey walked out from her sleeping chamber. Kevin's look of speechless appreciation re–defined the compliment.

The dress fit Lindsey's body like it had been sewn on to her. Her cleavage was displayed most advantageously above the low neckline of the gown, her waist looked so small that Kevin was sure he could span it with his hands, and the hem of the filmy, shimmering material kissed the floor around her. The dress covered the clear, acrylic, high-heeled shoes she wore on her small feet.

Kevin drank in the beauty of his date; her upswept hair a mass of curls piled high atop her head, with long, wavy tendrils falling over her shoulders and laying at rest against the soft, round globes of her breasts. It was several moments before he could find his voice, and Lindsey felt herself begin to blush under the intensity of his burning gaze.

"I had no idea you were so beautiful," he breathed.

The questioning lift of Olivia's brows alerted him to the fact that he may not have chosen his words well. "I mean, I knew you were beautiful, Lindsey," he tried again, "I just didn't know you were that beautiful." At Lindsey's somewhat confused look, he decided against an attempt to further clarify, and simply said, "the dress looks lovely on you."

Olivia chuckled, and he had the impression she was enjoying his discomfiture, "You two just have a good time," she offered with a smile.

Ten minutes later, Kevin and Lindsey were still gliding along in his Centurian, and she was beginning to wonder if he was taking her to the other side of the country. Kevin found himself unable to remove his eyes from the vision sitting next to him, and before the craft touched down, he found that he could no longer abstain from kissing her mouth deeply, leaving them both feeling slightly shaken from the passion that kiss evoked.

Just as Lindsey, who had not been paying much attention to the virtual-panel screens in Kevin's' vehicle, thought they were going to land, she felt the Centurian continue to descend, and wondered what altitude they had been traveling at. When she finally took note of her surroundings, she gasped. They were descending through a transparent tunnel of sorts, and all she could see was the familiar blue-green color of the sea. The lights of the Centurian flashed on, as its censors detected the darkening of their environment, and as recognition dawned, Lindsey realized Kevin was taking her back to the same underwater city where they had met the professors.

"Are we going to visit Trent and Thad again?" she asked with some confusion.

"I imagine they'll be here," was his cryptic reply.

It was then that they left the tunnel and settled comfortably in a parking area she had not noticed on their previous venture. The vehicles it contained were parked four tiers high, and they were very expensive looking conveyances indeed.

Kevin placed is hand on the small of Lindsey's back in the gentlemanly gesture that was becoming pleasantly familiar to her, and led her to the transport–walk. "I wanted to surprise you," he offered, "but since we're here now, I should tell you that Thad confided to me when we were here that there was a special, pre–grand opening of the city tonight for the investors and many government officials. I decided then to keep it a secret and bring you myself. You can't know how concerned I was that IBAT wouldn't lift the communication restrictions in time.

"Oh Kevin," Lindsey replied, feeling like the most special woman in the world, "I can't believe you did this, how wonderful!" She couldn't help herself from turning to him, and standing on her tiptoes, kissed him deeply. "But Kevin?"

"Yes?"

"Won't I be just a little out of place in this gown?"

"No, but I will be out of place in this," he answered, looking down at his thoroughly modern attire.

"How so?" asked Lindsey, "Do you expect everyone else to be dressed in twentieth–century attire?" Her giggle was most charming.

"Actually, yes," answered Kevin, with a chuckle of his own. "In keeping with the twentieth century theme of the home interiors here, that shop that your dress came from, 'Back to the Past' wasn't it?" She nodded her assent and he continued, "Well the shop owner and her husband are hosting tonight's pre–grand–opening, and the guests will all be donning twentieth century clothing, including us."

"Us?" asked Lindsey with a quizzical look, as she took in Kevin's very chic and very trendy attire.

"Yes," he smiled, as he bent to kiss his date gently on the tip of her nose, "we shall seek out the good professors and I will leave them to keep an eye on you while I change. I secured a loaner suit through Trent when I first learned of the costume dinner tonight. I didn't want you wearing a rented gown though, Little Miss Lindsey," he said with a beaming smile. "I wanted you to have one you could keep forever."

"That's not all I want to keep forever." The words slipped out of her mouth before she even realized it, and she felt an embarrassed flush creep across her cheeks.

Kevin turned to Lindsey as the transport carried them along toward the Town Square, and took both of her hands in his own. "I'm glad you said that Lindsey. Very glad."

Lindsey didn't have time to ask him exactly what he meant by that, as she glanced ahead and saw to her sheer delight, a large group of people milling about the square in elegant suits and gowns of the twentieth–century period. "Oh Kevin!" she almost squealed, "I can't believe it, they all look so beautiful. It's like stepping back in time." She placed her hand around his upper arm, noticing that her fingers didn't come close to encircling his biceps. She felt his muscles tighten at her touch and a shiver ran through her at this man's incredible masculinity.

Chapter Seven

Kevin steered his stunning date off the transport walk and led her toward the gathering crowd. He noticed that several couples had arrived after he and Lindsey, slowly gliding toward the square from the same direction they had come from. Many of the men turned their heads and then did obvious double takes when they saw the virtual goddess in white on his arm. At that moment, Kevin Sanders felt like the luckiest guy on the planet.

They stood on the sidewalk and Kevin began to feel a slight twinge of jealousy at the way some of the other men were looking at Lindsey. It was apparent on the faces of their wives and girlfriends that they too shared Kevin's feeling.

The building before them was enormous, and stood several stories high. He and Lindsey had commented on its architecture when they had returned from the entertainment center with Glen some months ago. The elegant gold lettering above the etched glass doors, announced its name as, 'The Blast from the Past – Fine Restaurant and Lounge.'

Just then, the glass doors opened to admit the still growing crowd and the two found themselves ushered inside en masse. Trent and Thad were in the lobby and had apparently been watching for their young friends' arrival. Both men were attired in twentieth-century tuxedos, complete with tails. They greeted the couple warmly, their genuine compliments on Lindsey's stunning appearance nearly causing her to blush. Taking her arms, one on each side, the two distinguished scholars led her away, while Kevin went to collect and don his rented suit.

"And what would be your pleasure this evening, Little Miss Lindsey?" asked Thad with his ever-present smile, as they made their way across the lush foyer, with its simulated twentieth-century furniture of gold and blue brocade, toward the open arch that led to the lounge.

The heels of Lindsey's acrylic slippers made tiny, temporary indentations in the beautifully crafted, thick carpeting that covered the floors. She had never seen such carpeting first-hand, and took in every line of the Neptune–under–sea pattern, done primarily in monochromatic shades of blue, green, and gold.

Before Lindsey had time to think about what beverage she might like, Trent broke in and jovially demanded that he be allowed to pay for her drink. Although Trent's black–silk covered belly kept him from getting as close to the bar as Thad and Lindsey, he had his credit chip at the ready.

The attractive young bartender not much more than a boy in his very early twenties, couldn't seem to take his eyes off the filmy white vision that stood on the opposite side of the simulated mahogany bar. He meant to ask the trio before him what they wanted to drink, but couldn't quite stop staring open–mouthed at the breathtaking woman standing before him.

Lindsey stared back as the young man's mouth moved, but nothing came out, "Are you all right?" she asked.

"Uh, I … yes," he finally stammered out, "what can I get for you?" His lop–sided grin was boyishly charming.

Trent and Thad both looked to Lindsey for her reply, but she so seldom drank liquor she didn't know the names of any drinks, or what they had in them. She tried to remember what the bartender had suggested for she and her mother at Sal's the night she first met Kevin, but couldn't recall what it had been. "Why don't you two suggest something for me?" she asked lightly.

"Okay, consider it done," smiled Thad, as he turned to the young barkeep. "How about three Rising Nebulas?"

"Coming right up, Sir," was the young man's instant reply. He turned around to prepare the drinks, all the while, trying to catch a glimpse of Lindsey out of the corner of his eye. The other three bartenders had already begun taking and preparing orders for the new guests that continually filtered in.

A few moments later, the young bartender returned with three very colorful drinks, each glass layered with red at the bottom and then separate layers of orange, yellow, and green above that, in a most interesting spectrum. Trent rendered his credit chip for payment, and once the bartender had returned it to him, the three sought out an empty table to sit at while they waited for Kevin's return.

As they sat down, Lindsey noted with some amazement that

the red liquid at the bottom of her drink had risen to the surface and the orange layer was now at the bottom. A moment later, the orange had risen to the top and the yellow was at the bottom. Curious, she sipped the effervescent orange liquid at the top of her drink and found that it tasted much like an orange, with a bit of a bite, but it was very flavorful and not at all unpleasant.

Lindsey couldn't seem to take enough in. She watched the men and women now seated at several of the tables and in the lines that had formed at the bar. The be-gowned women were beautiful in their simulated twentieth-century attire of various styles and colors, and the men equally well adorned in suits and tuxedos that were quite handsome. Lindsey truly felt almost as though she had somehow been transported back in time.

It was then that a very tall, extraordinarily handsome, blond man walked through the open archway, wearing a black tuxedo with black velvet double lapels. Lindsey's breath caught in her throat, and she nearly choked on the orange liquid in her mouth when she realized that the stunning man walking toward them was none other than Kevin himself. Of course, Lindsey couldn't help noticing that virtually every woman in the room stopped mid-sentence to watch this elegant man with the cat-like grace as he crossed the room.

Kevin failed to notice either the appreciative looks from the women, or the envious ones from the men. He saw only one person when he entered the lounge, and that was Lindsey. She sat between Professors' Farrier and McRae as though she was a queen holding court. Her beautiful chestnut curls, piled high on her head gave her a regal quality, and he found himself drawn to her like he'd been pulled into a tractor beam.

"Thank you for keeping an eye on my date," Kevin smiled as he approached their table, "one must keep an eye on the most beautiful woman in the entire city." He looked directly at Lindsey when he spoke, no hint of his words having been spoken lightly.

A waitress in a 1940's gown of gold lame' had spotted Kevin as soon as he had entered under the open archway, and virtually followed him to the table. He had no sooner exchanged chairs with Thad, and sat down next to Lindsey, than the waitress approached the table.

"Can I get you something tonight sir?" The dark haired woman asked.

Lindsey took note of the fact that the woman virtually ignored everyone but Kevin, and the look in her eyes was almost one of unabashed lust.

"Yes, thank you," was Kevin's polite reply, "I'll have what my lovely lady here is having." He took Lindsey's hand in his own and kissed her fingertips without so much as a glance at the attractive waitress. Lindsey felt shivers go through her spine at his touch, and looked up to see his eyes settled intently upon her.

The waitress turned on her heel and headed toward the bar, clearly stung at Kevin's unwitting rebuff.

Trent and Thad shared knowing looks and smiled. It was obvious that their young companions were falling, or had fallen in love. It was most pleasant to watch their newfound feelings for one another unfold.

They spoke briefly of the work being conducted at IBAT in hushed tones, but with the volume of people being seated around them, and the rapidly filling tables, the four thought it better to change the topic to more light–hearted and non–sequential banter.

An hour later, dinner was formally announced, and the guests began leaving their tables in the lounge to be ushered into the dining hall. Six sets of double doors were opened on the far end of the richly decorated room, and the crowd began to filter through them. Kevin kept Lindsey close to his side, and she took in her breath at the magnificent, four–story restaurant, with its tiered balcony's of tables leading up to the clear, domed roof.

Because of the height of the building itself, the patrons were afforded a view through the top of the dome, to the outer dome of the city itself. Spotlights were positioned so that the sea directly above the restaurant was lit up. High backed, antique reproduction chairs stood around hundreds of tables with mermaid–shaped candles on each lace–covered tabletop, and several aesthetically pleasing ushers in ecru tuxedos led the guests to their tables.

Lindsey was quite impressed to note that they were led to one of the main tables at the far end of the massive room, near a small stage, presumably set up for the speakers.

Dinner consisted of crabmeat salads and fresh fruit, followed by an array of shellfish with lemon and drawn butter, then beef and pork steaks with several kinds of steamed vegetables and half a dozen twentieth–century popular desserts. The steaks were marvelous, and Kevin determined that if they were simulated steaks, as most were these days, the chef had certainly done an excellent job.

Lindsey ate as much as the tightly fitting bodice of her gown would allow, and listened with interest as each speaker in turn took the stage during the 'Pre–Grand Opening' ceremony. As the night wore on, she found herself wishing more and more that she could have just a few minutes alone with Kevin. She wanted to touch him, to kiss him, and to be held in his arms at least for a brief time.

The ceremony was interesting, and though nothing whatsoever was mentioned about the information necessary to construct it having come from the tablets and scrolls found in the Library of Knowledge, much of the architecture itself was explained and described. The businesses within the city and their individual specialties were announced, and those who had already purchased their own private dwellings sight unseen, would be allowed to visit them for the first time following the ceremony.

After a holographic presentation of the city, including several views from every conceivable angle of both the inside and the outside, a bottle of 1999 vintage wine was uncorked and the new underwater city christened, 'Atlantica,' to a loud round of applause and cheers from the dinner guests.

When both the ceremony and the dinner had ended, Kevin suggested that he and Lindsey might enjoy another drink in the lounge, and invited Trent and Thad to join them. The older men declined, stating that they were not accustomed to such long evenings, and said their "good–byes."

It seemed that many of the other diners had the same idea with regard to an after dinner drink, and the lounge quickly began to fill up. Kevin had secured a small, romantic table in the corner, and ordered two more 'Rising Nebulas,' his eyes seldom leaving

Lindsey's as they enjoyed their drinks and each other's company. All the while, Lindsey couldn't help noticing the women at some of the other tables, starting unabashedly at Kevin. When their glasses were empty, Kevin took Lindsey's hand and escorted her through the lounge and lobby area, exiting through the main doors.

They made their way to the transport–walk and allowed it to carry them deeper into the city, where they enjoyed window shopping, along with many of the other dinner guests. A few of the shops were open for business, clearly hoping to make some early profits.

Kevin and Lindsey wandered through many of the brightly lit establishments and noted with delight that most of them were geared toward the twentieth–century way of life being embraced by this new city. There was one rather large establishment however that did not carry merchandise in keeping with this theme. It was an Android Center, called 'Modern Living,' offering exceptionally human–like, android 'home–assistants.'

While these were certainly nothing new, and the wealthy had been utilizing 'droids' in their homes for some years, Lindsey had never seen one up close and in person. Taking Kevin's hand, she fairly pulled him off the transport–walk and led him through the doors of the establishment. The droids were so realistic it was almost uncanny, and for the most part, these human lookalikes were extremely attractive, although there were a few specifically designed to look older, even a couple of nearly bald male droids.

"I rather like this one," exclaimed Kevin, with a twinkle in his eye as he indicated a blonde droid housemaid, with exceptional curves and very long legs.

Lindsey had no sooner looked to where Kevin was pointing, before she pushed him away and crossed her arms in front of her. "Really," she teased in return, "then I think you should buy her and take her home with you."

Kevin knew that Lindsey was just joking with him, but still, he rather liked that bit of jealousy he heard in her tone. He'd never cared much for the jealousy some of the women he had dated in the past had displayed, but in Lindsey, he found it charmingly endearing.

"Perhaps I shall take this one home with me." Lindsey stopped before a male droid that looked like Adonis. His thick, rather longish dark hair, and bare upper body, displaying a massively muscled chest and arms, made Kevin almost squirm. The thought of this droid even being in Lindsey's presence, real or not, was most unsettling. Kevin had never felt so much as a twinge of insecurity in his life, and now he felt himself almost squirming over a droid!

Near the back of the shop, stood a droid created to look like an elderly, heavyset woman with graying hair and small, bright eyes. Lindsey was fascinated with the realism of these animatronic devices that looked so incredibly human, and knew that if she ever had one of her own, she would want this one. There were even age lines on the droid's forehead and around the corners of her eyes and mouth. Lindsey reached out and touched the droids arm, noting that the flesh–like covering even felt real, except that unlike human skin, it was cold to the touch.

After an hour or so, Kevin led Lindsey to yet another walkway, which she assumed would take them back to the main parking area. Instead, she found Kevin leading her off the transport–walk and up to the front door of the dwelling inhabited by Trent and Thad. Rather than using the intercom next to the door to announce their presence however, Kevin placed his hand on the identification panel and the door slid open.

"Are Trent and Thad here?" asked Lindsey speculatively, as she perused the living and kitchen area.

"No, I don't believe they are," responded Kevin with a grin. He took her hand and led her to the familiar back yard. On impulse, she kicked off her shoes and again reveled in the feel of the grass under her feet. The ocean outside the dome was lit up nearly as bright as day, with all the lights of the city now fully functioning, and the marine life seemed to have shown up en masse to explore this newly illuminated area of their normally dark world.

Kevin led Lindsey to the edge of the yard where it met Atlantica's dome, and stood looking out. After a moment, he turned to her and took her in his arms. His mouth came down on hers so quickly; it took her by surprise. His kiss was deep and lingering, his tongue parrying with her own. After a moment, he stood back and looked down into her bright blue eyes. "Lindsey," he started, suddenly seeming quite nervous, "I know we haven't known each other very long…."

Lindsey felt her heart constrict. This was the part where he was going to tell her he wasn't ready for a relationship, that it wasn't her; it was he…and that he felt they should see other people. It had all been too perfect…she should have seen this coming.

"I've never asked this of another woman in my life," continued Kevin, reaching into his coat pocket, and fumbling around inside. "But I want to ask you to be my wife," he finished, almost blurting out the last few words.

It took a moment for what he had just said to register in Lindsey's mind. He wasn't breaking up with her; he was asking her to marry him!

The tears had started falling before Lindsey even realized they had formed. She threw herself into Kevin's arms and held him close to her, "Yes my love," was her immediate reply, "I can think of nothing I would rather do than become your wife."

"Thank God," breathed Kevin in relief, "I wasn't sure what you're supposed to do if the woman says 'no.'"

His broad grin met his eyes, and Lindsey could read the relief written in their depths. Having nearly forgotten the small box he'd fished out of his pocket, Kevin gingerly opened it to display quite possibly the largest diamond ring Lindsey had ever seen. She couldn't even guess at its worth, but knew the heart-shaped engagement ring had to be at least two carats in size, and the wrap-around wedding band contained another carat or two in smaller gems.

Kevin slipped the ring on Lindsey's finger and then kissed the back of her hand. "I know this seems rather sudden, since we really haven't spent much time together, but I think we're both old enough to know our minds…and our hearts."

"I've never been so happy in my life, Kevin," replied Lindsey, "I don't know much about being a wife, but I will try to be the best one I can."

"Just be you, Lindsey," he replied. "I don't need a wife in the literal sense of the word, I need you in every sense of the word. I want to live with you, grow with you, have children with you, and I'm scared of missing one single second of time with you."

Lindsey's tears intensified and she let out a small sob as she embraced him yet again. "I had no idea you were going to ask me this Kevin," she said through her hiccups, as she continued holding him.

"That's not exactly the only surprise I had in mind though," he offered.

"What else could there possibly be?" she asked, her eyelashes wet with more unshed tears, "I don't know if I could stand any more surprises just now."

"I think you'll like this surprise quite a bit," he replied, as he took her arm and led her back through the house to the cleansing room. As they stood looking down at the seashell tub Lindsey so adored, Kevin put his arm around her and smiled, "this is your bathing tub now Little Miss Lindsey."

It took a moment for his words to sink in. "My, my tub?" she questioned, "how is it my tub? It belongs to the professors," she finished, still sniffling.

"It used to belong to the professors," offered Kevin, "but it seems their work is done here and they have no more need of it. I was lucky enough to be able to purchase this house through them. It belongs to us now Lindsey. This is our house, our yard, our furniture, and your tub."

"Ours?" she repeated, her eyes widening as understanding began to dawn. "You already bought it for us?" She was unable to believe any of this was happening to her...unable to believe a man existed that was so perfect, so wonderful.

"I guess all that's left now, is for us to decide on a date for our wedding, and then move our things in here." He turned to face the vision of loveliness beside him and knew in his heart there was nothing he could ever deny her. "You know," he offered, there's plenty of room here, and I know your mother has been living with you in your condo, so I want you to know that she is perfectly welcome to live here with us. I don't want to separate you from her."

"My mother will be wanting to go back to Colorado in a few months," Lindsey explained, "about the time the next lease is due to be signed."

"You want to wait several more months to get married then?" asked Kevin, the disappointment clear in his voice.

"You couldn't pay me to wait a few months," managed Lindsey with a laugh, "I want to marry you right here and right now."

"Well," he chuckled, "I don't think we could get a preacher here on such short notice, although if I'd known you felt this way, I'd have had one waiting here for us."

"You do realize though Kevin, that we won't be able to have an extravagant church wedding. We'd never be able to get that kind of time off work."

"I'd marry you anywhere, any time, any place," he smiled in response.

"And what if I'd have said 'no'?" she teased.

"Then I guess I'd be living in this big house all alone…with that blonde droid." He teased back. He received a playful punch in his arm, causing him to yowl in mock pain and rub the assaulted appendage.

Lindsey was totally consumed with her love for this incredible man before her. She took him by the hand and led him to the bedroom she had once slept in. "Can you help me with the zipper of my dress?" she asked coquettishly, when they'd reached the bed.

"Help you with…." Glen grinned as he understood the full meaning of her simple question, and reached out to do her bidding.

When the dress had fallen to a frothy pile of shimmering white around her feet, Kevin drew in his breath and felt a pull at his loins that could not be denied. Lindsey had worn nothing underneath the gown, and stood before him fully naked, her full, up-thrust breasts tapering to a flat stomach and tiny waist. It was like looking at a living statue of the goddess Venus.

It took only seconds for Kevin to divest himself of his tuxedo and the trappings that went with it. Once in the twentieth–century reproduction bed, the couple were lost in all but each other, as their love culminated into an explosive union that nearly consumed them both.

Glen could hardly believe the magnificent home that was Sal's. Set high on a decorative pillar, nearly one hundred feet up, the two-story dwelling was nothing short of a mansion. The entire second tier was a clear dome filled with virtually every kind of plant and vegetable Glen could imagine.

Sal had taken Glen on a tour of his home that left his guest gaping in awe of the lavish and expensive furnishings and interior. Glen noticed that there was an attractive man and woman standing in the corner of the living room, their faces expressionless, neither moving nor speaking, and assumed they must be in Sal's employ, perhaps as maid and butler. Clearly, Sal's restaurant and lounge did quite well indeed.

The two men had no sooner sat down on Sal's comfortable 'hanging sofa,' when a young, dark haired boy of about six came barreling through the front door, followed by an attractive dark haired woman of about forty-five.

"Daddy!" exclaimed the boy, as he threw himself into Sal's open arms. "We went to the zoo, and I got to touch a monkey! The boys' excitement was evident in his flashing dark eyes, as he climbed up into Sal's lap. "There's not very many monkeys left," he supplied, as though revealing a great secret.

Glen began to feel uncomfortable. The dark haired woman, obviously the boy's mother, stood just inside the doorway; her arms folded in front of her. If her body language was a reflection of her mind-set, it didn't bode well.

"I see your entertaining," she said cattily, giving Glen the once-over and obviously finding him lacking. "Perhaps we should have stayed gone a bit longer." Her highly arched eyebrow lifted in a knowing look, as she stared down her nose at Glen.

"Not at all, Manerva," answered Sal calmly, as he ruffled his son's already tousled hair, "we were just about to enjoy some dinner, would you care to join us?" Sal's solicitous demeanor did not reach his eyes, and Glen could almost feel the tension between his new friend and this woman, Manerva. He wondered if they were married...if he had completely misjudged Sal's position, and began to feel uncomfortable to the point of wanting to make an excuse to leave.

The dark woman saved him from having to do so, as she spun on her heel and turned back toward the entry door, "Kindly do not allow our son to bear witness to any of your foul habits," was her parting remark.

"Daddy," exclaimed the boy, "can I go to Skyler's house and play?"

"It's too late to go play now, Dimmi, dinner is going to be served shortly, and we have a guest this evening."

The curious boy looked over at Glen as though seeing him for the first time. "My name is Dimitrius, what's yours?" he asked with childish innocence.

"This is Glen," broke in his father, "he is my friend and our guest for the evening."

"Hello Glen," offered Dimmi, as he extended his hand in the grown–up greeting he had obviously been taught, "do you own a restaurant like my daddy does?"

Glen could hardly respond through his confusion. It was becoming painfully obvious that Sal was not gay after all, and Glen flinched at the realization that he had made a horrendous mistake in assuming so. "I am a scientist," he finally managed.

"Do you work at IBAT?" asked the boy excitedly. "I want to work there when I grow up and do experiments!"

Before Glen could form another reply, the man and woman he had seen earlier standing against a wall, approached from behind, and the woman announced that dinner was served. Glen hadn't even seen them move from their earlier stations. His quizzical look brought a smile to Sal's face.

"They're droids," he explained, "I detest housework, and they give me more time to spend with my son. Dimmi demands a good deal of my time, don't you son?" He smiled down at the dark haired boy, with eyes so like his own. "His mother is Greek, and we named him Dimitrius after her father," he offered, as he pushed himself down from the sofa. "Are you hungry Glen, there's enough food to feed half the country in the dining room."

Glen could only nod, and follow his friend into the dining room. He'd never seen such an array of rich foods, pastas and pastries in his life, and he knew that none of the food was simulated. Their conversation was limited to very general topics, although Dimmi plied Glen for information about IBAT, it's size, and whether or not any experiments on deep–space exploration were being conducted.

Glen found himself opening up to Sal's son as their meal went on. Dimmi was truly quite bright and very articulate, and Glen couldn't help himself from laughing at the boy's exuberance and energy.

After dinner had been finished and Dimmi tucked into bed for the night, Sal ordered his male droid, whom he called Andreas, to bring them drinks, as they retired to the sitting room to watch a holo–movie. They paid little attention to the movie.

"I apologize Glen," offered Sal when they had seated themselves and were sipping their drinks, "I had expected Manerva to bring Dimmi home before you arrived. She's never been known for her promptness though."

"She is your wife then?" questioned Glen.

"Was. She was my wife," answered Sal, "there's no point in beating around the bush here Glen," he continued, "I'm gay, and have always been gay."

Glen breathed a sigh of relief with the realization that he hadn't misjudged this man after all.

"I tried for years to be normal," he continued, "but deep down, I guess I always knew who and what I was, I just didn't want to admit it."

Glen knew exactly what Sal meant.

"I got married," continued Sal, "and we had Dimmi. I never knew anything could bring so much happiness as Dimmi has brought into my life, but every time I went to bed with Manerva, I felt like I was putting on an act. I was faithful to her, and of that I have no regrets, but eventually, I knew I'd have to tell her the truth?"

"And how did you do that?" asked Glen, genuinely interested.

"I just told her," replied Sal, "one night after we'd put Dimmi to bed, I sat her down right here where we're sitting now, and told her that I was gay."

"I trust she didn't take the news well," intoned Glen rather sadly, knowing what Sal and his wife must have gone through that night.

"She accused me of having been unfaithful to her, screamed

every obscenity known to man, and stormed out of the house in the middle of the night. Two weeks later, I was served with the slide–tablet notifying me she had filed for divorce."

"But how did you end up with Dimmi?" questioned Glen.

"It's a bit uncomfortable to talk about really." Sal sighed heavily, "Not to mention embarrassing, but I went to a doctor and had him examine me. His report stated unequivocally, that I had never had physical sex with another man. I had to present those documents in court, and believe me, it was the most humiliating moment of my life."

"But it's not against the law unless you're caught in the act," stated Glen, why did you have to prove it?"

"Dimmi," was Sal's single response, "Manerva threatened to take him away from me for good, and I couldn't bear the thought of never seeing him again."

"So you'd never made love with another man?" questioned Glen.

"Not at that point. I knew that I would eventually, but I wouldn't be unfaithful in my marriage. I couldn't do that to Manerva or Dimmi. I waited for another year after our marriage had ended and the courts had granted me custody of our son. My former wife was never the real 'motherly' type," offered Sal, "She takes Dimmi places and buys him things, but she's never been the type to hug him or show him a great deal of motherly love. And I honestly don't blame her for her bitterness towards me, I imagine I would have reacted much the same way, were our positions reversed. I really don't fault her for anything."

"What about after your divorce," queried Glen, as he looked at the handsome Italian man next to him, over the top of his glasses, "did you find a man to care about after your marriage ended?"

"The first physical encounter I had with a male confirmed every feeling I'd ever had," explained Sal, "I knew without a doubt that I was gay, and would always be gay. Unfortunately, my relationship with the man didn't last very long. He seemed to be more interested in my personal possessions than in me. Since then, I've had a few relationships, but my work demands a good deal of my time, and this always seemed to be the factor that caused those relationships to end."

"I can certainly identify with that," explained Glen, pushing his sliding glasses back up his nose, "I virtually live at the lab, which really puts a damper on my personal life."

"Well, you're here now," smiled Sal, "and that's all that matters." He set his drink on the floating table next to him and turned towards Glen, "you're here now," he repeated.

Lindsey awoke from a dreamless sleep and felt Kevin's warm body beside her in the huge, four–poster bed. She felt happier than she'd ever been in her life, and had to look at the ring on her finger once again to reaffirm to herself that she hadn't dreamt the whole thing.

They had made love several times during the night, and always fell to sleep entwined in one another's arms. If this was just an inkling of what married life would be like, Lindsey had no doubt she would fall into it quite nicely.

Kevin stirred beside her, and then opened his eyes. "So it wasn't a dream!" he smiled. "You're still here and we're still engaged to be married. What more could I ask for?"

Lindsey brushed a stray lock of hair from above his eyes, and then kissed him sweetly on the mouth.

"Shall we make love again before we start our day, wife to be?" he questioned with a lift of his brow.

"We can," she answered almost shyly, "but I have to admit, I'm still a bit sore." She lowered her eyes and Kevin smiled down at her. Even with her make–up completely gone, and her hair tousled about her, she was a stunning beauty.

"In that case, I guess a nice hot bath might be in order," he said, kissing her forehead lightly.

"Oh, a bath!" exclaimed Lindsey like an excited child, "yes, a bath sounds wonderful!"

Fortunately, the shell–shaped bathing tub was large enough for both of them, and although Lindsey still fought a certain amount of shyness at being fully naked in front of a man, Kevin had a way of putting her at ease and making her feel more comfortable.

"You know," he said, as he ran the bathing sponge over

Lindsey's back and shoulders, "the only clothes we have to wear today are the gown and tux from last night. I left my regular clothes at the restaurant dressing room when I changed into the tux. I have to have the thing back today, but it's in a wrinkled heap on the floor…so I guess we'll just have to spend the day naked."

Lindsey knew he was teasing, and played along. "Well, maybe we'll start a new fad walking around the city completely naked," she giggled like a playful child.

Kevin knew she was teasing him, but just the thought of another man seeing her naked, caused a rush of blood to his head. "I think I'll have to make some arrangements," he amended.

After their bath, they donned the fluffy, twentieth-century bathrobes left behind by Trent and Thad. Even as well built as Kevin was, Thad's robe hung off him in bags and folds that were nothing short of comical. He wasted no time in heading for the link-panel, and put in a communication to the Blast from the Past Restaurant. In seconds he had made arrangements for someone to pick up the suit and bring him his street clothes. He also requested that some modern attire be picked out and brought to the house for Lindsey.

In less than half-an-hour, the home-control-center announced an approaching visitor, and the monitor screen above the front door, indicated the approach of a delivery boy carrying a satchel.

The garment brought for Lindsey was quite beautiful, and obviously very expensive. The luminescent blue jumpsuit fit her body like a second skin, and fortunately, there were shoes to match, although they were a half-size too large. Lindsey loved the look and feel of the sheer, body-hugging fabric.

"Are you hungry?" Kevin called out from the kitchen, while Lindsey finished dressing.

"Famished," was her laughing reply as she made her way toward him down the hallway. I guess this means we'll have to go out to breakfast," grinned Kevin, opening the cupboards to indicate the empty shelves within.

"Before we go Kevin, I'd like to link to my mom and let her know the good news." He kissed her lightly on the forehead and gave her a loving pat on her backside as she turned and headed for the link-panel.

Olivia was beside herself with excitement. "It seems incredibly soon," her mother stated, and then with an outrageous grin, "but I can't say I blame you for accepting, I'd snag him myself if I weren't almost old enough to be his mother." Lindsey beamed her delight at her mother's quick acceptance of this very sudden engagement. Life was truly good.

Minutes later, the two young lovers were back on the transport–walk heading toward the center of town, in search of a restaurant open for breakfast. They couldn't take their eyes off one another, and knew that this weekend would be entirely too short.

Chapter Eight

Monday morning came entirely too quickly, and though much of the work had slowed down at IBAT, there was still a great deal to be done. Lindsey and Kevin had arrived together, and neither of them was terribly eager to go their separate ways. Glen had arrived just after they had, and Kevin noticed immediately, the positive changes in his friends' demeanor. Glen looked happier and more content than Kevin had ever seen him, and he was glad for whatever turn of events had led to his friend's transformation.

Lindsey couldn't help noting the curious faces of the seamstresses when she returned to the 'creativity room.' It didn't take long for the huge diamond ring on her finger to be noticed by the women around her. For the next twenty minutes, she good naturedly answered their questions about how and when Kevin had proposed. Although most of the seamstresses showed genuine happiness and congratulated her, there was one in particular who looked quite sullen, and almost angry.

Amara had heard the rumors that Kevin was probably gay, but she never really believed any of them. Besides, if he was, she had no doubt of her ability to turn him 'straight.' He had smiled at her twice when she had passed him in the hallway, and she was certain that given enough time, he would ask her out. He had to. She wanted him. He was everything she had ever wanted in a man. Why he would want to marry this skinny little woman with her mousy–brown hair, Amara could not understand. It wasn't too late though; she would just have to find a way to get close to him. Once she had him in bed, this Lindsey woman wouldn't have a chance. She vowed to herself that she would find a way to get his attention.

For the next few hours, Amara kept her head bent over her work, hardly able to think past the seething hatred that was beginning to build inside her. How dare this woman sweep into IBAT and steal Amara's potential husband? How dare she? Her hands trembled with her rising anger as she tediously plied the trim on a gown meant for the cloned Egyptian princess.

Lindsey noted Amara's angry countenance and had no idea

why the woman was so obviously upset with her. Perhaps she was simply having a bad day. Lindsey vowed not to allow anything to dampen her happiness, especially not the pouting seamstress.

The schedule at IBAT was beginning to resemble normalcy again, and regular lunch breaks had finally returned to the hectic agenda. Kevin found a moment to link to Lindsey and ask her to meet him in the nutriment court. The knowledge that she would see him for even just an hour brought a smile to Lindsey's face. As the transmission was terminated and she turned from the linking–panel on the wall, her smile did not go unnoticed by Amara. Lindsey would have been shocked had she seen the look of hatred in the other woman's eyes.

Shortly before the lunch break announcement was made, Amara slipped quietly from the room, unnoticed by all but Lindsey, who wondered about this voluptuous blonde woman, and the intense dislike she'd seen on her face earlier. Perhaps the woman's attitude would change after lunch.

"Watch out for that one," offered the sweet–faced Stephanie, who had the position of head–seamstress. "She's had her eye on your young man since the day she arrived." The older woman's concern was apparent on her soft features.

"Ah, so that's what's wrong with her," Lindsey responded, as she began to understand Amara's angry looks earlier, "I thought she simply didn't like me."

"Oh, she liked you fine until Dr. Sanders came here to see you last week. That ring on your finger only escalated her bad disposition. I can terminate her if you like," offered the older woman. "I don't care for her much myself."

"Thank you Stephanie," responded Lindsey with a smile, "but I don't think that will be necessary. I'm sure she'll get over it soon enough." It was then that the computer–generated, feminine voice that came from everywhere and nowhere announced it was time to break for lunch.

Kevin couldn't seem to shake the blonde woman off. The minute she had seen him sitting at a table for two in the nutriment–court, she had attached herself to him like a leach. Sitting down next to this gorgeous blond doctor on the small bench, Amara launched into her most seductive voice, "I'm glad we finally found a minute to get to know each other," she purred. "I've seen you many times and have wanted to get to know you a little better." Reaching up she smoothed a stray lock of Kevin's blonde hair into place.

"To be honest, Mara...." Kevin began, but found his words cut short.

"It's Amara," she cooed, scooting even closer so that a piece of cellophane could not have been slid between their bodies. "I was named after the Amara star in the Llormora Galaxy discovered shortly before I was born."

An attendant appeared at their table and deposited two nutriment meals on the table top, then went on to complete his rounds at the remaining tables.

"Well, Amara," continued Kevin, not wanting Lindsey to enter the nutriment–court and see him with this clinging woman nearly sitting on his lap, "the truth is that I'm waiting for someone just now."

"Oh, I'm sorry," said the blonde, as she brushed his arm with her large breast, and then let it linger there for a moment. "I'll leave just as soon as he gets here," she smiled charmingly.

It was then that Kevin looked up and saw Lindsey standing a few feet away, the look of disappointment and disbelief apparent on her beautiful face. Before he could say another word, Lindsey had turned on her heel and disappeared into the throng of employees just entering the nutriment–court.

"I'm sorry, Kevin," cooed Amara innocently, "was that who you were supposed to meet for lunch today?"

"Actually, yes, that was the person I was supposed to meet." Kevin's extremely irritated tone made it glaringly obvious that he was quite unhappy about this turn of events.

"Well, don't worry about it Kevin," smiled the blonde woman, as she looked sheepishly into his eyes, her own gray eyes holding the promise of much comfort to be had. "I work with Dr. Larimer, and can certainly explain to her that we were just sharing a friendly chat, nothing more."

"I think I'd better go talk to her myself," stated Kevin, as he started to rise from the table.

"Wait!" Amara's hand went around Kevin's arm before he had fully made it to his feet. "It will just make you look guilty of something if you go running after her apologizing. And we know you haven't done anything wrong don't we?" Her tone was almost sickeningly sweet. "Trust me, I'll talk to her right after lunch and tell her she has nothing to worry about." She had not removed her hand from his arm, and fairly pulled him back down onto the seat.

Kevin did not want to hurt this woman's feelings, he had never intentionally hurt anyone, but he certainly did not want his fiancée to think he couldn't be trusted away from her. 'Would he look guilty of something if he went after her?' he wondered. It amazed him that his knowledge of women was apparently no where near the level he'd thought he possessed. He'd had many relationships with many women since shortly after entering puberty, and although he'd hurt some of them when he'd decided to end the romance, it had always bothered him greatly.

Now Kevin was afraid he'd hurt the one woman who meant more to him than all the rest put together. "I'm sorry, Mara," he said, shaking off her hand and rising, "I'm afraid I'm not very good company right now." Amara stared after him with narrowed eyes as she watched him walk out of the nutriment–court.

"Hey, Lindsey!" She heard her name being called as though through a thick fog.

Lindsey had decided to skip lunch and was returning to the 'creativity center,' her chest burning, and her mind feeling caught somewhere between intense anger and wanting to sob, leaving her wondering what she was supposed to do now.

She was desperately in love with Kevin, but could she really trust him? Did she really know him well enough to pledge the rest of her life to him? He'd been sitting so close to Amara, it had almost looked like they'd been kissing. Stephanie had warned her to watch Amara, but surely Kevin could have disengaged himself from the clinging blonde.

"Lindsey!" She heard her name being called again and forced herself to look up. Glen was coming toward her down the hallway, his glasses at half–mast, "How have you been?" he asked jovially, his ear to ear smile making him look several years younger.

"Oh, back to work as usual." Lindsey tried to make her tone as light as possible. It was obvious that Glen was in an exceptionally good mood, and Lindsey did not want to do anything to reduce it for him. She tucked her left hand behind her back so that he would not see the sparkling diamond ring on her finger. That would lead to questions she wasn't prepared to answer just now.

"Did you do anything special over the weekend?" he asked politely.

"Well, actually, uh, yes, but," Lindsey felt herself stammering like an idiot, "gee Glen, I'm sorry, Dear, I really have to get back to my work station, I left something there I need." She turned to go with a forced smile, "We'll talk later." As she started back down the hallway, she felt rather bad for her abrupt dismissal and turned back toward the somewhat confused looking Glen, "Hey, how about meeting me for dinner in the Doctor's Lounge later," she forced another smile, "about seven or so?"

"Seven it is!" was his jovial response. "See you then."

Lindsey made her way back to her workstation and began to review some of the pattern designs. She really didn't know what she was looking at, and found that she couldn't concentrate on much of anything…but the memory of Kevin and Amara seated so comfortably, and disturbingly close.

When the seamstresses began to filter back in from lunch, she noted that Amara was the last to arrive, and wore a satisfied grin as she breezed past Lindsey without a word. Throughout the next few hours, Lindsey could hear bits and pieces of Amara's whispered conversation with the woman at the next workstation. She was clearly bragging on her lunch 'date' with Kevin, and at one point, Lindsey overheard the other woman ask Amara about Kevin's recent engagement. "It seems that he's still on the market, if you know what I mean," was Amara's conspiratorial reply.

Lindsey wanted to slap the smug look off the blonde woman's complacent face. Stephanie couldn't help observing the happenings around her, and shook her head slowly; a look of disgust leveled at Amara, that made the younger woman flinch slightly.

It was near the end of the workday when Professor St. Germaine entered the room and made his way toward Lindsey. He asked to be shown the completed garments and loudly exclaimed his appreciation of the excellent results under Lindsey's knowledge and supervision.

"I think you'll be happy to learn though, Dr. Larimer, that tomorrow, you'll begin spending your work days in the nursery. The cloning process itself has been complete, and the infants are rapidly growing." His smile gave away his satisfaction and pleasure in the achievement of the first, and most important phase of the project.

Lindsey was ecstatic to learn that not only was the project a success thus far, but that she would be moving on to another level of her position at IBAT, and away from the smug countenance of Amara. "Excellent," replied Lindsey with a genuine smile, "I will look forward to tomorrow. I'm certain Stephanie can finish up the rest of the work here quite nicely." She looked down at the older woman, who was diligently overlooking the work of the seamstresses, and they exchanged smiles. For a moment, Stephanie reminded Lindsey of the droid with the gray hair they'd seen in the underwater city.

Lindsey's gaze settled on Amara's face for a brief instant, and she couldn't have missed the narrowed eyes of the blonde woman had she tried to. In a rare moment of cattiness, Lindsey couldn't help but get in a dig of her own, "Thank you so much Professor St. Germaine," she smiled broadly. "It will be wonderful to be more directly involved with the project and to work more closely with Dr. Sanders."

"Yes, yes!" exclaimed the jovial St. Germaine. "I understand the two of you recently became engaged and would like to extend my congratulations. It's all Kevin could talk about this morning."

The snickers of the women behind her brought yet another smile and a twinkle to Lindsey's eyes. That had to have rankled Amara. A quick glance in the woman's direction confirmed that Professor St. Germaine's unwitting comment had made its mark on the blonde seamstress.

For the next few hours, Lindsey chatted light–heartedly with Stephanie, feeling much better by the moment. She knew Kevin had been an innocent pawn in Amara's twisted game, and realized that she was not angry with him. It had bothered her greatly to see him sitting so close to another woman, especially one that Lindsey did not care for one whit, but she no longer blamed Kevin, and would set things straight just as soon as she saw him.

Lindsey smiled down once again at the monstrous diamond of her engagement ring, which had to have cost Kevin a fortune. Clearly, he had been serious in his proposal, and she knew without a doubt that she loved him with all of her heart.

It was shortly after seven o'clock that evening that Lindsey met Glen in the doctor's lounge for their evening nutriment. The older man still seemed as happy as he had earlier in the day and for the first time Lindsey really wondered what had caused this sudden change in Glen's normally staid demeanor.

"You're looking well, Glen," she greeted, as she joined him at the small table he had already pulled out from a section of wall, "if I didn't know better, I'd think you met someone special over the weekend."

Her knowing smile caused Glen a moment of discomfiture. He wanted so badly to share his newfound relationship with someone, but he had to be extremely careful whom he talked to about it. It was impossible to know anyone's mind-set on the matter, until the words were spoken. He really didn't know this woman that his best friend was so obviously in love with, but something in her eyes told him she was not the judgmental type.

"Well, actually," he began, his voice scarcely louder than a whisper, "I did get to know an acquaintance a little better over the weekend." There was an undeniable twinkle in his eye, and he looked almost incapable of not smiling.

"And so is this acquaintance an incredibly attractive man?" Lindsey knew she was not treading carefully, but had a gut feeling that simply could not be ignored.

"Oh yes, yes, he…huh?" Glen stopped mid-sentence, his looked of stunned shock was almost comical, "How did you know?" he asked in a whisper, looking nervously around as he did so.

"Let's just call it women's intuition," was Lindsey's smiling response, "that doesn't matter though. What matters is whether or not this guy really makes you happy, and from the look on your face lately, I would venture to say that he does." Lindsey was simply glad to see Glen happy. She didn't know him well, but she did like him a great deal.

"Am I that transparent?" he grinned broadly...his glasses nearly having made it to the tip of his nose.

"Quite," laughed Lindsey outright.

It was then that several others began to converge on the lounge, preparing to take their evening nutriment. Lindsey looked up in the hope of seeing Kevin, but he was not amongst the group of new arrivals.

"I guess you and Kevin have gotten much better acquainted," Glen's voice broke into Lindsey's perusal of the growing number of doctors entering the room. She looked up and noticed that Glen was looking at her engagement ring, both eyebrows lifted and his glasses dangerously close to slipping off his face entirely.

"Oh, yes," she smiled, wanting to see Kevin very badly at that moment, "Kevin asked and I accepted without a second thought. I love him very much...." her voice trailed off for a moment. "If you'll excuse me for just a second, I'll try to find him so you can share your good news with him as well." Lindsey moved to rise, but was momentarily stopped by the concerned look that crossed Glen's face.

"Not to worry," she smiled down at him, "Kevin will be just as pleased as I am." At least she hoped he would.

Lindsey had no sooner made it out the door and halfway down one of the many corridors that made up the labyrinth of the science unit, when she heard a familiar feminine voice just around the next corner. She'd been smiling to herself with the knowledge that she was beginning to learn her way around IBAT quite well, but the voices caused her smile to freeze.

"Oh, come on Kevin, it will do us both good to get away from here for awhile. We're not expected to report for work again until tomorrow morning, and I know a great restaurant not far from here. I'll buy." The over done, sickeningly sweet voice of Amara was unmistakable, and Lindsey felt anger at the self–asserting woman began to burn her cheeks. She started forward, and then stopped as she heard Kevin's voice.

"Listen Mara,"

"Amara," Lindsey heard the woman correct, and giggled softly to herself. Kevin didn't even remember the woman's name.

"Listen Amara," he corrected, "I don't want to hurt your feelings, but I've only recently become engaged to a woman that I love a great deal, and I'd really like to spend some time with her." He sounded almost exasperated. "So if you don't mind, I'd like to go find her now."

It was as he was disengaging the clinging blonde from her hold on his upper arms, that he saw Lindsey walk around the corner. His head fell back briefly and his eyes closed. She would see this and throw the ring back into his face. He wasn't quite ready for the beaming smile that lit up her countenance when he opened his eyes and looked at her.

"Well there you are Kevin," she said charmingly, completely ignoring Amara's glare. "Glen and I wanted you to join us in the doctor's lounge for nutriments." Kevin wasn't quite sure why Lindsey was no longer angry, but he wasn't about to question a good thing.

"I'd love to join you," said Kevin, with a meaningful smile, as he placed his hand on the small of her back and began to lead her down the hall in the direction she had come, without a backward glance at the now seething Amara.

Once around the next corner, Kevin turned toward Lindsey and pressed her back gently against the corridor wall. "Tell me your not angry with me Lindsey. I can't stand the thought of you angry. I couldn't care less about that woman, she's...."

Kevin did not get the chance to finish his sentence, as Lindsey stood on her tiptoes and kissed him soundly. "You have nothing to apologize for, Kevin. I'm the one who acted like a teenage idiot. I know how that woman is, and still allowed myself to become angry with you. Can you forgive me?"

Her kiss continued and Kevin was left feeling that he'd forgive her for cutting him in half with a laser. "There is nothing to forgive," he smiled, "only memories to be made." His voice took on that familiar husky quality that seemed to affect Lindsey down low in the pit of her belly.

"Oh!" she exclaimed, squirming out of Kevin's grasp and taking a step back. "Glen is waiting for us."

"Is that all? I thought the building was on fire for a moment there." Kevin grinned, his even white teeth and the slight dimple on his chin making him look even more devastatingly handsome. "Glen can wait for a bit, can't he?" All Kevin wanted to do was kiss this beautiful woman until she was out of breath.

"Well, actually, no," she grinned. "I just left him sitting alone in the doctor's lounge and told him I'd find you and come right back. He was in the process of sharing something with me, but before we go, there's something I need to tell you." Lindsey searched his eyes for a moment, and then continued, "Glen is gay," she said bluntly, watching his face for his initial reaction.

His grin made her smile, "I've known that for quite some time now Lindsey."

"How? Did he tell you? When?"

"Just call it a friend's intuition," he chuckled. "I'm actually quite glad that he is to be honest, because if he wasn't, I'd have to watch him around the woman I love."

Glen was still seated at the pullout table when Kevin and Lindsey entered the lounge a few minutes later. Many nods and smiles from the other doctor's, most of whom Lindsey did not know announced that everyone at IBAT apparently knew of their engagement.

Lindsey slid onto the small bench opposite Glen, and Kevin sat down on her right. He greeted his friend and then with a rather sly look said, "So, I guess we both have good cause for some celebration."

Glen almost blushed, and cleared his throat as he slid his glasses back up his nose to meet his eyes. Clearly, Lindsey had already told Kevin, and Kevin seemed to have no problem with the news whatsoever.

"Congratulations Kevin," smiled Glen sincerely. "I hope you and Lindsey live happily ever after and have a wonderful little Kevin or Lindsey." He bent his head slightly to take another bite of food, and his glasses began their familiar slow descent.

"Thank you Glen!" exclaimed Kevin, "and the same to you."

It took a moment for his words to sink in, but once they did, all three burst out in friendly, happy laughter.

Glen was unable to relay just who the special person in his life was, or to share his experiences of the weekend, as the tables around them were quickly filling with people. He changed the subject to a topic that everyone was quite interested in.

"I guess you two heard the news today that relations between the US, Russia and China are looking much better. It seems the peace talks they've been conducting just might be getting somewhere." Glen informed.

"Yeah," responded Kevin, as he reached around Lindsey to make his nutriment selection from the menu panel on the wall. In a moment, a small polished metal door slid open, revealing a hot nutriment pack of pasta and vegetables, "I heard about that this afternoon, but I rather had other things on my mind at the time." He cast Lindsey a sideways look and winked.

"I can certainly understand how one's mind can become cluttered with more important things than world peace," Glen chuckled.

"Well I for one was most happy to have heard that announcement today," chimed in Lindsey, "especially after our conversation with Trent and Thad." She paused thoughtfully for a moment, "Do you suppose the government will still be in such a hurry to complete our work in light of this turn of events?"

"Undoubtedly," answered Kevin in low tones between bites, "our work still means progress for the United States, and besides, we never know when the possibility of war might rear its ugly head again, and the information we will have learned could still be put to use."

"I don't know," whispered Lindsey, as she finished chewing a mouthful of simulated pork roast that left much to be desired in the taste department, "the idea of such high–tech power is almost frightening."

"Yeah, especially in the hands of the government," Glen snickered in a low tone.

That evening, alone in one of the small apartments afforded the medical and research staff at IBAT, Lindsey told Kevin that she would begin working in the nursery first thing in the morning. "Professor St. Germaine came to me today and told me to report there for the next segment of the project. I'll get to see you more often," she smiled.

"It's about time," Kevin responded, "I don't think I could go several more weeks here without seeing you all day long. Or without kissing you," he said, as he leaned forward and their lips met.

The kiss had barely ended when Lindsey remembered she'd wanted to ask Kevin a few questions about the current status of the Reclamation Project, so she'd be a little more up–to–date on something besides the costumes she'd been overseeing.

"They're children now, did you know that?" he asked.

"Children," she repeated, "you mean the clones of King Tut and Ankhesenamun?"

"None other," he replied, "and they're about the equivalent of two–year–olds, very bright two–year–olds might I add."

"I can't believe it's happened so fast," said Lindsey thoughtfully, "I can barely believe it's happened at all."

"Well that makes two of us," smiled Kevin. "We've had the ability to do it for about two–hundred and fifty years now, it was just a long time in getting the paperwork signed," he chuckled.

"Those governmental wheels do turn slowly don't they?" Lindsey laughed in return. "So have you seen them? The children." she clarified.

"Yes actually," he said, reaching for his champagne, "they're pretty children, although Tut seems to be much more aggressive than his little counterpart, Ank. And by the way," he added, "don't call her that."

"What? Ank?" questioned Lindsey.

"Yes. It's sort of a nickname we made up for her, since it's much easier than saying her full name, but she'll let us know quickly enough not to address her as such."

"What do you mean, she'll let you know?"

"Well, I haven't really worked with them directly, since it's not part of my job, but I have had the occasion to interact with them briefly. When I addressed the little princess as 'Ank,' she let me know that she would much prefer to be addressed by her full name, which of course she knows, since she's heard it many times since her creation."

"Surely she didn't use those exact words," exclaimed Lindsey with a disbelieving look.

"Actually, she did," he responded quite seriously, "I believe her exact words were, 'I would much prefer to be addressed by my proper name, Dr. Sanders.'"

"You can't be serious!" Lindsey could hardly believe her ears.

"You'll see for yourself tomorrow," Kevin assured. "Their level of intelligence is much higher than we had anticipated, which is one of the reasons St. Germaine wanted you to begin teaching them their own language. They already have an excellent grasp of English, that's for sure," he commented somewhat uneasily.

"Are you worried about something then?" asked Lindsey quizzically.

"Just the usual things a scientist would worry about," he answered with a smile. "How long we can allow them to grow at this rapid acceleration rate, what adverse effects it might have on them, if slowing down their physical growth rate will alter the level of intelligence they have already achieved…just the usual," he signed with a lopsided grin.

"Well, I'm certainly looking forward to meeting them for myself," said Lindsey truthfully. "What is it exactly that makes little Tut more aggressive?"

"I don't really know, but the two of them have definite character differences. Of course there's no way of telling if this is the way the original Tut and Ankhesenamun were when they were children, since they have already been exposed to so many differences in their present environment and interactions."

"He's not a mean little child is he?" asked Lindsey.

"Not exactly mean," supplied Kevin, "just somewhat demanding I guess you could say."

"What does he demand?"

"Anything. Everything," responded Kevin thoughtfully. "He even demanded at one point that he be served his meal first and

Ankhesenamun should wait for her meal until he was finished."

"He didn't!" exclaimed Lindsey.

"He did," answered Kevin. "He's also hit little Ank twice now while they were playing together, and their nurse wasn't quite sure what to do. They're surrounded by lab techs or monitors at all times, so he'd be stopped before he could actually hurt the little girl."

"Well, this sounds quite interesting indeed. Makes me glad I asked," smiled Lindsey with a slight shake of her head. "I can hardly wait to meet the little darling."

"And I can hardly wait to see this," Kevin laid his hand gently on her flat belly, "puffed out to here with our child inside."

Lindsey almost choked on the mouthful champagne she had just taken. "What!" she exclaimed, "did you just say?"

"I'm sorry," Kevin looked chagrined. "I guess I shouldn't just blurt out the first thing that comes to my mind. I just didn't realize how ready I was for marriage and a family until you came along."

"No," she said quickly. "Don't be sorry. It just took me by surprise and was one of the sweetest, most endearing things you could have said." She felt tears coming to her eyes, but wasn't quite sure why.

"You want one then?"

"Want what?" she said with a momentarily unclear mind.

"A child," he said with a grin. "You do want a child don't you?" His eyes explored her face for an answer.

"More than anything," she assured him, "as long as it's yours."

His mouth covered hers before she had completed her sentence. His tongue parted her lips and explored the sweetness within, but as his hand moved upward toward her breast she pulled away. "What?" she teased, "Did you want to start our family here on the couch?"

Kevin grinned at this beautiful, exciting woman that was his fiancée, and knew without a doubt he'd enjoy starting their family on the tabletop, the floor, wherever. His words were in contrast to his true feelings, "I suppose it would be a good idea to get married first, wouldn't it?"

"Yes," smiled Lindsey, thinking how lucky she was to have found love with such a handsome, intelligent man…a man who wanted to spend the rest of his life with her and to raise a child together.

"Have you given any thought to setting a date?" he asked with a lifted eyebrow.

"Actually, in light of our mutual friend Amara's escapades today, I really hadn't had the opportunity to give it much thought."

"I'm really sorry that had to happen, Lindsey," returned Kevin sincerely. "Please understand that there is nothing about that woman that appeals to me." He reached out and took her hand in his own, the engagement ring sparkling even in the dim light. This was his fiancée, the woman he would spend his life with. The knowledge that he could love so deeply, so intensely, was both new and overwhelming.

"I think maybe we should wait until our work on the project has been completed," Lindsey said thoughtfully, "otherwise we'd never have time to make all our plans. Of course," she offered, "we could just go before the Justice of the Peace and be married in a couple of days."

"Which I would certainly prefer," he intoned. "There is no way you will become my wife fast enough to suit me." His smile met his eyes and Lindsey thought she might just melt, "but I'm sure your mother and my parents are going to want the whole church ceremony and all the trappings. Not to mention the fact that I would very much enjoy watching you walk down the isle toward me in a traditional wedding dress."

"I'd like to wear the white dress that you bought me," she smiled, "maybe even have a twentieth–century theme."

"There's a good sized church in Atlantica you know," offered Kevin. "We could always think about having the ceremony there."

"That's an excellent idea," Lindsey exclaimed. "I just wish we had the time to start making some plans for it now. It's going to kill me to wait."

"It's going to kill me to wait on making your belly swell with our first child," Kevin chuckled. "But I guess for proprieties sake, we'll have to wait until we actually tie the knot, don't you agree?" He leaned forward and began to nuzzle Lindsey's neck softly; trailing his lips down her ear lobe, her chin, and her neck. "If it's not already too late," he added between kisses.

"Yes, I think we should be more careful until then," she answered. "It would be the proper thing."

"Right, the proper thing," repeated Kevin, as his lips moved back up to her own. Neither of them thought about what was proper or not proper over the course of the next couple hours, as they lost themselves in exploring one another and their newfound love.

Chapter Nine

Ankhesenamun was the most beautiful little girl Lindsey had ever laid eyes on. Having never had siblings of her own, her experience with children was quite limited, but that didn't stop her from forming an almost instant bond with the little dark haired clone, whose physical appearance suggested that of a two-year-old.

Expecting to hear but a few newly learned words, or perhaps a sentence, Lindsey was quite taken off guard, and completely astounded by the little girl's articulate skills.

"Will you come every day to see me?" asked the little Ankhesenamun. "I like you Dr. Larimer," she offered with childish innocence. "Will you teach me the ways of my people?"

"Your people?" asked Lindsey questioningly.

"Yes," replied the child, her huge amber eyes looking deeply into Lindsey's blue ones.

"The Egyptian people."

"Oh, yes," replied Lindsey, "I will teach you everything that I can."

"Will you make them let me darken my eyes with kohl, Dr. Larimer? In the pictures I have seen of my people, their eyes are darkened. I should like to darken mine too."

"Have you already asked to be able to darken your eyes?" questioned Lindsey.

"Yes," replied the child almost petulantly. "I asked our nurse, Zamalda, but she said I was too young, and would have to wait until I am much older. I do not wish to wait. I think I would look very beautiful with my eyes darkened. I think you would too."

The child's incredible grasp of the English language, and a wisdom that far surpassed anything Lindsey would have expected of one so young and so small, made the fact that the girl was only cloned a couple short months ago all the more overwhelming. Lindsey made a mental note to speak with this nurse, Zamalda as soon as possible. She didn't have long to wait.

"I don't care what you say! You are not my boss! I do not have to listen to you. I wish to be given my sweets now. You will get them!"

Lindsey whirled around to see a tall, thin woman with gray hair and a thin, bony face enter the room. A little boy with shoulder–length hair and flashing black eyes that could only be the little King Tutankhamun stomped along at the woman's side.

"You must be Dr. Larimer," offered the older woman, as she stopped before Lindsey's chair and extended her hand in greeting. "I am their head–nurse." She paused and frowned down at the male child beside her, "Zamalda Dunaway is my name." Her tone made it clear that she found her position as quite a chore indeed.

"It's nice to meet you," smiled Lindsey, returning the woman's cursory handshake. Will…."

The older woman continued talking as though Lindsey had not spoken, "I hope you have more luck with these two than I have." This time she clearly scowled at the frowning, very small version of the once famous king off Egypt. "That one there," she continued, indicating Ankhesenamun with a brief wave of her hand, "isn't too bad, though she can be wayward."

Lindsey opened her mouth to reply, but the dour Zamalda cut her off without taking a breath, "This one!" She glared at the little Tut; "This one needs to have his backside whipped!"

Lindsey's brows lifted nearly off her forehead at such flagrant animosity, declared in the full presence of the children, and as though they weren't there. "Truly," she began, fully intending to remind this woman of her position and the fact that this was a matter certainly better discussed in private. Her words were cut short yet again.

"I've never seen a more ill–tempered little brat in all my life, and I have six grandchildren of my own." Two small, pulsating, blue veins were becoming more and more visible in Zamalda's neck, "If it were up to me, I'd lock this little heathen up! Demanding demon seed that he is." She virtually hissed the last words down at the narrowed eyes of the two–year–old Egyptian clone, his pudgy little arms folded before him in a stance of absolute defiance.

"I really…." again, Lindsey's words were ignored, as the gaunt faced woman continued her verbal tirade. Lindsey couldn't help noting that the boy's eyes darted between them, as though trying to discern their individual thoughts through their expressions.

She also noticed that little Ankhesenamun looked sad and remained perfectly still and very quiet, her head bowed slightly, and her delicate hands folded in her lap.

"I don't envy you one bit trying to teach them the Egyptian language." The older woman's hands on her skinny hips were wrinkled and heavily veined. Lindsey noted that Zamalda Dunaway wore no wedding ring, and wasn't at all surprised. "You should hear the way this one here talks to me!" A nod of her long thin nose indicated she was again referring to Tut.

Lindsey glanced down at the olive-skinned boy with the almond-shaped black eyes. He was a handsome little guy, though he had an intensity in his eyes that was almost unsettling, and suddenly she found that she'd heard enough of this rude woman's diatribe. Without fully thinking about her words before she spoke them, Lindsey opened her mouth and almost shouted, "Enough!"

The skinny woman stopped speaking as though she had been slapped. Her eyes widened, and her eyebrows almost met in the middle as her scowl deepened. This time it was Lindsey who took the reins of the conversation. "Before you continue," she stated firmly, "and subject yourself to a burst blood vessel," little Tut's attention was riveted on Lindsey, "I'd like to remind you that there are children present, and neither your tone, your words, or the subject of this conversation are appropriate."

The woman was visibly taken aback at the authority in Lindsey's voice. She started to speak and found that for the first time in her life, she was interrupted.

"As for Tutankhamun speaking to you badly, it's no surprise, given the way you speak in front of him." Lindsey's accusation hit home, and Zamalda found herself momentarily embarrassed. "And as for your having six grandchildren," Lindsey continued, "they each one have my deepest sympathy. I can't imagine Professor St. Germaine subjecting these children to someone who appears to have been recently baptized in lemon juice."

Zamalda's pursed lips went nearly white, making the age lines around them look even deeper. She didn't want to lose her position at IBAT. Even though it was temporary, she wasn't ready to retire just yet. She had no one to go home to, and neither her children nor her grandchildren ever visited. She opened her mouth to speak again, not quite sure of what to say, but certain that she would have to find a way to glaze things over. "Well, I will have you know Dr. Larimer, that I have every confidence in my ability to continue caring for and teaching these children."

"Clearly," Lindsey responded, "there is a very thin line between confidence and arrogance. I will speak with Professor St. Germaine straight away about this incident," she announced seriously. "And I have no wish to discuss it further just now. Thank you."

Lindsey's tone and words of dismissal brooked no negotiation. Without a backward glance, Zamalda turned on her heel and stormed out of the room.

Tutankhamun's dark eyes, with their thick fringe of blue–black eyelashes, bore into Lindsey's own until she was sure the little boy could see her brain.

"You have some authority," he stated matter–of–factly. "This is good."

Lindsey had worked with Ankhesenamun and Tut every day since she had first met them, and had convinced Professor St. Germaine that Zamalda had been genuinely mean to them. The normal jovial countenance of the portly executive had changed to one of immediate anger upon Lindsey's recounting of what had happened during her brief meeting with the woman, and he wasted no time in sending the mean–spirited nurse packing. Besides, the children had grown much faster than originally anticipated, and were no longer in need of a nurse.

Ankhesenamun had taken to Lindsey in such a way that brought out maternal feelings Lindsey didn't know she possessed. She felt strangely protective of the fragile child, and noted with delight that the little dark haired girl, with the expressive big eyes, caught on to the Egyptian language like she had been born speaking it.

Little Tut, although demanding, as Kevin had warned her of early on, also caught on easily, though not as well as his female counterpart. During their lessons, Tut would pout or stamp his little feet if Lindsey corrected his pronunciation or the inaccuracy of a word he would use, but he would always come around, albeit slowly, when his teacher would speak to him softly and calmly. His grasp of numbers, fractions, hieroglyphics and hieratics was almost startling to Lindsey, and he seemed to revel in her sincere praise of his accomplishments.

It seemed to Lindsey that the children were growing at an almost alarming rate. In just a week's time, they had already grown visibly taller. Kevin had explained to her that during the cloning process, a chemically altered AGC, or Accelerated Growth Cell, was introduced during the embryonic stage. If accepted, the cell would result in an accelerated growth process, thus causing the clone to mature at the rate of one year for every month of life. Each day, the clones would be injected with an agent that allowed them to keep the AGC in check, and preventing their bodies from dying of old age within a very short period of time. Accordingly, in a mere three more weeks, these particular clones would be the equivalent of three years old.

It was difficult for Lindsey to fully grasp such an incredible concept. To her, they were children, and she found that as the days went by, she looked more and more forward to spending her time with them.

Of course, the primary work that Kevin and Glen had performed early on was no longer necessary, since the cloning process itself had been fully completed. Their work now consisted of monitoring the children's growth to keep the acceleration rate under control. It was understood that once the children reached the equivalent of about eighteen years old, the acceleration process would be retarded and the clones would then begin to age at the same rate of a normal birth–human.

It seemed that the cloned children grew out of the wide array of garments constructed for them, before they could wear each garment more than once or twice. The on–staff seamstresses would have to remain at IBAT for many months to come, working around the clock to keep Tut and Ankhesenamun in clothing.

As time passed, Lindsey found herself even further endeared to little Ankhesenamun, especially when she arrived one day with a stick of black kohl that she used to line the child's eyes. It seemed so strange when she stepped back and looked into the amber eyes of the very pretty little girl. The darkly lined, almond-shaped little orbs stared back at Lindsey. They were intelligent eyes…intelligent and full of life and wonder.

In short order, little Tut demanded that his eyes be darkened with the pencil as well, and Lindsey obliged him accordingly. His eyes too were intelligent, but there was something else in their black depths that Lindsey felt unsettling, a calculating, almost cunning look. She wasn't certain that she was reading the little boy correctly, but there were times when the intensity of the child was quite disturbing.

Over the next few weeks, Lindsey continued to spend ten to twelve hours a day teaching the children about Egyptian culture, beliefs, religion, art, textiles and customs. They both learned quickly and read every book on Egypt provided to them. Consequently, finding time to spend with Kevin was not an easy feat for the busy young woman. He still had his regular duties, combined with the constant monitoring of the children's growth, and Lindsey's days were so busy, there were evenings when she simply wanted to fall into bed and sleep.

She had eagerly anticipated working more closely with him, but found that while they were now working in the same unit, they were not necessarily in the same room for more than a few minutes. Still, it was better than not seeing him at all for days at a time. It seemed that he filled up the room with his very presence, and the physical attraction between them made it difficult not to want to touch one another whenever an opportunity arose.

The work had progressed to the point that the staff members could return to their homes in the evenings if they chose to. Sometimes she and Kevin would stay in one of the sleeping rooms at IBAT, and other times, returned to their separate dwellings, allowing Lindsey time to spend with her mother, whom she found herself growing closer to all the time, in spite of their extended time apart.

Olivia had been having many second thoughts about returning to Colorado. After all, her daughter was engaged now, which meant that a grandchild might not be too far off. Olivia found she looked forward to the prospect of being a grandmother, and didn't want to be residing in another state when the big event occurred.

Not wanting to cramp her daughter's life-style, Olivia had offered to find an apartment of her own, but Lindsey would not hear of it. She'd spent the majority of her life idolizing her father, and had come to realize that in doing so, she'd missed much of the intensely close relationship she was now enjoying with her mother. Knowing that once she and Kevin were married, they would move to Atlantica permanently, she encouraged her mother to stay with her, and then keep the condo for herself once Lindsey had married and moved out.

At the beginning of the fourteenth week of Tut and Ankhesenamun's life, Lindsey found that she and Kevin would be able to spend an entire weekend together. A substitute would be brought in to take Lindsey's position for those two days, and she and Kevin wasted no time in planning an excursion to the 'Sun Center.' The fact that it was Friday, the thirteenth made no difference whatsoever, their work, however important, had kept them apart entirely too long.

Professor St. Germaine had been enjoying the mid-day nutriment with Lindsey and Kevin, when they had decided on what to do and where to go on their free weekend. While the older professor had never been to the 'Sun Center,' he'd heard of it often, and decided that such an outing might be just what he needed as well. The professor couldn't remember the last time he took any real time off work. "Not to worry kids," he'd smiled jovially, "I won't hang around and bother you. I'm sure you see enough of me here every day of your lives!"

It was Kevin's idea to invite Olivia. "I'd really like to get to know her a little better," Kevin had suggested. "I've hardly even spoken to her since Lindsey and I started dating, and since she's going to be my mother-in-law, I think it would be nice for us to all spend some time together."

"Have I mentioned just how incredibly much I love you?" smiled Lindsey. "I can't imagine any other man actually wanting to include his future mother-in-law in his recreational plans." Her genuine look of love and admiration elicited a beaming smile from Kevin.

The 'Sun Center' was absolutely huge, and both Lindsey and Olivia were impressed beyond words. The ground level, dome–shaped building was the equivalent of six stories high, it's soft, white exterior glistening in those rays of the sun that could reach through the present layers of smog. It was a poor air quality day, and the trio hurried from the cramped quarters of Kevin's compact Centurian, to the protective interior of the entertainment center.

Once inside the mammoth dome, Lindsey and Olivia were equally impressed at this family–oriented, in–door playground. The entire floor of the building was covered in two feet or so of deep, white sand. A simulated ocean, complete with waves took up nearly one–half of the entire structure, and above their heads, affixed to the very center of the dome, hung a huge glowing orb that made up the artificial sun. The true sunlight effects the architects had in mind had definitely hit their mark. The inner walls displayed real–time panoramic scenery, the pounding waves and surf at one end, and palm trees blowing in the breeze at the other, making the experience more like being at the beach than being at the beach.

Several rows of relaxation chairs lined the edge of the replicated ocean, and an eatery stood off to the left, boasting both nutriment–packs and expensive real meat and vegetable meals. Scantily clad young men and women in matching swimwear carried trays of cold drinks to the vacationers.

Inasmuch as spending any quality time at a real ocean was simply not done, due to air quality, few people owned any type of swimwear. Fortunately, such attire could be rented at the 'Sun Center.'

Kevin, Lindsey and Olivia settled themselves comfortably on the relaxation chairs, and enjoyed watching children and adults alike swim and frolic in the warm, salty surf…yet others were riding the waves atop small boards, periodically falling unceremoniously and providing further entertainment for the observers onshore.

The simulated sun was very warm, and Lindsey soon felt pulled toward the irresistible refreshment promised in the gently rolling waves. She and Kevin made their way to the edge of the surf, holding hands and laughing like kids. The surf was cool and inviting as the two waded in until the water became deep enough for them to swim. They frolicked, dove, and played like children, laughing aloud at their own uninhibited antics. Kevin wanted to pat himself on the back for this idea. Lindsey looked incredible in the tiny little, rented swimsuit, it's upper and lower pieces joined at the center with a small ring, accentuating the curve of her narrow waist and flat tummy.

The ground beneath the dome had apparently been dug down at a steep angle on one end, allowing the 'ocean' to exceed a depth of more than fifty feet. Kevin pulled his beautiful bride–to–be gently under the water and kissed her with an intensity that would have made him gasp even if he hadn't been holding his breath the entire time.

Olivia found herself smiling as she watched her daughter and Kevin. It wasn't difficult to see that the two were very much in love, and she said a silent "thank you" to the Lord above for bringing this fine young man into her daughter's life. She only hoped that Lindsey would be as happy in her marriage as Olivia had been with Lowell. She still missed her husband incredibly, even though he had been gone for many years, and her one wish was that he could have been here to see his precious daughter's immense happiness, and to give her away at her wedding.

"You must be Lindsey's mother."

Olivia looked up to see the smiling countenance of a very large man, wearing a very brief pair of swimming shorts. It was impossible not to appreciate the good looking body of this stranger. Although large, and with a bit more stomach than truly necessary, he was certainly not unpleasant to the eyes, and Olivia found it difficult not to stare at the bare expanse of chest, covered lightly with a smattering of slightly graying hair. It was a moment before she could find her voice.

"Yes," she responded questioningly, "Lindsey is my daughter. Do you know her?"

"I certainly do," responded the man, as he sat in one of the relaxation chairs next to Olivia's, his slightly wet hair and the water still glistening on his body gave evidence that he had recently enjoyed a swim. "I'm the CEO of IBAT, Professor Garreth St. Germaine, but please," he offered, "do call me Garreth." The large man extended his hand and Olivia accepted it in greeting.

"Well, it's quite lovely to meet you Garreth," she smiled. "My name is Olivia Larimer, and I too much prefer a first–name basis."

"Good, good," he grinned, not being able to help but notice that for a woman in her fifties, she wore the rented swimsuit quite nicely. Her long, shapely legs ended in daintily tapered feet and well–manicured toes. "Well, I must say that it is now perfectly clear to me why Lindsey is such a beautiful young woman. It's obviously due to the fact that she has such a beautiful young mother." His good–natured flattery elicited a broad smile from Olivia. "I don't mean to impose, it's just that I heard the kids talking about this place the other day, and thought I might like to take in a little relaxation myself."

Professor St. Germaine sat back comfortably in the neoprene–covered lounge chair. It did indeed feel good to bask in the warm rays of the sun, simulated or otherwise, and the pretty fifty-something woman sitting next to him was quite attractive. Unmarried, like many of the workaholic doctors and professors that comprised the staff at IBAT, the professor realized just how pleasant it was to enjoy the companionship of someone outside the work environment.

"I'm certain it does you a world of good to get out now and again, if you work as many hours as my daughter does," she said, glancing back out at Kevin and Lindsey, still playing like kids and diving like dolphins in the surf. "It's good to see them enjoying some time together."

"How well I know it," her new companion sighed. "Our work never seems to stop, but sometimes, you've just got to get away from it even for a day." Garreth's smile was disarming, and Olivia found herself drawn to the enigmatic professor with the lovely British accent.

For the next hour, the two enjoyed a stimulating and witty conversation, discussing many topics from politics to history, to current events. It had been a long time since Olivia had enjoyed the company of a man over thirty and under seventy. Garreth was both engaging and intelligent. It again dawned on Lindsey's mother that she greatly missed the long, intellectually stimulating talks she and Lowell had shared during their twenty-seven years together.

"Mom, Professor St. Germaine, you've met!" exclaimed Lindsey, as she and Kevin approached with the water still glistening on their skin, and running in tiny rivulets down their bodies. "It's good to see you Professor," she smiled, and Garreth realized again the strong resemblance between the two women.

Kevin greeted St. Germaine with a pat on the back, "Why don't you and Olivia enjoy a swim," he suggested. "The water feels incredible, but our stomachs are feeling neglected." Kevin reached for a towel and began to massage it through his hair. "I thought we might wander over and have a bite of lunch. Of course, you're both welcome to join us."

Olivia glanced over toward the nutriment bar, and then returned her gaze to the endless waves and inviting ocean surf. "I think I'd like to avail myself of a nice refreshing swim," she smiled in response, "and maybe have a little something to eat later."

"How about dinner tonight in town?" suggested Garreth. Lindsey glanced at Kevin with a sly grin and raised brow. "I do mean the four of us, of course," he offered, slightly embarrassed for having been looking squarely at Olivia when he'd asked. "There are several nice restaurants not far from here."

It took only a moment for Olivia to accept this unexpected offer, both Kevin and Lindsey nodding their agreement as well.

"In the meantime," smiled Garreth, "why don't we enjoy a nice swim, while the kids get something to hold them over until dinner." Olivia took his procured arm, and together they strolled towards the waters' edge.

"Kids huh?" Kevin chuckled. "I wish."

For the next several hours, the four alternately sunned themselves, and swam in the cool ocean water. Fortunately, the Sun Center was fully equipped with grooming rooms, allowing the fun-seekers to change, and the women to reapply cosmetics and have their hair dried and reconfigured. It was dark outside by the time they left the Sun Center and made their way back out to the parking area. Since both Kevin and Garreth owned economy cars, they decided to call an air-transport cab to take them to dinner, agreeing to have it return them to their respective vehicles later.

Sal's Place was bustling with activity, and the four were concerned that they might not find a table. It was then that Kevin thought he saw Glen just ahead of them, disappearing around the corner into the restaurant area. He hurried to catch up with his friend, wondering if perhaps Glen would like to join them for dinner, but realized shortly however, that Glen was not alone. He seemed to be accompanied by an olive-skinned gentleman with a young boy, and the three of them were heading toward a large table at the far end of the dining room.

"Glen," called Kevin when he was within earshot. His friend turned around, surprise and then recognition dawning on his face. "Lindsey is here, and so is her mother and Professor St. Germaine. We just left the Sun Center and thought we'd come by for dinner, but I'm not sure we'll find a table. I guess we should have called for reservations."

"Nonsense," offered Sal, "of course you will join us for dinner. I shall have the staff enlarge this table and bring more place settings."

At Kevin's rather questioning look, Glen made the necessary introductions, and relayed that Sal was none other than the Sal that owned the establishment. It occurred to Kevin that this was the special man in Glen's life. If he made Glen happy, then he was happy for his friend. On a personal level, he would much rather have Lindsey.

Dinner was superb, and Sal found himself the recipient of compliments from everyone at the table. He had enjoyed meeting Kevin and his lovely fiancée. Lindsey's mother was charming and Professor St. Germaine was an interesting dinner companion as well. Dimmi delighted in the two women's exclamations of how handsome and grownup he was.

When Sal announced that the sumptuous and very expensive dinner was on him, he became everyone's immediate favorite. It wasn't difficult to see that Glen's face fairly glowed above the rims of his ever-sliding glasses when Sal looked at him...and Sal looked at him often, though the necessity of absolute discretion was foremost in both their minds.

Kevin glanced across at Professor St. Germaine, who was seated on Olivia's right. If he had noticed the attraction between the two men, he hadn't let on.

The work progressed at IBAT, and as the weeks turned to months, Lindsey's bond with the children deepened. When Christmas came, Lindsey presented Ankhesenamun with a silver bracelet that had a delicate thin chain, attached to a finger–ring, it's intricately engraved Egyptian motif elicited a gasp of delight from the child.

For Tutankhamun, she had purchased two ornately engraved arm cuffs, depicting ancient Egyptian hunting scenes. The pieces were replicas of actual artifacts found in Egypt, and Lindsey had commissioned them directly from a friend of her father. The man specialized in creating duplicates of the famous pieces that were on display in the Museum of Antiquities in Cairo, Egypt.

While Ankhesenamun had hugged Lindsey in appreciation, Tut had merely nodded his acceptance of the expensive gifts. Lindsey noticed with a smile however, that he immediately attached the cuffs to his upper arms.

In truth, she had wanted to purchase some of the portable, virtual–reality games that were so popular with kids these days, but Professor St. Germaine had delicately denied her request.

"I'm sorry Lindsey," he'd said. "I know Tut and Ankhesenamun would enjoy such things, but it would not be in their best interest. The government officials have made their position on the children's up bringing quite clear. They seem to find it necessary for them to be reared in such a manner so as to not expose them to too many modern influences."

It had been explained to the cloned children, as delicately as possible, who they had once been. It seemed both the United States and the Egyptian governments had come to the decision that doing so might in some way, better serve their ultimate purpose.

Surprisingly enough, the child–clones were not the slightest bit disturbed by this information. They both took the news quite matter–of–factly, and Tut especially, felt exceedingly important to be the subject of such an undertaking. And though the clone of the famous boy–king continued to display sullen periods, alternating with occasional outbursts of unprovoked anger, there were also times when the child could be quite charming, with an almost hypnotic quality to his voice.

Ankhesenamun on the other hand, was a very soft spoken, gentle child. By late December, and at the equivalent of six–years–old, she promised to be a great beauty. The dark haired little girl had long since taken to lining her eyes every morning by herself, and the older she grew, the darker and more elaborately she enhanced them.

"Allow me to paint your eyes," she prompted Lindsey. "You've never let me do so before, and I've so wanted to." Ankhesenamun's pleading always pulled at Lindsey's heart, but she had refused the child's offer each time, thinking she would look quite silly with those black lines around her light blue eyes.

"No, Miss," replied Lindsey. "It is time to work on your numbers."

"Can I not paint your eyes first and then do my numbers?" The girl's bright smile illuminated her aristocratic little face.

"I believe your appearance would be much improved," broke in Tut.

"Well thank you very much for that great compliment," was Lindsey's facetious rejoinder.

"You are most welcome," replied the boy.

It was difficult to tell if the child was serious, or exercising a rare bit of humor, but it didn't seem much was going to get done if she didn't just do it and get it over with.

It took Ankhesenamun about fifteen minutes as she artfully applied the kohl stick to the lids of Lindsey's eyes, and the underside of her lower lashes, fanning the edges out just a bit at the corners.

Lindsey looked at her reflection in Ankhesenamun's mirror. It wasn't horrible, but she didn't find it particularly attractive on her own, light blue eyes…perhaps with some brown lenses.

"A great improvement!" exclaimed Tut, with a mischievous glint in his eyes.

"I'm glad you think so, now let's see if we can make some great improvements in your math skills."

Tut pulled a face and plopped himself unceremoniously into

his instruction chair, the screen lowering before his face. Lindsey chose the appropriate slide–tablet and inserted it into a slot on the side of her 'Instructor's Cube.'

The lesson had barely begun when Lindsey looked up to see Kevin striding towards her from the main door and rose to greet him.

"It's been awhile since we've had any real time together," he said. "I thought you might like to ring in the New Year at our place in Atlantica."

Just the mention of Atlantica brought a rush of excitement, as did the mention of our place. She missed the beautiful, aquatic city, and since her mother had met Professor St. Germaine, they'd been almost inseparable. Lindsey was sure the two of them had already made plans for the big night. "Oh, Kevin," she exclaimed, "that sounds wonderful, I'd love it."

"Well, it seems you'll have yet another opportunity to wear your white gown," he smiled. "I understand the Blast from the Past Restaurant did so well on their twentieth–century theme pre–grand opening, they want to repeat that theme for the New Year's bash they're throwing. And," he paused, "I have dinner reservations already set up for earlier in the evening, before the party starts."

The giggles coming from Ankhesenamun's chair caused Kevin to pause and grin at the charming little girl. "Are you learning lots of things today Ankhesenamun?" he asked, stepping toward the study area.

"We are studying numbers and fractions today," she supplied sweetly. "And after this, we will work on our hieratics."

"Ah, I see," replied Kevin, with an understanding nod of his blonde head. "Then I trust you are doing well?"

"Oh, quite, thank you," replied the little replica of the long–dead princess.

Even with all Kevin's knowledge of science and technology, the fact that he was standing there talking to this child was truly a miracle in itself. "Can you show me what you've learned?" he asked, eliciting a smile and a nod from the little girl.

"This," she said, drawing a short, straight, vertical line, "is the number one, but that looks like your regular, Arabic one. This," she continued, as she drew an up–side down 'U' on her tablet, and then glanced up at her monitor screen to make sure the symbol was perfectly even on both sides, "is the number five in Egyptian. And this," she said, drawing what looked like a 'Pac–Man' figure from one of the ancient video games in the antique shop down town, and then adding a line below it, attached to something resembling a flower pot on the bottom, "is the number for one–thousand."

"Why that's quite impressive indeed," smiled Kevin.

Feeling encouraged, Ankhesenamun continued, drawing a figure that looked like an upright finger with a fingernail at the tip, and announcing it to be the number ten–thousand. A picture that resembled a bird sitting on an invisible branch, she declared to be the number one hundred thousand.

"That's just stupid stuff," broke in Tut, clearly feeling left out. "I can write your birthday for you, if you want me to."

Ankhesenamun threw her male counterpart an irritated look for his rudeness.

"I'd love to see my birth date in Egyptian," replied Kevin. "It's April the fifteenth, twenty–two hundred and thirteen."

The tip of the boy's tongue peaked out through the corner of his mouth as he went to work, drawing four ones, the upside down 'U,' followed by three ones on top and two below. Following this, were two of the Pac–Man characters, with two backward looking nine's underneath, and three more ones below another overturned 'U.'

"That's quite amazing indeed!" exclaimed Kevin. "It's certainly good to know that Dr. Larimer is doing her job so well."

"Why thank you Kevin," Lindsey smiled.

"I can show you how your name is written in hieratics," beamed Tut, clearly pleased with himself.

"I'd love to see that, young man, but I'm afraid I'm needed back in the lab. Perhaps you can show me tomorrow when the two of you are scheduled for your regular exam. Just bring your tablet with you," he offered. Turning his attention back to Lindsey, he fought the urge to kiss her, "I'd better head back," he said instead. "By the way," he reminded, "since New Year's eve falls on Wednesday, we'll want to leave here early tomorrow evening. I've already received permission from St. Germaine. Unfortunately though, I'm needed back here by Thursday, but at least we'll get to spend a few days together." His grin promised that those few days would indeed be well spent, "I'll see you tonight to discuss the details," he said.

"I can't wait," she replied, and then watched him walk away, his broad shoulders and narrow waist took her breath away every time she saw him.

Just before he reached the door, Kevin suddenly turned back toward her and grinned broadly. "Oh, and incidentally, Dr. Larimer, I rather like the Egyptian look you've adopted today." He was out the door before it dawned on Lindsey that Kevin had been referring to the dark lines of kohl Ankhesenamun had applied to her eyes. Having forgotten about the eyeliner, Lindsey was still chuckling when she heard Tut's angry voice.

"You are a show off!"

Lindsey turned to see that Tut was glaring at Ankhesenamun, as he spat his accusation at her.

"You are a bigger show off," replied the girl petulantly.

"Shut up!" screamed Tut.

"I don't have to shut up," stated Ankhesenamun bluntly.

"You do because I say you do, and I was the King!"

"You were the king, but you're not the king now, so you are no one's boss, especially not mine." The girl was clearly able to hold her own.

"Children," chided Lindsey, "calm down now. There's no need to argue and bicker."

"I wouldn't argue with her if she would shut up when I tell her to!" fumed the boy.

"I told you that you are not my boss," reminded Ankhesenamun.

"You never listen to me!" Tut fairly shrieked, "you don't listen to me now and you didn't listen to me then!"

As though he suddenly realized what he had said, Tut's mouth clamped shut and his eyes darted to Lindsey. The shocked look on her face told him she had caught his words and understood them. Her eyes flew from the set face of the boy to those of Ankhesenamun, and she noted that the girl fidgeted slightly in her chair. When Lindsey did not break eye contact, the child lowered her head, and in a barely audible voice whispered, "We remember who we were. We have from the beginning."

Chapter Ten

"It's impossible Lindsey, we didn't clone their souls, we cloned their bodies, they can't possibly remember anything more than they've been taught."

"I'm telling you Kevin," Lindsey replied, "Ankhesenamun told me they remember who they were!"

"Please understand, Honey, I don't doubt that she told you that, I just don't understand how it could possibly be."

"Think about it for just a minute, Kevin," Lindsey tried to calm herself. Ankhesenamun's quietly spoken words had slammed her in the chest like a ton of lead. "As far as we know, no one has ever cloned a human being before. I know they cloned some animals back in the twentieth, and twenty–first centuries, but animals can't talk." She ran her fingers though her hair, and plopped herself down on the air sofa in Kevin's sleeping–room at IBAT.

"It just seems so incredibly far–fetched, Lindsey." Kevin joined her on the sofa, putting an arm around her shoulders. "I mean, this is against every scientific principle of the cloning process. It simply cannot be."

"But it is. It is Kevin, and I fully believe that they do know who they were, I just don't know who else we should tell about this."

"Well, definitely St. Germaine," he responded. "He has to know. He's responsible for submitting a daily report of any and all progress on this project, I just doubt he'll believe it."

"Whether he believes it or not, we've got to tell him."

"I can't believe it!" exclaimed Professor St. Germaine, "Are you absolutely certain that's what she said, Lindsey?"

"Absolutely!" was the emphatic reply.

St. Germaine let out a low whistle through the gap in his front teeth; "This is quite a revelation indeed." He shook his head as though to clear it, "I'll write out a report for the government. I imagine they'll want to send in their own team of experts to conduct some tests on the children." His brow furrowed, "In the meantime, you two go ahead with your plans for the New Year. Your mother and I have plans of our own, you know," he smiled, but his eyes still reflected a somewhat far away look, as his mind fully absorbed this startling change of events, "I don't imagine there's any reason for anyone to cancel anything. If I know these government officials, it will take a month for them to assemble a team of examiners. In the meantime Lindsey," he cautioned, "just conduct their lessons as usual and say nothing more to them about this incident. But do listen carefully to any conversations between the two from this point on."

"Certainly," she replied. "This is just almost impossible to comprehend."

"That it is," replied St. Germaine, that it is."

By the time Kevin picked up Lindsey on Tuesday evening, Olivia had already left with Garreth.

"At this rate, you might end up with Professor St. Germane for a step–father," Kevin joked, as he handed Lindsey's luggage to an attendant waiting outside the front door of her condominium. The young man placed the baggage on the moving walkway and moved along with them to where Kevin's Centurian awaited.

"As long as he makes my mother happy, I'm happy," Lindsey replied truthfully. "She's been a widow for quite sometime now, and with you and I planning to marry and move to Atlantica after the project is completed, I don't know," she paused, "I just don't want to see her alone, and you know she'd never come live with us. My mother is far too independent for that."

The traffic was horrendous, and Lindsey was almost afraid to look at the virtual–panels, as Kevin's vehicle wove its way through and around air–cabs, transport vans, sky–cycles, and an array of other vehicles all fighting for flying space. It seemed that everyone in the entire city was scurrying somewhere to celebrate the New Year.

The tall, circular homes, condos and businesses, some of them still decorated with brightly lit Christmas ornaments, flew by in a blur, at least what could be seen of them between the seemingly endless sea of transport–crafts. At one point, the traffic came to an absolute standstill.

"Gee, I wonder if St. Germaine would want you to call him

'Dad' at work," teased Kevin.

"You're very funny Dr. Sanders," she retorted, reaching over to tickle Kevin lightly in the ribs, satisfied when it caused him to squirm. "But I'm serious, I think it would be wonderful for my mother and Professor St. Germaine to get married. I'm certain my father wouldn't expect her to spend the rest of her life without a companion. I will always miss him with every breath I take, but my mother is still very much alive and deserves as much happiness as she can find."

"I agree fully, you know. I was just thinking the other day when you kissed me, that I had all this happiness hoarded up for myself and it just wasn't fair to everybody else."

"Oh, you're just a funny, funny kind of guy, you are." Lindsey reached over and tickled him a little more fervently, eliciting an outright shriek of laughter.

For the time being, the two were focused solely on one another; all thoughts of the Reclamation Project temporarily erased from their minds.

Atlantica hadn't changed a bit, and Kevin and Lindsey were both glad to be back. There were even more people milling about the city than there had been at the grand opening, and the transport walks were incredibly crowded.

"I still don't know how you managed to secure reservations on such short notice, Kevin, but I can't tell you how happy I am that you did." Lindsey paused thoughtfully for a moment, "Do you suppose the professors will be here tonight?" she asked.

"Actually, they will," he replied, as they made their way from the tiered parking area to the moving walk–way and joined the throng of others moving along past the shops, businesses and dwellings. "To be honest, it's only because those two have so much pull here in Atlantica that I managed to get the reservations. I don't think there's anything they can't get."

"Excellent," she replied with a nod. "I know this trip is strictly for fun and pleasure, but I'm dying to know what they might think of this new turn of events."

"Well, you can certainly ask them tonight," answered Kevin.

"But for now, my primary concern is just getting to spend some time alone with you."

"You took the words right out of my head," Lindsey laughed.

The house was the same as they had left it, the snacks and nutriment packages they had purchased in town on their last trip, were still in the old fashioned, simulated wood cupboards.

Lindsey had been eagerly awaiting the usage of the bathing tub, the backyard, and later, the four-poster bed. She still couldn't believe this house belonged to the two of them. There were people with countless wealth who had not been able to buy in, because of the tremendous demand for condominiums and individual dwellings. Kevin had told her earlier that even the hotels in Atlantica had been booked for New Years before the city itself had been completed. It seemed the perfect prelude for she and Kevin to start their life together.

"Lindsey, come here and look at this!" Kevin exclaimed from the back yard.

Lindsey hurried through the transparent sliding doors, not sure what she expected to see on the other side. Kevin, with grass up to his knees, was not one of the scenarios she would have envisioned.

"Now I really feel like a homeowner!" The excitement on his face caused him to take on the exuberant appearance of a happy child. "I can't believe this!" he exclaimed. "Look how tall it's grown!"

Lindsey could only stand and grin as she watched her fiancé shuffle his feet through the tall, lush thickness of their own, private lawn. "You know," she offered, "I'm certain they must have a service that one can obtain to keep up with the yard when we're away."

"Are you kidding?" he asked, as though she had to be joking, "I'm going to buy one of those gadgets to keep it cut and trimmed myself. I can't wait."

Lindsey walked toward him and stepped into his arms. She could feel the heat of his body through the thin material of his form-fitting shirt. "You're sounding terribly domestic Dr. Sanders," she teased. "You'll have everyone thinking I have some sort of a spell over you."

"You do," he grinned. "And hey, domestic is good. Nothing wrong with domestic. I can see it now, I'll be right out here," he gestured with a wave of his hand, "trimming up the grass, while you sit over there," again indicating an area nearer the house, "with our laughing, healthy child on your lap, as we watch the whales mate."

"Kevin, what has gotten in to you today?" she giggled. "You seem almost giddy."

"Giddy, is it?" he laughed, wiggling his eyebrows at her.

In one swift motion, he swung his arm around her and pulled her gently to the ground, following her with his own body. Lindsey giggled and squirmed, but Kevin silenced her mock protests with a deep kiss, finally rolling over and laying next to her, as they both gazed out through the mammoth, transparent dome to the aquatic wonderland beyond.

"You know Lindsey," he said thoughtfully, "speaking of feeling domestic, I've been doing a lot of thinking lately." He turned his head to look directly into her eyes, "I just don't think I can stand waiting much longer to make you my wife."

"What?" asked Lindsey, not quite believing what she'd just heard. "What are you saying, Dr. Sanders?"

"Just that I can't see waiting until after the project is complete for us to get married, Linds. I think we both know it's what we want. Unless of course, you want to wait for a formal church wedding. I'd be just as happy with a Justice of the Peace."

"I don't suppose we'd be any more married if we had a church wedding, or any less married with a Justice of the Peace."

"True," supplied Kevin, "and I'm sure there is a Justice of the Peace down here somewhere."

"You mean you want to get married here in Atlantica? Now?"

"Yes, here and now. If you're willing to become my wife. Are you Linds?" he asked, searching her eyes," Are you ready to be my wife now?"

"I think I've been ready since the first time you kissed me," responded Lindsey huskily.

"Then why don't you go enjoy a nice hot bath, which I know you've been dying to do, and I'll see if I can't make some arrangements."

"Umm," replied Lindsey. "A bath sounds delightful. But Kevin, tomorrow is New Year's Eve, I can't imagine you'll be able to find a Justice of the Peace to perform the ceremony on such short notice."

"Well," he thought aloud, "I did see what I think was a wedding chapel on our last visit, maybe there's still someone there, I'll look up their link code. You just enjoy your bath."

Lindsey started to pad off down the hall toward the cleansing room with the seashell bathtub, when she suddenly stopped short, "Kevin," Lindsey turned back around, "what about my mother? I hope she won't want to kill me for getting married on the spur of the moment without her even being there."

"Well, we can always promise her we'll have a church wedding sometime next year," he offered. "I'm sure she'd rather you make an honest man of me, than to sleep with me like some play thing."

Lindsey's laughter could be heard even after she'd entered the cleansing chamber and closed the door behind her.

At 8:00 PM, on Tuesday, December 30, 2250, Kevin and Lindsey stood before the Justice of the Peace in the underwater city of Atlantica, and repeated the vows that would forever make them man and wife. And it was on that day that Dr. Lindsey Larimer became Dr. Lindsey Sanders.

"Oh, Kevin," exclaimed Lindsey, as they left the tiny chapel, "I can't believe we did it, I can't believe I'm your wife."

"Well, I think I've known from the day I met you that you were the woman I've been waiting for all my life. And might I add," he included with a grin, "it took you long enough to come around. Hell, here I am getting married for the first time in my life at the age of thirty-seven!"

Lindsey giggled as they stepped onto the moving walkway, and gingerly lifted the train of her now twice-worn, replica gown. "Is this Mr. Humorous guy something new, or something you've been keeping from me until very recently?" she teased, "I rather like it, you know." Her smile and the light in her eyes were definite evidence of her immense happiness.

"I guess maybe it's you that brings it out in me," he returned, still grinning like a kid. "I told you, it's because you are the only right person on the planet for me."

"I hope I'm the only person under the ocean for you too," responded Lindsey, as she flexed her own wit.

"The only person in the universe!" he exclaimed... successfully ending the debate.

"I don't know," responded Lindsey, a mock-questioning look on her face, "Amara seemed to think she was the right person for you." Her eyes twinkled, and the muscles in her face worked as she tried to keep from laughing aloud.

"Oh, who's the funny one now?" returned Kevin, as he encircled her small waist with his arm and pulled her close.

Lindsey looked down at her left hand, the diamond wedding ring now intertwined with the engagement ring, while Kevin's finger sported the plain, gold band he had purchased the same day he'd bought her wedding set.

The shops, entertainment centers, and nutriment bars that lined the streets in Atlantica bustled with activity. There were people everywhere, some in plain, modern clothing, and others attired in the twentieth-century theme clothing so prominent here in this enchanted city. Once again, Kevin had managed to rent a replica-tuxedo for the occasion, the suit fitting his well toned, muscled body like it was made just for him.

Much of the activity around the newlyweds went unnoticed, as they glided along the transport-walk toward their own home. The surreal experience settled in on both of them, making Lindsey feel like one of the fairy-princesses in the fables her father had read to her in her childhood.

Evening was settling on the city as the pair arrived at the front door of their home. The light emanating from the dome had been made brighter, and seemed to attract the ocean life like mosquitoes to a flame. Dolphins frolicked; as though putting on a show for the city's inhabitants, and schools of colorful fish performed their aquatic ballets that seemed almost choreographed.

Kevin took Lindsey by complete surprise as he lifted her off her feet and carried her over the threshold. "This is the first time we've entered our home as man and wife," he reminded her, returning her gently to her feet. The door slid shut with the familiar 'whoosh' sound, and Kevin looked down into the eyes of his wife. He couldn't remember ever seeing a woman as beautiful as Lindsey. Just knowing that she was the one he would spend the rest of his life with, the one who would bear his children and grow old with him, filled him with a feeling of such intense love for her, that is was almost overwhelming. "You know," he reminded softly, "this is also the first time we'll make love as man and wife."

Lindsey felt as though her heart were about to burst. She loved Kevin more than she would have ever thought possible. Her body ached with need for him, and within moments, the two stood next to their replica–bed.

Kevin pulled his new bride to him and kissed her forehead, her eyes, her nose, and then his lips came to rest upon her own, with a passion that was growing stronger with every passing second. His kiss deepened, until Lindsey felt that her knees might just buckle right out from under her. His hand moved from her waist to her breast, and he kneaded it gently.

Lindsey tilted her head further back and matched the thrusts of his tongue with her own, as her hands moved over his back, his shoulders, and his arms. The muscles rippled beneath his clothing, sending chills through her body.

In a few fluid movements, her gown lay in a heap on the floor, and Kevin's tuxedo followed. Lindsey felt herself lowered onto the softness of the twentieth–century bed while Kevin's mouth went lower, as he kissed her chin, her throat, her neck, and then finally moved slowly down to encircle the rose colored nipple of her breast with his tongue.

Lindsey felt like she was on fire, and only Kevin could quench the flames, the same flames he was fanning wildly at the moment. Lindsey reached down and gently touched the root of his manhood, his sharp intake of breath attesting to his arousal.

In seconds, he was within her, moving slowly at first, kissing her deeply and passionately. Every fiber of Lindsey's being screamed for release, and she felt a moan of sheer pleasure escape her throat as his thrusts began to deepen. Nothing else in the world existed…nothing else mattered but the feel of Kevin running his hands over her body, cupping her breasts and driving into her in a rhythmic motion as old as time itself. Their union took them to dizzying heights, as their fervor reached an unequaled crescendo. With an indescribable ecstasy, they attained their release simultaneously, spiraling back down from the peak of their mutual passion.

Kevin and Lindsey made love many more times during the night, each time just as ardent and fulfilling as the time before. It was early afternoon by the time the two had bathed and dressed.

Lindsey heated two nutriment packs, and enjoyed brunch on a blanket in their back yard with her husband, the tall grass around them making the atmosphere seem quite out–doorsy.

Every manner of ocean fish and sea mammal glided about outside the dome, and the newlyweds frequently pointed out various types of plant life and corral splays, constantly marveling at the unearthly beauty that they were so fortunate to behold first–hand.

The day passed far too quickly, and Kevin found himself unable to make love to his wife often enough. The blanket, spread out on the grass provided a soft cushion for the two lovers, as they tasted, explored and shared themselves with one another.

It couldn't have been more wonderful…until Kevin looked up to see a sea–rover craft full of tourist's glide by, its inhabitants pointing and grinning out the portals. He hoped this was just a New Year's special, and not a regular event. At that moment, he was glad the grass had grown so tall. Kevin didn't say a word to his wife as the visiting tourists disappeared from view. She would have been mortified beyond recovery.

When the evening came and it was time to prepare for the New Years dinner and party, Lindsey felt almost too weak to bathe and dress herself.

Their dwelling, having belonged initially to two men, lacked a 'Coif–Configurator,' and Lindsey stood before the mirror in the cleansing–room, struggling unsuccessfully with her freshly washed mane of chestnut curls. She didn't hear Kevin walk up behind her, until she felt his arms slide gently around her waist.

"We just received a link from Trent and Thad," he said, nuzzling her neck, "they are waiting to see my new bride."

"But my hair looks terrible Kevin. I haven't got the first clue how to fix it, and there's no Coif–Configurator here. I can't let them see me looking so awful."

"Surely you jest!" he exclaimed with a laugh. "You're so beautiful right now, it's all I can do not to ravish you again." The tops of her firm breasts above the neckline of her gown were reflected in the mirror, and Kevin felt his loins beginning to stir with desire yet again. "As a matter of fact," he added, "if you don't stop looking so sexy, I'm not sure we'll make it out of the house tonight."

"But Kevin," she started to protest.

"Not to worry, Mrs. Sanders," I'll take care of everything just as soon as you come speak with the professors.

"We're delighted beyond words!" exclaimed Thad.

"Absolutely." chimed in Trent. "We knew from the moment we met you that you kids were meant for each other."

"We're sending a wedding gift right over to you," announced Thad.

"Oh, you don't have to do that," broke in Lindsey, "after all, it was a very spur of the moment decision."

"Be that as it may," replied Trent, "your gift will arrive shortly, and we'll look forward to seeing you two tonight."

Trent signed off before Lindsey could render any further protest, but the link had no sooner been disconnected, than Kevin pressed the indicator panel with his index finger.

A young woman's face appeared on the screen. "Desiree's Salon, may I assist you?" asked the pretty shop clerk with a smile.

"Yes, please," responded Kevin. "My wife and I have recently moved here to Atlantica, and she is in need of a Coif–Configurator, do you have any?"

"We have several," offered the clerk, "would you like to see our display?"

"Yes, I would thank you," was Kevin's reply.

The clerk reached toward the link–device on her end and pressed the selector panel; the full line of Coif–Configurators was instantly displayed on the screen.

"Which one would you like my love?" asked Kevin, as he

pulled his wife closer to his body, and the link–machine screen, affording her a better view of the selections.

"Oh my, Kevin," she exclaimed, "the prices are horrendous! I can't believe how much they're asking for these things."

"Don't you worry about the price, Mrs. Sanders," smiled Kevin in return, "just consider it my wedding gift to my lovely new bride."

"But I haven't gotten you a gift yet," she reminded him.

"Oh, you've given me all the gifts I can imagine ever wanting," was his honest and heart–felt reply.

Lindsey perused the selections on the screen, finally settling on one that looked the most similar to the one in her condo and pressed the area of the link–machine displaying that model.

In a moment, the redhead's smiling face returned, "Thank you for your selection, sir," offered the clerk. "With tax, your total purchase comes to four–thousand and twenty–two credits," she advised. "Would you like to insert your credit chip now?"

Kevin reached into the pocket of the tuxedo he had donned once again and withdrew the chip, placing it in the slot provided on the link–machine panel. In a moment, the chip rose back up through the slot.

"Your purchase is complete," concluded the clerk, "and we can deliver your item to you on Thursday, the second of January."

"Thursday?" repeated Kevin. "I apologize for not having mentioned it earlier, but my wife is in need of the configurator immediately."

"Oh, I'm very sorry sir," responded the clerk, "our shop will be closing in less than an hour, and we won't be back in until after the New Year."

"Would it be possible for me pick the item up?" questioned Kevin.

"Oh, that would be fine, Sir, but please do hurry," she replied.

"I'll be there in just a few moments," Kevin responded, as he disconnected the link.

"You are already the most wonderful of all husbands," said Lindsey sincerely, as she held Kevin to her and placed her face on his broad chest. "But I don't expect you to jump up and rush to buy every little thing I need."

"I didn't jump up and rush," Kevin reminded her with a smile. "I merely walked casually over here to the link machine and pressed this thing right here, and...."

"I love you Doctor Sanders," Lindsey said into the lapel of Kevin's tux.

"And I love you Doctor Sanders," replied her husband.

"I rather prefer the Mrs. Sanders you referred to me as earlier," said Lindsey, as she stepped back and gazed into the handsome face of her new husband. "It has a rather nice ring to it, don't you think?"

"Oh yes, I definitely like the sound of the Mrs. part." Kevin kissed his wife deeply, before leaving her to her toilette, and heading into the heart of the city to pick up the configurator…their first purchase as man and wife. Kevin almost whistled as he walked along the transport, allowing him to move twice as fast toward his destination.

At this point in his life, Kevin couldn't imagine being any happier, although some of his sense of fulfillment was overshadowed by the possible outcome of The Reclamation Project. For some reason, he just couldn't shake the feeling that they were dabbling in things that might be well out of their control. Kevin forced himself to shake off the momentary sense of imminent gloom that always surrounded him when he allowed himself to think about where the project was ultimately going.

Kevin had no sooner left the house, than Lindsey turned back to the link machine and pressed the menu key on the selection panel. Having found the necessary link–number, Lindsey input the information into the machine. In a few seconds, an older man with bushy white eyebrows came into view.

"Neptune's Garden, may I assist you Madam?" he asked politely.

"Yes, please," responded Lindsey. "My husband and I are in need of a mechanism for trimming the grass in our back yard. Do you have such a thing?"

"We have only three models to chose from Ma'am," was his reply, "but there are several in stock. Oh, and just so you know," he said as an afterthought, we do have a lawn service that can come around once a week for a small fee."

"Thank you for the offer, Sir, but my husband is quite adamant about wanting to trim the grass himself." Lindsey smiled at the mental picture of her handsome husband's face when he'd seen how tall the grass had grown in their yard. "May I look at your selection screen?"

"Certainly, one moment." The man reached forward and she was immediately connected with the requested screen. It seemed that the twentieth–century gizmo required to trim the grass was called a 'lawn–mower.' Lindsey remembered having heard of them before, but she'd certainly never seen one firsthand.

Perusing the proffered list, Lindsey noted that two of the lawn mowers offered by 'Neptune's Garden,' were fully automated, with built–in sensors so that human–operation was not required. She knew Kevin would be disappointed if he weren't able to do the work himself, and pressed the frame indicating her choice of the manual version. According to the verbal description accompanying the picture, this unit would even catch and store the clippings for garden mulch. That bit of knowledge gave Lindsey another idea, and before she had finished shopping she had ordered several fruit–bearing and flower–bearing clippings, plants and bulbs, and a book on how to care for a garden.

Feeling quite confident in her choices, Lindsey hardly winced at the total bill of well over eight thousand credits. This time it was her own credit chip that purchased the order, and she smiled contentedly as she returned to the cleansing room to apply her cosmetics.

Lindsey hoped Kevin would be pleased with the wedding gift she would present to him, at least she knew the lawn mower was something he could use. The proprietor had assured her that for an additional fee of only eight hundred credits, he could have her purchase gift–wrapped and delivered within the hour.

No sooner had Lindsey returned to the mirror in the cleansing room, than the feminine voice of their home–control center announced an approaching visitor. Thinking it must be someone delivering the wedding present from Trent and Thad, Lindsey opened the door to find herself looking directly into the twinkling blue eyes of an elderly woman. The lady's face seemed somehow familiar, but Lindsey couldn't quite place her.

"May I help you?" asked Lindsey.

The older woman smiled pleasantly, and presented Lindsey with a slide–tablet, "If you read this, all will be explained." The woman's smile was absolutely adorable, and without hesitation, Lindsey invited her in, taking the procured tablet. She pressed the upper right hand corner, and almost immediately Trent and Thad appeared on the small screen. The two men sat side by side on an air–sofa; the fat little Deuteronomy ensconced comfortably between them.

"Here is your wedding present!" beamed Thad with a smile.

"Her name is Moira," chimed in Trent, "and she comes directly from the 'Modern Living Shop' here in Atlantica."

"Kevin told us she caught your eye the last time you two were here," offered Thad.

"And Moira can provide any household services you can name," grinned Trent. "Which will give you and Kevin more time to enjoy your honeymoon."

Deuteronomy lifted his head and meowed, as though to corroborate Trent's words and both men laughed.

"Moira is fully programmed," offered Thad. "So she can find her way around the city and perform any shopping you don't wish to do yourself, but the following pages contain information on program extension services, in case there is a specific service you would like her to perform."

"Right," confirmed Trent. "Like being a nanny when you and Kevin have a child." The two men practically beamed at the mention of children.

"You know," grinned Thad, "we're both available to be designated god–father, god–grandfather, or god–whatever other kind of father position might be available when the time comes."

Lindsey was still laughing outright, when the pre–recorded message ended and the tablet went blank. She turned to Moira, who still stood behind her with a large case in her hand, still smiling brightly.

"Well Moira," said Lindsey, "you are a very lovely gift."

"Thank you Mrs. Sanders," responded the incredibly life–like droid. "My programmer was not sure from the limited profile he had to work with, whether to have me refer to you as Mrs. Sanders or Dr. Sanders."

"Oh, please call me Mrs. Sanders," Lindsey answered. "We were only just married yesterday, and I rather like hearing it."

"Then Mrs. Sanders it is," beamed the charming woman. "Where shall I put my things?"

"What did you bring," inquired Lindsey.

"I come complete with two uniforms, cleaning supplies, miscellaneous household tools, a bath and cosmetic gift bag, courtesy of 'Modern Living,' and my solar–recharger, which I can utilize independently from your back yard," Moira replied.

"But we're under the ocean, Moira," Lindsey reminded. "How does a solar–recharger work under the ocean?"

"Oh, it's highly sensitive Mrs. Sanders," she explained. "What bit of the sun's rays filter through are plenty sufficient, even if you can't see the sun's light, it's there. I will only require three, five minute intervals per day to remain fully efficient, and I don't require food, water or sleep. I can provide any cleaning services not already performed by your pre–installed home–care system, including the full preparation of meals, and assistance with personal grooming."

"My goodness!" exclaimed Lindsey. "You are quite the perfect gift, aren't you?"

"I come complete with a life–time guarantee that covers all moving parts, re–charger replacement and biannual maintenance visits. The tablet contains a user–friendly manual that explains how to re–program or alter my personality and vocabulary skills."

Lindsey found it quite difficult to believe that this woman who stood before her was not an actual human being. Felling compelled to touch the realistic skin of the droid; Lindsey reached out and rubbed her fingers on Moira's arm. The covering even felt like real skin, except that it was still much colder than the flesh of a living being.

"You mentioned that you were able to assist with personal grooming?" questioned Lindsey.

"Yes, Mrs. Sanders," answered the droid. "I have extensive knowledge of cosmetic application, coif–configuration and coordinating garments and accessories."

"Do me a favor Moira?" asked Lindsey with a smile.

"Yes, Mrs. Sanders?" replied the woman.

"Don't tell Mr. Sanders you have the ability to dress my hair."

Less than twenty minutes later, Lindsey stared back at her reflection in the mirror with a feeling akin to awe. Her skin tone appeared flawless, and the cosmetics Moira had artfully applied to her eyes and lips brought out her features in a most stunning fashion. She vowed to purchase more of the cosmetics from the shop that provided the samples included in the customer gift bag.

The housekeepers' ministrations were not lost on Kevin. When the control–center announced his approach, Lindsey almost ran to the front door to greet him. She had no idea she could miss someone so much in such a short period of time. It seemed that marriage had served to even deepen her love for her blonde Adonis.

"My God, Lindsey!" he exclaimed, almost dropping the large package he had tucked under his arm. "You look positively stunning!"

"Why thank you husband," teased Lindsey. "I hope you will still greet me so sweetly fifty years from now."

"And I hope you don't look so damned desirable fifty years from now. Hell, I wouldn't have the strength to fight off all the young guys that would be trying to steal you away from me," he joked, handing her the package. "It's your wedding gift," he announced, as he kissed her on the cheek, and then moved his lips lower to nuzzle the lobe of her ear.

Lindsey giggled, and then noted that Kevin suddenly went quite still, "Who is that?" he asked, looking past her toward the living area.

Knowing whom her husband was referring to without turning around, Lindsey informed him that Moira was a gift from Thad and Trent. "Apparently," she advised, "my chatter–box husband told the good professors that a particular droid had caught my eye the last time I visited Atlantica."

"That's where I've seen her before," he remembered aloud. "But I was going to buy her for you myself, I certainly didn't mean for them to purchase her. My God," he lamented, "these droids cost a fortune, I can't believe those two spent so much on a wedding gift."

"We'll have to name them as joint god–fathers of our child you know," smiled Lindsey. "They rather hinted at it on the slide tablet that came with Moira."

"Moira," repeated Kevin, "that's quite a nice name."

"She does everything," supplied his wife. "She cooks, shops, cleans, provides minor home repair work, and even applied my make–up."

"Well if she does as good a job with the rest of those things as she did with your make–up, I think she'll do quite nicely. You do know though," he added, "that you're perfectly stunning without cosmetics."

"My goodness, Honey," laughed Lindsey. "You're just racking them up aren't you?"

"Racking what up?"

"Points; good Points."

"Great!" he teased, "when can I redeem them?"

In less than five minutes, Moira had single–handedly installed the Coif–Configurator next to a cloth covered vanity table in the cleansing–room. "Shall I assist you in choosing a hairstyle?" asked Moira.

"By all means, please," Lindsey answered. "The last time I wore this dress, my mother and I chose an upswept–style with bits of my hair hanging in long spirals."

"Oh, that sounds lovely, Mrs. Sanders," offered the pleasant Moira. "Would you like me to look for a similar style?"

Within moments, the two had chosen a configuration that swept only the right side of Lindsey's hair back and upward, securing it with the diamond hairpins she had inserted into the accessories–panel. The remainder of her tresses were then curled into masses of long spirals by the configurator, with the top of the hair on the left side being swept back slightly and secured. The end product definitely had the desired results, and as Lindsey gazed at her reflection in the mirror, she felt more like a princess than she ever had before.

Rising from the vanity stool, Lindsey was just about to call out for Kevin to see her new hairstyle, when he appeared at the doorway of the cleansing–room. "You!" he charged, pointing his index finger at her, and causing her to stop dead where she stood. "You are the greatest, most wonderful wife any man on any planet could ever want or ask for!"

"So you like my hair then?" teased Lindsey. She knew full well that his wedding gift must have arrived while her head was ensconced in the Coif–Configurator.

"I love your hair," said Kevin, as he walked toward the vision that was his wife. "I love your eyes, your mouth, your face, your breasts, your body." He reached out and took her in his arms. "I love your heart, your mind and your soul," he breathed into her fragrant hair. "And did I mention I love your breasts?" he added, cupping one in his hand as he spoke.

"Yes," Lindsey replied dreamily. "I believe you mentioned the breasts."

"She's smiling," stated Kevin, as he realized that Moira stood but a few feet away.

"She always smiling. She's programmed to smile," replied Lindsey. "But it is a bit uncomfortable kissing in front of someone, even if that someone is a droid."

"Well, if we don't stop now," whispered Kevin, "we'll be doing a lot more than kissing in front of her."

The 'Blast from the Past' restaurant was just as Lindsey had remembered it, and she was overjoyed to be returning. Although many of the patrons wore modern, formal wear, Lindsey was pleased to note that the majority had donned period suits and gowns.

All eyes were on Kevin and his bride, as he escorted her through the main entrance and into the massive dining area, where they had enjoyed the grand–opening dinner with Trent and Thad.

Side by side, the newlyweds followed the young hostess to their table, Lindsey's dark mane a perfect contrast to Kevin's golden locks. In an aesthetic sense, they were by far the most attractive couple in the establishment, a fact that did not go unnoticed by the other patrons.

"I don't think I'd better let you out of my sight tonight,"

smiled Kevin, as he seated his wife and then took his own chair at the small table for two, "I think every man here has fallen in love with you on sight."

"I beg to differ, Husband, but I think it's the other way around."

"Do you mean to tell me that after less than two full days of marriage, you've gone and fallen in love with every man in this room?" he teased.

"There's that funny guy again," returned Lindsey with a grin.

The New Years Eve party was unlike any event Lindsey had ever been to before. The restaurant owner had spared no expense on entertainment, and the drinks flowed freely, as the sea of guests danced and partied into the New Year.

It was nearly 11:30 PM, when Kevin finally spotted Trent and Thad at the other end of the ballroom, and taking Lindsey's hand firmly in his own, began to weave through the sea of revelers.

Lindsey stayed close behind her husband, unable to see around his broad shoulders. She nearly ran into him when he stopped suddenly, and was quite amazed when she heard him loudly greet Glen instead of the professors. Popping her head around Kevin's tux–clad body, she was pleasantly surprised to see Glen and his new companion, Sal.

Both men congratulated the newlyweds heartily, when Kevin broke the news of their recent nuptials, and Lindsey was pleased to see that Glen looked happier and even younger than the last time she'd seen him. His glasses were so near the tip of his nose, they almost fell off his face entirely when he hugged the bride.

"I can't tell you how happy I am Glen," said Lindsey, "I love being married, I love our house here in Atlantica, and I love this place," she finished, indicating the ballroom with a sweep of her hand.

"Well, I'll tell you a little secret if you promise not to share it with anyone other than your husband," Glen offered.

"I promise," was Lindsey's solemn reply.

"Sal owns this place, as well as his restaurant back in the city." Glen grinned broadly at Lindsey's wide–eyed look of astonishment,

"I was shocked too," he supplied, "it seems he bid for the building before the construction of Atlantica was even under way. Fortunately, his bid was selected. Sal confided in me that within the next year, he'll be a trillionaire."

Lindsey was incredulous, "you chose well, Glen," she grinned, "but he'd better make you happy or he'll have to deal with me."

Twenty minutes later, Kevin and Lindsey were once again winding their way through the crowd toward the figures of Thad and Trent. The two men greeted their young friends jovially, hugging Lindsey in turn and shaking hands profusely with the new groom.

After several more toasts to their happiness, health and fertility, Lindsey managed to steer her husband and the professors away from the main throng of guests and into a more private area in the lounge.

"There's something I must tell the both of you." She addressed Trent and Thad in a near whisper, "Something Ankhesenamun said to me the other day. I've been quite disturbed by it."

The New Years countdown had already begun, the revelers nearly drowning out her voice as they chanted from the ballroom, "twenty–five, twenty–four, twenty–three…."

The professors bent their heads and stood closer, both straining their ears to hear her voice above the din.

"She told me that they remember who they were." Lindsey tried to raise her voice enough to be heard without screaming.

"Fourteen, thirteen, twelve…." the chanting grew louder.

"She said they have remembered from the beginning," finished Lindsey, literally having to yell to make her voice heard over the clamor.

Not even the deafening roar from the crowded ballroom of 'Happy New Year!' and the ensuing thunder of stomping feet and applause could drown out the, "Oh my god!" that emitted from the two men in unison.

Chapter Eleven

It seemed strange to be inviting Trent and Thad into their home, when they had once been guests there themselves, but there was simply nowhere private enough within the city of Atlantica; the revelers having flowed out into the streets to continue their New Year merry-making. Even the backyard could not be considered a secure enough area in which to discuss any aspects of the Reclamation Project.

Although the four had returned to the ballroom immediately after Lindsey had shared the topic of her concern with the professors, they had stayed no longer than necessary to say their respective 'good-nights.' Just returning home on the transport walk was difficult. It seemed that everyone around them had been a little too full of good cheer. Many of the revelers were literally dancing in the streets. The four had smiled and waved, returning wishes of well for the New Year, all the while scarcely able to wait to discuss this highly unexpected turn of events.

Moira wasted no time in seeing to the comfort of her owner's guests. The four had no sooner seated themselves in the living room, than the housekeeper-droid bustled into the room with refreshments and snacks.

"Thank you Moira, you are most efficient," praised Lindsey, "but might I ask you to wait outside in the back yard until I call for you."

"Certainly, Mrs. Sanders," returned the gray haired maid, with the ever present sweet smile and twinkling blue eyes.

"Thank you so very much for your kindness in gifting us with Moira. We can't thank you enough, though I must say it's rather difficult to look at her and not see a real person."

The professors both nodded their acknowledgment of Lindsey's appreciation in unison.

"After Kevin mentioned you had seen them and found them so fascinating, we couldn't think of anything we'd rather give to your for a wedding gift," proclaimed Thad.

Trent sat down his drink and folded his arms over his rotund belly, looking decidedly uncomfortable in his rented tuxedo, and no doubt longing for the comfort of his robes. "We'd thought about that good–looking, tall male droid, but figured Kevin wouldn't appreciate that much!" Both men chuckled until quelled by the lift of Kevin's eyebrow.

"Well I realize she is only a droid," said Lindsey, sitting comfortably next to her husband, "but I just don't feel quite comfortable discussing this matter in front of anyone other than yourselves."

"Understandable," agreed Trent.

"I don't imagine we can be too careful," intoned Thad, "but please do continue with what you were telling us at the party. I can scarcely believe the girl told you they remember."

"In truth," replied Lindsey, "there's not much more to tell. Kevin had come by to see me, and the children wanted to show him how well they could write their numbers. When he left the room, little Tut accused Ankhesenamun of being a show off, and an argument ensued. It was then that Tut shouted at her that she never listened to him, and that she had never listened to him before either. As his words sunk in, I looked at Ankhesenamun and that's when she said it, her exact words were, 'We remember who we were; we have from the beginning.'"

"If anyone other than Lindsey had told me this, I wouldn't have believed it," said Kevin "This is completely at odds with everything we have ever thought we understood about cloning."

"Who else have you told about this, Lindsey?" asked Thad.

"Just Professor St. Germaine, the CEO at IBAT," she replied honestly.

"And what did he say when you told him?" queried Trent.

"He was just as amazed and shocked as you are," she told them, "and said that he would write the information in his daily report, and that the government would undoubtedly want to send their own team of professionals in to conduct some tests on the two clones."

"This is most frightening," intoned Thad.

"Yes," agreed Trent, "but also most fascinating. I mean, think about it," he said seriously, "if these two clones really do remember who they were, do you have any idea how many of the gaps they can fill in about the Egyptian history itself."

"You're right there, my friend," acknowledged Thad, "according to the scrolls we've read, both Tut and Ankhesenamun were reported to have had actual encounters with individuals from other planets. The governments are concerned with discovering how to utilize the pyramids as a weapon, they aren't exactly aware that they were also used for tele–transportation. Imagine the information they could provide. Still, I find that this information doesn't set well."

"I know what you mean," interjected Kevin, "and if the government sends a team out to run tests on them, and the children reveal this information, God only knows what the government might do with that it."

"Do you have any idea when these tests will be conducted?" asked Thad.

"I really don't," replied Lindsey, "but Professor St. Germaine did tell me that in the interim, he wants me to conduct their classes as usual and to say nothing."

"Then I would leave that to his good judgment," nodded Thad, but the look in his eye suggested otherwise.

Lindsey found it difficult to sleep. She and Kevin had gone to bed shortly after Thad and Trent had departed, after settling Moira into the second bedroom. The droid would not sleep, of course, but Lindsey simply did not know what else to do with her non–human housekeeper.

Kevin had made slow and passionate love to his wife, and for a time she laid in his arms, her head resting against his chest. He could sense that the news she had shared with Trent and Thad still weighed on her mind, and knowing Lindsey wasn't asleep, he asked her if she wanted to talk about it.

The two shared their thoughts for over an hour on the infinite number of ways the world might change, if indeed the clones were capable of remembering their earlier lives. Should Tut and Ankhesenamun truly be able to share information about advanced, intelligent life on other planets, heaven only knew where that might lead.

It was nearly 3:00 AM before the tired couple fell to sleep, but Lindsey's slumber was not a peaceful one.

It was dark; too dark to see where she was going. Staying close to one wall, Lindsey trudged onward. She was far below the surface of Giza; she imagined about halfway between the Sphinx and the Great Pyramid. The walled tunnel was so much more frightening a place when alone and with no lights. Her legs were feeling the strain as she forced herself to continue up the incline. She had to find her father, had to tell him something very important, but the information she had for him was beginning to fade from her mind. Suddenly Lindsey tripped and fell face down, skinning her knees as she did so. The floor of the tunnel had given way to stairs, but they were invisible in the pitch blackness that enveloped her in its folds. Having made it to the stairs however, gave Lindsey a renewed vigor. She was closer to her father, closer to saving him. Only what exactly was it she was supposed to tell him? Someone had told her to deliver a message…someone who glowed. Lindsey searched her mind, but it was like trying to concentrate through a drugged stupor. She had to relay something of the utmost importance to her father…something about him not continuing with something. He had to stop; that was it, he had to stop or all would be lost. What? What would be lost? Frightened, her breath coming in gasps, she forced her legs to obey her mind. Onward she climbed, feeling as though her limbs were made of lead, determined to find her father. Lindsey stumbled again when she brought her foot up to negotiate the next step, and realized there wasn't one. There were no rails to hold onto, and she felt a stabbing pain in her right ankle with the missed–step. She'd made it to the first landing; that realization spurring her on. It was hot, and her hair was soaking wet from her own perspiration, beads of sweat running in rivulets down the side of her face. There was a light up ahead and Lindsey knew she didn't have much further to go. Her knees burned from having been scraped, and every step she took was by strength of will alone. She heard her father's voice up ahead, and forced her aching legs to carry her to the edge of the light. Her father spoke with someone just outside her field of vision, but at the sight of his daughter, he stopped speaking and turned his attention toward her. He was alive!

Her father was alive and standing just a few yards ahead of her. What was it she was supposed to tell him? Who had given her this important information and why? He had to stop something. What in the hell did he have to stop? Lindsey's mind struggled to remember.

"You have to stop father!" she shouted, hurling herself toward his outstretched arms, "you can't find it, you can't let it happen."

She was almost near him now. Only a few feet to go. Her legs hurt…they were tired and felt heavier with each step.

"Stop!" The figure that appeared before her seemed to materialize from nowhere, blocking her way.

Heart stopping fear gripped Lindsey, as her eyes focused on a golden disk hanging from the neck of the shadowy form standing only inches before her. Her throat constricted and sheer terror consumed every cell of her body. This entity before her emanated evil, hatred and something even deeper, something Lindsey didn't want to be a part of.

Lindsey forced her eyes to move slowly upward, as her sweat-soaked body began to shiver violently. She didn't want to look, didn't want to know what she would see, but couldn't stop her gaze from moving further upward, until she found herself looking into the cold, black eyes of King Tutankhamun. He was no longer a little boy, but a full-grown man. His eyes shone like polished onyx, made even more sinister by the heavily black lined lids. The gold armbands she had bought him for Christmas adorned his upper arms; only they were much larger now.

"Be gone!" shouted Tut. His voice sounded synthesized, and seemed to reverberate off the walls.

Lindsey brought her hands up to cover her ears, and cowered as the horror overwhelmed her.

"Lindsey, what must you tell me, Darling?" Tut's presence blocked her view of her father, but his voice brought back a small bit of courage.

"You can't continue Father!" she shouted, "You can't let any of this happen, it's all up to you…."

"I said be gone!" Again the synthesized voice of King Tutankhamun filled the chamber, this time forcing Lindsey to her knees like the percussion from an explosion.

Lindsey dared to look up and wished that she had not. The towering king stood above her, legs parted...the gold cobra of his headpiece seeming to come to life. The blade came from nowhere, as had King Tut, and threw itself into his hand. The knife blade glinted in the seemingly sourceless, defused glow of light, as his arm arched upward. Lindsey screamed for all she was worth, just before he brought his arm down to strike a mortal blow.

"Lindsey. Lindsey! Wake up!"

From some far off place, Lindsey heard Kevin calling her. Her husband, Kevin... He was here. He would make everything all right, wouldn't he?

"Lindsey!" Kevin's voice took on a desperate, almost pleading tone.

Rising through a thick fog, Lindsey reached up and found that she was entwined in Kevin's arms.

"My God, Lindsey," said Kevin, "you're soaking wet with sweat."

Lindsey began to shiver and Kevin pulled his wife closer to the warmth of his own body, speaking softly, as he pushed the wet strands of her hair out of her face. "You screamed so loud, I thought someone was trying to kill you. What in the world were you dreaming about, Honey?"

"Someone was trying to kill me," replied Lindsey, her mind still shrouded in a mist of confusion.

"Well you were obviously having a nightmare, Linds. Who was trying to kill you Sweetheart?"

"I don't remember," Lindsey answered honestly, as the nightmare receded further into the realm from whence it had come.

In seconds, Lindsey had fallen back to sleep. This time, it was a peaceful, dreamless one, but Kevin lay awake for some time afterward, concerned about what had so scared his wife, that she had awoken him screaming. It was the scream itself that bothered Kevin so much. He'd never before heard anything so frightening in his life. It has been a shriek, a moan and a wail all at once, a soulful, terror filled sound that still made the hackles rise on the back of his neck.

It was almost noon when Lindsey awoke. Her head hurt and

every muscle in her body ached when she tried to stretch. Kevin's side of the bed was empty, and Lindsey was glad her husband had already risen. Her body smelled not at all pleasant, and a musty scent seemed to linger on her skin. She needed a good cleansing and would have to strip the sheets from the bed to be cleansed as well.

It dawned on Lindsey suddenly that she had Moira to take care of those unpleasant details, and smiled slightly as the true benefit of Thad and Trent's wedding gift set in.

Throwing her legs over the side of the bed, Lindsey winced and wondered why in the world her whole body felt so sore. She had no sooner begun to stand, than a sharp, almost knifing pain shot through her right ankle. 'For the love of God,' she thought, wondering if perhaps she and her husband should tone down the vigor with which they made love.

After a moment, the stabbing pain in her ankle subsided and Lindsey grabbed her comfortable half-robe from the foot of the bed and went in search of Moira.

The new housekeeper seemed to be busying herself in the kitchen area, but greeted Lindsey with her ever present smile and a warm greeting. "Your husband said to tell you he wanted to let you sleep in this morning. He's out and about in the yard just now. I was just going to prepare some lunch for him. Are you hungry?"

Lindsey still felt somewhat disoriented from her disturbed sleep of the previous night, and shook her head slowly. Somehow food didn't sound terribly appealing. "I think I'll just let Kevin know I'm up now and enjoy a nice hot bath."

"As you wish, Mrs. Sanders," was Moira's sweet reply.

Kevin looked so completely domestic; Lindsey couldn't help smiling to herself. There in the back yard, her handsome husband busily glided the new lawnmower back and forth through the overgrown grass. As he moved forward with the almost silent machine, the grass beneath his feet was short and trim.

As though sensing her presence, Kevin turned and saw his disheveled young wife in the doorway, her tousled hair, and the short bathrobe making her quite desirable indeed. Suddenly, the smile froze on Kevin's face.

"Kevin," questioned Lindsey with some alarm, "what is it?

What's the matter?"

With the touch of his finger, the low hum of the machine stopped, and Kevin set it down, heading across the yard toward his wife. "What in the world have you done Lindsey?" The look on his face was quite disturbing, and his wife wasn't quite sure what to make of it.

"I don't know what you mean, Honey, I haven't done anything but get out of bed and come out to let you know I'm up now."

"Did you fall down on the way out here?" he questioned seriously.

"No, I didn't fall," Lindsey paused, searching her husbands face for some clue as to what he was talking about.

"Your knees," he answered slowly, "what have you done to them?"

It was then that Lindsey looked down and noticed for the first time that both of her knees were scraped, dirty and covered with dried blood. The nightmare flashed back through her mind with an intensity that nearly took her breath. She had fallen on the stairs while trying to find her father in the dark recesses of the underground tunnel. Tut, a grown up Tut, had stood before her, blocking her way.

Slowly, Lindsey turned her hands over and looked at her palms. Both of them were swollen and slightly bruised. "Oh my God!" she exclaimed, "this can't be happening. It isn't possible!"

By Thursday morning, Lindsey had managed to shove the incident back into her mind and resume her duties at IBAT. The newlyweds announced their marriage to their collective colleagues at an early morning meeting, receiving a resounding round of good wishes. Lindsey had already telephoned her mother and was quite pleased at Olivia's joyous acceptance of the news.

Although the terror brought about by the nightmare itself had subsided, the bruises and scratches had not. Fortunately, the evidence of her bizarre and still unexplainable experience was covered by the full–body jump suit she wore under her lab coat.

Of course, Lindsey and Kevin had discussed the incident for several hours the morning after her nightmare, but no matter how long they discussed it, or how much they went over the details, nothing explained the scrapes and bruises on Lindsey's knees. Kevin had opined that perhaps she had slept–walked and fallen in her sleep. Even so, they both concurred that the scrapes and cuts could not possibly have occurred on the soft carpeting throughout their home in Atlantica. The circumstances remained a mystery, and Lindsey could but hope there would not be a repeat performance. She and Kevin had both decided it would be an incident best kept to them.

Just as Lindsey and Kevin were heading toward their respective work areas, Professor St. Germaine caught up to them, "It seems," he advised, "that the government wasted no time in conducting the testing on Tut and Ankhesenamun." At Lindsey's surprised look, he continued, "They arrived here on New Year's Day and put the two through some very rigorous tests."

"And?" prompted Kevin.

"And, strangely enough," continued St. Germaine, "their technicians have determined that the two of them remember nothing more than they have been taught here at IBAT."

"But she admitted it to me," intoned Lindsey, "I certainly didn't imagine it."

"Well, perhaps it's for the better," returned St. Germaine with a thoughtful nod, "there's no telling what the government might have done had they determined the children could remember anything about their original lives."

Kevin could see by the look on his wife's face that this news bothered her. There was something happening that he was beginning to feel very uncomfortable with, and it was clearly affecting his wife. He made a mental note to pay close attention to Lindsey. He felt extremely protective toward this woman, and did not want to see her any more upset than she already had.

"For now," instructed St. Germaine, "say nothing to little Ankhesenamun about her remembering anything, but do keep your ears and eyes open, and report anything to me that seems out of the ordinary."

As the weeks turned into months, Lindsey truly began to wonder if she'd imagined Ankhesenamun's declaration of a remembered past–life. The children grew at a seemingly astronomical rate, and Lindsey was astonished from one day to the next at how rapidly the two clones matured, but never had Ankhesenamun mentioned another word of any prior memories.

As Tutankhamun grew, so too did his arrogant demeanor. The armload of garments made daily by the seamstresses never seemed to suit the young man. They were not elaborate enough, not adorned richly enough, not up to his high standards. The older the boy grew, the more indifferent he seemed to become to Lindsey, going through his daily lessons with all the ambition and finesse of a droid. Ankhesenamun on the other hand, seemed sweeter and kinder with each passing day and Lindsey found herself growing closer and closer to the young Egyptian girl.

By the second week in October of 2251, Lindsey had determined that there was simply not much more she could teach either Tut or Ankhesenamun. Both clones had an excellent working knowledge of the English and Egyptian language, numerical systems and culture.

It bothered Lindsey a good deal that Tut, now the equivalent of a sixteen–year–old young man, looked incredibly like the full–grown King Tut she had dreamed about months before. The once slender body of the male clone had somehow sprouted biceps and abdominal muscles that one normally only saw on men who worked their bodies, or took body–toning supplements, yet she knew the young man did neither. It also disturbed Lindsey greatly when she would catch the extremely handsome boy staring at her with a mysterious, almost hungry look in his eyes, though those looks did not frighten her as much as her body's own reaction to them.

Lindsey had taken to spending as little time alone with Tut as possible. Fortunately, Ankhesenamun was never far, but there was an attraction to the young man that Lindsey could neither ignore, nor give in to. It seemed that as time went on, thoughts of Tutankhamun would flitter, unbidden through her mind at times when she hadn't been thinking of him at all, as though he somehow had the ability to penetrate her thoughts. It wasn't exactly something she felt appropriate to discuss with her husband, but Lindsey resolved to remain as professional in her interactions with Tut as possible.

Professor St. Germaine had gathered the doctors and professors still working closely on the Reclamation Project for a special meeting in the last week of October. It seemed the US and Egyptian governments had decided the time was near to test the fruits of their labors. All the scrolls and tablets had been deciphered, and the two clones were perfectly healthy in every way; the acceleration process kept constantly in check.

Until now, Tut and Ankhesenamun had been completely unaware of the full reasons for the governments' initiation of the Reclamation Project, and both had assumed they had simply been chosen as the subjects of this new–age cloning concept. As Lindsey had the closest relationship with the two however, the IBAT board and the respective governments had decided that she would be the one to explain the real purpose of the project to them. It was apparently felt that Tut and Ankhesenamun would be more receptive upon learning the full depth and purpose of the true course of the governments' intended course of action. After all, they both played very important roles.

It was late in the afternoon when Lindsey made her way to the area formerly known as the 'Nursery,' where Tut and Ankhesenamun resided. She hadn't felt well all day long, and kept telling herself it was simply due to lack of sleep. Although she hadn't experienced any more nightmares, she'd been sleeping fitfully for the past couple weeks, and her appetite had become almost non–existent.

"There is something that I have to explain to the both of you," she began, once Tut and Ankhesenamun were seated comfortably across from her. "There is more to the Reclamation Project than we have revealed to you thus far."

Tut lifted a dark eyebrow, "Somehow that doesn't surprise me," was his smug retort.

"Tutankhamun, that is rude," admonished Ankhesenamun, "allow Lindsey to tell us what she has come to say." As always, the startlingly beautiful young woman spoke softly, her liquid brown eyes reflecting both her intelligence and an inherent femininity that seemed to have been lost on modern day women for a number of decades.

"Speak then," Tut's words were more of a command than an assent to Ankhesenamun's gentle reprimand, "and do not tell me what to say." His last words were directed at the dark haired beauty next to him, though his eyes were unreadable.

"I have come to tell you," continued Lindsey, "that the two of you are much more than the subjects of the first successful human cloning experiment, and both the US and Egyptian governments require your assistance in a matter of great importance."

For the next hour, Lindsey relayed the full purpose and extent of the Reclamation Project, explaining the necessity of the 'human–keys' spoken of in the scrolls and tablets. She described the Library of Knowledge as she remembered it from her first–hand experience, and then told Ankhesenamun about the amulet that had been found on her corpse in the Takla Makan Desert. "It is believed that either, or perhaps both of you, can engage the power of the pyramid through the use of the amulet. The government has only waited this long because negotiations with Russia were successful. It seems however," she continued," that they are now preparing to proceed with the project."

"And if we do not wish to be of assistance to the government," smirked Tut, "what then?"

"I don't know exactly," replied Lindsey honestly, "I don't believe it has occurred to the government that you might refuse."

"Of course we will help in any way we can," spoke Ankhesenamun, her darkly lined eyes met Lindsey's and she smiled warmly. "But for now, Lindsey, I think that you should rest."

"Rest?" repeated Lindsey.

"Yes," replied Ankhesenamun, "you need to rest just now."

"I don't understand what you mean," Lindsey was beginning to feel slightly queasy, and her temples ached slightly, "I'm fine, really." Her words were spoken as much to convince herself, as Ankhesenamun.

"I have told you before," interjected Tutankhamun, as he turned and glared at his female counterpart, "do not speak for me!" Tut rose from his chair, the new golden armbands around his upper arms, straining against his sinewy biceps, and throwing shards of light into Lindsey's eyes.

The nausea rose up again, threatening to overwhelm her. She laid her head back against the chair and closed her eyes for a moment, hoping her stomach would settle again. It seemed that her eyes wanted to close of their own accord and she could hear Tut's voice in the background becoming louder.

"How dare you continually speak for me!" his voice boomed, "You are as insolent as you were over four thousand years ago, and I'll tolerate it no more now than I did then!"

"Be careful what you say," whispered Ankhesenamun, "Lindsey will know we remember."

"She will know nothing more than I wish for her to know!"

Lindsey tried to open her eyes, and fought to lift her head, but the nausea swept over her yet again, leaving her too weak to move.

"It is not necessary for anyone to know, Tutankhamun, you said that yourself," even Ankhesenamun's voice was growing agitated.

"They already know of the pyramids! They want us to show them how to harness and channel the power. It is not their right! They will misuse it!"

"As you did once?" the anguish in Ankhesenamun's voice was the last conscience thought Lindsey had.

"Where am I?" Somehow Lindsey's voice sounded small and weak even to her own ears, a bright light source above her, forcing her to close her eyes once again.

"You're in the infirmary just now, Dr. Sanders," responded a deep, masculine voice, "it seems you gave Professor St. Germaine quite a fright. He carried you in here himself you know."

Lindsey struggled to sit up, but an unseen hand pushed her gently back. "Don't be alarmed, Dr. Sanders," assured the physician, as he stepped into view, "your husband has been sent for, and you have a clean bill of health, but there is a matter or two I would like to discuss with you here in private."

"Is she all right?" gasped Kevin, as he virtually flew around the corner and through the open door of the infirmary waiting room, to be met by a nervously pacing Professor St. Germaine.

"Your wife seems to be fine, Kevin, but I'm sure as hell not doing too well." The older man almost fell back into a body molding chair against the wall, worry etched clearly on his face, "I can't imagine what I would have said to Olivia if Lindsey hadn't of been alright."

"It's me you'd have to worry about, not Olivia," Kevin said seriously, "just tell me what happened."

"I was walking down the hallway on my way to the Nutriment Court, when Ankhesenamun burst through the door into the hallway, saying that Lindsey had fainted. Tut was right behind her, with your wife in his arms. The two of them assured me that one minute your wife had been fine, and the next minute she rose to stand and then just passed out. I took Lindsey into my own arms, yelled for an intern to notify the infirmary, and ran straight here. I don't know anything more about what caused it than that, but the physician has assured me she's going to be just fine. I wanted to see her for myself of course, especially since I'm having dinner with her mother tonight, and this isn't exactly something I can keep from her."

Just as Kevin had turned toward the door leading to the infirmary itself, Glen rushed into the room. "What happened Kevin? I just heard Lindsey fainted in the clones' living center!"

"I'll let you know as soon as I do," said Kevin, as the door to the infirmary slid aside, allowing him entry.

"How did you know what happened?" asked Professor St. Germaine, as Glen took a seat next to him, his glasses almost hanging off the tip of his nose.

"A Code Blue Infirmary Order was announced, and I heard it in the lab," responded Glen, "so what happened?"

"You scared me half to death, you know," chided Kevin, as he helped Lindsey from the Centurian and led her into his apartment. Having lived between Lindsey's condo, his apartment and the Doctor's living quarters at IBAT for the past several months, Kevin resolved to either buy a larger apartment closer to IBAT, or move to Atlantica with his wife permanently, and deal with the commute to work.

"I'm so sorry, Kevin," she apologized, as the two made their way to the living area and engaged the air couch. Once sitting comfortably next to her husband, Lindsey explained that she really couldn't remember anything more than beginning a conversation with Tut and Ankhesenamun, and then waking up in the infirmary. "I do believe I know why it happened though, if you'd like to hear it."

"Well of course I would, Lindsey," replied Kevin, "my wife passes out cold for no apparent reason whatsoever, and I don't know that it won't happen again. Something had to cause it, so what do you think it was?"

"The fact that I'm a little more than two months pregnant," responded Lindsey with a smile, "I'm going to have our baby."

Chapter Twelve

Kevin thought he himself might pass out after hearing his wife's news of their impending parenthood. He couldn't seem to hold her close enough, touch her enough, and love her enough.

"I guess this explains quite a bit then, doesn't it?" asked Kevin with a smile, as he gently kissed the top of his wife's head. He'd been worried about Lindsey for the past few weeks, and was relieved to hear that there was a perfectly logical explanation for her fatigue and inability to sleep well.

"I believe my mother once told me that she felt tired all the time when she was pregnant with me. I suppose I shall have to ask her," said Kevin thoughtfully.

"Perhaps we should link to her and let her know she's going to be a grandmother in a few, short months," smiled his wife in reply.

It seemed that the knowledge of her pregnancy had energized Lindsey. The color was beginning to return to her cheeks and she felt more and more like her old self with each passing minute. By the time she and Kevin arrived at her condo, Lindsey felt better than she had in weeks.

Olivia's face showed her concern when she met her daughter and son–in–law at the front door. "I just received a link from Garreth St. Germaine," she said, taking Lindsey into her arms and hugging her close, "what happened to you today, Honey?" The worry lines etched into Olivia's brow made her look momentarily every bit her age.

"Oh, Mother," there is nothing whatsoever to worry about," Lindsey paused, looking directly into her mother's eyes, "unless finding out your going to be a grandmother upsets you in any way."

Kevin nearly had to cover his ears with his hands to protect his hearing from Olivia's loud shrieks of delight. His mother–in–law threw her arms around his neck and hugged him so tight, he felt his eyes were in danger of popping out of their sockets. Seeing his wife's happiness as her mother's tears of delight streamed down her face, Kevin decided it was almost worth losing both hearing and sight for.

"Lindsey, you've made me happier than I ever thought possible," sniffed Olivia, "and I think you should tell Garreth right away."

"Professor St. Germaine?" asked Lindsey, "why should I tell him right away?"

"Because he's going to be the baby's step–grandfather."

"Oh my God! Mother! I can't believe it! You're going to marry Professor St. Germaine!" Lindsey was beside herself with unadulterated joy. Her mother had been a widow for a very long time, and while no one could ever replace Lindsey's father, she knew her mother deserved any happiness and companionship that came her way. This day had turned out quite nicely indeed.

Lindsey was exhausted by the day's end and felt that she might finally be able to enjoy a good night's sleep. After stepping from the cleansing tube, and wishing fervently there was a bathing tub in Kevin's small apartment, she joined her husband on the air bed. Sleep came within moments, and Kevin smiled to himself when he heard his wife's even breathing.

At that moment Dr. Kevin Sanders felt more content and fulfilled than he had at any other time in his entire life. He was married to a beautiful and intelligent woman, he would be a father by the following Spring, and he actually liked his mother–in–law. Within minutes, he too had fallen into a deep and peaceful slumber.

It was dark, but the light was just ahead. Lindsey could hear her father speaking, but couldn't make out the words. There was someone else speaking as well, a voice she knew, as Lindsey struggled to force herself forward. Her legs felt heavy, each step a concerted effort, as she entered into the outskirts of the light.

"You involve yourself with things beyond your own comprehension!" The words were shouted as though many voices spoke at the same time, and Lindsey shuddered, huddling close to the edges of the darkness.

"I could not have known," was the simple response. It was her father's voice, the words spoken low, almost in a whisper. Lindsey forced herself from her crouched position and stood upright. She had to go to her father, to stand by him no matter what the cost.

He came from nowhere. One second, Lindsey had taken but half a step forward, and the next, the acrimonious countenance of King Tutankhamun stood but inches from her. Had she completed the step, she'd have walked directly into his muscled physique.

"And you! You condescending weakling!" The voices emanating from the enraged king when he spoke were almost physically painful to hear. "You are just as guilty!" he roared but inches from her face.

Lindsey closed her eyes, unable to look at the face of this man who frightened her to the core of her being. Tears fell from her lowered lashes and ran in warm rivulets down her cheeks.

"In all of your arrogance, did you think you could sweetly talk me into handing you the power that is rightfully mine!" The dim glow behind him glistened off the gold of his armbands, reflecting bright shards of light across Tut's angry countenance.

Lindsey would have fallen to the floor, but it was then that she realized she was no longer standing on her own power. Daring to open her eyes and look down, she found that her body had levitated several inches from the ground, her feet dangling in mid air.

"Do not hurt her husband." The gentle voice of Ankhesenamun came from nowhere and everywhere at the same time.

Again Lindsey opened her eyes and saw to her amazement that Ankhesenamun, richly garbed in a gown Lindsey had never seen before, stood slightly behind the angry king.

In a flash, Tutankhamun turned his full wrath on the stunning Egyptian princess, and Lindsey's feet hit the stone floor. Intense, indescribable fear overwhelmed her, and she felt as though her body were trapped in a vise.

"I have told you before," boomed the legion of voices that sprang forth from Tutankhamun, as he addressed the princess, "do not interfere, and do not speak for me!"

Lindsey looked toward her father, only a few yards away from her. Moving slowly, so as not to attract attention from the enraged king, Lindsey scooted forward on all fours toward her father.

"Our time to use the knowledge has come and gone Tutankhamun!" returned Ankhesenamun's voice, "they have found the library and it is their right to use the power now! It was written! We must help them. You must help them." Though still soft, her words seemed somehow magnified when she spoke, as were Tut's.

Finally, reaching her father, Lindsey thought for a moment that he might disappear from her sight, but when she extended her hand to him, he enfolded her into his arms. "I am so sorry Lindsey," his voice caught in his throat. "Can you ever forgive me for making you a part of this?"

"Oh, Father," sobbed Lindsey, "I miss you so much, and I'm so frightened of him. We have to get away from here. Come with me now." Lindsey pulled on her father's arm and he followed her toward the opening through which she had come in. Hugging the wall with the irate king's back to them, Lindsey and her father made their way to the entry door and exited the room, away from the light; away from the still booming voice of Tutankhamun

"How dare you continually speak for me!" his voice thundered. "You are as insolent as you were over four thousand years ago, and I'll tolerate it no more now than I did then!"

"Be careful what you say," whispered Ankhesenamun, "Lindsey will know we remember."

As Lindsey and her father disappeared further into the dark recesses of the tunnel, she struggled to remember where she had heard those very same words spoken.

"She will know nothing more than I wish for her to know!"

Lindsey's legs felt like lead, she wanted to run, wanted to get her father as far away from this place as possible. The words of the Egyptian king and princess were still right behind them, as thought there was no distance between them at all.

"It is not necessary for anyone to know, Tutankhamun, you said that yourself," Ankhesenamun's voice was growing agitated. "They already know of the pyramids true purpose!"

Ahead of her, Lindsey saw her father begin to ascend a dimly lit stairwell that had not been there before. "No father, no!" screamed Lindsey, "Do not go that way! Stop!" She screamed with all her might, but it was too late, her father had reached the top step just as the staircase caved in, and he disappeared from her view.

"Nooo!" screamed Lindsey, "Dad…come back!" She dropped to the cold stone floor and sobbed. She had lost him again; her father was gone.

"They will misuse it!" she heard the thunderous voice of Tutankhamun shout out.

"As you did once?" was the soft reply.

"Lindsey!" Kevin shook his wife in an attempt to wake her from an obvious nightmare, her chilling scream having awoken him from a sound sleep, "Lindsey, Honey, wake up!"

"Kevin?" Struggling up from the sea of fog that seemed to surround her like a shroud, Lindsey fought to focus on her husband.

"You had another nightmare, Linds." The worry was apparent in Kevin's voice, as he held his wife close. "What were you dreaming about?" he asked gently.

"My father," Lindsey choked out, nearly sobbing "My father was there and I was trying to get him away from King Tutankhamun."

"Oh, Honey," soothed Kevin, "I think this project is becoming a little too much on you. I think maybe we should ask St. Germaine to give you a few days off to rest."

"No," came Lindsey's immediate reply, "I am needed now more than ever."

"Why, Lindsey?" prodded Kevin. "Why are you needed there now more than ever?"

"I don't know. I just am." With these last words, Lindsey's eyes closed, and Kevin realized she had fallen back to sleep. He hoped that this time, she would sleep more peacefully.

Lying awake for over an hour, Kevin found himself dwelling more and more on his wife's physiological condition. He had hoped that discovering her pregnancy might somehow put an end to her restless nights and constant fatigue. Perhaps this was all simply the result of her physical condition, but still, something didn't seem quite right, and it didn't set well with Kevin at all.

"Are you sure you feel up to working today, Linds?" asked Kevin, as he and his wife underwent the required sterilization process, prior to entering the main lab area at IBAT.

"I'm fine, Kevin. Really," she responded, "I feel great. It was a bad dream, nothing more."

"Well I want you to link to me immediately if you start to feel faint again," he chided gently, "and take good care of our baby."

Lindsey beamed and blew her husband a gentle kiss as she made her way to Ankhesenamun and Tut's domicile. She remembered the conversation the two had been engaged in yesterday, just before she lost consciousness. It had all come back to her clearly in the dream, every word the two had spoken. They remembered their original lives and she was sure of that now, regardless of what the government test results revealed.

Determined to find out once and for all what was going on, Lindsey swallowed hard, and entered the outer chamber that had served as a schoolroom for many months. There on one of the comfort chairs sat Professor St. Germaine, speaking with both Tut and Ankhesenamun. He looked up when Lindsey entered and rose to his feet immediately.

"Lindsey," he greeted, "I didn't expect you to come in today. How are you feeling?" His concern was genuine and Lindsey could see the worry in his eyes.

"Oh, much better," was her honest reply. She looked past the tall man to see Tutankhamun watching her with his sharp, black eyes.

"Listen," Lindsey almost whispered, "could I talk to you for just a moment in your office?"

"Why of course, my Dear," replied St. Germaine, as he led her out of the room and down the hallway to his office.

"Firstly," began Lindsey, once the door had closed behind them, "I understand congratulations are in order. Mother told me last night that you two are going to be married, and I wanted you to know I couldn't be happier."

"Thank you Lindsey," replied St. Germaine, the gap between his front teeth becoming more prominent when he smiled. "It means a lot to me to know that we have your complete blessing. Your mother has told me how close you were to your father, and I was a bit concerned that you might not be accepting of our marriage." Garreth found that he was already beginning to feel the stirrings of fatherly love toward Lindsey. Had he ever had children of his own blood, he would very much liked to have a daughter like her. "I had dinner with your mother just last night you know, and she said you had something you wanted to tell me. Was that it?"

"Not exactly," Lindsey grinned in return, "I just wanted to tell you that you're actually getting a package deal."

"A what?"

"A package deal," repeated Lindsey, "you're going to get a wife and a grand–child all within a couple months' time."

St. Germaine was elated, and took his soon–to–be stepdaughter in his huge arms, hugging her gently. "I am truly a happy and fulfilled man!" he exclaimed honestly.

"I would like to ask just a tiny favor from you," Lindsey began, as she stood back and looked up into the professor's still–smiling face.

"Anything," he replied without hesitation, "would you like to take a few days off to spend with Kevin in Atlantica?"

"Oh, thank you so much for the offer, it sounds wonderful, but I realize the project is too close to completion for Kevin or I either one to take any time off just now."

"We could make arrangements," offered St. Germaine, "for the sake of your health."

Lindsey couldn't help but smile in response, "Truly, thank you very much for the offer, but I really feel that I need to continue my involvement in the project. What I'd like for you to do is to find some way to remove Tutankhamun from their domicile for a bit, so I can speak with Ankhesenamun alone."

"I certainly don't think that would be a problem," replied the professor, "but why do you feel it necessary to speak with the girl alone? Has Tut caused you a problem in any way?"

"No," Lindsey lied, "I just have a feeling that I can glean a great deal more from her than I can from him. It almost seems as though Ankhesenamun can't speak freely in his presence, and I still believe the two of them remember who they were." Lindsey couldn't explain the nightmare she'd had, and the words that had come back to her, "I honestly don't know how much of the true purpose of the project I told them yesterday before I fainted."

"I briefed them both just this morning," replied St. Germaine, "just before you entered the room a few moments ago. As I said, I didn't expect to see you today."

"How did they take it?"

"The news?" asked the professor. Upon Lindsey's nod of assent, he continued, "well Tut took the news without a word," he advised, "and the girl just smiled and nodded, saying that they would help in any way they could."

"Good," Lindsey nodded again, "I would still like to speak with her alone."

"Done," replied St. Germaine, "I'm sure I can find a way to keep the boy busy for a while, but I do want you to share any information you may ascertain with me."

"Of course," she replied.

Lindsey had no sooner returned to the clones' domicile, and sat down across from Tut and Ankhesenamun, when a young guard entered and advised that Tutankhamun was required in the lab for acceleration–testing.

"I have undergone the testing but yesterday," returned the young man replied testily.

"It seems further tests are required," responded the guard, "I have been instructed to escort you to the lab."

Shooting a look of contempt toward Lindsey and one of warning toward Ankhesenamun, Tut rose and followed the guard from the room.

"I know the two of you remember who you were, Ankhesenamun," stated Lindsey bluntly, "and I don't know why you feel it necessary to keep that fact from me."

The young Egyptian woman lowered her lashes and spoke softly, "We remember nothing more than what we have learned from you, Lindsey."

"No."

The single word brought the girl's eyes up to meet Lindsey's. "Why do you speak in the negative?" she asked, "I have told you that we do not remember."

"You mean Tutankhamun told you not to tell me you remember, am I right? Just like he told you not to speak of your memories to the team sent in by the government to conduct the tests last week. I am right aren't I?" Lindsey paused, and searched the younger woman's face for a sign of the truth.

Again, the girl lowered her dark eyes, but then raised them almost immediately to meet Lindsey's light blue ones, "It does not feel right to tell you an untruth," she admitted, "you have been a friend to me and I care for you."

"I care for you too, Ankhesenamun," Lindsey rose and sat back down next to the beautiful young woman. The girl's blunt–cut shoulder length hair was styled in the popular ancient Egyptian manner, with tiny braids running through it from root to end. Her soft, brown eyes encircled with the dark kohl made her look far older than her equivalent age of sixteen.

"Has he come to you in your dreams?" asked Ankhesenamun.

A chill coursed down Lindsey's spine, "How do you know this?" she asked, almost holding her breath for the younger woman's response.

"He comes to me in mine," was her simple answer.

"How?" questioned Lindsey, "how does he do this? Was he able to do it before, in your original lives?"

"Not at first," replied Ankhesenamun, "not until after he summoned the others."

"The others?" questioned Lindsey.

"The gods," she replied, her darkened eyes darting about the room, as though expecting Tut to appear at any given moment, "he broke the law of Amun Ra, and used the pyramid in an attempt to call upon the Annuaki."

"I have heard of the Annuaki," said Lindsey, almost to herself, "Thad and Trent spoke of them, and of Tut's misuse of the pyramid. But why, and how did he do it?"

"The Annuaki had been coming and going from this planet since the beginning of time itself," explained Ankhesenamun. "They set forth the laws by which the people of Earth lived, and offered us protection against other cosmic travelers who might seek to make the earth their own. The Egyptian Kings of Egypt had the blood of the Annuaki in their veins, lending them the position of demi–gods among our people. It was Amun Ra himself who I was truly in love with."

"Amun Ra?" questioned Lindsey incredulously, "you mean

you were in love with the Sun–God, Amun Ra?"

"Yes," replied Ankhesenamun earnestly, "and he loved me too. At that time, the Annuaki were the 'peace–keepers' of the universe. Whenever a planet or people have been threatened, it was the Annuaki who stood against that threat."

"Sort of like cosmic police?" questioned Lindsey.

"Something like that," answered the young woman, "for the most part, the Annuaki had stopped visiting the earth unless specifically needed. The pharaohs ruled in the name of the gods and through their authority, so the Annuaki were not needed on earth. They had returned to their own home planet, with the promise that they would return periodically. They did return right after my marriage to Tutankhamun, but all was well at that time. Unfortunately, not for long," finished Ankhesenamun, her eyes downcast sadly.

"Why," asked Lindsey, "what happened?"

"Well, at first," began Ankhesenamun, "I was pleased about my marriage to Tutankhamun, as my father, Akhenaten had been taking my sisters and I to his bed from our earliest memories. I despised his touch, and although my mother, the Queen Nefertiti, was not pleased with my father's insatiable lust, she loved him so greatly that she would turn her eyes and heart away from the truth. I became pregnant with my father's child when I was no more than twelve, and bore a female who I named Princess Ankhesenpaaten Tasherit, but my mother, considering the child an abomination, had her secreted away and I never saw her again." A shadow of sadness crossed the young woman's face as she continued, "when my sister Meritaten died, the responsibility of marrying her husband, Smenkhkare fell to me. I did not like him, and did not trust him, but I performed the duty of my position and married him. When Smenkhkare died not long afterward, he was succeeded by his then eight–year–old brother, the King Tutankhamun. Again, my position dictated that I marry the boy, and when he was in his tenth year and I in my thirteenth, we were wed. This time however, I was pleased about the union."

"You wanted to marry a ten–year–old boy?" asked Lindsey.

"He was quite handsome, even at ten," smiled Ankhesenamun, "and promised to be even more handsome with time. He seemed gentle and kind, and in truth he was, until he became older and his position as King of Egypt went to his head. I think he started believing he was himself a god, even though his original bloodline connection was by then, well diluted. We began to quarrel violently when Tutankhamun reached manhood. He blamed me for my inability to provide him with heirs, in spite of the fact that he used my body most urgently several times every day in an attempt to get me with child. He made certain that all the pictorials of us together were drawn to depict a married couple enjoying wedded bliss. It was not so," the almond–eyed beauty lowered her head and a momentary sadness crossed her face, "he was vain and spiteful, and every day I spent with him was miserable."

"What led him to misuse the pyramid, Ankhesenamun?" asked Lindsey.

"I am sorry to speak for so long without answering your question, but you must know these things to fully understand the course of events," explained the dark eyed girl.

"No, I apologize for interrupting," responded Lindsey, "please do continue."

"Several years after my marriage to Tutankhamun, the god Amun Ra, whose given name is Emmesharra, visited Egypt with an envoy from Orion. They transported through the pyramid and one day simply appeared seemingly from nowhere."

Lindsey listened intently, remembering the name of 'Emmesharra' having been spoken by Trent and Thad.

"I had never met Emmesharra before," continued Ankhesenamun, "but I knew the moment our eyes met that I would love him for all eternity. I had never before or since, met a more handsome man, nor one who can love so intensely."

"And did Emmesharra feel the same," queried Lindsey.

"Oh, yes," replied Ankhesenamun, "he felt the very same way." Her eyes took on a distant, almost dreamy quality that Lindsey much preferred over the girl's sad countenance of a moment before.

"How did you keep this from Tut?" asked Lindsey. She noted the momentary smirk on Ankhesenamun's face.

"He hates to be called that you know," she smiled, "but to

answer your question, I think he knew the moment I did. The attraction between Emmesharra and myself was a tangible, almost electric feeling that I believe Tutankhamun sensed from the beginning. He dared say nothing of course, but his dislike of me soon grew into hatred. When I became pregnant with Emmesharra's children, I thought Tutankhamun would kill me."

"You what!" exclaimed Lindsey. "You got pregnant with Emmesharra's children?" her astonishment was so clearly apparent that Ankhesenamun almost laughed out loud.

"Please understand Lindsey, that Emmesharra and I loved one another beyond description. Can you imagine what it felt like to be loved by a god, who was himself worshipped by nearly all of Egypt?"

Lindsey was taken aback by the reality of what the girl was telling her. For the god Amun Ra to fall in love with a mortal woman was a possibility she would never even have considered. "What happened when you bore his children, and what became of them?" she asked.

"They were stillborn," answered Ankhesenamun sadly. "You must understand that Emmesharra, was a direct descendent of a Jupitarian Angel. He was born a god, and will never die. The Jupitarian's were a race of what we on earth considered to be giants. Emmesharra himself is nearly seven feet tall, and I am but a small woman. The children that grew within me grew too fast and too large, and had they not died, I would have. To save face, Tutankhamun publicly recognized the infants as his own and had them mummified. In keeping with Egyptian custom, their corpses were placed in his tomb with him when he died."

"Ah, yes. I knew that there were two mummified, infant corpses found in his tomb, but I assumed, as did the rest of the world, that Tut was their father. "And speaking of which," blurted Lindsey, "how did King Tut die? That has been a mystery for several hundred years now."

"That I do not know." Ankhesenamun shook her head slowly as she spoke, "Tutankhamun began to fall ill in his eighteenth year. He suffered from constant headaches and a sick stomach, but the physicians could never seem to find the root of his illness. They administered many remedies that may or may not have prolonged his life for a brief time, but shortly after his nineteenth year, he died. Many suspected he had been murdered, but no one really knew for certain, not even I."

"But he attempted to harness and utilize the power of the pyramid before he died?" asked Lindsey.

"Yes," affirmed Ankhesenamun, "much to my heart's dismay, Emmesharra and his envoy could not remain on the earth for long. They only came to check on our progress periodically, and after a short three months, they returned to the pyramid, and from there, to the stars. Before leaving however, Emmesharra presented me with an amulet, the one you found buried with me, and told me that in time of emergency, I could place the amulet on the table in what later became the Great Library Of Knowledge, and summon him. When placed just so, the amulet acts as a link to the Orion Nebula, and can bring forth the Annuaki. Emmesharra cautioned that the amulet was not to be used lightly, and only in time of great emergency or catastrophe."

"Speaking of the amulet being buried with you, Ankhesenamun," said Lindsey thoughtfully, "why in the world were you buried in the Takla Makan desert in the first place?"

Ankhesenamun smiled, "I was wondering how long it would take you to ask me that question. To answer it," she paused briefly, a sad smile forming on her full lips; "it was because during my life with Emmesharra, I befriended another woman from earth who's people had migrated to China during the time of my original life as the Princess Ankhesenamun. Kishara too, had fallen in love with a descendent of the angels and had vowed to stay with him for the rest of her life. As the descendants of the angels do not die, and humans do, she had decided early on that when her life ceased, she wished to be returned to earth and buried with her people. I, on the other hand," sighed Ankhesenamun heavily, "had no wish to be buried with mine, and upon my death, Emmesharra returned me to earth and buried me next to Kishara, with the amulet he had given me."

"But Tut found the amulet before he died, and tried to use it himself?" questioned Lindsey, "is that what happened?"

"Not exactly," responded Ankhesenamun, "but you're close. To be honest, I secreted the amulet away, and I do not believe

Tutankhamun knew of its existence. Though he did know that the power within the pyramid was purposely designed to be both harnessed and channeled by the use of the golden ark. As he became more and more ill, he also seemed to become almost petrified of the thought of dying. Were he to die childless, he knew that the direct male bloodline of the 18th Dynasty was extinguished for all time. Tutankhamun felt that if he were to summon Amun Ra, the god could make him well again."

"Well, I suppose I could understand that," reasoned Lindsey.

"But you know our culture well enough to know that we look at death as a part of life, a pre–ordained part of life that cannot be denied or altered. Amun Ra himself handed down these dictates. If King Tutankhamun were meant to die, then it was his destiny to do so. His attempt to summon the gods to free him from his illness was not in keeping with our teachings or beliefs, and made him nothing less than a coward. This is why I did not offer to use the amulet."

"So did Tut have an ark built?" Lindsey was growing more and more fascinated with Ankhesenamun's recounting of events that occurred hundreds of years ago, but still remained as fresh in the girl's mind as they had been at the time of their occurrence.

"Tutankhamun had the ark constructed and took it to the transport room. The ark worked, but not as he had planned."

"What happened," questioned Lindsey, practically on the edge of her seat.

"The Annuaki did not come."

"But I thought you said it worked."

"It worked, but the Annuaki did not come."

"Then how can you say that it worked?" Lindsey was becoming confused.

"Because although the Annuaki did not come, the Utukki did."

"The Utukki?" Lindsey knew she sounded like an echo, but the information she was hearing was truly history, and she did not want to miss a word.

"Descendants of the entity Christian's refer to as the fallen angel, Satan."

"You can't be serious!" exclaimed Lindsey incredulously.

"I am quite serious," replied Ankhesenamun. "You see, I followed Tutankhamun to the transport room, part of me hoping against hope that what he was attempting would not work, and part of me praying that it would. I was frightened to death that misusing the power so could have horrendous repercussions, but at the same time, if there was even the smallest chance I might get to see Emmesharra again, I couldn't stand the thought of missing it."

"What happened when the Utukki arrived instead?" asked Lindsey, as she searched Ankhesenamun's eyes for answers to questions she never even knew existed.

"It was the most frightening experience of my life." The dark haired beauty closed her eyes, but Lindsey could see the tears that were forming in the corners.

"I'm sorry to ask you to relive things that were obviously so unpleasant to you, Ankhesenamun, but truly, this information could be of the utmost importance to the safety and continuation of this entire planet."

"I understand Lindsey, and I will tell you the things you need to know, but for my own piece of mind, I must leave out certain details that are simply far too painful to be re–lived. I hope you understand," replied the young woman. At Lindsey's nod, she continued, "the Utukki are what could only be described as a reptilian culture. They walk upright and have the same basic body structure as we do, but there skin looks and feels like that of a reptile. Their eyes and tongues are between that of humans and snakes, and they are evil incarnate. It was primarily the Utukki that Emmesharra and his angels protected other races from."

"Did Tut attempt to interact with these monsters?" asked Lindsey; her heart racing at the intensity of what she was hearing firsthand.

"He had no choice," responded Ankhesenamun, "he was in the room when they arrived, and though he was every bit as frightened as I was, he was also very ill, and his need for life was greater than his fear of the Utukki. He told them why he had summoned them, told them that he was ill and did not want to die. They laughed at him and threw him to the floor, then turned and headed straight for me."

"Oh my God!" exclaimed Lindsey, the goose bumps rising on her arms at the thought.

"There were seven of them, and I will never know how they knew I was hiding just out of their view, but they did; as though they sensed my presence all along. They all used me violently, and I thought I would surely die. Before they transported back to whatever hell they came from, they threw an amulet at Tutankhamun, who lay vomiting where they had thrown him. I believe it was an amulet that could be used to call them forth without the ark, though why anyone would want to contact them intentionally is beyond me. I know that Tutankhamun took the amulet, but I never saw it again. From that day until the day of his death, I hated him with an intensity I never knew I possessed."

"Did you not use the amulet from Emmesharra then to summon him?" asked Lindsey, certain that she would have done so with all due haste.

"No," was Ankhesenamun's solemn reply, "I had been injured, but the physicians were able to treat me, and though they were never told of the actual circumstances, they were sworn to secrecy under the threat of death. My shame knew no bounds, and I could not face Emmesharra with what had happened. Within two months, Tutankhamun died, leaving me a twenty–two year old widow, and the last surviving member of the House of Thebes. I had outlived my entire immediate family, and the throne of Egypt was vacant for the first time in two hundred and fifty years. As the Royal Heiress, I would confer Pharaonic authority to my next husband, which presented yet another problem."

"Finding a suitable husband," interjected Lindsey, completing Ankhesenamun's train of thought.

"Exactly," answered Ankhesenamun with pursed lips, as she remembered another time and place, "the only real candidate at the time was the Vizier Aye, who was well into his seventies, and my great–uncle. He had no desire to rule however, and even had he wished to, he was far too old to have ruled for long."

"Which would have left you back at square one," completed Lindsey.

"Yes," confirmed the sad faced young woman, "but I chose him nonetheless. The other alternative was Horemheb, who felt that the god, Amun Ra should be replaced by the god, Aten, the same God my father worshipped. In truth, it was Tutankhamun who restored Amun Ra as the rightful god of Egypt in the eyes of the people you know." At Lindsey's nod of assent, the girl continued." I tried to find another husband by sending word to King Suppiluliumas and begging him to send one of his sons to become my mate and rule at my side. But his son was killed on his way to join with me, and I had no choice but to marry Ay."

"Oh Ankhesenamun," signed Lindsey, "I know so much of what you say from our history books, but it is so very different to hear these accounts first hand. What a nightmare it must have been for you."

"It was a sorrowful time for me," replied Ankhesenamun honestly, "Ay was frail and ill most of the time. He was too weak to rule, and by then, so was I. I knew that I was of no use to the people of Egypt, and finally, out of desperation and the sheer need to extricate myself from the hell that had become my life, I used the amulet and summoned Emmesharra."

Lindsey held her breath, clinging to every word of Ankhesenamun's recounting of a story never before heard by anyone on earth.

"At first, I didn't believe the amulet had worked," the girl continued, "I had followed Emmesharra's instructions, but nothing happened. With my heart heavy in my breast, I turned to leave, but a bright flash of light stopped me, and I suddenly felt as though the air was being drawn from my lungs. I turned back around, and there he stood."

Lindsey closed her eyes, trying to imagine what it must have been like; standing before the sun god, Amun Rah himself, within the confines of the oldest and most magical structure in the world. She listened intently as Ankhesenamun continued, and hung on to her every word when she did.

"When I told Emmesharra what Tutankhamun had done, and what had happened to me at the hands of the Utukki, he went livid with anger. I waited as he and his emissary of angels gathered all the information ever written about the power of the pyramids, and all other secrets of the planet. Then I watched as those scrolls and tablets were laid out inside the transport room. Before my very eyes, and in a manner most unexplainable, I watched as the stone walls were covered with gold and etched with hieroglyphic engravings. Emmesharra set in place what you would call the elevator platform, and then sealed the tomb from the inside. He explained to me that should man ever discover the location of the library and find a way to harness the power of the pyramids, the Annuaki would return and assist mankind in achieving the next level of knowledge. If misused however, the result would undoubtedly be the total destruction of the planet earth. Emmesharra said that this was in keeping with the command of God himself. I left with him then, and stayed at his side until the day I died."

"Oh, Ankhesenamun, sighed Lindsey, "I had no idea what you had truly gone through," she paused and shook her head, "no one did. What you have shared with me is a part of our history unknown to us completely. Did you ask Amun Ra to take you with him?" she asked.

"Oh, no," replied Ankhesenamun, with a look of surprise on her face, "I could never have been so presumptuous as that. I was hopeful only that Emmesharra could place me somewhere far away from Egypt itself. The memories there were simply far too painful for me to go on living a normal life, had a normal life even been an option. No, I did not ask him," she repeated, and then smiled broadly, "which is why there are no words to relay how happy and relieved I was when Emmesharra asked me to leave with him!"

"I'm certainly glad he did," affirmed Lindsey, "what was it like to live with him? Where did you live?" It seemed that every question brought forth yet another question, and Lindsey wasn't quite sure what to ask first.

"It was a place that can only be experienced, but I do not believe it could be described," was Ankhesenamun's cryptic reply.

It was then that the two women heard movement in the hallway just outside the door, and the dark young beauty stopped speaking in mid–sentence.

"There is nothing to worry about," Lindsey assured her, "he has no way of knowing what you and I have been discussing."

"Oh, he'll know," assured Ankhesenamun, "he'll know."

Chapter Thirteen

"So it doesn't seem that Tut's assistance is required nearly as much as Ankhesenamun's is," finished Lindsey, after having just relayed her conversation with the young, Egyptian clone to St. Germaine and Kevin.

She had linked to her husband first; asking him to meet her in Professor St. Germaine's office, where they had both arrived at the same instant. The professor sat at his desk, leaning forward in his chair, his anticipation at hearing the information Lindsey had to share, was evident in his questioning look.

Lindsey felt almost weak from the volume of knowledge she had gleaned from Ankhesenamun, and as she stood next to Kevin, who was still slightly out of breath from his sprint to St. Germaine's office, she wasn't even sure she knew where to begin. She herself had not even had time to fully comprehend the depth, scope and breadth of where this information might lead. Now in the security of the sparsely furnished, stark, white room, she found that she was far too exhilarated to even sit down. Taking a deep breath, Lindsey attempted to recount, in as much detail as possible, all the things Ankhesenamun had shared with her earlier.

Professor St. Germaine let out a low whistle through the gap in his front teeth; "This is certainly far more than I ever expected to hear."

"Well, it's certainly against the laws of physics," interjected Kevin. "Apparently, the information we have always accepted as scientific truths, have been nothing more than scientific conjecture." He ran his hand through his blonde hair and shook his head slowly.

"I'm just not certain how much of the information Ankhesenamun shared with me should be shared with the respective government entities involved here," said Lindsey. "If we simply utilize Ankhesenamun and her amulet in place of the human–clone, the Annuaki will be summoned forth, and the governments may interact with them accordingly."

"I believe you may be right, Lindsey," replied Professor St. Germaine, as he sat back further in his office chair and intertwined his fingers, "these Utukki don't sound like a race the earth should be involved with in any manner. Knowing some of the bizarre decisions our government has made in the past, I don't know that I would want to relay this information to them. God only knows what they might decide to do with that bit of knowledge."

"I'm so glad you agree," sighed Lindsey, "that was certainly my concern as well."

"This amulet that was given to Tut by the Utukki was never found in his burial chamber was it?" queried Kevin.

"No," answered Lindsey, "Ankhesenamun's recounting was the first I've ever heard of any such amulet."

"Well," interjected St. Germaine, "let's just hope it's never found."

"Amen to that," responded Kevin, his hands jammed into the pockets of his lab coat. He didn't like any of what he was hearing, and he certainly wasn't comfortable with his wife spending any length of time with the clone of King Tutankhamun. The boy sounded like he could be quite evil–tempered. Kevin knew one thing for certain, if the young man ever laid a hand on Lindsey, Kevin would personally send him back where he'd come from.

"You do realize," intoned St. Germaine in a low voice, "that what we are discussing here could be considered treason against our country."

"How so?" questioned Kevin, with raised brows.

"We have just agreed to purposely withhold information and facts relative to this project from the very government who is responsible for it. We will have to keep what we know to ourselves and speak of it to no one else."

"Agreed," stated Kevin firmly.

"You certainly have my word," affirmed Lindsey, "I am worried about Ankhesenamun as it is. She seemed quite frightened that Tut would somehow know what she had spoken to me about, and retaliate against her in some way."

"Well, I for one don't particularly care much for this business of the boy being able to invade people's dreams," stated Kevin flatly, the look on his face attesting to the depth in which this bothered him.

"Ankhesenamun said he was not able to do so until after his

encounter with the Utukki. Apparently, it left him with some sort of strange psychic ability."

"Personally," interjected the professor, "I know the boy is not being honest when we conduct the regular psychological examinations. I have always felt that there is more to this young man than meets the eye. I think it would be a good idea to keep a very close watch on him from this point on."

"An excellent idea indeed," agreed Kevin, with a glance at his wife. He was feeling especially protective of Lindsey now that she carried their child, and his blood almost boiled at the thought of her even being in the presence of the arrogant, young Tut.

"Perhaps I should check in on Ankhesenamun just to make certain that she hasn't had any problems with Tut since we spoke," offered Lindsey.

"Well, their sleeping areas are completely separate, so she certainly doesn't have to interact with him should she choose not to. And of course, their every movement has been watched constantly through the monitoring system. Should he attempt to harm her in any way, our security personnel would intervene instantly."

"It does make me feel a little more comfortable to know that," replied Lindsey, "but I think the young Tutankhamun has more subtle ways of extracting revenge."

"Listen, Lindsey," I just don't feel comfortable with you around that guy after everything I've heard." He put his hand up slightly as Lindsey started to interrupt him, "I realize it is your job, and I would never presume to try to change you or your work ethic in any manner, I just worry about you, Honey." His last words were spoken softly, and Lindsey knew that he truly had every right to be concerned.

"He's right you know, Lindsey," spoke in St. Germaine, "at this point, we really don't know what the young man is capable of." The professor rose from his chair and straightened to his full height. Looking down on his soon–to–be stepdaughter, he implored her, "Please do be careful," he said earnestly, "I would never forgive myself if anything happened to you, and what's more," he paused, "your mother would never forgive me."

"I promise to take every precaution when Tut is anywhere near me," replied Lindsey solemnly.

"I think it might be a good idea to beef up security a bit around their compound just in case," said St. Germaine thoughtfully, with a look toward Kevin. The younger man's nod affirmed his agreement.

As Lindsey neared the entrance to Tut and Ankhesenamun's domicile, she noted two security officers in the hallway not far from the door. It seemed that Professor St. Germaine had wasted no time in posting additional security as a precautionary measure.

Within a foot or so from the door itself, Lindsey thought she heard what sounded like a number of voices speaking at the same time. As the panel slid open to allow her entrance however, she saw only Tut and Ankhesenamun sitting across from one another in the very chairs she and the young girl had occupied earlier. Whatever conversation had been taking place prior to Lindsey's entrance, ceased abruptly.

"You look well, Dr. Larimer," purred Tut, the softness in his voice not quite reaching his slightly narrowed, black eyes, "It seems that being with child suits you."

"And just how is it that you are aware of my personal condition?" questioned Lindsey.

"Why it literally radiates from you Dr. Larimer," stated Tut softly, as he rose and walked slowly toward her.

Lindsey was instantly uncomfortable with his nearness, but vowed not to flinch so much as a muscle as he approached to within inches of her.

"I have always found women in the family way to be most attractive," he said huskily, never removing his eyes from her own, "except for that one," he fairly spat, as he turned slightly to indicate Ankhesenamun.

Lindsey could feel his breath against her skin, and it seemed he had grown another couple of inches, for she found herself craning her neck to meet his eyes. "Thank you for sharing that bit of information with me," she replied with thinly veiled sarcasm, "and please remember to address me as Dr. Sanders," she reminded him.

"There is much more I could share with you Dr. Sanders," his voice deepened as he almost whispered his words, "if you would but follow me to my private quarters."

Lindsey knew she should be outraged as the full meaning of his words sank in, she should push him from her and tell him he was entirely out of line. She should, but for some reason, his words brought a shiver to her and a strange, warm sensation began to unfold in the pit of her stomach.

"Tutankhamun!" Ankhesenamun's voice cut through Lindsey's faltering senses, bringing her out of her momentary lapse.

The young man spun around and glared at his female counterpart, "Stay out of it woman, it is not of your concern."

"Lindsey is my friend, so it is very much my concern," was her matter–of–fact reply.

"I merely came by to let you know that more garments have been completed and will be delivered to you tomorrow," said Lindsey, with a forced lightheartedness she did not truly feel.

"Well thank you for sharing that important information," replied Tut facetiously, "perhaps you could return and share additional information with me later." His sly smile and the look in his eyes made it clear to Lindsey exactly what it was this assuming young man wanted to share with her.

Though Ankhesenamun's verbal intervention had broken whatever momentary, and bizarre hold Tut had over Lindsey, the tension between the two seemed almost tangible.

"Dr. Lindsey Sanders, please report to Professor St. Germaine's office." The voice page was a welcome announcement, giving Lindsey an excuse to extricate herself from the presence of the pompous and frighteningly intense Tut.

"Ah, there you are," said Professor St. Germaine, as Lindsey entered the office she had left only a few minutes earlier, "please, have a seat and make yourself comfortable," he offered, motioning to one of the vacant chairs across from his desk.

Lindsey had no sooner sat down, when the door slid open and Kevin entered. "Weren't we here just a few moments ago," he joked, "or is it just me experiencing a moment of de–ja–vue?"

St. Germaine chuckled deep in his throat; "You two had no sooner left here when I received word that the respective governmental entities in charge are preparing for the final stage of the project."

"You mean they're ready to move on to the pyramids?" asked Kevin. He'd known it wouldn't be much longer before the final stages of the project were underway…before their work would come to fruition. Still, he couldn't ignore the sinking feeling that the outcome could ultimately be more than anyone had bargained for. Kevin glanced at his beautiful, young wife seated next to him. He didn't want her to be a part of this, didn't want Lindsey to be subjected to any form of danger, and this project had been dangerous from the very beginning. He also knew that there was nothing he could say or do to dissuade her from making the journey to Egypt.

"When, Professor St. Germaine?" asked Lindsey, "when will we be leaving?"

"Just as soon as the appropriate teams have been assembled," he replied, rubbing his temples as though to ward off an impending headache. "The government officials have decided they want to schedule the trip for November twelfth, the day our clones will become the equivalent of seventeen years of age."

"November twelfth!" echoed Lindsey, "but that's only a week away."

Kevin swallowed hard, the nagging feelings of trepidation he'd been experiencing were rapidly upgrading to all out fear, not for himself, but for the safety of the woman who had come to mean everything in the world to him.

"Apparently," sighed St. Germaine, "all the necessary preparations have been made, and the teams have been assembled and are being readied at this very moment. I think you'll both be pleased to know," he added with a slight smile, "that both Professor Farrier and Professor McRae will be part of the team actually entering the Library Of Knowledge, which it seems was agreed upon when they were initially approached to perform the translations." Professor St. Germaine chuckled softly as shook his head; "Those two know how to negotiate."

For reasons unknown to even himself, Kevin somehow felt slightly better knowing that the two men he and Lindsey had come to care about and trust would be present.

"Thad and Trent!" exclaimed Lindsey, "that's wonderful. I'm

sure they're both thrilled at the prospect. I can't wait to see them again." It was then that the thought struck her, "Will Kevin and I be part of that team?" she asked, almost holding her breath for St. Germaine's answer. Although Lindsey certainly shared Kevin's concerns about the adverse possibilities of the project, somewhere inside her, she knew she had to be a part of the outcome, had to be there to witness first hand the results of the project that had already changed her life in so many ways.

"You will be," was St. Germaine's half-hearted reply, "though I wish it were otherwise."

"That makes two of us," interjected Kevin, "God only knows what we might be getting involved in."

"I only wish I had been chosen as part of the team as well. I don't like the fact that I won't be there to help you watch out for Lindsey," replied the professor. Switching his worried gaze to his future daughter-in-law, he spoke to her directly, "If your mother had even the slightest inkling of the implications of this project, she'd kill me for allowing her daughter to be a part of it"

"Look you two," responded Lindsey with as stern a tone as she could muster, "I'm a big girl, and I can take care of myself quite well. I love you both dearly, and I sincerely appreciate your concern for my health and wellbeing, but I assure you, I'm quite capable of facing whatever comes." She only wished she felt as confident as her words made her sound.

"Of that I have no doubt," replied St. Germaine softly, "I would just feel a good deal better about the whole affair if I were there to keep an eye on you along with your husband."

"Speaking of which," responded Kevin, "why won't you be a part of the team, and how many of us from IBAT will be?"

"Well," responded St. Germaine, "aside from yourself, Lindsey, Ankhesenamun and Tut, Glenn will be the only other member of IBAT on the first team. Since you and he will be required to constantly check the accelerated growth process of the clones, and Lindsey is the only member of the project to have already entered the library, the three of you are absolutely necessary to the completion of the project. As the CEO of IBAT, my involvement has been much more indirect than your own, so naturally my presence is not required. I understand the remaining seven people that will comprise the first team have been selected by the Egyptian and US governments. There will be three teams of twelve individuals actually making the trip, but only the first team will enter the library. One team will remain on the landing just outside the library, and the third team will be stationed outside the pyramid itself."

"I wish you could be there with us," replied Lindsey honestly.

"Has Glen been told yet that he'll be part of the team entering the library?" asked Kevin.

"No, I'll be telling him shortly," answered St. Germaine, "he had a medical appointment this afternoon, but he's due back in the lab in an hour or so."

"Nothing serious, I hope," stated Kevin with a slight frown.

"No, I don't believe so," replied the CEO as he rose from his chair and stretched his large frame, "at least he didn't give me any reason to believe so when he asked for a few hours off," he added. "I imagine he'll be back soon, and I can tell him then. By the way," he said, as though on an afterthought, "I also want to invite the three of you to join me for dinner tonight. I've already asked your mother," he advised, addressing his future daughter-in-law, "so we won't be able to discuss anything about the project of course."

"I think that would be quite nice," answered Lindsey, her clear blue eyes confirming her sincerity, "I would enjoy a night out with my family."

"And some time away from the projected," echoed Kevin, as he and Lindsey rose from their seats and followed the older man to the door.

"Good, good," smiled St. Germaine, as the three stepped into the hallway. "Then I'm sure you'll be glad to hear that I've arranged for the two of you, and for Glen, to take a three-day leave starting tomorrow."

"Oh, Professor St. Germaine!" exclaimed Lindsey, "you are an incredible, wonderful man!"

"Here, here," seconded Kevin, "I could use some quality time with my wife."

"I thought you might feel that way," the professor grinned.

Fortunately, it was a weeknight, and Sal's wasn't terribly busy. Kevin and Lindsey had waited in the lounge with Professor St. Germaine and Olivia until Glen arrived.

Lindsey was the first to look up and see Glen stroll in through the front door, though she had to look twice to make certain it was he. Gone were the black–framed glasses that were forever traveling up and down the bridge of his nose, and the gray in his hair at his temples seemed to have fled with his spectacles. Instead, a younger and much more confident Glen made his way toward the awaiting group at the bar. Even his step seemed jauntier, so different from his usual rather shuffling gait. Lindsey smiled to herself. It seemed that being in love suited Glen quite well.

It didn't take the others long to notice the marked difference in the professor, but only Lindsey and Kevin knew the real reason for it.

"Well I must say, Glen," remarked St. Germaine, "it seems I should have given you a few hours off a long time ago. You look ten years younger!"

Glen smiled broadly, "I guess it was time for a change," he quipped.

Once seated at the elegantly set table that St. Germaine had reserved in advance, the five chatted amicably and ordered their respective meals from the extensive menu. Now and again, Lindsey noticed Glen's eyes darting about the restaurant, undoubtedly hoping to catch a glimpse of Sal.

"I just can't get over the change in you, Glen," remarked Olivia from across the large, round table with its pristine white tablecloth. "Whatever it is you've done, please do share your secret with the rest of us." Her tinkling laugh was infectious, and Glen nearly blushed at the continued compliments being directed his way. He was not a man accustomed to being complimented, with the exception of the praise he received for his work.

"Well," he offered, "I can only say that I finally decided to have a bit of minor eye surgery to correct my vision, and a little permanent color to scare away the gray. In truth, I wish I'd have had the surgery years ago. I didn't realize how much of a pain those glasses were until I got rid of them."

"It wasn't painful was it?" asked Kevin, "the surgery, I mean."

"Not at all," responded Glen, "as a matter of fact, the entire procedure took all of eight minutes, and was entirely painless. Like I said, I wish I'd have had it done a long time ago."

Olivia smiled broadly, "Now tell us the truth, Glen, have you met someone special that perhaps prompted you to make these magnificent changes?" Her eyes crinkled at the corners in anticipation of his response.

It was then that Sal appeared at the table, standing between Glen and Kevin. "Ah," he exclaimed, "it's good to have you all back again. I have warned the chef that if he does not please you with his culinary skills, he will be reduced to waiting tables!"

His comment elicited chuckles from his five guests. "I hope you like the recent changes we have made here in the dining hall." Looking up, he indicated the false night sky above, which had only been recently installed.

Until that moment, the group had been too busy chatting among themselves to notice, but following Sal's uplifted gaze, they observed immediately that the ceiling had been converted to a miniature replica of the milky way, complete with twinkling stars, and shooting comets.

"It's beautiful!" exclaimed Lindsey and her mother in unison.

"You've really outdone yourself," interjected St. Germaine, as he perused the sparking lights and tiny planets above them.

"Oh, but I'm not quite finished just yet," advised Sal, his lips stretching into a wide grin above his perfectly manicured mustache. "I plan to move all my Italiano memorabilia into the lounge area and convert the entire dining area into what I shall call the Cosmic Room. Of course, this will necessitate closing the restaurant portion for a week or so, but I think it will be worth it in the long run. I hear they're opening a theme restaurant just down the street," he said with a conspiratorial wink, "so naturally I have to keep up with the competition."

Professor St. Germaine laughed loudly, the gap between his two front teeth making him look almost boyish, "Well, never fear my good man, we would never patronize your competition!"

"In that case," laughed Sal in return, "your deserts will be on the house." It was then that he looked down and met Glen's eyes directly for the first time since he'd arrived at the table. The looks in his own brown eyes clearly stated that he liked what he saw; though he masked it almost immediately. "Glen, my friend," he stated with a warm smile, "I see you underwent the vision–correction process, and there is more face where those glasses used to be!"

Glen returned Sal's smile. He could tell Sal was truly pleased with his transformation, and the knowledge boosted his spirits even further.

"If you ask me," grinned Olivia broadly, "I think Glen has met a special woman."

Lindsey was glad she hadn't been taking a drink or chewing food, certain she would have choked. Kevin squeezed her hand slightly, and she knew he too was fighting off a grin.

Sal looked momentarily taken aback, but recovered quickly, and Glen seemed to be at a total loss for words with which to form a reply. Professor St. Germaine, always having been highly intuitive, did not fail to miss the look that passed between Sal and Glen. If his instincts were correct, such a situation could lead to a good deal of trouble.

"Well then," interjected the handsome Italian, "I shall have to return to the kitchen and check on the cook's progress. And I also wanted to let you know that I am now offering dinner entertainment seven nights a week, that will commence in about fifteen minutes. I do hope you all enjoy your meals, and I'll send over a complimentary bottle of wine." With another wide grin, and a slight bow, Sal left the table and made his way back toward the kitchen at the far end of the dining hall. Within moments, an attractive young woman wearing the 1940's garb exclusive to all the employees of Sal's, brought a large bottle of wine to the table.

Sal's choice of entertainment was by far and away some of the best to be offered, and consisted of a young Italian couple with flashing dark eyes, that sang haunting ballads of love found and of love lost, their voices blending in the most perfect harmony imaginable. The diners were clearly enthralled, so that even Kevin hardly noticed when Glen excused himself to use the restroom.

Once Glen had left the dining area and made his way to the

outer hall, he turned left and headed away from the restrooms and directly to Sal's private office. His attractive Italian counterpart was seated behind his large desk, but stood up immediately at the sight of Glen standing just inside the doorway.

"I wanted to see you if only for a minute," smiled Glen, as he strode softly across the richly appointed office.

"I'm glad you came," responded Sal, as he stepped into the circle of Glen's open arms and the two embraced warmly. Standing back slightly, he gazed wistfully at the enormous physical change in this man he had come to love with an intensity that even he would not have imagined possible. "You know," he said in almost a whisper, "I love you with or without your glasses and graying temples, but now that they're gone, you're even more incredibly handsome."

"I'm pleased that you approve," smiled Glen sincerely.

"Yes," grinned Sal in response, "I most certainly do, but now I don't know if I should kiss you or be jealous of you."

"Well I must say," chuckled Glen, as he reveled in the sincerity so evident in Sal's dark eyes, "I would rather have the kiss, especially in light of the fact that I'm going away for a few days and won't be able to contact you." He hated the crestfallen look he saw on Sal's face, but there was nothing he could do about it. Before meeting this very special man, Glen's job had filled his life and consumed every waking moment of his time. Now, he found himself wanting to spend far less time at the lab, and far more time with the handsome Sal.

"Is it your work that takes you away from me?" asked Sal softly.

"Unfortunately it is," replied Glen, "though were it for any other reason, I would ask you to accompany me."

"I will miss you while you're gone," said Sal, his long, dark eyelashes fanning his downcast lids, "but I know you said from the beginning that there would be times I would not see you for lengthy periods, so I can only wish you a safe and successful journey." Sal raised his eyes and mustered his best smile, but his heart seemed to have sunk a little lower in his chest.

"If things were different," smiled Glen almost sadly, "we could live together and see each other whenever we weren't working. I can't think of anything that would make me happier."

"Nor could I," agreed Sal, "nor could I."

"Well there you are!" exclaimed Olivia. "We were just about to send a search party for you."

Glen had arrived just as the young entertainers had finished a more lively and energetic number, to the rousing applause of the patrons. "Yes, it would seem that the entire restaurant is glad to see me back," he chuckled, as the applause died down around him.

Olivia giggled engagingly; "Well you missed a truly lively number just now. I think I may have worn a spot in the carpet from all the toe–tapping I did."

As their meals began arriving at the table, accompanied by yet another complimentary bottle of wine, St. Germaine apprised Olivia of the fact that Kevin, Lindsey and Glen had just been granted a three day leave of absence. After which the three would be out of town for a few weeks to work on a particular project.

"A three day leave of absence?" questioned Glen; his brows lifting like a child who had just received a coveted treat. "When did this happen?"

"We just learned of it this morning," chimed Lindsey, "and were most pleased I might add."

"And I think a couple of days in Atlantica would be most relaxing," intoned Kevin.

"Oh Kevin," beamed his clearly excited wife, "do you mean it? Can we go to the house in Atlantica?"

"Is after dinner too soon for you to start getting ready?" he grinned in response.

"Need you ask?"

Olivia and St. Germaine exchanged knowing grins, and both were pleased that the young married couple would be able to spend some quality time together. St. Germaine was the only person at the table to notice Glen's brief glance in the general direction of the kitchen and office area, and the momentary longing in his eyes. It was then that the professor knew his earlier impression had been correct. He hoped he was the only one who had picked up on what was clearly happening between Glen and the Italian Restaurateur. If knowledge of such a relationship were to become public, both young men would be sent to one of the prison stations that perpetually orbited the earth's atmosphere. All of Glen's training and knowledge would be wasted if such a thing were to happen, and he could only fervently hope that the two young men would be as discreet as possible.

Both Lindsey and Kevin were glad to see that Atlantica hadn't changed a bit since their last visit, and were greeted at the front door of their dwelling by the ever-pleasant Moira. It felt good to be back in their very own home again, and Lindsey wasted no time heading directly for the coveted seashell bathtub.

Kevin made his way straight to the back yard and had the lawn mowed and trimmed to perfection in less than fifteen minutes. After pausing momentarily to admire his handiwork, he decided to make use of the cleansing chamber just off the master bedroom. He wanted to make the best of the next three days with his wife, and mentally prepared an itinerary that included a trip to the Entertainment Center, as well as dinner and a wardrobe infusion for both he and Lindsey. In spite of the many plans he was even now forming to keep he and his wife entertained, Kevin still couldn't fight off the nagging feeling in the back of his mind that life as they knew it was about to change irrevocably. Little did he know that he and Lindsey shared much the same thoughts at that moment.

The water was silky soft and incredibly soothing, as Lindsey sank lower into her oil-scented bath. She tried pushing all thoughts of the Reclamation Project from her mind, and enjoying the fact that she was in her very favorite place in the world, and about to spend a wonderful and romantic few days with her handsome husband. Still, it was hard for her not to wonder where the project might lead and how it would inevitably change the future of the world itself. She remembered in vivid detail the story Ankhesenamun had shared with her, and felt a chill in spite of the warmth of the water around her. Strengthening her resolve not to dwell on the project, Lindsey sunk even lower into the deep tub, so that the water rose to cover her neck. Closing her eyes, she concentrated only on letting the warmth relax her body and her mind to drift toward more peaceful thoughts.

She was back in the darkness of the tunnel, climbing upward

toward the library, her feet and legs aching from the effort. The dim glow of light appeared in the distance and she knew it wouldn't be much farther now. Whispered voices came from everywhere and nowhere, as Lindsey continued forward, her legs becoming weaker with every step, her breath coming in short gasps as she forced her body to move. When she entered the outer circle of the indiscernible light source, the voices grew only slightly louder, but it was still impossible to pinpoint their source.

Finding herself at the base of the twelve steps leading to the landing, and the entrance to the Library of Knowledge, Lindsey realized that it seemed the wall itself was emanating a soft yellow–green glow, not unlike the dwellings in Atlantica. Atlantica, she was in Atlantica with Kevin. They were taking time off together before…before what? Struggling to focus, to clear her befuddled mind, Lindsey tried to remember what it was she and Kevin were supposed to do, and how she could possibly be in this tunnel now, when she was supposed to be in Atlantica. She shook her head slowly and closed her eyes as a wave of nausea overtook her. The harder she tried to think, the more nauseated she became. Summoning strength she did not know she possessed, Lindsey forced herself up the stone steps, dropping to her knees to crawl up the last few. She could feel the stones scraping her bare flesh, but still continued climbing until she had at last reached the landing that she knew to be the scale–elevator.

There was knowledge to be had; to be reclaimed…that's what she and Kevin had to help do soon. Was this it? Had the project started already? Another bout of nausea engulfed her and she couldn't bring herself to stand up. Had she become separated from the team? Where was Kevin and why had he left her here alone? More nausea. She had to stand, had to do whatever it was she had come here to do, though she couldn't remember exactly what that was.

Pushing herself against the softly glowing wall, Lindsay labored under the strain of simply trying to pull her body into at least a semi–upright position. How would she work the elevator? It required twelve bodies to lower to the library door, and she weighed only a hundred and ten pounds.

The whispers started becoming louder and with their increased volume, a throbbing pounded in her temples. Lindsey strained to hear what the voices were saying, and the throbbing increased. Pressing her fingers to her temples, she forced herself to concentrate on whom the voices belonged to, and what was being said. They were clearly male, but only one of them sounded vaguely familiar. She couldn't be certain, and it seemed that they were speaking from somewhere in the distance...below in the library perhaps. Yet another wave of nausea nearly dropped Lindsey back to her knees, as she fought back the urge to vomit. It was then that the whispered words around her began to take form.

"She told her everything! She is to blame for this. It is because of her that the spineless inferiors with their diluted blood will become enlightened!

It was Tutankhamun; of that there was no doubt, and it seemed that he voice was coming from below her. Had the group entered the library without her? How would she ever be able to join the others from her present position, alone on the landing? She leaned her head back and felt the coolness of the stone wall beneath her splayed fingers. As if by magic, the landing begin to slowly lower, and Lindsey nearly lost her balance. She tried again to clear the fog from her mind and to focus on why she was here.

The library door was open, and Lindsey could see light emanating from the room as the top of it became visible above the lowering platform. The voices stopped abruptly followed by a shuffling sound. As the platform came to a stop, a single figure stood in the doorway of the library to greet her. Lindsey struggled to focus, but the figure was scarcely more than a silhouette, standing as it was in the center of the light source.

Lindsey stepped forward hesitantly, as her eyes slowly adjusted to the light. At that same moment, the figure stepped closer and reached toward her. She raised her head slightly and squinted into the face before her. This was not Tutankhamun; it was...bluish–green and scaly.

Lindsey sucked in her breath in sheer terror at the sight of the form that stood only inches away from her. The elongated face and shiny black eyes were more snake–like than human. The creature blinked and for a fraction of a second a translucent layer of skin covered its eyes from the corners, not unlike that of a reptile. The creature's nose was flat and round, though the chin and lips appeared to be human...until it opened its mouth to speak and a long, purplish-black tongue appeared, to accentuate every syllable with a deep hissing sound.

"It is you and your meddling father that are to blame for the havoc you have wrought," came the wheezing hiss, "and it is you who will be blamed for the ensuing insurrection." With lightening speed, the creature slammed Lindsey full force against the wall behind her. Her breath left her entirely and a white hot pain shot through her abdomen, as she hit the hard stones and then fell to her knees. There was suddenly blood everywhere, soaking into the soft, white material of the bathrobe she hadn't realized she'd been wearing until that moment. She looked down and realized the blood was coming from her ... she was losing the baby!

Lindsey opened her mouth and tried to scream, but no sound came forth. At that moment, Tutankhamun appeared from behind the reptilian creature. He looked down at the blood-soaked robe and sneered, "This is where your interfering has gotten you now, Dr. Sanders," he spat. "Kill her," he said flatly, and turned back toward the open library door.

"With pleasure," hissed the creature, as his hands encircled Lindsey's throat.

She couldn't breathe; she had lost her baby and would die here at the hands of this hideous creature. Too weak to defend herself against the attack, Lindsey went limp and submitted to her own death.

Choking on a mouthful of water, Lindsey opened her eyes and realized she had fallen to sleep, and had slid too far down into the bathtub. Jerking her self to a sitting position, and soaking the carpet below in the process, Lindsey put her hands on her chest and choked out the water that had found its way into her mouth.

Her heart racing, Lindsey forced herself to look slowly downward, half expecting to see the water red with blood, a sigh of relief leaving her chest as she saw that the water was still crystal clear.

Ruth Marie Davis

She didn't notice the scrapes on the backs of her elbows, or the ones just below her wrists, on both of her palms.

Chapter Fourteen

Wednesday, November 12, 2251

It seemed to Lindsey that she and Kevin had no sooner arrived in Atlantica, than it was time to pack up and head back to the lab.
    Now, as she stood amid the throng of workers busily loading the government transport vehicles that would take them to Egypt, she found herself unable to shake the feeling of dread that seemed to hang in the air like a pall. It wasn't difficult to see that both Kevin and Glen shared her feeling, and even Professor St. Germaine's usual good humor was missing, as he stood with his arms folded before him, watching as the last transport was loaded.
    "Nervous?" asked her husband; as they settled themselves into one of the sleek, black vehicles and felt it smoothly leave the ground.
    "I'd be lying if I said I wasn't," she returned honestly, glancing out the virtual–panel. It was another very poor air–quality day, and the city seemed to be surrounded by a gray cloud, much in keeping with the general mood. Secretly, she was glad Tut was not in the same vehicle as she, Kevin and Glen. She didn't want to be in his overbearing presence any more than absolutely necessary. Lindsey knew that Ankhesenamun was probably enjoying the trip immensely…from the way every one of the all-male members that made up the second and third teams had been fawning over her from the moment she stepped into view. It had also been abundantly clear that Ankhesenamun welcomed the attention greatly, and just as clear that Tutankhamun was for some reason, incredibly irritated by it. Lindsey smiled to herself at that thought.
    "I'll be glad when the project is over," included Glen, "though we have no way of knowing just how much this thing might affect us all afterward." He gave his friends a side–long look, "To be honest, I'm almost hoping that it doesn't work, and we can all pack it up and go home."
    "'Don't feel bad," replied Kevin, "I've been thinking the same thing all day long." He took his wife's hand absently and began to

gently knead her soft flesh. He didn't like this at all…not one bit. He had awoken that morning with a feeling of dread that was almost tangible.

"I don't know what I think at this point," said Lindsey quietly, more thinking aloud than anything. "My father worked his whole life to find the Library of Knowledge. He always believed that great things would come if the library were to ever give up its secrets, and that mankind would benefit immensely." Lindsey gazed up into her husband's green eyes, and blushed slightly at the memory of their intensely passionate love making the night before in Atlantica. Not having been able to bring themselves to leave their home any sooner than they had to, the couple had traveled straight from the underwater city to IBAT first thing that morning.

As though reading her mind, Kevin favored her with a Cheshire cat smile, as they momentarily shared the memory of their intimacy. "I do hope your father was completely correct in his hypothesis," Mrs. Sanders, "a better world to raise our child in would be a wonderful and welcome change indeed."

The feeling of dread was suddenly intensified by Kevin's words, as Lindsey's mind flashed back to the nightmare she'd had in Atlantica. She had lost her baby in that horrible dream and the overwhelming grief she felt upon waking up far outweighed her fear of the creature that had wreaked such havoc upon her.

Less than half–an–hour after the convoy of government vehicles had left IBAT, they touched down at the temporary encampment already constructed by the government, and awaiting the three teams.

Lindsey was somewhat surprised to note that the encampment had been constructed in the Giza Plateau, not far from the giant Sphinx of Chephren, a place she had been to many times before, and knew like the back of her hand. Now it was known to be the starting point of the journey through that long, dark, tunnel, to the Pyramid of Cheops…and the library. The tunnel certainly had more significance to Lindsey, than to any other human being on the planet, and as she entered the massive interior of the fully transparent, air–quality protection dome, she couldn't help the involuntary shudder that ran through her.

Glen, Kevin and Lindsey had no sooner stepped over the threshold into the encampment, than they were pleasantly startled to see two smiling, and very familiar faces. Thad and Trent stood side by side just inside the dome entrance, waiting to greet their young friends; a bored looking Deuteronomy languishing in the crook of Trent's folded arm. The enthusiasm on their respective faces made them look like children in a candy shop.

Wasting no time, Lindsey fairly threw herself into the arms of two men, their very presence somehow alleviating her fears by half. Had Lindsey looked at the expression on her husband's handsome face at that moment, she would not have failed to see he fully shared that feeling. Stepping back to peruse her two dear friends from head to foot, and to scratch Deuteronomy's head and ears, Lindsey noted that both men had adopted almost identical khaki jumpsuits, the front enclosure of Thad's threatened to burst open above his rotund belly at any moment.

"How in the world did you get the military to agree to letting Little Dude come along?" Lindsey fairly squealed. "I can't believe they would allow such a thing."

"Ah," smiled Trent, as he stroked his pointy beard with his free hand, "that was a contingency we set forth before we agreed to head up the translation of the documents found in the library."

"Where we go, he goes," chimed in Thad, "and we're here now." His jovial smile lit his round face; the part of it not covered by his bushy beard.

"Well, I must say that you two have got to be astounding negotiators." Lindsey laughed and lowered her head to kiss Deuteronomy on the tip of his little black nose.

"How do you like that?" questioned Trent, as he looked his large friend in the eye with mock seriousness.

"The little ingrate," returned Thad, feigning great displeasure, "we bring him along and he stills our limelight."

Glen and Kevin had no sooner shook hands with Thad and Trent, when a rather short and stocky young MP appeared out of nowhere, "Excuse me gentlemen, and Ma'am," he added as though in afterthought, with a nod to Lindsey," I've been sent to show you to your berthing quarters." With a stiff, smart turn, the young soldier spun on his heels and began to lead them briskly down a walkway, lined on both sides with temporary structures somewhere between tents and over-sized, round-top boxes covered in cloth.

"Our berthing quarters," repeated Lindsey with a giggle and a sidelong look at her husband, "but I'm not due until May."

Glad that his wife was still able to find her sense of humor, Kevin smiled back into her sky blue eyes, "Have I mentioned lately that I love you more with every day that passes?"

"Actually, no," was Lindsey's quick reply, "but if you keep talking like that, I may have to let you show me later just how much you love me."

Kevin couldn't help the brief chuckle that escaped his lips. His wife still had the knack for making him feel like a high school boy on prom night.

The temporary "berthing" units as the military personnel referred to them as, were actually quite well appointed quarters indeed. Although Lindsey imagined the respective military entities had begun preparing the area many months earlier, she had somehow envisioned spending the night in hastily constructed field tents. She was truly quite surprised to discover that she and Kevin's quarters consisted of a unit with three small rooms containing a sleeping area, small kitchenette, complete with fully stocked nutriment cabinet and re-hydrator, and a very small cleansing chamber. The water rations were proportionately small as well.

As both the Egyptian and US governments had agreed upon from the beginning, they shared equal responsibility for the direction of the Reclamation Project. This apparently necessitated the appointment of two Commander-in-Chief's, as they were referred to by the multitude of military personnel housed within the confines of the protective dome.

Lindsey, Kevin and Glen had been introduced to both Commander Jackson Anglin, a tall and intensely distinguished gentleman of thin build, with a neatly trimmed salt-and-pepper beard, and Commander Sekhem Morad, a slighter built, dark-skinned man in his forties, with a black, pencil-thin mustache. The two men were equally impressed with Lindsey's perfect command of the Egyptian language, as well as her ability to speak and interpret several of the ancient dialects, not spoken in centuries.

In friendly, yet authoritative fashion, the two leaders explained that they would jointly head up Team One, and that all three teams would rendezvous at the base of the Sphinx at o–six–hundred on the following morning. It seemed that all key members of the Reclamation Project would be required to attend a briefing after the evening meal, or 'chow,' as Commander Anglin referred to it, which would be served in an area the military personnel called the 'mess hall.' Lindsey found it a bit difficult to follow all the martial jargon, and found many of the terminology's almost comical.

The evening meal was served in a mammoth Quonset–hut type building, covered in what appeared to be a tan colored canvas. Lindsey was left to wonder why the military had seen fit to stock the small kitchen in their berthing space, if meals were to be taken in this building referred to as the "mess hall." She and Kevin had scarcely finished their last few bites, when all individuals not part of the actual teams were asked to return to their quarters, so that the much anticipated briefing could commence.

Within seconds after the last non–team member left the chow hall, tables and benches had been reorganized in a circular fashion. Beginning with Commander's Anglin and Morad, each individual was asked to state their name, rank if appropriate, team number and purpose. Both Glen and Kevin, neither having ever served in the military, felt more than a little out of place.

During the ensuing exchange of information, Lindsey, Kevin and Glen learned that aside from themselves, Tut and Ankhesenamun, Team One consisted of both Commander Anglin, Commander Morad, The Professor's Farrier and McRae, and a middle–aged Army Major by the name of Corwin Armstrong. Apparently, Major Armstrong was some sort of 'negotiator.' In addition, there were two rather beefy Security Officers in their mid–twenties. The two members could have nearly been twins, and introduced themselves as Lieutenant Michael Kauffman, and Lieutenant Jake Fox, respectively.

"All three teams will be taken by transport to the entrance–way at the base of the Sphinx," began Commander Anglin.

"Upon arrival," chimed Commander Morad, "Teams One and Two will follow the lead of Commander Anglin and myself...."

The words had no sooner left Commander Morad's lips, than Commander Anglin finished his sentence, "And Team three will take and maintain position outside the entrance."

"Once inside the tunnel itself," continued Commander Morad, the pencil–thin mustache lining his upper lip, moving in rhythm to the opening and closing of his mouth, "we will walk in single file to the foot of the twelve steps leading to the scale–elevator...."

"At which time," Commander Anglin concluded, "Team One will be lowered to the library entrance, and eleven of the twelve Team Two members will take place on the platform as soon as it rises."

"This way," supplied Commander Morad, "should an emergency arise in the library, the remaining member of Team Two can take position on the landing, lowering the entire team."

Lindsey, Kevin and Glen smiled at one another periodically as they listened to the Commanders' continually finish one another's sentences. It was as though the two men shared one collective thought process. And while maintaining a professional, military bearing, they still seemed to interact with each other in a friendly, outgoing manner. At least there didn't seem to be any professional or authoritative animosity between the two leaders.

"We have in our possession the amulet that was found with, ah, Princess Ankhesenamun," said Commander Anglin. He looked slightly discomfited by the knowledge that the amulet was actually discovered on the corpse of the long–dead mummy of Ankhesenamun; yet that very same, exceptionally beautiful young woman, sat not far from him at this very moment. "We have decided that the amulet should be placed on the table in the library by the individual who last possessed it."

"That would mean of course," supplied Commander Morad, entwining his slender, brown fingers on the table top before him as he spoke, "that Princess Ankhesenamun herself will do the honors."

Ankhesenamun smiled shyly as all eyes turned toward her. Of course, most of the young men present had not yet taken their eyes off the raven haired beauty, and found it impossible to believe that this woman, and the sullen young Egyptian man sitting at her side, once sat at the throne of Egypt, literally thousands of years earlier. From the looks being cast her way, a pesky little thing like she being a clone, could be easily over-looked by virtually every one of the unattached, male team-members present.

"And I, Commander Morad," interrupted Tutankhamun sharply, "where do I fit in to this chain of events?" His flat tone held a note of disrespect that brought all eyes sharply into focus on his saturnine countenance and a rather questioning look from both Commanders.

"You will stand with Ankhesenamun when she places the amulet on the table," returned Commander Morad, appearing fully calm, if not a slight bit condescending in tone.

"If we do in fact achieve some level of communication with advanced life forms," included Commander Anglin, "we want the two of you to be the first individuals seen by whomever we contact."

Tut's black eyes shifted nervously for a moment, as though perhaps remembering briefly his encounter with the Utukki. Lindsey's gaze settled upon Ankhesenamun, and she wondered if the girl was remembering that horrible day so long ago, when the Utukki had violated her so hideously. Or was she perhaps remembering another time, locked tightly in the arms of the Sun God Ra?

Suddenly, the memory of the scaly creature from Lindsey's nightmare, flitted, unbidden into Lindsey's mind, forcing an involuntary shudder to course down her spine, and the hackles to rise on the back of her neck. Could this have been the monstrous Utukki Ankhesenamun had spoken of? It was more likely, thought Lindsey that she had simply been dwelling on the younger woman's words, and had conceived the figure from the mental picture she had derived. That thought made her feel abundantly more secure.

Nonetheless, it was Ankhesenamun's amulet that called upon the Annuaki, and it was Ankhesenamun's amulet that would be placed on the table in the library tomorrow. Lindsey smiled to herself, determining that rather than fear her participation in the events that would soon take place, she should be reveling in the fact that she was fortunate enough to be a part of them.

After another hour of going over the details of the final steps of the Reclamation Project, which included Lindsey recounting to the group her first ever experience in the Library of Knowledge, she found herself answering the barrage of questions that followed.

It was nearly eight o'clock that evening before the team members shuffled out of the Mess Hall. Looking up through the dome top, Lindsey noted that it was raining quite heavily and there were no stars out. She'd always found the rain rather romantic, but was glad for the protective dome nonetheless. It wasn't healthy to stand in the rain for very long.

Professor's Thad and Trent hugged Lindsey warmly, and then shook hands with Glen and Kevin, before excusing themselves from the group and heading toward their own quarters, "We're old and have a big day tomorrow, Kids," smiled Thad warmly, the lines in his slender face deepening as he did so.

"We'll see you first thing in the morning then," yawned Trent, as he and Thad headed off in the direction of their berthing units.

"Honey," said Kevin, turning toward his wife, and noticing how the dimly lit artificial light sources, made her hair look alive with a fire of its own, "Glen and I have to conduct full check–ups on both Tut and Ankhesenamun this evening. We've been just a little concerned with Tut's AGC process…his Accelerated Growth Cell," clarified Kevin at his wife's momentary questioning look.

Lindsey nodded slowly, "Yes," she confirmed, "I remember you mentioning it before. Is there is real problem."

"We don't know just yet," chimed in Glen, "but it does seem that we're finding it more difficult to control the cell growth in Tut than we are in Ankhesenamun."

"Do you want us to walk you back to our quarters first?" asked Kevin, "or would you like to accompany us to the medical area the military has constructed for us to conduct the check–ups in."

"Actually," replied Lindsey with a smile, "I would much rather accompany my two favorite guys than go back to our quarters alone."

"Careful now, Dr. Sanders," cautioned Glen, his new glasses–free, gray–free look seeming to have transformed his entire demeanor to one of a much more outgoing individual with a good deal more confidence. "I've heard you say the very same thing to

Farrier and McRae. You'll soon have us all fighting over who is really your favorite." His teasing chuckle elicited a quick smile from Lindsey and Kevin both, as the three wound their way through the rows of temporary structures, to the one set aside for the IBAT personnel to conduct whatever tests and exams were necessary.

Lindsey hadn't realized she'd missed spending time with Ankhesenamun, until she was hugging the girl in greeting, "It seems you've been the primary focus of most the young men in the complex here," smiled Lindsey sincerely, "I think in another day or so, these guys will be fighting over you."

Ankhesenamun laughed outright, her kohl–lined eyes crinkling slightly at the corners. "I must admit it is very flattering indeed," confided the olive–skinned beauty, as she flipped a thick lock of her tawny mane over one shoulder. "There is only one man I am interested in seeing though," she lowered her voice to a conspiratorial whisper, "and I pray that tomorrow will bring him to me." The light in her eyes told Lindsey that this young woman was truly and deeply in love with Emmesharra, and continued to harbor a love that had transcended time itself. Lindsey desperately hoped that Ankhesenamun would have her wish, because she certainly didn't want to think about the alternative.

"I just don't know exactly what we're going to do if we can't get a handle on Tut's AGC," said Glen with a worried frown, as they left the medical unit and made their way back toward their respective berthing quarters. "At this rate, he'll die of old age in another year."

"I know, Glen," responded Kevin, "but you saw how Commander's Anglin and Morad took the news, as long as Tut is there and in place tomorrow, they're happy. There doesn't seem to be any real concern for what happens to him after that point."

"Why that's horrible," retorted Lindsey, as the trio passed several groups of soldiers milling about and playing cards not far from their own quarters, "he's a living human being by virtue of the fact that we have made him one, with full authority and participation by the military itself."

"I suppose it does seem rather callous on their part," agreed

Glen, "but the military is the military and their concerns undoubtedly differ immensely from our own."

"But isn't there something you two can do to control the cell growth?" asked Lindsey.

"Not with the limited facilities we have to work with here," responded Kevin, "I'm not even sure there's much we could do at IBAT."

"The only thing that will retard the process to an acceptable level, is the equalization–serum we've been injecting Tut and Ankhesenamun with from the beginning," interjected Glen, "but we're already administering the maximum dosage to Tut."

"That's right, Lindsey," confirmed Kevin, "too much of the serum could result in the involuntary collapse of Tut's central nervous system, so we're damned if we do and damned if we don't."

"It appears that either way we look at it, he won't live through the year." Glen's eyes were downcast at the helplessness he felt. "Although Kevin and I have been discussing the possibility of modifying the serum itself, we can't do anything until we get back to IBAT."

"In the meantime though," Kevin's slightly monotone voice left no doubt that he too was struggling with the helpless feeling of not being able to correct a situation he was in essence, directly responsible for, "the tissue cells will continue to degenerate, taking the equivalent of weeks off his life."

The trio had made their way to the entrance of Kevin and Lindsey's quarters, and Kevin placed his eyes on the retinal–scan panel, causing the door to slide open silently. Their quarters were in the top–secret, heavily guarded area of the encampment, causing Lindsey to feel both secure, and slightly nervous at the amount of weaponry surrounding their compound. "Won't you come inside and visit with us for just a bit before we retire?" she offered, "I think I saw some dehydrated coffee is the kitchenette."

"To be honest, I was hoping you'd ask," answered Glen with a grin, "for some reason, I'm just not terribly tired right now, and don't particularly relish sitting alone in that damnable little box they call my berthing unit."

Lindsey couldn't help noticing that Glen wasn't half bad looking without the nerdy black glasses and the graying hair. She knew he was undoubtedly lonely without Sal, and linking was not allowed from the confines of the dome, unless authorized by either Commander Anglin or Morad, and then only in an emergency. It seemed that the Reclamation Project was such a top-secret operation that only the military members directly involved even knew why they were there.

"You are an incredibly lucky man to have such a wonderful wife," offered Glen, as Lindsey disappeared behind a small door into the kitchen area. He and Kevin sat down on the portable airbed, the only furniture in the sleeping room, which also served as a living area of sorts, "I hope you treasure every moment with her."

"Oh, believe me, I do, my good man, I do." Kevin grinned so wide; Glen couldn't help laughing outright. "Sal makes you happy doesn't he?" Somehow the subject of Glen and Sal made Kevin incredibly uncomfortable to speak about with his best friend. He supposed he'd never given it much thought before Glen was actually seeing someone. Of course, he had known about his friend's sexual preference for quite some time, but it had never directly affected him before now. Lindsey had spoken of it to him many times, most recently, during their last trip to Atlantica. He didn't remember what had brought Glen up in the first place, but he did remember that he and Lindsey had been settled comfortably in their lawn chairs, watching the fluid movements of the indigenous sea life that provided endless hours of mellifluous, aquatic entertainment from outside the domed city.

'How awful it would be if we couldn't love openly,' Lindsey had said, 'wouldn't it be horrible to love somebody so much, yet have to hide it from the entire world?'

'What do you mean, Honey?' he'd questioned, 'we don't have to hide anything. I love you and would happily proclaim it to the world.'

'I think you already have,' she'd smiled back sweetly, as she padded her still flat tummy, 'It's Glen and Sal I was referring to.'

That uncomfortable feeling had reared its ugly head at the mention, but Kevin knew Lindsey was absolutely right. He couldn't imagine hiding his love from his beautiful, intelligent wife, couldn't imagine having to sneak around to see her, knowing that were he caught, he would most assuredly spend the rest of his life on one of the prison space stations. Just the thought made him shudder. Now, as he sat across from his best friend, he could almost feel the longing within Glen that came from being separated from the one person he wanted to be with more than anything.

"I know it's got to be incredibly difficult not being able to contact Sal," he said slowly, meeting Glen's brown eyes as he did so.

For a moment, Glen was entirely taken aback by Kevin's casual broaching of the subject. He'd never really discussed it with his friend, except for briefly over a meal at IBAT some months earlier. Glen had somehow sensed then that Kevin wasn't entirely comfortable with the subject of homosexuality, and was hetero to the core of his being, of that, Glen had no doubt. He suddenly saw his long-time friend in new light. Clearly, Kevin cared about him, and such a friendship was to be both respected and revered above all others. "Thank you, Kevin," responded Glen honestly, "it means a lot to me to know that you understand."

"Being married to Lindsey has helped me to understand a lot of things," reflected Kevin. "She's helped me understand the depth of true love for one thing. I'm learning to fully appreciate the importance of life, and the creation of life." His voice trailed off, as his mind flashed on both the pending birth of his child, and the impending death of another life he had helped to create...that of the once-boy-king of Egypt.

"That is much to learn in such a short time as you have had together," smiled Glen sincerely in agreement, "she must be a hell of a good teacher."

"The best," replied Kevin, just as the subject of their conversation reappeared, her hair pulled back and secured with some sort of clip, and a small tray containing three steaming, military issue mugs. He wanted to make love to her then and there, but couldn't begin to bring himself to ask their friend to make his exit after having just invited him in.

"It must be terribly lonely for you, not being able to link to Sal," said Lindsey meaningfully, as she handed the two men their coffee mugs.

"We were just discussing that very subject," returned Glen,

taking a sip of the steaming, black liquid.

"You were?" asked Lindsey, feeling a sudden, almost overwhelming urge to kiss her wonderful husband smack on the lips, "I imagine Sal feels much the same way."

"I would like to think he does." Glen's grin broadened, just before his face puckered, "Please don't hit me Lindsey, but this is quite possibly the worst coffee I've ever tasted in my life."

Lindsey laughed aloud, as she settled herself comfortably next to her husband, her feet dangling in mid air over the edge of the invisible perimeter of the small airbed. "I apologize deeply, but as with the unidentifiable mystery dinner they served us in the appropriately named Mess Hall, the coffee is equally distasteful." She laughed pleasantly, "Had I known taking 'chow' there was not a requirement, I'd have re–hydrated some of the nutriment packets in the kitchenette."

"Those are military issue too," pointed out Glen, so I seriously doubt they'd be any more palatable. And only three more days of the military's exceptional culinary skills," he finished with a grin.

"Ah," interjected Kevin, "and now the real reason for you missing Sal comes out," his grin was contagious, "you miss his cooking don't you?"

"Kevin, shame on you," admonished his wife, "though I'd kill for just one of Sal's deserts about right now."

"Here, here!" agreed Glen whole–heartedly, "I'll even toast that with this hideous coffee."

"I don't know if I can handle three more days eating and drinking this stuff," Kevin sighed, looking questionably at the dark liquid in his cup. "I don't understand exactly why they've decided we have to maintain position here for three full days. Whatever happens will undoubtedly happen tomorrow morning."

Lindsey felt the now familiar chill run through her at the mention of the culmination of their work about to come to fruition, but she wasn't quite certain if it was a chill of anticipation, or a chill of doubt.

"Makes you wonder what the old boy who built those pyramids over there would think," intoned Glen, with a gesture toward the general direction of the structures in question, "if he knew that we were about to make use of his architectural masterpiece in the twenty-third century."

"Well, actually Glen," corrected Lindsey, "it was three old boys that constructed those pyramids on the plateau. Of course, now we know that they had a good deal of help."

"I stand corrected," replied Glen, feigning the look of one who had been properly, and sufficiently chastised. "Please do enlighten me further," he invited, his warm smile encouraging Lindsey to say whatever was necessary to keep their friend smiling, and momentarily detoured from his thoughts of missing Sal.

"Well, it can get quite boring to someone who hasn't spent their entire life studying it," she smiled. "But to render a brief synopsis; the pyramid containing the Library of Knowledge, which is the Pyramid of Cheops, or the Great Pyramid, was built by an old boy named Khufu, who was more often referred to as Cheops, that being the Greek form of his name."

Glen laughed outright at Lindsey's intentional, casual use of his earlier slang; Kevin just wanted to kiss his incredibly awesome wife. He found both her wit and her intelligence immensely attractive. Her face and body were a definite plus as well.

"And the other two gentlemen?" asked Glen, orally upgrading the individuals in question to a much improved status, his smile replaced immediately by yet another grimace, as he took another swig of the dark liquid masquerading as coffee.

"Well, those two came along quite sometime later. It seems they liked the location Cheops had chosen, and in their own times, each built a pyramid on the same plateau, a short distance to the south. These were kings of the Fourth Dynasty, Chephren and Mycerinus. Of course there was certainly more to their building site than location, given the esoteric significance."

"I love it when you speak with an accent," her husband grinned adoringly.

"And on that note, I shall take my leave," chortled Glen, rising from the airbed and handing his still half-full cup to Lindsey. "Thank you for having me in," he offered, as he turned toward the door. "I don't think the coffee will keep me up," he intoned with a lopsided grin. "Though I just might pass out in a dead faint from the aftertaste." He stepped out into the night air, and the door slid quickly closed behind him.

Glen's own hut, as he thought of it, would be unoccupied, save for himself, and he truly hoped that sleep came quickly. He missed Sal incredibly, and kept trying to envision the darkly handsome face in his mind. Just when the mental picture would become clear, it would slip into fuzziness again. He could never spend enough time with Sal, and would give anything he owned to be able to love Sal openly, and without fear of repercussion.

Glen entered his quarters, and pressed the panel that activated the portable airbed. The resulting rush of air was accompanied by a low humming sound. Throwing himself down on the portable apparatus, Glen noted with displeasure that the air streams being emitted were uneven beneath him and most uncomfortable at best. Closing his eyes, Glen remembered waking up next to Sal after their first night together, in Sal's incredibly comfortable airbed. He missed the strong, handsome Italian, with the amber colored eyes.

If only things were different, if only President Albanion had not been elected over Emmett Hines, who had been an excellent leader, and who was definitely most worthy of another term in office. Hines was certainly far more liberal than the devious woman whose victory had come with as many questions about the legitimacy of the ballot counting, as the infamous Bush, Gore election back in the year 2000. There had been a series of incidents linking Albanion to several Mafia affiliated organizations, but nothing had been proven. Still, it had seemed to everyone that Hines was by far and away the more popular of the two candidates, and had spoken out openly for gay rights, even though he himself was a married man with several children. Had he been elected, perhaps Glen and Sal would have enjoyed the luxury of proclaiming their love for each other openly. He couldn't imagine anything that would make him happier or more content. Those were his last thoughts, before he drifted into the arms of Morpheus.

"Do you have any idea how incredibly much I love you?" asked Kevin, as he gently nuzzled his wife's ear. Her naked body against his ignited an intense passion within him unlike any other woman before her had ever done.

"Oh, I have an inkling," was her teasing reply.

Kevin placed his hand on Lindsey's bare stomach, "How long before I can feel our child move about?"

"Another eight weeks or so, I would imagine," replied Lindsey, smiling to herself as much from the joy of knowing their child continued to grow within her, as in the simple fact that her husband wished to know.

Kevin suppressed a chuckle. Since his wife had become pregnant, months no longer seemed to exist; she measured every event in weeks now. It seemed to Kevin that he couldn't get enough of this woman who now carried both his last name and his child. He had never known it was possible to love anyone so much. He found it equally amazing to discover how much he could love a person that hadn't even been born yet.

Moments later, words became unnecessary, as the couple came together in a union that was nothing, if not the joining of souls. Both carried the knowledge within them that the events of tomorrow could very well alter life as the entire planet had come to know it. The uncertainty that knowledge brought fueled their passion for one another to an unequaled crescendo; their need to cling together on this, their last night of absolute certainty of their place in the universe, would bring them closer together than even their own child could.

Chapter Fifteen

Thursday, November 13, 2251

"It's colder than a well–digger's ass in the Klondike!" Lindsey heard one of the young soldiers exclaim, as all three team members filed out of the field–dome, and into the transport vehicles that would carry them to the base of the Sphinx.

It did seem to be unseasonably cold, and the ominous black clouds above were threatening to bring forth another deluge of rain at any moment. Lindsey found herself empathizing with the disgruntled looks of the Team Three members, who would be left to stand in the cold outside the entrance to the Sphinx until Teams One and Two emerged.

"You okay, Honey?" asked Kevin, as the transport lifted silently off the ground and hovered for a moment, before gliding effortlessly toward the direction of the Great Pyramid.

"As okay as I can be," Lindsey returned with a forced nonchalance she really didn't feel at all. Another wave of nausea rose up, and she swallowed hard, unsure if this was the ever present morning sickness that accompanied her pregnancy, a horrendous case of nerves, or a good deal of both.

"Are you having morning–sickness again, Linds?" asked Kevin, more concerned about his wife's well being now than ever. He didn't like the fact that she would be within the confines of the Library of Knowledge if something should happen. There was only one way in and out of that room, and no way to evacuate it quickly should an emergency arise. Although all members of Team Two and Three were heavily armed in the event of an unforeseen crisis, the only members of Team One that would be in possession of any weapons were Commander's Anglin and Morad, their Negotiator, and the two Security Officers.

"The nausea rather comes and goes," returned Lindsey, "but the doctor says it should stop soon." Lindsey was just thankful she'd been able to sleep the night through dreamlessly, and without any of the horrific nightmares that had started plaguing her not long after she began work at IBAT. Of all the nights since then, she had actually almost expected to find herself in the throes of a nightmare last night. Instead, she had made the most wonderful, passionate love to her husband ever, and had drifted into a peaceful sleep. At some point, in the very early morning hours, Lindsey had awakened for no apparent reason, and reached out to her sleeping husband. The two made love again until they were breathless, and were still joined when they both fell back into the depths of slumber.

Trent and Thad who were both seated directly across from Glen, Lindsey and Kevin, noted the pale countenance of the usually radiant, fresh-faced Lindsey. Without the need for words, the two communicated their concern for her to each other.

'She doesn't look healthy today, does she Trent?'

'No, Thad, she's too pale and there's no color to her cheeks. I don't like the fact that she's going in.'

'Nor do I, Trent,' Thad returned by mere thought alone. After all, it wasn't polite to discuss people openly, when they were sitting right before you. 'You know she has to be present though, she's a part of it, and just think about what would happen were she not to go in with the rest of us.'

'I know, I know,' responded Trent silently, the only indication of his thought energy, a slightly pulsing, light blue vein, barely discernible near his right temple, 'but why was the baby she carries not foreseen? It could change things. I don't know friend,' he thought back in response, 'I have been much concerned by this unexpected turn of events. I am most pleased that the two of them are to have a child, but equally displeased that this was not known to us from the beginning.'

'We shall have to watch her closely, my friend.' Thad's thoughts were heavy. He found the older he got; the less time he was capable of communicating with Trent by sheer will alone. It was becoming more strenuous for him to expend the amount of energy required to impart his thoughts without the use of words.

'We'll have to watch her closely indeed,' replied Trent, 'we cannot risk having anything happen to Lindsey. It is most disconcerting.' Trent glanced down at the khaki jump suit he wore, missing his long-time feline friend immensely, the one concession that the military refused to allow. 'I am gravely bothered that

Deuteronomy is not with us, as we were lead to believe by the Realm he would be.'

'I too am at a loss to understand why the military demanded that Dude remain at the compound during this stage of the project,' answered Thad, his head beginning to ache from the strain of thought–sharing, 'he was in the Sight.'

'Yes,' answered Trent, the light blue vein on his temple beginning to darken, as he too found his thoughts becoming too heavy, 'but the Sights are often left to some degree of interpretation, and not always as clear as they could be. We are becoming more diluted with age my friend.'

'True,' returned Thad, his thoughts were becoming far too heavy to continue without use of the spoken word, 'but it won't be long now until we are fully recharged.' He couldn't withhold the involuntary smile that crept to the corners of his lips.

"Are you sure you'll be all right, Lindsey?" asked Trent solicitously, glad to feel the heaviness of his thoughts recede by the use of his voice. "You look a might pale today child."

"Oh, I'll be fine, truly," answered Lindsey lightly, "I'm sure it's just Kevin's child acting up."

"Oh, it's my child when it acts up!" exclaimed Kevin in mock astonishment, affording his wife a sidelong look and eliciting a giggle for her. He loved this woman more than life itself, and didn't care much for the fact that her normally pink cheeks now held no color whatsoever. He hoped to hell that this phase of the project wouldn't take long. His thoughts were punctuated by the landing of the transport van less than fifteen feet from the entryway to the Sphinx, and to an unknown future.

Unlike in Lindsey's nightmares, the passageway was brightly lit. All the individuals that comprised team's one and two had been issued light tubes, and all twenty–four of them illuminated the thick stone walls, so that every crack and chisel mark was clearly visible.

Lindsey was pleased beyond words to discover that her initial excitement at being a part of this project was beginning to return. Surrounded as she was by so many others, again, so unlike her nightmares, Lindsey began to feel the adrenaline rush coursing through her veins that always accompanied a new archeological discovery. It was that rush that had pushed her father to discover the Library of Knowledge in the first place, and she to follow in his footsteps. Now, she was about to be a part of something that her father had only dreamed of, the discovery of the true purpose of the Great Pyramid.

"Come on men," she heard Commander Anglin exclaim, "keep the pace, we have a long way to go yet!"

"Are you doing alright, Linds?" asked Kevin from directly behind her, in the single file line, as the passageway began to wend upward, requiring much more effort to negotiate.

"To be honest," returned Lindsey, between regulated breaths, "I feel better than I have in quite some time."

"If you do need to stop, or to slow down, I want you to say something," replied her concerned husband, "we're not in the military, and I don't want you pushing yourself beyond your limits."

"Don't forget, Dr. Sanders," stated Lindsey evenly from over her left shoulder, "I've made this trek before."

"But not while you were three months pregnant," retorted Kevin.

"True," was her giggling reply.

The Commander's didn't call for a break until both teams had arrived at the first landing, at which time they called for a half–hour rest and chow break. By that time, Lindsey was more than happy for the respite. Though tired, the nausea had subsided completely, and the rest would give her sufficient time to rub the mild cramping out of her calves. There was still a long way to go, and instead of the flat surface they had been traveling until now, the remainder of the journey upward would require climbing hundreds of stairs. Lindsey knew from first–hand experience just how arduous that climb could be under the best of circumstances.

"How are you feeling, Lindsey?" Ankhesenamun's soft voice was a welcome sound, surrounded as she was by so many men.

"I am feeling well, Ankhesenamun," replied Lindsey honestly, "though my calves are aching a bit."

"Allow me to rub them for you then," offered the younger woman, "I am worried that this climb might be too difficult for you in your delicate state."

"I honestly don't feel the slightest bit delicate," replied Lindsey truthfully, noting that the other team members began dropping to the ground, or leaning back against the stairs and walls, as they ate their rations and talked amongst themselves.

Ankhesenamun smiled, as she settled herself next to Lindsey, and began manipulating her overworked muscles.

Lindsey let out a sigh of relief, as Ankhesenamun's soft hands and fingers worked the stiffness from her aching calves. She couldn't help thinking about the irony of her situation at that moment; sitting on a step somewhere deep underground between the Sphinx and the Great Pyramid, leaning casually back against the wall, while the clone of a long–dead Egyptian princess tended to her legs like a dutiful servant. She also couldn't help noticing that the olive–skinned young beauty had chosen to wear her best gown and jewelry, and had used more kohl to darken her eyelids than usual. Clearly, the girl wanted to look her absolute best in the event she should realize her desire to see the only man she had ever loved.

Lindsey glanced over at the sulking countenance of Tut, leaning back against the wall several stairs above, and on the opposite side of where she, Kevin, Glen and Ankhesenamun had settled. "He doesn't look happy," commented Lindsey in a whisper, with a nod in Tut's general location.

"Is he ever?" asked Ankhesenamun in return, her eyes meeting and locking with Lindsey's in a shared moment of understanding. "I think he is more afraid than anything," confided the woman who once ruled this very country at the young, pouty mans' side. He is worried that Emmesharra will come, and does not know how he himself will fare should that happen."

"Ah, Trent," came Thad's slightly winded voice, "you see, we get here late and all the good jobs are taken!" The portly Professor McRae lowered his broad frame onto the wide, stone step a foot or so next to where Ankhesenamun sat rubbing Lindsey's over–worked calf muscles. He was joined momentarily by a smiling Professor Farrier, staring questionably down at the half eaten contents of his nutriment package.

"Well, she has got two legs, Professors," smiled Ankhesenamun from over her shoulder, "and I can but work on one at a time."

The Egyptian beauty was rewarded by a loud chuckle from both Trent and Thad. Having been introduced to the portly professor and his reed thin sidekick only just that morning, she'd felt an instant draw to them, as though she had known the two wise and learned men forever.

From somewhere up the stairway, where many of the young Team Two solders sat consuming their nutriment meals, was heard exclamations of, "My legs are really hurting from all that walking," followed by a round of laughter and several other voices adding, "mine too!"

Ankhesenamun smiled meeting Lindsey's eyes as she did so. "Your time is so different from mine," her liquid brown eyes were soft, as though her mind had been momentarily drawn back to a bygone era, "the men of my time would never have spoken so freely in my presence," her smiled widened, "but I'm not complaining, mind you."

"But you were a princess then," grinned Lindsey broadly, "they dared not speak so freely around you."

"Which is precisely why I do not mind living in your time one bit," giggled Ankhesenamun in return, briefly turning her head to scan the group of young men lounging about on the stair steps above them, "but none of them are Emmesharra," she added wistfully.

"Are you sure you're going to be able to make it the rest of the way up?" asked Kevin, as he finished the last of his bland lunch, and began to roll the wrapper briskly between his palms, until it had fully dissolved.

"I think I'll be just fine now," responded Lindsey, "thanks to Ankhesenamun." Reaching up, she brushed an errant strand of the younger woman's ebony hair from her face, and again smiled her gratitude.

"Whatever happens when we reach the library Lindsey, I want you to know that I will always think of you as a friend." The sincerity in Ankhesenamun's eyes was unmistakable.

"And I you, Ankhesenamun," replied Lindsey, in flawless, ancient Egyptian.

The twelve massive steps that heralded the end of their

journey were as familiar to Lindsey as if she had seen them only yesterday. Of course, she had seen them in her nightmare in Atlantica.

Stopping at the base of the massive, precision cut, stone stairs, Commander Anglin raised his hand and spoke loudly enough for even those team members who had not yet reached him to hear, "Everyone assume their scheduled positions."

"All Team Two Members will have weapons at the ready, as a precautionary measure only," interjected Chief Morad, his own baritone voice in contrast to his slight size and build.

Lindsey, Kevin and Ankhesenamun stepped forward simultaneously followed closely by Thad, Trent, Glen, and the still sullen countenance of Tutankhamun, with Major Armstrong and the two young Security Officers, Kauffman and Fox, bringing up the remainder of Team One.

It seemed that Trent and Thad could hardly contain their excitement as they took their places on the scale elevator. Their eyes circled the room, taking in every stone, every angle, as though to commit this place, and this moment, to memory.

Commander Morad had been the first to step onto the platform, followed by Commander Anglin, and a brief wave of nausea formed in Lindsey's stomach when it was her turn. Without even realizing it, she took an involuntary step back. The cool stone of the wall behind her felt familiar, and she leaned her head back, experiencing a moment of de–ja–vu as she did so. In her nightmare, she had leaned against the stone and the elevator had lowered, with her alone on it. No sooner had the memory returned, than she found her gaze forced to the stern face of Tutankhamun, standing just on the other side of Major Armstrong. With narrowed eyes, and a set jaw, Tut shook his head from side to side slowly, and Lindsey swallowed hard.

It was at that moment that the twelfth member of Team One stepped up onto the platform, and it slowly began to lower.

Kevin pulled Lindsey forward, to spare his wife from being scraped against the wall, and put an arm around her. He had resolved not to let her out of his sight for so much as a single moment.

When the scale–elevator stopped, a collective gasp escaped the eleven members of Team One, who unlike Lindsey had never before beheld such a sight. The light–packs carried by each of the twelve people illuminated the solid gold doors before them, so that they glowed like molten lava, the intricately carved hieroglyphs looking as though they had been chiseled out only recently.

"As indicated in our agreement," stated Commander Anglin, as he turned his attention to Trent and Thad, "the two of you shall have the honor of opening the entry doors to the Library of Knowledge."

"This is the entrance to the Great Library here before us, is it not?" questioned Commander Morad, his expectant look settling upon Lindsey.

"Yes, Sir," replied Lindsey with a nod, "it is one in the same."

"Then by all means, gentlemen," nodded Commander Morad crisply, "please afford us entry at this time."

The two Commander's stood stiffly, side–by–side, as though at attention, as Trent and Thad stepped forward. Standing on either side of the massive golden portals, each took one of the handles, and then settled their eyes simultaneously on Lindsey as they gently pulled the ancient doors open.

A low whistle emanated from someone in the group near her, but Lindsey scarcely heard it. She had half expected to see some hideous, scaly monster emerge and begin choking her. Much to her relief though, the only thing staring back at her was the memory of the day she stood next to her father, as these doors were opened for the first time since they had been sealed.

As the lights from Team One illuminated the room, the brilliant reflection of the gold–paneled walls was as though walking through the gates of heaven, and for a moment, even the normally assertory Commander's were unable to do more than stare in awe.

Stepping forward slowly, all twelve members were finally ensconced in a structure that was older than recorded time, most of them staring in wide–eyed wonder at hundreds of hieroglyphic and hieratic etchings.

The opulence of the relatively small room was awe inspiring, the walls and ceiling, and even the shelves, that now stood empty of the ancient writings, glowed as though a white–hot fire burned beneath the outer layers; a glow that even the passing of many centuries had failed to dull.

Commander Anglin tapped the communication device on his left wrist, and relayed their exact position, as he and Commander Morad had done routinely since having entered the doorway at the base of the Sphinx.

"This is Team Two, Sir, Lieutenant Commander Bennett speaking," came the return transmission, "we read you loud and clear, though we seem to have lost you on our monitors when you stepped into the target room."

"Team Three, Sir, Lieutenant Commander Sisler here," broke in a second voice, "that's a ditto from our location."

The transmission from the Team Three leader was broken up intermittently, and Commander Anglin tapped his wrist device again, "Lieutenant Commander Sisler," he returned, "give me an element report."

"Yes Sir," came the crackling reply, "the wind is whipping up pretty...."

All eyes were on Commander Anglin as he strained to hear the remainder of the Team Three leader's report.

"Say again," requested Anglin in a louder voice, "I'm losing your transmission."

"The wind sir, it's really interfer...."

More crackling sounds made it impossible to hear the rest of the transmission.

Commander Morad exchanged looks with his co-Commander-in-Chief, and nodded his head slightly.

"Lieutenant Commander Bennett," he fairly barked, "do you still read me?"

"Loud and clear, Sir," was the immediate reply.

"Good," responded Commander Anglin, "we're about to carry out phase two of the operation. Consider your team members to be on yellow alert. I'll keep my communication port open, as will Commander Morad. In the interim, have your junior officer attempt to make contact with Team Three. If the wind is interfering with communications, move the team into the base of the Sphinx, just inside the entry way."

"Consider it done, Sir," was the instant reply from the Team Two Leader, "communication port to remain open, end of verbal transmission."

"Lieutenant Kauffman," stated Commander Morad, with a nod toward the negotiator who stood only a few feet away, "the amulet if you will."

Ankhesenamun drew in her breath, as the golden amulet glistened in the reflection of the light beams being trained on it, when Lieutenant Kauffman extracted the ornately inscribed disc from a folded piece of leather he'd kept hidden until that moment.

The last time she had laid eyes on the amulet was shortly before her own death, when she and Emmesharra had held it in their hands together, and she took her final breath.

A flood of emotions swept through Ankhesenamun as the amulet was placed into her trembling hands, and a tear escaped from the corner of her kohl–lined eyes, to trail it's way slowly down her olive skinned cheek

Kevin clutched his wife's hand so hard, Lindsey thought he might have broken some of her metacarpals, as Ankhesenamun and Tutankhamun took their respective places before the round table with the indentation carved smoothly into its surface.

"We are ready to proceed," stated Commander Anglin, with a nod of confirmation from Commander Morad.

Slowly, her fingers quivering, Ankhesenamun lowered the amulet into the circular indentation on the table.

Tutankhamun clenched his jaw, his white knuckled fists balled at his sides. Kevin clenched his teeth and pulled his wife closer, while Lindsey flashed on a mental picture of her father's smiling face that day so many years before, when she had stood next to him in this very same room. Glen's mind was instantly awash with thoughts of Sal and his son, Dimmi, while Professor's Farrier and McRae were riveted to the spot, wide–eyed with wonder.

The light, when it came only moments later, seemed to come from nowhere and everywhere at once, it's whiteness nearly blinding the twelve fascinated, yet frightened individuals enfolded in its beaming intensity.

Ankhesenamun's long, straight, ebony hair stood out around her head like a halo, as a static electricity filled the room with a tangible charge.

Commander's Anglin and Morad tapped frantically on their communication devices to no avail. Not even static was heard in response.

It seemed that the light became even brighter, until everyone present had to cover their eyes from its blinding glare.

"Ankhesenamun," came a resonate voice that no one in the room had ever heard before.

Lindsey lifted her head slightly and fought to open her eyes against the intensity of the white–hot glow of light.

A man stood before Ankhesenamun; a man bathed in golden light, as though his skin were made of burnished copper. Lindsey blinked the protective tears that were rapidly filling her eyes, unable to see the figure's face clearly. She knew that the others were fighting for a clear glimpse of the figure that had appeared seemingly from nowhere.

"Emmesharra," returned Ankhesenamun breathlessly, "you have come."

"You have called me here, and I am pleased beyond explanation to see that you live, but tell me how it is so, when I buried you myself and have searched for your re–born soul to no avail."

"The Great Library of Knowledge has been discovered, my lord, Ra, and the Reclamation has begun. I was brought forth by the people of this time to assist them in contacting you."

"It is truly time then," stated the perfectly chiseled male form that glowed with a light of his own from head to foot, "it has come full circle."

"Yes," came Ankhesenamun's soft reply.

"And you," spoke Emmesharra, his deep, rich voice like perfectly played musical notes, "what is your part here?" his tone was even, and changed not an octave when he addressed the cowering form of Tutankhamun.

"I too am here at the will of the people of Earth," responded the once great boy–king of Egypt meekly, his head bowed low.

"I fail to understand why you would be required," stated Emmesharra just as evenly as a moment before.

"Sir, uh, Ra, uh, if I may?" came the voice of Major Armstrong from somewhere behind Ankhesenamun, "I am Major Armstrong, I am here to speak on behalf of the people of Earth."

"Then you may do so," was Emmesharra's immediate response.

Major Armstrong fought to look at the incredibly tall and well built figure that stood before him, blinking his eyes rapidly to clear the constant accumulation of tears. The intensity of the light was overwhelming, and he could but catch a glimpse now and then of the visage he presently addressed. This person would be an imposing sight, one to be revered, to say the least in any era.

Major Armstrong stepped gingerly forward, motioning for both Thad and Trent to join him, as he took a position just to the left of Ankhesenamun, "We have found the ancient writings, Sir, er, Ra. That is...."

"You may address me as Emmesharra," returned the entity before him, in a voice that was perhaps a fraction softer than a moment before.

"Yes, thank you," replied Major Armstrong, "I have here with me the learned scholars, Professor Trenton Farrier and Professor Thaddeus McRae," he indicated with a sweeping gesture toward the two older men who now stood at his side, heads lowered reverently. "They are responsible for having translated the writings left here in the library."

"Then they are truly wise and learned indeed." Was there an inkling of humor in Emmesharra's deep voice? "I will convene with the elders of my planet," he continued, "and will return with an emissary in two days' time to discuss the full content and impact of the writings you have translated. Before I return however, you must again contact me to confirm that all your world leaders will be present upon our arrival."

"Yes, but Sir," Major Armstrong cleared his throat, and again attempted to look into the face of the glowing persona he addressed, "Emmesharra," he corrected, "we have come to you as a joint act between the United States of America and the Union of Greater Egypt. The other world leaders are not, uh, that is," stammered the flustered Major Armstrong, "they're not exactly aware that we have discovered the ancient writings."

"The knowledge you seek was meant for the descendants of the sons of man and the descendants of the sons of God. The blood of both is mixed amongst the sons and daughters of the Earth. Have all your world leaders not agreed to be present in two days' time, you must contact me again and state so. The history of the planet Earth has shown that your weapons grow much faster than your wisdom. You have discovered the writings, and the people of Earth may now rightfully reclaim that knowledge which was lost to them. Unless all world leaders agree to be present however, we shall neither elaborate on, or discuss the documents you have found until this dictate has come to pass."

"And how will you return here Emmesharra?" asked the Major, his head still lowered, eyes closed in an attempt to control the flood of tears caused by the blinding, white light, "will you require us to return here to this place?"

"It will not be necessary," replied Emmesharra, "now that you have summoned us, we will come through this portal to you. You will know us when we arrive."

"Very good then Sir, er, Emmesharra," corrected Major Armstrong once again, "we shall make contact with the other world leaders immediately."

"That would be most advantageous indeed," returned Emmesharra, "but before I leave your presence, I must know one thing," the tone of his voice indicated that he meant to have an answer posthaste.

"Yes, Anything," replied the negotiator, hoping upon hope that he would have an answer for whatever question this imposing figure before him might present.

"How is it that you chose to bring life to Ankhesenamun, and how came you by the amulet I see before me?"

"Her mummy was found quite by accident," replied Major Armstrong, "in a country far from her birth, and hence the amulet. We assumed her or Tutankhamun to be the human–key mentioned in the ancient writings."

"Any Egyptian Pharaoh could have acted as your human–key, even one from this time who was descended of a Pharaoh. The amulet was not necessary to bring me forth. It was originally meant for Ankhesenamun to call upon me had she the need to do so, and was buried with her as a matter of the heart."

"Then might I ask, sir…Emmesharra," began Major Armstrong, "if not the amulet, then what object could we have used to activate the power source herein?"

"You need have constructed a simple arc to place upon the tabletop" replied Emmesharra stoically, "be prepared to meet in two days' time. I shall wish Ankhesenamun to be present then." With these last words, the light began to slowly dim, the static electricity in the air to lessen, and the room to return to some semblance of normal.

Long after the image of Emmesharra had vanished, the twelve member of Team One stood wide-eyed, the last remnants of tears leaving their eyes, to run in unchecked streams down their faces.

This had been an experience, a revelation, unlike anything that anyone could possibly have expected. Contact had been made; contact with a race so advanced, they had been responsible for the very pyramids and structures that modern man was still incapable of duplicating.

With a low whistle, Commander Morad tapped his wrist device, "Team Two," he said almost breathlessly; "this is Commander Morad. Contact has been made, I repeat, contact has been made." The resounding cheering that greeted his transmission forced him to wait a moment before continuing, "We will be joining you momentarily and returning to base-camp with all due haste."

Commander Anglin stepped closer to his co-Commander-in-Chief, "This is commander Anglin, Team Two," he said, not bothering to utilize his own communication port, "have you made contact yet with Team Three?"

"That is negatory, Commander," came the reply from Lieutenant Kauffman, "we did advise Team Three to take shelter inside the Sphinx, Sir, but we don't know if they received that transmission."

Commander Anglin afforded Commander Morad a stiff nod, "Let's head top-side then, shall we?"

"We'll be heading topside now, Team One," stated Commander Morad into his wrist-device, "end of voice transmission, maintain open communication ports."

"Ten–four, Commander," sounded the reply.

The exhausted, and still somewhat stunned members of Teams One and Two, emerged through the passageway opening, into the base of the Sphinx, to be met by an anxious Team Three leader.

"Commanders Anglin and Morad," greeted Lieutenant Commander Sisler with a smart salute, as he stepped toward the joint Commander–in–Chief's, "good to see you back safely, you had us worried there for a bit when we lost contact."

"Same here," replied Commander Morad as he exchanged glances with his co–commander, "but we understand you did receive Team Two's transmission to take shelter here within."

"Thankfully we did, Sir," replied Lieutenant Commander Sisler with all sincerity, "the wind whipped up out of nowhere. It was all we could do to stay on our feet. I guess it wasn't until we returned inside and Team One exited the Library that full communications were restored."

"Well, in any event," interjected Commander Anglin, "the operation was a complete success, at least this phase was," he included, casting a slightly worried glance at Commander Morad, "there is much more to be accomplished."

"And in a very short period of time," returned Commander Morad, "I think we'd better return to the compound and start putting in links to certain other individuals."

With a nod, Commander Anglin motioned to all team members to move out to the waiting transport crafts for immediate return to the protection of the domed military encampment.

The transport–van rose effortlessly and hovered for a moment before turning about and heading in the direction of the encampment. Lindsey, looking back through the virtual–panel at the Sphinx couldn't help the exclamation that rose to her throat, "Look," she pointed out to Kevin, Glen, Thad and Trent, "the wind is suddenly dying down to nothing."

"Why it is!" exclaimed Glen, "hell of a coincidence isn't it?" he expounded.

"I should say so," agreed Kevin, following his wife's gaze, to where only a few slight gusts of wind now stirred the sand at the base of the Sphinx.

"It's almost as though we brought it with us," stated Thad.

'Didn't we my friend,' thought Trent, and saw his friend's slight nod of agreement.

The mood at base–camp was one of exuberance upon the arrival of all team members, as word began to spread through the compound that the Reclamation Project had gone well.

Of course, all team members had been cautioned against revealing the details of their day's mission to anyone outside of the key members of the project itself, and all of them knew the final outcome still remained to be seen.

Rallying together the world leaders included the leaders of China and Russia, and with current relations so unstable, it was not a task either envied or coveted by anyone. Of course President Albanion was probably being advised at that very moment of the outcome of the meeting with Emmesharra, and would undoubtedly do whatever was necessary to attain China's President Lee and Russia's President Yelinov's participation. For that matter, President Albanion and Egypt's President, Ahad Kameel would also certainly incur the wrath of the remaining world leaders, for having kept the entire Reclamation Project from them in the first place.

It seemed that the chow hall food was only slightly more palatable than the night before, but as with all the team members, Kevin and Lindsey were weary to the bone from their strength–sapping experience. As tired as Lindsey was, she chose to accompany Glen and Kevin anyway, when they announced they would need to run a short series of tests on Tut and Ankhesena-mun.

Finding her young friend bright–eyed and in exceptional spirits brought a smile to Lindsey's face, and Ankhesenamun could seem to speak of nothing or no one except Emmesharra, though Tutankhamun looked tired, haggard and still wore the same dour expression he'd displayed all day.

As with the last tests Glen and Kevin had conducted, Lindsey could tell by the looks on their solemn faces, that they did not like the results they received, but for some reason, they didn't discuss those results, and she didn't ask. At that moment, her mind was focusing on sleep and nothing more.

"Let's take a look at him again first thing in the morning," Glen suggested, as he left Kevin and Lindsey at their front door, and made his way to his own berthing quarters.

"Around seven then," replied Kevin, as he and Lindsey entered their own unit.

"Gone!" barked Commander Morad, his deep voice booming, "what in the hell do you mean he's gone, and just where in God's name is there for him to go?"

"We don't know, Sir," responded the Chief Security Officer, with a shake of his head, "the IBAT staff came in to examine him and Ankhesenamun a few minutes ago, but he was gone."

"Well, I certainly hope you have all available personnel out searching for him," hollered Commander Anglin, entering the room just in time to hear that Tutankhamun had gone missing, "just how in the hell did he breeze right by every body here and leave?"

"Well, uh," stuttered the Security Officer, "the compound was designed to keep people from gaining unlawful entry, not necessarily from leaving, with all due respect, Sir."

It was at that moment that a half-dozen security personnel entered the compound that had maintained Tut, Ankhesenamun, and the examining facility. "We just found one of our guards sir," announced one of the group, "he's been hit over the head with something hard, and his uniform taken from him."

Ankhesenamun looked alarmingly at Lindsey, and both knew they shared the same thought at that moment. Had Tutankhamun hidden the amulet he had used to call the Utukki, and was possibly seeking it out at this very moment?

Lindsey's face went white, and Ankhesenamun's wide, kohl-lined eyes were the last things she remembered seeing, before the room around her began to swim and darkness enveloped her like a shroud.

Chapter Sixteen

Friday, November 14, 2251

Lindsey awoke to a wave of nausea that caused her to lurch abruptly upright and lose the contents of her stomach.

"Lindsey!" Kevin fairly shouted, his fear for his wife's well being, evident in the frown lines creasing his brow. Wedging himself behind her, he braced her body upright with his own, holding her hair back away from her face, while Lindsey continued emptying her stomach into a container held by none other than Ankhesenamun herself.

Purged and exhausted, Lindsey allowed herself to fall back into the comfort of her husband's strong arms.

"Lindsey," he repeated in a calmer, yet still clearly unnerved voice, "are you alright Honey?"

Lindsey nodded slowly, feeling weak, as though every ounce of blood had been drained from her body, and instinctively placed her hands over her still flat belly.

"The baby is fine," Kevin stated softly, in reply to his wife's maternal gesture, "you were out for a few minutes there Honey, and I performed a scan on you."

"With these primitive, military–issue instruments," added Glen derisively, as he stepped into Lindsey's still hazy field of vision.

"Where is everyone?" asked Lindsey, looking around the small examination room that was empty, save for her, her husband, Glen and Ankhesenamun.

"Almost everyone from the base camp has gone to search for Tutankhamun," supplied a clearly worried Ankhesenamun.

"But we weren't about to leave you here," interjected Glen. The fact that he too was truly concerned about his best friend's wife, and his own co–worker, was apparent on the deep frown lines between his black eyebrows. "There's a couple hundred military personnel out looking for him now, and Trent and Thad both joined the search as well."

Lindsey's mind jolted into action, as full recollection dawned, and the reality of their circumstances hit her full force. "Oh dear God," she stated almost breathlessly, her frightened blue eyes locking with Ankhesenamun's darkened amber ones. "We've got to find him, no one else is aware of what he might be capable of doing... except us," she finished in a whisper, her eyes searching the room again to assure herself that no one else was present to hear her words.

"We," repeated Kevin, "is not even an option."

"Kevin!" responded Lindsey, "I have to help find him, you know as well as I do why he must be found quickly. If it's not already too late," she added, the decisive look on her face brooking no further argument, "just help me up, we've got to go now!"

There were only two guards and a beleaguered Deuteronomy at the main portal that led out of the domed encampment.

"Meeeow," the mournful wail from the professor's feline companion sounded again, as he sat before the nearly transparent door that remained closed, refusing him exit.

"Deuteronomy!" exclaimed Lindsey, as they reached the security officer's post.

Reaching down gingerly to retrieve her friend from near their feet, Lindsey felt the blood rush to her head with the effort, and she fought to maintain her equilibrium as she rose with the heavy, black, furry Deuteronomy held securely in her arms.

"I'm afraid our orders are not to let anyone in or out until Commander's Anglin and Morad return to base–camp," supplied one of the security officer's, who was a redheaded young man in his twenties, with thick, chapped lips.

"We're Team One Members of the project," returned Kevin sternly, "our presence is both needed and required just now, I can assure you."

Looking uncertainly to his cohort, and receiving a questioning look in reply; the redheaded officer tapped his wrist device and made voice contact with Commander Anglin.

"Allow them to pass immediately, and allow them any remaining vehicle!" the Commander fairly barked, "and give Doctor Sanders your communication device, I want to remain in contact with her from this moment on!"

With an expression of utter amazement, mixed with an equal amount of unbridled respect, the young officer removed his wrist device and handed it to Lindsey, opening the door for the small group as he did so.

"Uh, Ma'am," stuttered the security officer that had remained quiet until that moment, "Commander Anglin didn't say anything about the cat going out too."

"The cat goes with me," returned Lindsey flatly, "you may return to your duties," she stated over her shoulder, as she passed through the open doorway with her husband, Glen and Ankhesenamun suppressing grins as they followed her outside, and into the night of the Giza Plateau.

Lindsey could have sworn she saw Deuteronomy stick his tongue out momentarily at the security officer, and there was certainly no mistaking the indignant look on his feline face.

"This is the only remaining vehicle!" exclaimed Kevin, an almost stunned expression on his aquiline features, as the four stood looking down at the dark green hovercraft that stood alone just outside the dome. "My God, this thing is older than your Vette Glen!"

"Yeah," agreed his friend, lifting the rounded, darkly tinted Plexiglas type hood, and helping Ankhesenamun into the back seat, before joining her in the cramped compartment, "and it looks like they've been using it for target–practice," he concluded.

"Oh I see," replied Kevin, as he helped his wife, who still clutched Deuteronomy tightly, into the small front seat of this antiquated craft, "and you're going to leave me to operate it."

"Better you than me, my friend," returned Glen, "better you than me."

"Computer," stated Kevin, as he closed the dark cover over their heads, and noticed that his own head still touched the cold hard surface.

No response.

"Computer," Kevin commanded louder.

No response.

"It's broken!" shouted Kevin in total frustration.

"Try pushing that button," suggested Lindsey, indicating a small white raised area on a darkened control panel, just barely discernible in the diffused light emanating from the domed encampment.

Reaching forward cautiously, Kevin pressed the tip of his index finger lightly on the white button, and was instantly rewarded with the illumination of the control panel, and a rather loud, uneven humming sound as forced air from underneath the craft begin to lift it slowly from the ground

"Okay," nodded Kevin, tongue in cheek, "that wasn't too hard. I imagine these arrows on the instrument panel are direction indicators," he added, scanning the dimly lit instrument panel yet again, "so we'll just push this one to go forward...."

The words were no sooner out of Kevin's mouth, when he pressed the button marked by an arrow, and was instantaneously thrown back in his upright seat.

Lindsey and Ankhesenamun screamed in unison, Glen was certain his spine had snapped, and Deuteronomy's eyes widened, as the hovercraft pitched forward as though NASA had launched it.

Kevin released the button and the craft halted immediately; it's occupants, having been thrown forward, sat in petrified silence, with all eyes on their stunned pilot.

"It's okay, it's okay," Kevin repeated, "It seems the buttons indicate the speed as well as the direction."

"It seems that way," replied Glen, still rubbing the back of his neck.

Bracing himself, and pressing the button more gently, Kevin maneuvered the craft haphazardly, in the general direction of the Sphinx.

"Does anyone know if the search party will be heading toward the library?" asked Lindsey, as she gently stroked Deuteronomy's head.

"They said there were guards posted at the entrance to the base of the Sphinx," supplied Glen, "and that there was no way he could gain entry."

"Yes," responded Ankhesenamun, "but he is dressed as a military security officer himself, so he might be able to gain entry without being stopped."

"The moment he was discovered missing, a message was relayed to the guards at both the Sphinx and at the base of the Great Pyramid. They were forewarned that Tut had stolen the uniform of a security officer," intoned Kevin, as he clenched his jaw in an effort to maintain control over the lurching craft.

"But there is no way of knowing how long he was gone before he was discovered missing," replied Lindsey, "there is a possibility that he had already gained entry before the guards were alerted."

"Perhaps you should contact Commander Anglin or Morad on the communicator," suggested Glen, "they might be able to tell us whether or not anyone passed by the guards prior to their having been notified of Tut's disappearance."

"Excellent idea," agreed Lindsey, as she tapped on the wrist device. Even adjusted to its smallest possible size, the apparatus was still too large for her thin wrist.

"Yes, come in, this is Commander Anglin," came the return transmission.

"Commander Anglin," repeated Lindsey, "this is Dr. Sanders. We're on our way to the Sphinx right now. Can you tell me if anyone entered there before the guards were alerted to the young man's disappearance?"

"That is affirmative," responded Commander Anglin, his voice indicating that he was slightly out of breath, "it seems that a guard did join those already stationed near the base of the Sphinx at about six-hundred hours this morning, but managed to slip away unnoticed, and cannot be located now. We are relatively certain it was Tut, which means he had more than an hour head start. We're heading in the direction of the library at double-time speed right now. I don't believe there is any way you could catch up to us at this point, unless you know of another way in there."

"I only wish I did Sir," was Lindsey's disheartened reply.

"To be honest, Dr. Sanders," replied Commander Anglin, continuing to control his breathing and still maintain the conversation, "I don't know what good it will do the young man should he reach the scale–elevator, since it takes twelve people to lower it. There is no other way you are aware of to lower that thing is there?"

Lindsey's mind flashed back to the nightmare she'd had in Atlantica. In that phantasy, the platform had lowered when she'd leaned against the wall, then yesterday, when she tried leaning back against the wall again, Tut had shot her a look of almost pure hatred. Could there actually be some means by which just one person could utilize the scale–elevator? "There is no other way to lower the platform that I am aware of," responded Lindsey. After all, it had been a nightmare, a dream and nothing more.

"Very well," responded Commander Anglin. "Do keep us posted should you see or hear anything, and I will advise you if we manage to apprehend our young runaway. Commander Anglin, over and out."

"Lindsey," said Kevin, as his wife again tapped the large wrist device, fully terminating the transmission, "couldn't there be another way in to the library through the Great Pyramid? I mean," he clarified, "doesn't the library sit directly beneath the pyramid itself?"

"Well, yes," responded Lindsey thoughtfully. "The library is under the pyramid, but there's no evidence of an entrance directly from the pyramid to the library itself. Archeologists have been searching for such an entrance for years."

"Still, with the search party more than an hour ahead of us, we don't have a chance of catching up to them, and we haven't got anything to lose," he added. His wife's nod of consent spurned him to veer the craft in the direction of the Great Pyramid of Giza.

"No unauthorized personnel have been here since my shift started," supplied one of the security officers at the base of the Great Pyramid. The outer perimeter was lit up almost as broadly as daylight by the artificial lighting installed by the military.

"We're members of Team One," offered Kevin, "and we have authorization from Commander Anglin directly to assist in this search in any way we see fit. We'd like to look around inside the pyramid itself."

A quick transmission to Commander Anglin confirmed Kevin's words, and the foursome were handed portable light units, and assigned four security officers to accompany them into the darkened interior of the pyramid.

Ducking to enter the three–foot, eleven–inch doorway, the group descended into the pyramid, continuing on for several–hundred feet, until the corridor became level and terminated into an unfinished chamber. Additional corridors leading outward from this chamber had been lost secrets until shortly after her father and his workers had found the Library of Knowledge. Since that time, a direct access from the pyramid to the library had been sought, but as yet, undiscovered.

Lindsey, juggling Deuteronomy in one arm, and attempting to focus her light–source with the other, trailed behind her husband and the security officers, with Glen and Ankhesenamun close behind. Having been inside this mammoth wonder of the world on many occasions, Lindsey knew the interior of the structure like the back of her hand, and she knew there was no direct entrance to the Library of Knowledge from this location.

A wave of nausea crept up nearly to her throat, accompanied almost simultaneously by a throbbing in her temples, causing Lindsey to stop in her tracks.

"Linds!" exclaimed Kevin; "this is too much for you. You've got to stop now and rest for awhile. I can't have you jeopardizing your health or the health of our child."

Kevin's tone left no question as to his sincerity, "But I've got to help find him," argued Lindsey. Her voice sounded weak even to her own ears, and she knew that further argument on her part would be futile.

The group had just entered through one of the many, and seemingly endless passageways "Please, Honey," he intoned, "just wait here for a few minutes, while we check out some of these passageways. Deuteronomy will keep you company, and you have your light," he sounded like a father speaking gently to a contrite child, "we won't be long, okay?"

Lindsey nodded almost dejectedly. She had little strength left, and didn't posses the energy to argue. Settling herself on a large, square–hewn stone in a recess near the chamber, Deuteronomy held close to her breast, Lindsey settled in to wait for the return of her husband and friends, as she heard their voices becoming dimmer from whichever corridor they had entered down.

The silence was almost unnerving. As many times as Lindsey had been in this very structure, she had certainly never been in it alone at night. The feeling was both eerie and slightly unsettling.

"Meeeow," wailed Deuteronomy from deep in his throat, as the feline began to squirm in Lindsey's arms.

"What's the matter, Little Dude?" asked Lindsey in her softest voice.

"Meeeow," sounded the mournful reply, as the black ball of fur began to twist and squirm until he had freed himself from Lindsey's grasp. With green eyes glinting, Deuteronomy padded off in the direction of the unfinished chambers, and disappeared down one of the corridors before Lindsey could stop him.

"Meeeow," she heard from the passageway just to her left.

"Deuteronomy!" shouted Lindsey, "come back here you little heathen!"

No response.

"Dude!" she shouted again, "I mean it, you'd better come back here right now, or I'm telling Trent and Thad!"

'Lord,' thought Lindsey to herself, 'I'm threatening to tattle on a cat!'

"Meeeow," she heard, as a bushy, black tail disappeared around a bend in the corridor ahead of her.

Onward Lindsey trudged, as the corridor seemed to descend downward gradually, Deuteronomy never far ahead, but never allowing her to catch up. Her breath was beginning to come in gasps from trying to keep up with the elusive feline, and the nausea rose and fell with nearly every step.

Lindsey didn't know how far she'd gone, when Deuteronomy stopped dead at the end of the passageway. There was nowhere to go from here, the corridor ended in a solid rock wall, and the black ball of fur she had been chasing, sat licking his paws and running them over his face and head. His green eyes met Lindsey's as she approached him, admonishing his evilness with every step.

"Now see what trouble you are?" she said, reaching down to pick up the object of her exhaustive search, "If Kevin has returned to find me missing, we're both in for it."

Just as Lindsey's hands began to encircle Deuteronomy, he

leapt to the side and Lindsey stumbled forward. Placing her hands before her to stop her fall, Lindsey was astonished when the entire wall suddenly pivoted with a scraping, groaning sound, to reveal a small room on the other side.

As quick as a flash, Deuteronomy ran through the opening and into the small chamber, stopping at the far wall near a raised, stone platform.

"What in the name of…." Lindsey entered the room, sucking in her breath as she did so.

"Meeeow," wailed Deuteronomy, his eyes having taken on an almost yellowish glow in the single light Lindsey carried to ward away the pitch–black darkness of the room.

"I don't understand 'Meow,' Dude," admonished Lindsey, again reaching down to retrieve her feline friend.

Again Deuteronomy sidestepped Lindsey's efforts, and instead, pounced upon the small stone platform and looked up at the exasperated woman whom he'd just lead on quite the merry chase.

"Okay Dude, enough is enough!" said Lindsey sternly, as she stepped onto the platform to retrieve her wayward charge once and for all.

A grating sound below her, alerted Lindsey to the fact that she was about to discover a good deal more about this small chamber.

Slowly, the platform began to lower, and Lindsey reached out to steady herself, scraping the palms of her hands on the wall as she did so.

In a matter of moments, the small scale–elevator had lowered to an even deeper subterranean level, and another corridor that seemed to stretch endlessly before her. Deuteronomy wasted no time exiting the small platform and heading off down the passageway, as though he traversed this route daily, leaving Lindsey no choice but to follow him as closely as possible.

On and on Lindsey stumbled in her effort to keep up with the flighty feline, and it was sapping every bit of her remaining strength. The aching in her temples, coupled with the continued bouts of nausea, were almost more than she could bear, but Lindsey continued on.

"Meeeow," the sound came from somewhere ahead of her in

the distance.

Lindsey's hand-held light pack was beginning to dim a bit, making it hard to see her way over the rough, loose stones beneath her feet. Twice she fell and managed to pick herself up again, and twice scraped her legs and knees in the process.

It seemed that the tunnel would never end, and Lindsey wasn't sure she could go much farther. Then suddenly, a series of roughly hewn stone steps appeared before her, and just as in her nightmares, Lindsey struggled up each one, her breath coming in gasps as she fell again, placing a hand over her belly as she did so, and crawling up the last few steps.

A platform, not unlike the scale–elevator that lead to the door of the library, met her at the top of the twelve stairs, and using every ounce of her remaining strength, Lindsey forced her weakened and bruised body to stand.

"Meeeow," sounded another cry from Deuteronomy.

Lindsey looked over at her only companion, who was at that moment, standing at the base of the far wall, staring up at the many hieroglyphics etched there thousands of years ago.

"I think it's clear your trying to tell me something here, Dude," said Lindsey breathlessly, "there's a way to make this thing work, isn't there?"

"Meeeow," was the only response.

Lindsey trained her dimming beam of light on the wall and tried to read the inscriptions, 'By the glory of Ra,' was all the writing said.

Reaching out with both hands, Lindsey began to push on the surface of the wall, first one place and then another, until she felt the platform beneath her give a brief jerk, and begin to lower.

Half expecting to see the entrance door to the library before her, Lindsey was disappointed to see yet another corridor instead. This one however, was only about twelve yards long, and ended into a solid gold wall!

Unsure what she might find on the other side, Lindsey raised her wrist to tap the communication device, and contact Commander Anglin. She had no idea how close the others were to the library, but something told her she was even closer.

Her wrist was empty. Lindsey realized then that the

communication–device must have fallen off somewhere along the way. The missing wrist–device made Lindsey feel suddenly much more vulnerable.

Deuteronomy now sat at the base of the golden wall; the metal glinted in the dim glow cast by her rapidly diminishing light, and seemed to reflect off the feline's unblinking eyes. These were the same exact inscriptions as those on the far wall of the library, and Lindsey couldn't help reaching out to trace the hieroglyphs with the tip of her index finger.

Before she knew what was happened, the entire wall began to turn like a huge revolving door, and in an instant, Lindsey found herself standing inside the Library of Knowledge, and staring straight into the face of the devil.

"We are so pleased that you could join us," hissed the reptilian–like creature, whom Lindsey, until this moment, had convinced herself was a figment of her mind's own invention.

Tutankhamun stood just behind the creature, a smug, yet somehow uncertain smirk on his unusually puffy face. At first, Lindsey thought he had darkened his lower lids with kohl, but then realized that his eye sockets were just horribly dark underneath…as though he were ill.

From behind the sickly, smirking Tut stepped yet another creature, nearly identical to the one who now stood only inches from Lindsey's face, forcing her gaze upon him, as his glassy eyes blinked side to side like that of a lizard.

Opening her mouth to scream, Lindsey was horrified when no sound came forth. The slanted gaze and hideous countenance consumed her as she stood before the man–creature. His bluish–green skin covered in small, barely definable scales, glinted in the muted glow of the room behind him.

With sweat rolling down her temples, and blood drying on her legs and knees, Lindsey tried desperately to tear her riveted gaze from the yellow eyes of this demon, whose stare seemed to be rendering her body incapable of obeying the commands of her mind.

"So like the sons and daughters of man," hissed the creature slowly, his 'S's lingering long after the words had been spoken, "when in the face of fear, your first instinct is to pull away and run, instead of standing and fighting for your own puny lives...."

The 'S' continued to linger in the air around her, and Lindsey felt her already queasy stomach began to rise again. Unable to fight back the wave of nausea that had suddenly consumed her senses even more fully than the gaze of this monster before her, she heaved forth, covering the creature's chest with what little remained in her stomach.

As though her bile burned his skin, the reptilian–like beast stepped back, a deep, growling hiss emanating from his throat as he did so.

As soon as their gaze had been broken, Lindsey filled her lungs with air and screamed for all she was worth, turning to run back the way she had come.

The golden wall was just before her, and Lindsey pushed with a renewed strength, in her effort to escape the hideousness that was her reality.

A long, scaly arm reached out as quickly as lightening and grabbed her, pulling her sharply up to his chest. The thick flesh–like layer of scales still bubbled from where her vomit had landed.

With an inhuman strength, the creature pushed Lindsey from him, her body slamming forcefully against the golden wall. The impact forced the wall to swing fully around, sending Lindsey flying through to land in a heap on the other side. The last thing she heard was a series of deep hissing sounds followed what sounded like a man screaming.

Deuteronomy enclosed now in the library with the two Utukki warriors and Tutankhamun wasted no time. Jumping onto the face of the creature that had pushed Lindsey, the hissing feline bit and scratched until the evil one was on the floor writhing in pain from a series of open gashes. No sooner had the second Utukki stepped forward, then Deuteronomy leapt up and sunk his teeth into its scaly arm, refusing to let go.

With an unearthly screech, the creature reached down to pull his companion to his feet, and with a biting, scratching Deuteronomy still hanging from his arm, the warrior pulled his comrade toward the yawning portal from which they had evidently emerged.

A long greenish-blue arm reached out for the amulet that had called them forth, still lying in place on the small table near the portal, just as both Utukki disappeared into the white light.

As the light from the portal began to dim, a furry paw emerged, followed by the rest of its owner, and a pair of intense green eyes stared up at the trembling, pasty face of Tutankhamun.

Deuteronomy never had to do more than stare at the once famous boy-king of Egypt, and the quivering man fell to the floor.

"That was Lindsey!" shouted Kevin, "I heard her scream somewhere up ahead!"

Running at full speed, stumbling over loose rocks and stones as they went, Kevin, Glen, Ankhesenamun and the four security officers continued on.

Kevin was beside himself with panic. When they had returned to the place where they'd left Lindsey, to find her missing, her husband thought he'd lose his mind. From somewhere in the distance, he thought he'd heard her calling out to Deuteronomy, and had followed the faint sound of her voice, and his own instincts. Now that he had heard her scream, his every sense was on edge, and he was perfectly ready to kill anyone, or anything who might harm her, and with his bare hands if need be.

The security officer's had been in constant contact with both Commander's Anglin and Morad, and had already informed the two Commander-in-Chief's that they were in a passageway inside the Great Pyramid that just might actually take them to the library.

The raised platform that had lowered Lindsey to the golden wall had now risen back up for lack of weight, but was too small for more than one person at a time to lower themselves down.

Kevin didn't wait for Glen, Ankhesenamun and the guards to follow. Before the platform had fully touched the ground below, he had leapt off and headed down the corridor in search of his wife, leaving Glen to await the return of the single-person, scale-elevator.

The guilded wall before him paled in comparison to his wife's crumpled body, lying in a heap on the hard stone floor. Kevin couldn't get to her side fast enough.

"Lindsey!" he shouted, falling to his knees and taking his

wife's limp body into his arms, "Oh my God, Lindsey," Kevin sobbed against her hair.

"I'm not dead Kevin," was her weak reply, "but I think I've lost our baby." Lindsey's face crumpled as the reality of their loss hit her full force, "Can you ever forgive me for losing our baby?" she asked through her tears.

It was at that moment, that Glen came to a sliding halt next to his friends, "Oh Jesus, Kevin," he exclaimed, as his eyes settled on the massive amount of blood on Lindsey's legs, and soaking into the dirt–covered stones beneath her.

"It was the Utukki," explained Lindsey quietly, "Tut called them here. He must have found the amulet he'd hidden so long ago. They're in there," Lindsey nodded her head toward the golden door, "but we can't tell anyone that we knew of the amulet's existence."

"I know, I know," replied Glen; "we won't tell a soul."

Ankhesenamun, followed by the four security officers, appeared breathless, just as Kevin lifted his wife into his arms, "Lindsey, oh my Lindsey," whispered Ankhesenamun, tears welling in her eyes at the sight of the blood, and the knowledge that her friend had lost the child she carried.

"My wife says there are others in there with Tutankhamun, and that they're dangerous," warned Kevin, as the security officers stepped toward the golden wall.

Both guards drew their weapons and began looking for a point of entry into the room that had to be on the other side.

"Just push there," said Lindsey weakly, her mind swimming from the amount of blood she had already lost.

The security officers had no sooner burst into the room, than Commander's Anglin, Morad, and the rest of the search party stormed through the doors on the other side of the ancient library.

Two groups of men stood facing each other, weapons at the ready, until their eyes were drawn downward to the still form of Tutankhamun lying on the floor at the base of the round table. The only other entity in the room was a purring Deuteronomy, who sat across from Tut's unmoving figure, licking his paws and running them delicately over his face and head.

Chapter Seventeen

Saturday, November 15, 2251

"It was an abscessed tooth," Lindsey heard from a voice somewhere far away, "the accelerated growth process simply caused it to manifest and deteriorate far more rapidly than it normally would have."

Lindsey thought the voice sounded like Glen's, but her mind seemed to be swimming in a thick fog, and she felt herself drift in and out of awareness.

"That's undoubtedly what took his life the first time around." It was Kevin's voice she heard, the familiar sound pulling at the edges of the hazy blanket of obscurity shrouding her senses. "Only he would have suffered with the abscess far longer than he did this time."

Glen sighed deeply, "Without having been administered his injection yesterday, his cells began to degenerate so rapidly, that he wouldn't have made it much longer anyway, I guess we've both known that all along."

"How ironic to think that one of the most famous kings of Egypt died from an abscessed tooth," returned Kevin. "Though it is in keeping with what Ankhesenamun told Lindsey about Tut's last days. His surgeon must have drilled a small hole in his skull to relieve the pressure."

"Ankhesenamun," breathed Lindsey weakly, "is she all right?"

"Lindsey, thank God!" Kevin fairly shouted, "we've been waiting for you to awaken all morning."

"What, what time is it?" asked Lindsey slowly, as she attempted to rise from her prone position on the examination table. They were clearly back at base–camp, and as full clarity returned, Lindsey gasped as the memory of the events she had just experienced flooded back.

"Let me help you up, Honey," offered Kevin, as he assisted his wife to a sitting position, "I've loaded you up with vitamins and energizers, so you should be feeling good as new in another moment or so."

Lindsey's hand flew to her stomach, and tears burned at the corners of her eyes, "The baby is gone Kevin, our baby," she sobbed, "I'm so sorry."

"Lindsey," chided Kevin softly, as he enfolded his distraught wife in his arms, "I just thank God that you're alive. There will be another child for us." Kevin swallowed the lump in his throat. He wanted to be brave for his wife, but his heart ached for the loss of their child.

Glen cleared his throat gently from behind Kevin, "It seems that Commander's Anglin and Morad are heading this way," he advised.

"They're wanting to ask you some questions, Honey," said Kevin softly, as he stepped back and brushed the tears from Lindsey's face, "do you feel up to it?"

"I think so," replied Lindsey with a soft hiccup, just as the entry door slid aside to admit the Joint–Commander–in–Chiefs.

"Dr. Sanders," greeted Commander Anglin, with a slight bow of his head, "we certainly hope you are much improved this morning."

"Yes, you gave us quite a scare there, Doctor," intoned the dark eyed Commander Morad, the concern on his thin features was evident.

"But we do have to ask you just a few questions, Dr. Sanders," said Commander Anglin apologetically, "in spite of fact that we don't like having to bother you at such a difficult time."

"I understand," returned Lindsey, with a slight nod, "I'll do my best to answer whatever questions you have."

"Excellent," smiled Commander Anglin, his eyes crinkling at the corners. "I suppose the first question we need an answer to, is whether or not you have any idea why in the world Tut would have ventured to the library alone in the first place, and what if anything, he might have expected to find there."

Lindsey's mind returned to the day she and Kevin had discussed this very subject in Professor St. Germaine's office at IBAT. Withholding information from the United States Government was treason, but admitting to this knowledge now could ultimately lead to imprisonment for at least four people that Lindsey could think of. Her mind whirled, searching for an explanation that wouldn't implicate anyone.

"Treasure."

The single word came from somewhere near the other side of the room, and it took Lindsey a moment to realize that Ankhesenamun had been sitting quietly in the corner all the while.

"He was searching for the treasure rumored to have been hidden near the Library of Knowledge," lied the young Egyptian beauty convincingly, as she rose from her chair and walked forward with all the regal poise of a true queen. "He had mentioned it many times," she continued, reaching the two commanders and standing before them, "even though I told him over and over that had the treasure ever existed, it would have been discovered when the library was."

"So this is the only reason you can think of for Tut stealing away from base-camp and entering the Sphinx on his own?" asked Commander Morad, the effect of the stunning raven haired woman before him, causing him to flush slightly.

"I am certain of it, Commander," purred Ankhesenamun. Her full lips took on a pouty quality that so flustered the Egyptian Commander-in-Chief, he nearly stammered out his next question.

"Do you uh," the normally matter-of-fact man of authority before her, suddenly felt most inadequate in the presence of one with such rare beauty, and such a fascinating past. "That is, are you aware of how Tutankhamun might have gotten inside the library without the use of the scale elevator?"

Lindsey found herself almost stunned speechless, as she watched Ankhesenamun bat her lashes and cast side-long glances from Commander Morad to Commander Anglin and back again, and as her own eyes met with those of her husband, it was apparent that he too was attempting to conceal a grin.

"I honestly don't know of any other way in, except the way Lindsey discovered only yesterday," answered the dark eyed beauty in a husky voice.

"Yes," nodded Commander Anglin, clearly as every bit taken by Ankhesenamun's feminine wiles. "But Tut entered through the Sphinx, not through the Great Pyramid, so there simply must be another entrance somewhere."

"Yes, of course," agreed Ankhesenamun, lowering her eyes and turning her mouth down slightly at the corners, "but it seems that knowledge has died with Tutankhamun."

"I can see this is causing you grievous upset," stated Commander Morad, starting to reach a hand toward her, and then withdrawing it as though he had only just realized the involuntary gesture, "and we apologize for our poor timing."

"Ah, just one more thing," included Commander Anglin, as he turned to Lindsey, "the security officer's have stated that you told them there were others in the library with Tut yesterday when you were found. Who were these 'others' you referred to?" Commander Anglin's sharp eyes searched Lindsey's face as her mind whirled in search of an answer.

"I, uh, well I really didn't actually see anyone else," lied Lindsey, "I just heard Tutankhamun talking and assumed he was talking to someone."

"Please understand Commander," broke in Kevin, "my wife had just lost our child after Tut attacked her, and was only half-conscience and near delirium when we found her. In her confusion, it may well have seemed as though there were other's present."

"I see," replied Commander Anglin with a nod, "and again, we are terribly sorry to have to ask questions at a time like this."

"We do have to make another sojourn to the Sphinx," added Commander Morad, forcing himself to tear his eyes from the angelic faced, doe-eyed creature that stood entirely too near him, and turn his attention to Kevin and Lindsey.

"Yes, we will," said Commander Anglin with a nod. "President Albanion has advised us that she has been in direct contact with all our world leaders, including President's Chen Lee and Kaelsic Yelinov. Apparently, they have all agreed to join us here tonight."

"She stated that though they are both accusing the United States and Egypt of trickery and false pretense," added Commander Morad, "they are, nonetheless, afraid of missing something of such magnitude, in the event that there is any truth to what we have shared with them thus far."

"They are exercising as much caution as I am sure we would,

were our positions reversed," stated Commander Anglin, "to give credit where credit is due," he added.

"We shall set out within the hour to notify Emmesharra, as he bade us to," concluded Commander Morad, "do you think you are well enough to join us as a member of Team One, Dr. Sanders?" he asked.

"Yes," nodded Lindsey. "I believe that my health is much improved now…at least physically," she added the last, as though in afterthought.

"Very well then," stated Commander Anglin, as he and his co-commander turned to leave. "We shall assemble the teams and set out in thirty minutes, we've another long journey ahead."

"Ankhesenamun," smiled Lindsey into the kohl-lined eyes of the girl whom she had truly come to think of as a friend. "Thank you for your quick thinking, you saved us all from a good deal of trouble." Lindsey couldn't resist the urge to put her arms around the olive-skinned young woman, "I guess I'm just not a very good liar."

"A most admirable quality in a friend," responded Ankhesenamun, the maturity in her voice belying the mere seventeen years of her present life.

"I just pray that all goes well," said Lindsey seriously, as she stood back and looked thoughtfully at Ankhesenamun, "they didn't find Tutankhamun's amulet, did they?" she asked, knowing what the answer would be before the question had fully left her mouth.

"No," replied the woman that Lindsey could no longer think of as a clone. "It was the first thing I looked for when we entered the library yesterday, just after we had found you, but it was nowhere in sight."

"I wish Deuteronomy could speak," said Lindsey with a half-smile, "he's the only one who really knows. Kevin didn't know exactly what had happened to me until a few minutes ago, when there was finally a moment to explain it to him. He thought Tutankhamun was the one who hurt me."

"So did everyone else," answered Ankhesenamun, "but I knew the moment I saw you lying there, that it was the vicious Utukki who had harmed you. I cannot tell you how sorry I am that you have lost your child. I know exactly how you feel, since I lost my own children a very long time ago." Ankhesenamun's voice trailed off, as though the painful memory of that long–ago time had fully resurfaced to torment her.

"You two ready to head out?" asked Kevin, as he and Glen appeared in to doorway, "All three teams have been mobilized and are preparing to leave the compound."

"We're right behind you," replied Lindsey as light–heartedly as she could.

The sun was shining and not a breath of wind was evident, as the team members filed out of the dome and into the transport vans that would carry them to the Sphinx, and to the Library beyond, hidden deep beneath the Great Pyramid.

Though the entrance Lindsey had stumbled upon the previous day was a much shorter route, the passageway was also a good deal narrower, and the elevator that had carried her down to the library entrance could only carry one person at a time. Commander's Anglin and Morad had determined that under the circumstances, the original route would be most advantageous.

"Our condolences to the both of you," offered Thad, as he and Trent entered the transport van with Lindsey, Kevin, Glen and Ankhesenamun. "It broke our hearts when we heard of your loss last evening."

"Indeed it did," added Trent, as he settled Deuteronomy comfortably on his lap. The feline seemed to have other ideas with regard to his seating preference, and had no sooner looked up to see Lindsey across from him, than he left Trent's lap and jumped lithely over to ensconce himself in Lindsey's arms.

"Hello Little Dude," said Lindsey softly, stroking the sleek, black, ball of fur.

Deuteronomy sniffed Lindsey's stomach and let out a soulful meow, before laying his head comfortably into the crook of her arm and staring up at her in such a way, that Lindsey felt herself wondering if he somehow knew she'd lost her baby.

The transport just ahead contained both Commander's Anglin and Morad, the two Chief Security Officers, and the Negotiator, Major Armstrong, and had just begun to leave the ground, when what appeared to be a large, and fast moving black cloud came into view on the horizon.

"What in the world is that?" asked Glen, staring out the virtual panel as the cloud grew closer.

"Oh my God!" cried the pilot, as pieces of the cloud began to break away and bear down on the group of military transports. "Get back to the dome and get inside it now!" he screamed at his passengers. "We're under attack, and it's constructed to withstand air and ground strikes! Move now!"

The words had no sooner left his mouth when a number of shrieking sounds was heard, followed by bright, white flashes of light, and the immediate destruction of three transport vans, that had contained all members of Team Three.

Lindsey and Ankhesenamun screamed as one, just as Trent reached over to release the door, and with a lightening–quick motion, Lindsey would have thought impossible in a man his age, reached up and pulled her from her seat to the ground. It was up to the others to extricate themselves from the vehicle and follow.

The group had nearly reached the safety of the dome when Lindsey looked back and saw that both Commander's Anglin and Morad had exited their transport and were running full–speed toward the dome, the security officer's and Major Armstrong but a few paces behind them.

A blinding beam shot down from one of the hundreds of triangular–shaped aircraft above, striking the ground just behind Commander Anglin, and leaving a six–foot hole in the sand.

Major Armstrong was blown off his feet, and landed face down several feet away, while Commander's Morad and Anglin, oblivious to the Major's plight, continued their race toward the dome.

The security officers that had been only a few paces behind the Commanders' were both seared through a moment later, as the air strike rained down like mammoth fiery balls of hail.

"My amulet!" screamed Ankhesenamun, when she saw that the bag it had been contained in now lay several feet from the fallen body of Major Armstrong, whose care it had been in.

They had reached the dome, and Trent was hell–bent on

getting Lindsey inside as fast as humanly possible, "No!" she cried, just outside the entry door. "The amulet! We must retrieve the amulet!"

"Deuteronomy!" Trent shouted the single word, and the cat, that Lindsey seemed to have forgotten about when Trent pulled her from the transport, appeared from nowhere. "The amulet Deuteronomy!"

As though he understood his master's words perfectly well, the agile Deuteronomy turned and headed back they way they had just come, at a dead run.

The destructive beams flashing down from the ominous, black crafts above were searing through the transport vans, and leaving craters in their wake. The desert sand was being blown everywhere and mingling with a wind that had just begun to rise, blinding many of the team members who were attempting to seek refuge in the dome. Unable to see, and running from sheer panic, one after another of the team members and security personnel were being annihilated by the unknown enemy that had appeared from nowhere. Shrieks and screams of terror filled the air to mingle with the swirling sand, and the acrid scent of seared flesh.

"Inside, everyone, now!" screamed Commander Anglin, as he and Commander Morad breathlessly reached the dome's main portal and began pulling the individuals through that had made it that far.

Lindsey, Kevin, Glen and Ankhesenamun stood just inside the doorway, with Trent and Thad, the white–hot shafts of light being emitted from the wicked, triangular crafts, continuing to rain down upon the perimeter, as well as the dome itself.

Ankhesenamun screamed as she looked up and saw that with every ray of light that hit the dome, a small, groove in the dome itself would form, "They're going to get through!"

"That's all the survivors!" screamed Commander Morad to one of the door–guards, "close it up!"

"No!" yelled Trent, raising a hand as if to halt the Commander-in-Chief from closing the main portal. "Deuteronomy has the amulet!"

"The cat has the amulet!" screamed Commander Morad, as he and Commander Anglin squinted through the thick, transparent wall of the dome. They could make out nothing save swirling sand, and blinding flashes of light coming from what seemed to be every conceivable direction. Placing both their noses to the clear wall, the two men searched in vain for the return of the black cat.

No one was prepared for the bloody mass of human flesh that flew toward them to splat full–force against the surface of the dome, leaving bits of brain and entrails to slide in bright red hunks, down its smooth surface.

From somewhere behind Lindsey, someone began to retch, the contents of their stomach spewing onto the polished walkway, but the horror of their present situation had nearly numbed her into immobility.

"We've got to shut the door now!" screamed Commander Anglin at the top of his voice. "We don't know if they'll try to breach the dome! Close it!" he commanded the door–guard.

Without hesitation, the guard placed his hand on a panel atop his podium, and the door began to close.

Eight inches to go and Deuteronomy would be sealed outside for good, seven, six…

"No!" screamed six voices in unison.

Five inches, four, three!

"Meeeow!" Deuteronomy came through the mere three inch opening at such high speed he was unable to stop.

Just as it seemed the dirty, black feline, dragging the heavy amulet by its chain would stop, the fates united in cruelty, forcing him to slide through a puddle of vomit left by one of the survivors of the perimeter attack. When at last the disheveled Deuteronomy came to a stop against the wall of the infirmary, it was with the utmost of indigence that he shook his tail and trotted back to his owner, dropping the amulet at Trent's feet, and meowing soulfully.

"Is there another way out of here, Commander?" asked Kevin as calmly as he possibly could, addressing neither Commander Anglin nor Commander Morad, but rather both of them, at the same time.

Around them sounded the 'red–alert' warning alarms as soldiers rushed about, officers directing them to secure their stations. "There's only the 'sally–door,' but you can't leave the protection of the dome! We don't even know who we're dealing with here, but I have a good idea it's either the Russians or the Chinese."

Lindsey glanced at Ankhesenamun, and saw that her friend's face was a mask of worry, "Where is the sally–door?" asked Lindsey, her panic rising with every destructive beam that hit the outer surface of the dome.

"It's at the other end of the compound, but you're all under orders not to leave this dome!"

"Yes, Sir!" returned six voices, as the group turned on their heel and began to run at top speed down the main corridor toward the other end of the massive dome.

The small door was only a few yards away, but would clearly not accommodate more than two people side–by–side. Past the flurry of officers, soldiers and security guards, the group had no sooner reached the opening, when a blinding flash of light from above hit the ground just outside.

The six–foot crater was difficult to crawl out of, and with every effort made by the six runaways, the sand would force them to slide back down. Kevin placed a hand firmly on his wife's fanny, and pushed her upward with all his might.

Reaching up over the edge of the crater, Lindsey's hand closed around a piece of debris, and jamming it into the sand, used it to pull herself the rest of the way up. Once her head rose above the top of the high sand wall, she looked over to discover with shocked disgust that she had been clutching what remained of a charred human arm and hand. With an ear–shattering scream, Lindsey threw the blackened appendage.

With a heavy thud, something landed on Glen's back as he struggled upward, as though swimming in an ocean of sand. Thinking he had been attacked from behind by one of the horrifying Utukki creatures, Glen rolled over, prepared to defend himself any way he could. As he rolled, the arm fell off into the sand next to him, and with a shriek, he turned and scuttled up the remainder of the sand wall with lightening speed.

Breathless from the exertion, the remaining four climbers and a matted Deuteronomy made it to the top of the pit, only to be met with blood–soaked sand and mutilated body parts.

"Stay together, and look for a vehicle that's still intact!" shouted Kevin over the whine of the bat–like ships continuing to batter away at the dome.

"There!" yelled Glen. "There's one over there!" He pointed to a craft about ten yards away, barely visible in the sandstorm that had erupted with the arrival of the Utukki.

Dodging the fireballs that crashed down around them, the six horrified refugees wound their way through the blinding sand to the only vehicle unscathed thus far. It was the very same one Kevin had driven just the day before when they'd gone in search of Tut. There had scarcely been enough room for four, and now Trent and Thad were with them, not to mention the vomit covered Deuteronomy.

"This can't be happening!" screamed Kevin, pounding the vehicle with his fist, as though it would somehow be transformed into a nice transport van.

Only slightly more adept at operating the antique hover–craft than he had been the first time, only with knees and elbows ramming in to every one of his ribs, Kevin pressed the button he knew should guide the craft forward.

Deuteronomy let out a wail that seemed to have no end, as he found himself pasted to Trent's chest with the force of their take–off.

Like a beam of light, the ancient craft surged forward, narrowly missing a Utukki craft in the process of making a U–turn, and another attack on the dome.

Through sheer, blind luck alone, Kevin managed to land the craft just outside the entrance to the Great Pyramid.

"It's much faster this way," he shouted over his shoulder, as the six still petrified escapees climbed to the entrance of the pyramid, grabbing several light–tubes lying about on their way from the seemingly abandoned perimeter.

"We'll have to take the elevator one at a time, and watch your step we have no time to lose."

Deuteronomy jumped down from Trent's arms, running ahead of Kevin. "Just follow him," said Lindsey, "he knows the way like the back of his paw." In truth, she was desperately thankful that she wasn't making this trip alone with Dude again.

Grabbing Lindsey's hand, Kevin led her through the passageway behind their meowing guide, as they wound there way ever deeper into the bowels of the pyramid, and then the very earth itself.

When the group finally entered the library through the pivoting, golden door, they were gasping for breath and bone weary.

Retrieving the amulet from his pocket, Trent handed it to Ankhesenamun's' shaking, extended hand and she gingerly placed it in the groove on the table before her, while the group held their collective breaths.

The blinding white light that slowly began to emit from the wall behind the table was a welcome sight to the inhabitants of the library.

"I am returned," came the deep, soothing voice, "and I see that there is great trouble here among you. Ankhesenamun," said the glowing figure, "have you met with harm?"

"No, Emmesharra," Ankhesenamun replied softly, her head downcast to avoid the blinding light surrounding the near–silhouette before her. "But Tutankhamun is dead, and the Utukki are attacking the military even now. Can you help us Emmesharra?" she asked, tears running down her cheeks, "can you help us my love?"

"I can help no one save those before me now, for it is written," he stated in a clear, calming tone.

From just outside the main entrance doors came the sound of the scale–elevator beginning to lower. "They come for us now!" shrieked Ankhesenamun, as she reached her hand toward the light.

The dazzling brightness of the hand that came from the circle of light and took Ankhesenamun's own was reflected in every inch of the golden walls within, lighting the entire room to a blinding intensity.

Ankhesenamun disappeared into the light, and the hand was extended. Through the tears streaming down her face, Lindsey reached out and felt herself pulled into what felt like an electrified vacuum.

Fighting for breath, and feeling as though her lungs were about to burst through her chest, Lindsey was unprepared for the overwhelming sensation of total calm that engulfed her at the journey's end.

Turning her head to the right, Lindsey locked eyes with an even more stunning Ankhesenamun. The bright, vivid colors of the gold-trimmed gown she wore, were alight as though there were a fire somewhere near, though none was apparent. The dark eyed beauty was as perfect as an antique porcelain figurine, her skin flawless, hair shining as though it had been spun with tiny shimmery threads.

Kevin appeared next, and from the way he looked at his wife when he turned his head, Lindsey had the feeling that he was seeing her in an ever better, more beautiful light than ever before. His own chiseled features were alarmingly handsome, and Lindsey felt herself drawn as if by an unseen force, into her husband's welcoming arms.

Glen, Thad and Trent followed, but just behind Trent came a loud commotion and a hissing sound, followed by a beleaguered Deuteronomy, who hadn't been able to resist one last swipe of his claws across a Utukki face. Oddly enough, the feline, though covered with dried vomit and sand only moments before, now stood at Trent's feet, clean, sleek and shiny black.

With one hand on the small of Ankhesenamun's back, Emmesharra motioned for the group to follow him out of the intense glow of the transport room. Leading the survivors through several hallways that glowed with purplish-blue, gently pulsating lights, and scarcely taking his eyes from Ankhesenamun, the group finally emerged at what must have been the bridge of the ship.

There were six or so of Emmesharra's people performing various tasks, and though each of them smiled at the new arrivals, they did not speak, even to themselves. Lindsey had never seen such an attractive group of people in her life. The two women on the bridge were statuesque, with perfect skin and long silky hair, and the men looked like Greek gods. Still, when she turned to gaze at her own husband, he appeared even more attractive than these otherworldly beings before her.

The Annuaki, including Emmesharra, all wore floor-length white robes, each person's robe seeming to mold to their body like a second skin, though no seams were outwardly present. It wasn't until Lindsey eyes lowered to the bottom of the robe worn by one of the men standing near some sort of a control panel, that she noticed their feet were not quite touching the floor, nor were Emmesharra's. These advanced beings seamed to float an inch or two above the floor, as they went about their duties.

"Why did we not see your ship from the dome, when you can clearly look down on everything that is happening below?" asked Kevin, as he and Lindsey, followed by Glen, Ankhesenamun, Thad, Trent and Deuteronomy, looked out a panel of windows at the havoc being wreaked below.

"This craft is not meant to be seen," returned Emmesharra. "It is what you might refer to as a reconnaissance craft. It is for the purpose of watching and monitoring only, and is not equipped to intercede in anything of this magnitude," he finished, waving his hand at the destruction being carried out below.

The Utukki ships had breached the dome, and the inside was red with blood. Lindsey sobbed at the sight that met their eyes. No one could possibly have survived it. Everyone was gone, Commander Anglin, Commander Morad, everyone.

"I am sorry that we could not intervene, Lindsey," said Emmesharra, now clearly visible without the blinding light surrounding him. His hair was black as night yet seemed to cast an almost golden glow, and hung long, thick and straight down his back. The robe he wore was of the most pristine white, and his sandaled feet were perfect down to his toenails, which seemed to hover effortlessly above the soft glow of the floor beneath. When Lindsey turned and met his eyes, she nearly gasped at the perfection of his features. The man appeared to be a god, and Lindsey could easily see why the Egyptians had worshipped this divine personage.

Lindsey was surprised when Emmesharra called her by name, but from somewhere deep in her mind, it seemed natural that he should know it. "There's no saving them now," she said sadly. "But what about the rest of the world? Are they too at the mercy of these monsters?"

"I am afraid so," returned Emmesharra, his own voice sad. "Once they were called here, every living thing was at their mercy." He shook his head, his crystalline blue eyes again scanning the destruction below. "We cannot interfere…the Utukki were invited."

At that moment, a dozen or so Utukki fighter–craft broke away from the attack on the already breached dome, and veered off in the direction of Cairo.

"Nooo," choked Lindsey, as the worst possible scenario took place before their very eyes. Within seconds, flames and billowing plumes of black smoke erupted over the city of Cairo itself.

At a moment when it didn't seem that anything could make the present situation worse, the sky literally darkened with what seemed to be thousands of newly arrived Utukki craft, and chaos reigned as far as the eye could see.

Kevin put both his arms around his wife as he stood behind her watching the relentless attack on every living thing within reach of the Utukki, "Are they going to destroy the entire earth?" his anguished voice blurted forth.

"It is a certainty," returned Emmesharra, signaling for his navigator to prepare to leave the atmosphere.

Lindsey put her face in her hands and sobbed as she realized that she would never see her mother or Professor St. Germaine again, would never enjoy another day with Kevin in Atlantica, would never hold the child they had created together. She thought her heart would break at that moment. "What have we done?" she wept, "What have we done?"

Glen turned as white as a sheet. His last thought was of Sal's liquid brown eyes, as the craft turned effortlessly at a ninety–degree angle, before shooting out into space at a speed far beyond anything comprehensible by the inhabitants of the planet below…the planet that was fast becoming nothing more than a vanishing speck of light, in an endless sea of stars.

Chapter Eighteen

Lindsey was certain she'd awaken at any moment to realize that she'd just had a horrific nightmare. Nothing seemed real, as she stood on the bridge of this indescribable craft next to Emmesharra and Ankhesenamun; her husband's arms still around her. Her mind whirling, Lindsey took a mental inventory of the events that had led up to this moment, from her father's discovery of the Library of Knowledge, to the clone of King Tutankhamun summoning the Utukki, to the ultimate annihilation of the earth itself. It all sounded like a bizarre sci–fi movie, and she wanted nothing more than to open her eyes, and find her self emerged in hot, soothing bath water.

Lindsey closed her eyes for a moment, opening them to find the brilliant white lights flashing by them in a high–speed laser–type show not unlike some of the rides at the Entertainment Center in Atlantica.

Trent, Thad and Glen stood on Lindsey's right, watching in wide–eyed wonder as they streaked through outer–space, experiencing firsthand what the greatest minds of earth had only dreamt of, having not actually landed on the Earth's own moon until 2045.

The formal discovery of NASA's elaborately conducted hoax upon the world had finally broken wide open in 2005, when the set they had used to film the historic Apollo 11 moon landing in 1969, was uncovered in Area 51 in the desert of New Mexico.

In a bizarre and most unexpected twist of fate, several senators and congressmen had petitioned the government to allow key officials entry to the Area 51 hangar, to put to rest once and for all, rumors of little alien beings having been secretly kept there since the 1940's.

In the spring of 2005, with an official, governmental subpoena in hand, twelve elected individuals entered the Area 51 hangar. To their own shock and amazement, rather than finding extra–terrestrials, they discovered an entire movie set, complete with moon back–drop and the flag that had allegedly been planted on the moon by none other than Neil Armstrong, Michael Collins, and

Edwin Aldrin.

In the aftermath of the discovery of what ultimately became the most infamous hoax of all time, the inhabitants of Earth learned that no astronauts from any country had made it to the moon. It seemed that from an astronomical perspective, the people of Earth were decades behind what they had been led to believe.

When it came down to it, it seemed that travel to the Earth's own moon could not be achieved due to a radiation belt that made transporting human life past a certain point quite impossible. Apparently, that had been known by the United States from the very beginning, but when the Apollo 11 landing was broadcast on television, the people who witnessed it had no way of knowing they were watching a combination of movie set and Arizona desert at night.

Finally, in 2045, a scientist from Ohio by the name of Clive McKinstry, invented a material light enough to be used in the construction of a space–module, yet capable of withstanding the effects of the radiation belt itself, and protecting human passengers from it as well. Although McKinstry's invention had eventually made it possible for the firsthand exploration of Mars by 2110, a recession and subsequent lack of military funds had halted the mission in its early stages.

Now and then, Lindsey would notice Emmesharra nod to one of the Annuaki crew, and though the crewmember would nod back in apparent affirmation, no words were spoken between them. Stranger still, was the fact that this seemed to be occurring between Thad, Trent and the Annuaki crewmembers, or was she just imagining it? Lindsey's felt that her mind was on over–load, images of her past, her childhood, began to push themselves to the forefront of her mind, as the planets and stars flew by from without.

"You must be made ready for arrival on Ataneberu," stated Emmesharra from somewhere to Lindsey's left, "you will not survive the trip otherwise."

Lindsey felt the warmth of Kevin's arms dissipate slowly, to be replaced by something else, something that seemed to guide her slowly away from the bridge of the ship, down more corridors, and into a small chamber with a round ceiling, where several large glass tubes encircled the inner walls. The walls and ceilings were covered with inscriptions that vaguely resembled hieroglyphics, but Lindsey found herself unable to focus on the objects as she struggled to try to read them.

"You must take your place here," said Emmesharra softly, as the glass tube seemed to rise up from the floor with a mere wave of his hand. "You will be conditioned for the journey."

Slowly, as though in a trance, Lindsey stepped forward into the tube, and then turned around to face the tall, handsome form of Emmesharra, her vision beginning to blur. She had a vague sense that Kevin, Glen and the others were also being placed in these floor–to–ceiling tubes.

Her last conscience thought was of placing her fingers on the inside surface of the cylinder that had now closed down around her. The tube looked like glass, but when her hand touched it, it was neither solid nor liquid, but somewhere in between and a ripple formed where here skin made contact, much like the rings that form on the surface of the water by skipping a stone.

The oxygen that now filled her lungs inside the tube smelled like the air on earth just after an electrical storm, and there was a sense of lightness surrounding her. Lindsey's heavy eyelids began to close slowly as a trance–like state of sleep overcame her. Had she been able to look down at that moment, she would have noted that her feet were no longer touching the floor.

Huge airships resembling souped–up blimps lifted square–cut stones into the air, placing them with perfect precision atop a half–built pyramid. From somewhere far away, Lindsey watched the building of the massive edifice as though through binoculars. While she seemed far removed from it, she could view it in such great detail as to make out the tiny grains of sand that rolled down the slanted walls with every stone laid in place.

She watched in fascination as one after another, the massive stones were set and then trimmed at the perfect angle with a laser that came from the airship above. Lindsey found herself inexplicably able to control her view of the construction of the massive pyramid by sheer will alone, allowing her a three–hundred–and–sixty degree view of the building process. It was as though she had no form, no substance, but could zoom around in any direction to watch with avid interest and delight, as the pyramid rose up and took shape. She could will herself to see beyond the exterior, through the two–and–a–half ton blocks to the chambers and passageways within.

Suddenly, and without warning, Lindsey felt herself being pulled back away from the structure, "No," she cried out weakly, "it's not finished yet, I want to…."

Emmesharra stood looking down at her. Lindsey was no longer in the tall cylindrical tube, but was lying on a table in a brightly lit room with a strangely graduated ceiling. It appeared to be some sort of laboratory or examination room from the looks of the odd instruments lying about, none of which Lindsey could even attempt to identify.

"There you are Honey," smiled Kevin, as he stepped into her field of vision and stood next to Emmesharra. Lindsey noted with a smile that her husband wore the same body–molding robe, as did Emmesharra, and she liked the way it fit him…she liked it a lot.

Other voices to her left caused Lindsey to turn her head, finding herself not the least bit surprised to find that Trent, Thad, Glen and Ankhesenamun also now wore the glowing white garments donned by the Annuaki. Deuteronomy, held firmly in Trent's arms, still wore his shiny black fur, and Lindsey felt a slight giggle spring forth from her throat at the thought of the fat little feline wearing a small, white robe as well.

Emmesharra smiled, showing perfect, white, even teeth, "It seems your conditioning was quite successful, you are feeling well?" he asked.

"I feel wonderfully well," smiled Lindsey honestly. In truth, she'd never felt better, as she took Kevin's procured hand, and allowed him to help her slide from the table top, noticing as she did so that her feet did not touch the ground. He was so close, and so incredibly handsome that Lindsey felt herself drawn to him, as though she could somehow step inside the shell of his body to mingle her soul with his own.

'You can you know,' came Emmesharra's voice, though Lindsey noted that his mouth did not move.

'Can what?' asked Lindsey, as she suddenly realized she had

not formed the words with her mouth when she spoke them, even though she heard them as she said them.

'Can touch souls,' returned Emmesharra simply. 'When we mate here on Ataneberu, it is not just a sharing of the body, but a sharing of the souls as well.'

'This is what I saw happening between you and the others on your ship isn't it?' questioned Lindsey, referring with her thoughts to the Annuaki ability to communicate without using the spoken word, and not the least surprised when Emmesharra nodded in assent.

'Words are not necessary even on your planet,' he communicated, the deep blue pools of his eyes conveying a measure of mirth. 'Only the people of Earth are far too caught up in their own personal interests to explore such a thing fully, or to learn to put it to use.'

Lindsey looked up into Kevin's eyes, and then blushed deeply when she realized that everyone else in the room had probably picked up on the thoughts she was harboring when she looked into her husband's forest–green eyes.

'Your feelings for your mate are not to be ashamed of here on Ataneberu,' although Emmesharra's lips did rise at the corners in a smile, his mouth still did not move when he spoke. 'We are a pure race of people here, and the love for one's mate runs many times deeper, than it does on Earth, as you are no doubt experiencing now.'

It wasn't difficult to see from the reflection in Kevin's eyes that he was feeling quite the same as his wife, and Lindsey had to fight the urge to place her lips over his own.

'There is a place of rest for you and your friends, if you will follow me,' said Emmesharra as he turned and extended his arm to Ankhesenamun, who stood just behind him.

Although Lindsey's mind willed her legs and feet to walk, her body seemed to move forward with a will of it's own, as on a moving walkway, though nothing but mid–air itself rose between her sandaled feet and the dimly glowing floor beneath.

The small room Lindsey and Kevin were lead to contained no furniture, but somehow that seemed not at all strange. Suddenly, there was no door where the door had been, the others were no longer present, and Lindsey was finally free to hold her husband close.

Kevin's lips pressed down upon his wife's, her mouth tasting sweet and soft beneath his own. His hands explored and caressed her body, until the robe she wore seemed to fall away from her, baring her nakedness to him. It was a deeper; more spiritual bonding than either could have ever imagined possible.

Lindsey felt drunk with the sheer pleasure of her husband's body filling her own, their minds came together, thought for thought, feeling for feeling, mingling, consuming and culminating in a shattering fantasia of exploding senses...the sharing and the joining of two souls.

Lindsey and Kevin had no idea how long they floated together, fully entwined in the small room, drinking in all that there was of one another, until even the essence and the fabric of their spiritual selves was no longer a singular thing.

Emmesharra's voice came from the doorway that had again magically appeared, and when Lindsey looked down, she saw that she and her husband were once again wearing the long, white robes of the Annuaki.

'Would you like to see some of our world?' asked Emmesharra, his mouth still did not move, except to smile down at the radiant Ankhesenamun who stood at his side.

Lindsey and Kevin's minds came together in a single thought, that they were about to enter into yet another indefinable experience.

The walls of the corridor were much like the walls of the Annuaki craft that had carried the visitors to Ataneberu. Lindsey ran her fingers along them, watching the rings undergo a change of multiple, luminescent colors as they fanned out, leaving small trails where her skin made contact with the oddly glowing material.

Kevin sucked in his breath as they came to the end of the corridor and exited out into the heart of the city. Lindsey, following Kevin's gaze, noted with utter delight that every building in sight was a pyramid shaped structure. Some of the pyramids were no larger than a regular sized house on Earth, while others in the distance could easily have dwarfed the Great Pyramid of Cheops. There were no vehicles, and the lack of a need for them was evident in the number of beings floating about from place to place effortlessly.

'There is no hate here,' explained Emmesharra, 'only love for one another. We exist, as you can see, on a much higher plane than do the beings of earth.'

The entire city was awash in a purplish–blue light, much like the light emitted from the walls of the space craft that had carried them here, and many of the pyramid buildings had windows, in which Lindsey could see people moving about. There was a feeling around her of well being and happiness, but somewhere deep within her heart; Lindsey could still feel the loss of her mother.

'I know your heart, Lindsey,' communicated Emmesharra. 'Should you choose to stay here with us, the pain within you will dissipate.'

'Should I choose to?' asked Lindsey with her mind, while she drank in the wonders around her with her eyes. 'Is there another choice?'

'Possibly,' replied Emmesharra. 'It is being discussed by the elders at this moment, but is difficult to say what their decision will be.'

Lindsey seemed to be having a difficult time comprehending exactly what Emmesharra was saying to her, but as always, he knew her thoughts as soon as they had formed. 'Your confusion is the result of your brain attempting to adjust to the functional level of the plane you now inhabit. As that portion of the conditioning wears off, you may find it increasingly more difficult to concentrate, or to speak without the use of your tongue. Soon, I will provide you all with an infusion, or you would become unable to understand anything that I attempt to convey.'

Emmesharra spoke slowly in his mind, as one might to a small child, and Lindsey nodded her understanding.

'I shall leave you to explore, while I confer with the elders, but do not go too far,' instructed Emmesharra telepathically.

It was then that Lindsey noticed Glen, Thad and Trent, who had been hovering nearby, somewhere behind her, and smiled as she saw that even Deuteronomy's feet were nowhere near the ground.

Taking Lindsey's hand in his own, Kevin pulled her forth and willed himself upward, as Lindsey followed. Behind them came Glen, Thad and Trent, with Deuteronomy following closely, Ankhesenamun having gone with Emmesharra.

It was like swimming in air as they glided about over and around the hundreds of pyramid dwellings, all of them emitting the purplish–blue glow that seemed to light the entire city against the dark of the night.

Three very dim moons shown down from above, and were so close that Lindsey as though she could almost reach out and touch them.

As though they shared one collective mind, the five explorers enjoyed the wonder of this fantasy world in which they were now existing; all experiencing the love and well–being that was a part of the planet itself.

Many of the Annuaki people relayed a welcome to their fascinated visitors, and many waved their hands in greeting. All of them were beautiful beyond words, perfect in every way, and here and there, Lindsey saw small children staring back at them with wide eyes.

It was a place of perfection, of peace, tranquillity, love and calm, yet in the midst of the all–consuming euphoria that filled their senses, neither Lindsey, Kevin nor Glen could stop thinking of their own planet. Any thoughts on that topic held by either Thad or Trent were carefully veiled.

A pulling sensation brought the visitors back to the doorway of the pyramid building they had departed what seemed like only moments earlier. Emmesharra, with Ankhesenamun at his side, stood waiting for their return. 'I have spoken with the elders and am advised that we shall present your case to the Serandreals, the time keepers, and await word from them, their response may take some time, so an interim location for you will have to be decided upon.'

'The Serandreals?' thought Kevin.

'An interim location?' questioned Glen

'Can we not stay here?' communicated Trent.

'The Serandreals will help?' thought Thad excitedly, as Lindsey, Kevin and Glen all riveted their eyes on him at the same time, to further ascertain his thoughts.

'Too many questions from all of you,' interrupted a smiling Emmesharra, 'I shall do my best to explain what I can. Do remember though that your earthly bodies had to be conditioned for this trip in order for you to survive for any length of time in our atmosphere, but the conditioning will began to wear down soon and you will require an infusion.'

'An infusion?' thought Lindsey, 'there is too much information coming at me.'

Emmesharra's grin widened, 'An infusion is required to stimulate your Earth brains, so that you can continue to understand and return our mental communications.'

'Earth brains, eh,' teased Lindsey.

Emmesharra was mentally laughing, 'We communicate on a much different plane than you are accustomed to,' explained their celestial host, 'but you will only be capable of comprehension for a short time longer. One infusion is all you will, or can be administered, and before it's effects wear off, you will have to be transported to another realm, or planet as you would refer to it, until the Serandreals have made a decision.'

'But exactly where are we now?' asked Kevin, 'You have referred to this place as Ataneberu, is this the New–Neberu Thad and Trent found mention of in the scrolls and tablets from the library?'

'It is one and the same,' returned Emmesharra. 'Our Neberu was destroyed in the celestial battle many eons ago. The Utukki, who followed their fallen leader, Satan, and his right–hand minion, Set, devastated our realm through the destruction of our great pyramids. We had no choice but to move on to another realm as similar to our own as possible. We came to the Orion Nebula, settled here, in the realm formerly known as Mintaka, in the Delta Ori, and named it as you said,' he nodded to Kevin, 'New–Neberu, or Ataneberu.'

'But initially, it was the sister planet of Mars that you inhabited?' confirmed Thad with a question.

'Yes,' we came to settle near the entity that Egyptians have long referred to as Horus, the son of Osiris. Horus was the twin of the most evil Set, and did slay him in time. The realm of Orion is where the reincarnation of mortals eventually evolves to, until of course, they attain their karma and go to the final realm to join the son of the almighty Jehovah.' Emmesharra bowed his head in a moment of deference to the Creator of all things.

'The existence of God himself,' intoned Glen without a word.

'Have you ever doubted such?' asked Emmesharra mentally.

'I believe that even the most righteous of mortals has questioned His existence at one time or another,' replied Glen.

'Even though it is written that he should not,' Emmesharra shook his head almost sadly, 'even though there is evidence of his existence everywhere.'

'Though much of that evidence has been lost to man,' replied Trent.

'Yet much remains,' Emmesharra's thoughts were hard for a moment, as his mind was momentarily infused with anger at the thought, 'the very existence of our Pyramids in so many locations on your planet should be evidence enough,' he intoned. 'The bible was purposely left for the sons of man to know of God's intentions, and of his love,' he continued. 'In the book of Isaiah, chapter nineteen, verses nineteen and twenty, the people are told that, 'In that day shall there be an altar to the Lord in the midst of the land of Egypt, and a pillar at the border thereof to the Lord. Emmesharra lowered his head, 'the pyramids of Egypt are the very pillar that Lord spoke of, and communication through the Great Pyramid is clearly possible, as you know first–hand. After the first celestial battle, we were the guardians of Earth until the final days,' he paused, 'until the Revelation.'

'If you were to guard the Earth from harm until the Revelation, why has it now been destroyed by the Utukki?' asked Lindsey, 'why did you not save it from their destruction.'

'Because we no longer guard it,' responded Emmesharra. 'The Revelation is passed, it has already happened, and you are the descendants of the survivors. Many of the pyramids were destroyed, but somehow the Great Pyramid remained as evidence of what once was, the Great Pyramid, and the bible,' he finished with downcast eyes.

'So all the Christians awaiting the Armageddon are waiting for something that already happened?' questioned Glen.

'Yes,' replied Emmesharra, 'though the people of Earth are still God's people, and he still loves them and hears them, and we continue to carry out his will through the divine intervention of the Serandreals, who are the direct messengers of Christ himself.

'Think of all we could have learned, all the knowledge the people of Earth would have had to build from, had the devious Tutankhamun not summoned the Utukki,' thought Glen.

'There would have been no further knowledge forthcoming, even had Tutankhamun not summoned the Utukki,' stated Emmesharra rather flatly.

'But you were to meet with the world leaders to discuss the ancient wisdom for the good of all mankind,' interjected Kevin, 'why would there be no further knowledge forthcoming?'

'Because your own leader lied,' returned Emmesharra. 'She had not contacted the leaders of Russia or China, but had planned to replace them with others who resembled them, thinking that we would not know the difference. Her deception and greed would have precluded any elaboration of the records found.

It had always been thought that by the time mankind discovered the scrolls and tablets, they would be ready for the wisdom, and eager to share the knowledge, but that was not the case, and clearly your world was not ready.'

'What of the reincarnation you spoke of when you first arrived?' asked Glen.

'Unfortunately, much of the information in the bible with regard to the reincarnation of the spiritual self was eliminated by man many generations ago. The leaders of the church were afraid that people would assume they could make it to heaven on their own deeds and merits, with no assistance from the church or its leaders. They removed the direct references to reincarnation, and instead taught the masses that the gates of heaven were only open to steadfast churchgoers and those who contributed monetarily to the church. In truth, the soul will have many lives on Earth in which to learn the lessons of life and to attain oneness with their own karma. From that point, the soul is transported to another realm, or plane, where more lessons are learned. This will continue until the soul has attained a level of perfection, at which time there will be no rebirth, nor returning, but rather, eternity with the Lord God.' Again, Emmesharra bowed his head in reverence.

'But you, yourself were worshipped as a god in Egypt,' thought Lindsey, 'why was such a thing allowed?'

'We were sent to earth to assist the survivors and returnees after the Armageddon,' supplied Emmesharra. 'While I settled in Egypt, others were dispersed throughout the planet, where their own pyramids were constructed so that the people they were assisting would still have a method of communication. There were pyramids constructed in the places Earth dwellers have labeled China, Africa, Indonesia, and everywhere in between. Though many of them have since been covered by changes in the topography of the earth, still others remain undiscovered by modern man. Those of us who were sent, were sent to teach those who remained on earth the basic knowledge with which to better themselves. They were taught mathematics, farming and agricultural skills, astronomy, and all the things necessary for productive life. They were taught of Jesus and of his Father, yet for all these teachings, the people of earth began to worship us, the messengers. It was harshly discouraged, though some of those sent to share the knowledge, began to enjoy their status as gods. This angered the One True God, and we were withdrawn from the earth, and from rendering further assistance. Much of the divine teachings were lost, or mis–relayed to the next generations, yet the words of the bible and the pyramids remained as living proof of our deeds, and of the One True God himself.

It seems however, that the Egyptians came to believe they could be transported to the stars to literally join Osiris, in spite of the fact they were taught that it was Jesus they would join with, not Osiris,' thought Emmesharra harshly. 'They were also taught that it would take many lifetimes on earth before they would be sent, or reincarnated to that stage. Apparently, they somehow felt that because over time their blood had been joined with the blood of those who came with me to assist them, that they could attain such a level by virtue of their birthright alone. Their priests concocted elaborate incantations that they convinced the Pharaohs would transport them directly to Osiris, and our hearts were saddened by their presumptions. As the Atlantians before them, they elevated themselves to positions of importance they had not truly attained in the grand scheme of the universe.'

'I wish the Library of Knowledge had never been found,' thought Lindsey almost morosely. Her thoughts were becoming sluggish, and she was trying hard to maintain concentration on all she had just heard.

Emmesharra raised his head and stared into Lindsey's face for several moments, 'I believe it is time for an infusion,' he stated, 'your thoughts are beginning to dim.'

They were back in the room they had left not long before, and the infusions had taken only a few moments. Lindsey's mind again felt sharp and clear. She could clearly sense the thoughts of the others, although Trent and Thad were a little more difficult to read, as though there was a mask over their mental impressions.

'The Elders have decided that you are to be sent to Alnitak in the Zeta Ori,' advised Emmesharra. 'It most resembles the atmosphere of Earth, and the inhabitants are much like yourselves, only about two hundred years more technologically advanced. The inhabitants of Alnitak will know nothing of who you really are, and that information is not to be shared with them for any reason.'

'And will Ankhesenamun accompany us?' asked Lindsey.

'She shall remain with me and go where I go,' replied Emmesharra. 'She shares the blood of the Sons of God, and will remain here indefinitely; at least until she dies again of old age. It was not allowed for me to bring her back from the dead for my own purposes, but you have brought her back for me, and for that I am eternally thankful.' Emmesharra made a slight bow of gratitude. 'There will be only three of you going, Lindsey. Just yourself, your husband and Glen, but Thad and Trent will go on to their own home planet to join their people, the Serandreals.'

'What?' three identical thoughts branched forward from the minds of Lindsey, Kevin, and Glen.

'It is true,' explained Emmesharra, 'they were not born of the Earth, but have chose to exist there for many years in order to spread knowledge to the people of your planet. It is the choice of the Serandreal to do so. Because of their extensive time on your planet however, they're essence has been diluted. They require an infusion of sorts, that can only be obtained on their home planet, the Planet of Sight,' he continued as he began to lead Lindsey, Glen and Kevin down a hallway, and back to the room containing the cylindrical chambers. 'The infusion you, yourselves have just received shall serve to allow your minds to remain open for the knowledge that will come to you during your journey.'

'Like the construction of the pyramids?' asked Lindsey, 'I thought I had dreamed that.'

'It was no dream,' supplied Emmesharra, 'it was a journey of knowledge, and you shall enjoy another one shortly, as will your husband and friend.'

With his last words and the wave of his hand, Emmesharra sealed the tubes closed around Lindsey and her companions. A few moments later, the top of a mammoth pyramid opened, and a massive craft in the shape of a scarab lifted slowly from it's yawning peak, before disappearing into the stars.

Lindsey stared down at the clear blue water, watching in fascination as the unfamiliar looking crafts darted about in and out of its smooth surface. As with her visions of the pyramids, she seemed to be removed from the events transpiring before her, though could view them from any conceivable angle with the simple thought to do so.

Nearby stood what at first appeared to be a coliseum built of pristine white stones, with a gilded roof. As her mind zoomed in for a closer look however, she could see that it was rather like a huge condominium, where people resided in separate, enclosed cubicles, each cubicle much larger than her own apartment, with individual rooms inside for sleeping and eating. The large structure was circular in shape, holding a courtyard within that had gardens with virtually every type of flower and vegetable known to man, and in the innermost center of the garden sprung a fresh water fountain.

These were the Atlantians, the people that spawned a million legends, and Lindsey was watching them first–hand, as they frolicked, played and worked in their perfect kingdom; their aquatic Camelot. From somewhere in the back of her mind, she wondered if Kevin and Glen were watching this scene through the same window in time as she was.

Sensing, rather than seeing the mammoth crystal formation beneath the island the city had been constructed upon, Lindsey was fully aware of the power emanating from that endless source of energy. Clearly, the Atlantians had found a way to harness that power, and to channel it in such a way as to operate their many transport crafts, and provide light and pumps for irrigation.

The fresh water fountain that sprang forth from the middle of the island ran directly up through the very center of the crystal itself, which produced a healing quality into the clear, pure, life-giving liquid.

Three fresh water canals, leading out to the ocean that surrounded the island ringed the breathtaking city. Separating the canals were rings of green, lush land and smaller, private dwellings, with yet more vegetables and flowers growing in abundance.

Just off the island, many of the Atlantians amused themselves with water races, wherein their crafts skipped along the surface of the water at unimaginable speeds. As though with x-ray vision, Lindsey could see far below the surface of the water to the sub-cities situated on the ocean floor below; cities very much like her own Atlantica.

Suddenly, Lindsey seemed to find herself being pulled back away from the vision of Atlantis, as other visions began to appear before her in rapid succession. She saw a race of human-like creatures living deep within the center of the Earth, the nucleus of the planet substituting as a sun for their hidden world. Tides pulled at their oceans, clearly the bottom of the Earth's unmeasured ocean depths. These beings though small in stature and with huge, luminous eyes had adapted to their underworld environment since the Revelation, meaning they had once appeared fully human.

The expelling of the waste from this subterranean world resulted in the active volcanoes on the surface of the Earth, the lights of this massive underworld city escaping through the thinnest area of the earth and resulting in the Aurora Borealis. The inhabitants resided in cities far more elaborate than any on Earth, and Lindsey sucked in her breath when she saw that they came and went in flying crafts from several points, to exit the planet itself and travel to the stars beyond.

In a flash, her vision disappeared, to be replaced by the massive, mystical slabs of Stonehenge. From her present position, Lindsey could see a gathering of peoples from many planets, many eons ago. It was an area of great power, of intense energy; energy that could be drawn from and channeled. Many meetings had taken place at this memorial site, many nations from many worlds had rendezvoused here, and there was sufficient energy to power the entire planet for a million years, if only the inhabitants of earth could tap it.

As though a vacuum had been turned on behind her, Lindsey felt herself being sucked backward into a spinning, whirling void.

'I hope you enjoyed your trip,' smiled Emmesharra, as the cylinder rose and Lindsey glided forward, 'we are arrived at our destination.'

Following Emmesharra down the now familiar corridor of the ship, Lindsey, Kevin and Glen were curious to see this interim-city that their host had spoken of.

'Behold the realm of Alnitak,' said Emmesharra telepathically, with a wave of his arm toward the windows of his craft.

Kevin expelled his breath with a low whistle. Second only to Ataneberu, it was the most beautiful sight they had ever beheld.

The city glowed brightly against the backdrop of early nightfall, and the single moon was much larger and brighter than that of the Earth. The cities were built on the ground, unlike the most modern cities on earth, and the air appeared crystal clear.

Twilight on the city below cast an aqua glow, as opposed to the pinkish glow from that of Earth, and Lindsey found herself wondering what the inhabitants of this planet would be like.

'Much like yourself,' stated Emmesharra in response to her thoughts, 'except that these people work for the good of their communities and not for their own enrichment, and are constantly in the pursuit of higher knowledge and religious wisdom. It is how we had hoped the Earth would have evolved by now, but unfortunately, it was not to be.'

'And a sad thing that is,' interjected Glen

'Come,' communicated Emmesharra, as he turned and glided back down the corridor, motioning for them to follow him, 'it is time for you to transcend.'

Chapter Nineteen

Alnitak, it turned out, was inhabited by a race of people as inwardly beautiful as the exterior beauty of the planet itself. Lindsey, Kevin and Glen were placed into a dwelling and left to introduce themselves to the residents, while not giving away their true purpose, or any other details that could cause unnecessary questions.

The people of this irresistible planet were incredibly intelligent, and far more advanced than the creatures of Earth. Instead of linking to others, or relying on computers for information, each individual wore a small device that slid down over one eye. It acted like a tiny computer would, relaying and sending information, problem solving and communicating. Each person performed a specific task for the greater good of the collective community, and everyone effectuated prayer several times a day.

Lindsey was amazed to note that while there were as many variations of the worshipping practice as there were nationalities on Earth, all prayed to the same God; the One True God, though there were other names they referred to Him as. It seemed so much simpler here than the religious history of the Earth. There was no religious persecution, no spilling of blood in the name of one god or one religion over another.

The people who inhabited Alnitak had only goodness in their hearts. There was no evil, hence no need for police, jails or prisons, there was no violence, no hatred, no greed, vanity, corruption or confusion. There was no need for world leaders, senators or governors.

'If only the people of Earth could live in such peace and harmony as this, what a wonderful, wonderful place it would be,' thought Lindsey sadly.

Alnitak was a perfect world indeed, and the three visitors almost didn't want to leave when Emmesharra appeared a week later with Ankhesenamun once again at his side.

'We must make for Serandreal,' stated Emmesharra, once they had transferred up to his scarab–shaped craft. 'A decision has been made.'

It took a moment for Lindsey to accustom herself to communicating without the spoken word again, but she managed to do so relatively quickly, 'What decision has been made?' she asked.

'All will be explained in due time,' said Emmesharra, leading them to the room containing the cylinders.

'I could find this place with my eyes closed,' joked Lindsey, as she, Kevin and Glen followed closely behind their host, attempting to get used to moving about without manipulating their legs and feet again.

Stepping into the tube, Lindsey drew in the familiar electrically charged air, and within seconds, was soaring over the Earth, or at least, how the Earth had once been. Slowly, she began to descend to the planet, and looking up, witnessed a plethora of ships coming from every corner of the sky, and landing all around her. From these ships, many different beings emerged and fanned out around the planet. Every culture, every civilization was taken under the wings of these great beings that had come from the sun and the stars.

Vast teachings and the wisdom of the ages were shared with the people of the Earth, many marriages took place between these sons of God and the sons of man, and many children borne of those unions.

These beings were angels indeed; guardian angels of a sort sent to nurture and husband the people of Earth, to teach them, to guide them, and to sow the seeds that brought about advancement and the reinventing of an entire civilization.

The feeling of being swept backward and away from the fascinating scene was becoming more and more familiar to Lindsey. Although not awake, she was fully aware of her place onboard the Annuaki ship, and knew that within a few moments, the tube would rise, and she would step out and see Emmesharra, Glen and her incredibly handsome husband.

The tube did not open, though Lindsey's eyes finally did. She turned her head slowly to the right, and saw that both Kevin and Glen were still ensconced in their own transparent tubes, feet dangling in mid air and eyes closed. Both men looked incredibly peaceful in their trance–like states, as their visions seemed to continue.

The remaining transportation/conditioning cylinders that lined the circular room were empty, and Lindsey waited for what seemed like an eternity.

Still, the tube did not open, and no one came. Lindsey was starting to worry; starting to feel trapped as she floated within the confines of the narrow, upright coffin.

'You know better,' smiled Emmesharra, as he walked into the room, Ankhesenamun again at his side. 'Some things simply take more time than others.'

Lindsey couldn't help noting the pure joy on Ankhesenamun's face since she and her Ra had been reunited. She said so little, and her thoughts seemed to be solely on the wonder of the man at her side, and the depth of her own love for him.

Emmesharra's thoughts interrupted Lindsey's own, and when she looked into his face, his broad grin told her that he knew her mind, and was as pleased by Ankhesenamun's happiness as she was.

'There are people here who I wish for you to meet,' stated Emmesharra, 'but this meeting must take place here, with you as you are.'

'I cannot leave the tube?' communicated Lindsey.

'Not this time,' returned her host. 'The Serandreal Council have reached a decision after much communication and prayer, and will arrive momentarily to begin the time–cycle exchange.'

'Time cycle exchange?' Lindsey's mind searched for the meaning of Emmesharra's words, but none seemed to be forthcoming.

'The Serandreals have the ability to alter physical reality through a combination of their own will, and divine assistance, which enables them to cut through the time–space continuum, and to place people or objects in specific periods of time. The process itself is one that cannot be explained by either word or thought,' explained Emmesharra, 'but the results can be, so to speak, or think,' he included with a smile.

'Please think it for me then,' requested Lindsey. 'I truly want to know what is happening.'

'The council has agreed that the destruction upon the Earth was the direct result of the clone, Tutankhamun's treachery, not of man's,' explained Emmesharra. 'Though it was man's meddling with God's own creations that lead to the subsequent annihilation of a planet itself. On the other hand,' he smiled warmly, 'that meddling also brought Ankhesenamun back to me, and our love is legendary, even among the Serandreals…this is looked upon well, though the interference of man into the works of God is seen as an abomination. Though the president of your United States was prepared to lie to and deceive us, this in and of itself would not have resulted in the total destruction of Earth.'

'But what does this decision mean to me, to us?' asked Lindsey, with a glance toward the cylinders containing the upright forms of her husband and Glen.

'There is a chance that amends can be made Lindsey,' communicated Emmesharra seriously. 'But the responsibility will lie solely upon you.'

'Me?' was Lindsey's startled thought. 'How can I possibly make amends for the destruction of an entire planet?'

'The council is prepared to send you back,' explained Emmesharra. 'To a time before the Library was discovered. It will be up to you to see to it that it remains undiscovered.'

'But the discovery of the library was my father's life's work,' Lindsey's thoughts were hard. 'I could never convince him to set his search aside.'

'It is the only way.'

'Why can we not be sent back to just before Tutankhamun left the military compound and called forth the Utukki? We could stop him from calling them.' Lindsey could feel the desperation setting in. She simply couldn't be responsible for changing all that had happened.

Emmesharra sighed, 'But knowledge of the Great Library still existed, yet clearly, the people of Earth were neither prepared for, nor ready to receive the wisdom of the ages. This is the only way,' he finished firmly.

'If the library is not found, I will never go to IBAT, never meet Kevin, never marry him, or have his child.' Lindsey's heart began to ache; yet it also told her that these were selfish thoughts indeed, when an entire world full of people had been consumed by a race of monsters.

'I know how difficult this will be for you, Lindsey.' Emmesharra's own mind flashed to the time he had lost his beloved Ankhesenamun, and he felt a momentary physical pain at the memory.

'How will I make my father believe me?' asked Lindsey through the tears in her eyes and the lump in her throat that threatened to choke her. 'If I tell him all that has happened to me, he'll think I've gone crazy. Even I wouldn't believe such a thing.'

'You can't tell him.' Emmesharra shook his head slowly from side to side, 'It is forbidden for you to do so. You must find a way on your own.'

'But will I remember all this?' asked Lindsey, her thoughts becoming heavy.

'Only for a short time, and then the memories will fade away entirely, just as your ability to focus and function on Ataneberu did after a awhile, though there will be no infusion for you.'

'How long?' questioned Lindsey. 'How long will I remember?' It was getting harder and harder to think; to comprehend Emmesharra's mental communication.

'A week, maybe two, there is no real way of knowing, each person is different.'

'This has been done before?' asked Lindsey, incredulously.

Emmesharra smiled and stepped aside at the very moment several wizened old men entered the room. Their white robes were very plain and even threadbare in some places, and it seemed that they all had heavy, white beards.

Encircling the cylinder that contained Lindsey, the Serandreal council members joined hands and bowed their heads. Though the men spoke in low tones, their words seemed to reverberate in Lindsey's head, as though many people were speaking the same words out loud, over, and over again. Her thoughts became heavier, and she forced her head upright to take one last look at her beloved Kevin, her husband, and the man she loved to the depths of her soul, but would never see again.

Lindsey closed her eyes, tears rolling down her cheeks, as the grievous losses she had endured all came back to her at once; her father, her mother, her baby and now her husband. It was all too much for anyone to bear.

Blackness began to surround Lindsey's still form, only to be immediately replaced by an unimaginable searing brightness...and the tears continued to flow.

There was a most obnoxious sound coming from somewhere nearby, making Lindsey nearly want to scream. She buried her head deeper into the lumpy pillow; the hard neoprene–like cot beneath her was almost as unbearable as the cacophony of wailing that would not stop.

'Lumpy Pillow...' Lindsey tried to open her eyes, but they felt like they'd been weighted down with lead. 'Hard mattress?' Lindsey forced her eyes open, and sucked in her breath when she realized she was at that very moment in her small cottage just outside of Cairo.

Lindsey fairly leapt off the cot, and looking down at her own body, attired neck to foot in her dirt covered desert garb, sucked in her breath. She rubbed her eyes profusely, certain that this could not be real.

For a moment, a sweeping wave of dizziness nearly caused an already dazed Lindsey to sit back down. Placing both hands on her temples, she stood unsteadily on the dirt floor of the small, limestone hut, waiting to catch her bearings.

'Oh dear God,' she thought, 'this can't have been a dream.' Glancing down at the lumpy pillow she had been lying on only moments earlier, Lindsey realized that she had been sleeping on her travel bag, a bag now stained and wet from what looked to have been a million tears. She'd always refused to cart around a portable airbed here in the desert.

'The desert!' her mind screamed. 'What was the date?' Looking around at the walls of the tiny room, there was no indication of either the date or the time.

The raucous chiming sounded again, and Lindsey realized it was coming from a portable linking panel she kept on the floor near the bed.

Rushing to the machine, Lindsey bent down and placed her index finger on the panel. Her father's face appeared on the small screen before her, grinning broadly, "I thought I said you looked like you needed to rest a few hours. I didn't realize you were going to retire for the rest of the day and night." His last words were punctuated with laughter.

Lindsey choked back a sob. She hadn't seen her father for more than ten years, and now here he was alive, talking, laughing, "Oh, Daddy," Lindsey breathed. "It's so good to see you."

"What do you mean, it's so good to see me?" asked her father. "We've been together every day for more than a week straight."

Lindsey's mind was spinning, as she grasped for the right words, "I just, uh," she stammered, "I just love being with you all the time."

"Well, that's why you're my girl," her father grinned broadly. "We're going to do some digging near the Sphinx. I think we might be on to something there."

Lindsey's eyes darted for the first time to the end of the control pad of her link–panel, noting the date, June twenty–first, twenty–two forty, "Oh my God!" she exclaimed with a start. Her mind scrambled back to the day her father found the secret entrance at the base of the Sphinx. It was today!

"Lindsey, honey," said her father, a slight frown marring his forehead. "Are you alright my dear, is something wrong?" Lowell Larimer's head moved from side–to–side, as though trying to look around his daughter to see if there was anyone else in the room.

"No, Daddy," explained Lindsey, as light–heartedly as she could. "I just realized how late it was, that's all. I didn't mean to sleep for so long." A sudden, unbidden thought of Kevin swept through her mind, and Lindsey wanted to double over from the pain of losing him.

"Why is your face all streaked up like that, honey?" asked her father. "Have you been crying?"

"Oh, no Daddy," said Lindsey quietly. "I was just starting to wash my face."

"Well, that must be why you didn't answer me a moment ago," smiled her father. "You finish up and come join me. I'll see you in a few minutes."

The screen went blank, and Lindsey went white. She had thought for some strange reason that she should have been allowed more time in which to complete this impossible task.

Unrolling her travel bag, Lindsey withdrew her cleaning kit, and opening the black case, placed first her face and then her hands into the aperture, removing all vestiges of dirt and grime from her skin in a matter of moments. Not that it mattered really, Lindsey knew she'd be filthy again in no time at all.

The transport van had barely stopped, when Lindsey whisked open the door and fairly flew out and into her father's arms.

"Why Lindsey Marie, I can't imagine what's gotten into you today," said her father with a grin, as he held his beloved only child close to his chest. "I don't think I've ever seen you quite so affectionate, but I'm not complaining, mind you." Lowell chuckled deep in his throat. He'd never thought it possible to love anyone as much as he loved his daughter.

"I can't help it if I still haven't outgrown my love for my Daddy," Lindsey smiled up at her father "You're my bestest guy, remember?" If she could have gotten away with standing there at the base of the Giza Plateau with her father's arms around her forever, Lindsey would have done so.

"Well, I have some very exciting news for you," beamed Lowell. "One of our workers discovered a discolored area at the base of the Sphinx, just below the sand–line. This might just be what we've been looking for!"

Lindsey forced a smile, what was she supposed to say? 'No,' we shouldn't dig there'…he'd never understand such a thing.

Lowell turned to the dozen or so workers awaiting instructions, "To the Sphinx!" he announced for all to hear.

'This is madness,' thought Lindsey, as she sat beside her beaming father in one of the small, desert–roving, transport van's he employed for the specific purpose of traveling from one area of interest to another. 'I'm sitting here doing nothing whatsoever, when my very purpose was to stop this from happening.'

In a flash of brilliance, Lindsey formed a daring idea, and as the transport van began to lower at the base of the Sphinx, Lindsey opened the door and jumped out, hitting the hard sand below with a thud.

"Lindsey!" shouted her father, as the transport touched down fully, and he leapt out with the agility of a man half his age, "Lindsey, what were you thinking? Are you alright?" Lowell didn't stop to await the others as he visually examined his daughter's prone figure, and noted the odd way her right leg seemed to be twisted behind her. Thank God she was breathing, though her pulse was beating quite fast.

The pain was incredible, and Lindsey found that she didn't want to open her eyes; didn't want to face the fact that she'd broken her leg. It felt like a white–hot knife was being driven into her calf, and she clenched her teeth against the intensity of the agony it was causing her.

"Lindsey," pressed her father, "can you talk to me, honey?"

"Oh, Daddy," choked out Lowell's daughter, "it hurts so bad, please make it stop."

At that moment, Dr. Lowell Latimer felt more helpless than he had in his entire life. Had it been within his power to do so, he would take Lindsey's pain and suffered it himself, but that was not within his power. "Let's get her to Cairo immediately!" he barked.

Within minutes, Lindsey was received at hospital emergency unit, and administered medication to eliminate the pain, and send her into a deep sleep while her leg was set and the bone chemically mended. The entire treatment and healing process took less than half an hour, and the attractive Egyptian doctor pronounced Lindsey to be 'as good as new.' Her heart sank several inches.

"Dad?" Lindsey began, as they walked down the hospital steps and toward the waiting transport van. "Can we not do anymore searching today?"

"Why, Little Miss Lindsey," asked her father, with a smile. "Are you feeling unwell from your dive?"

"It's not that, Dad," returned Lindsey with a slight smile of her own, at her father's use of his pet name for her. "It's just that I would very much like to sit down and spend some quality time with you. We haven't really talked in awhile."

"Honey, we talk constantly," replied her father.

"But I mean talk, talk, you know," answered Lindsey, her own brow furrowed slightly, "really talk."

Lowell shook his head, this just didn't seem like Lindsey at all. She hadn't been the same since she'd taken a nap that afternoon, and he'd only suggested it because he thought she'd looked tired, and had perhaps been exposed to the outside air for too long. For some reason, his little girl just wasn't herself today, and Lowell resolved that if she felt the need to talk, they would talk until the sun came up.

"If it's important to you to spend some time talking with your old pops, then it's important to me too," smiled Lowell, as he helped his daughter into the awaiting transport, and instructed the driver to return them to his hut near Lindsey's own. He vowed to keep an active vigil on his curiously behaving offspring.

"Thank you so much for understanding, Dad," said Lindsey, as she snuggled up as close as she could to her father. Being so close to him after having to live with the untimely death of her mentor, made Lindsey feel like a child again. She just couldn't seem to get close enough to this man, who had been the center of her world from the moment of her birth, yet her mind screamed out that she would lose him again, if she didn't think of a plan posthaste.

Lowell put his arm around his daughter and held her close, as the transport lifted smoothly from the ground and ascended several feet, before heading in the direction of the Giza Plateau.

Lindsey's mind whirled with a thousand questions that she could ask no one. If she convinced her father not to search for the fabled library any further, would he live to a ripe old age? Could she truly ever forget her life and experiences with Kevin, Trent, Thad, Ankhesenamun, and Atlantica? Emmesharra had said it would be a week or two before all memory of what had transpired before her return to this time would vanish from her mind completely, yet was it honestly possible to forget so much? What would her life be like without Kevin? Would she marry someone else? And what if she couldn't convince her father to set aside his lifelong quest? Would she be relegated to reliving the entire experience over again? If so, what then would be the outcome? What would happen to Kevin and Glen in the meantime? Would she spend the rest of eternity coming back to convince her father to end his search? Lindsey's head began to ache, there were far too many questions, and no answers for any of them. The one and only thing that she was sure of at that moment, was that she had a mission to accomplish, and she couldn't allow herself to fail.

"Have you been missing your mother, Honey?" asked Lowell solicitously, as the transport landed lightly within a few feet of his temporary desert abode.

Lindsey thought of her mother's smiling face the last time she'd seen her. It had been at Sal's Restaurant just before she, Kevin and Glen had left for Egypt. Olivia had been so happy, almost glowing with her newfound love for Professor Garreth St. Germaine. A momentary pang of guilt reared its ugly head as Lindsey thought of her father, who was even now pulling two small chairs together for them near a small table.

The mental picture of Kevin, her mother, Professor St. Germaine and Glen all sitting together, enjoying their meals and one another's' company, flashed through Lindsey's mind, leaving a lump in the back of her throat. She wondered if she wouldn't feel a good deal better if she were able to just sit down and cry for an hour or two. Unfortunately, time was not on her side, and the luxury of a good cry simply wasn't an option. "I do miss Mom terribly, Daddy," Lindsey replied, as she settled herself in one of the ancient, wooden chairs. "Could we go back home and spend some time with her?" she asked lamely.

"Go home?" asked her father incredulously. "To Colorado? Honey, why in the world would we want to do such a thing when we're so very close to achieving our life's work? I just know we're about to succeed, I have a feeling in my bones."

"But Dad, we have to stop the search!" Lindsey had blurted out the words before she'd realized her brain had formed them.

"What?" exclaimed Lowell, a look of shock crossing his otherwise distinguished features. "What do you mean stop the search, Lindsey Marie? I've been searching for the library all my life, why in the world would I want to stop now?"

What could she say? Lindsey's mind grasped for an explanation, an elaborate lie, something, anything, "We just have to, Dad," was her weak reply.

"Lindsey," said her father gently, as he took the chair opposite her own and handed her a small glass of his cherished cognac. "I don't know what has gotten into you, but maybe you'll feel better if you drink this."

Lindsey took the proffered drink, "Thank you, Dad," she responded. "But I think it's going to take a little more than this to make me feel better. Another sharp memory of Kevin making love to her in the soft warmth of their bed in Atlantica, flashed through her mind and Lindsey could not control the sob that sounded in her throat.

"Lindsey, I am truly at a loss," said her worried father. "You were fine this morning, and every bit as excited about this dig as I have been. What in the world happened between then and now to change everything so much?" Lowell leaned forward in his chair, wishing above all else that he could read his daughter's mind.

"I can't explain it Dad," replied Lindsey slowly, her head downcast, the glass of cognac clasped in her hands all but forgotten. "I can't tell you why. I can only beg you to give up this search now and forget about it for all time."

Lowell rose and paced the room slowly, rubbing the back of his neck as though it would somehow help him to understand why his daughter had changed so very much in the course of only a few hours. "Lindsey," he said, turning slowly to face his daughter. "Do you know what you're asking me to do? Do you have any idea how much of my life is tied up in this pursuit? I can't just walk away from it and forget all the years of searching, seeking and working for the very day when I would make the greatest discovery of all time. What about the grants I've received for this project, all the money that's been poured into the research alone?" Lowell came to stand before his daughter and then bent down to meet her eyes; "I wanted you to be at my side when that day came, Lindsey. I wanted you to share in it with me, because I thought that's what you wanted too, I thought it meant as much to you as it does to me."

There were tears beginning to form in her father's eyes. She had never seen him cry in his entire life, and now he stood before her, suddenly looking incredibly old and haggard. "I'm so very sorry Daddy," Lindsey sobbed. "Please don't hate me for this, it's just something I know we can't allow ourselves to succeed in. God is my witness in that I would never do or say anything to hurt you, but please, please, Daddy, grant me this, and stop the search now." Lindsey could hardly speak through her sobs, as the tears rolled unchecked down her flushed cheeks.

His daughter's tears were more than he could bear, and Lowell enfolded Lindsey in his arms and rocked her back and forth. "I'll offer you this, Lindsey," he said into her soft hair through his own tears. "We'll go back to Colorado for one month and spend some time with your mother. We'll talk about it and think about it, and make a decision at that time."

'A week, maybe two,' was what Emmesharra had told her, when she asked how long she would remember. Surely, she would completely forget everything at the end of a full month! What if all knowledge of the outcome was erased from her memory and she stood by her father's side when he discovered the library? But this was a start, and it was more than she had anticipated, Lindsey vowed that she would write down her entire experience in vivid detail as soon as they arrived home in Colorado, so she wouldn't forget, couldn't forget. The thought had no sooner manifested, than another part of her mind seemed to warn her that she needed to forget…that she couldn't allow herself not to forget. Somehow Lindsey knew that she couldn't go through the rest of her life living in the shadow of what might have been, couldn't compare every man she met to the paragon of perfection that she had found in Kevin. It hurt to think of forgetting it all, hurt deeply, but somewhere deep inside her heart, Lindsey knew that she had to let go and start over fresh. Resigning herself to the dictates of her conscience, and resolving to see to it by whatever means were available to her that the library remained undiscovered.

"I love you so much Daddy, there aren't any words for how much," she blurted.

"And I love you too, Little Miss Lindsey, with all my heart." Lowell stood and walked a few steps to his travel bag. Opening the brown satchel, he began to place his miscellaneous belongings inside. "Perhaps you should link to your mother and let her know we're on our way home."

He didn't want to go and Lindsey knew it. The pain she had caused her beloved father stabbed sharply at her own heart, and there was nothing she could do about it. Lindsey lifted the glass to her lips and drained the contents, feeling an immediate warmth rise up from the pit of her stomach. Glancing across to her father, his back to her, shoulders slumped as he packed his few belongings, she knew that she had hurt him deeply. Her father, who had always been there for her, loved her, encouraged her, had been deeply disappointed and discouraged by her words. Lindsey had hurt the one person that had been her strength, her security, her teacher, and her mentor since first she had drawn breath, and in doing so, she had nearly destroyed herself.

It was with a heavy heart that Lindsey pressed the control panel on the link machine, and then nearly burst into tears again when her mother's smiling face appeared on the small screen.

"Is everything alright Lindsey?" she asked curiously. "You look like you've been crying, dear."

"I, uh, fell earlier and broke my leg," replied Lindsey, for lack of any other excuse. "But Dad got me to the hospital, and I'm all better now. I, uh," she stammered, "Dad wanted me to let you know that we're going to come home for awhile."

"You haven't reached a dead–end have you, Honey?" asked Olivia with a slight frown. "Your father was so sure you were about to make the great discovery any day now."

"No, it's not that Mom," replied Lindsey, feeling more guilt than anything for the hurt she had caused her father, and the deception she was now offering her mother. "We just miss you and want to come home and spend some quality family time."

"Well Honey," responded Olivia, "I can't think of anything I'd like more, it just seems an awkward time to want to come home. I've never known your father to pick up and leave in the middle of a dig before."

"I know, Mom," Lindsey replied, unable to meet her mother's eyes on the monitor. "We just miss you, that's all."

Lindsey couldn't shake the overwhelming depression that had settled over her like her own dark cloud. She could see the Sphinx in the distance through the one virtual–panel in her father's small hut, and her heart felt heavy at the knowledge that she and she alone was pulling her father away from the beckoning, ancient monument.

"Lindsey," said her father suddenly, as though a revelation had suddenly struck him, "have you been approached by anyone today about our research?"

Lindsey searched for an answer, but her mind betrayed her, "Uh, what do you mean, Dad?"

Lowell strode the few paces to where his daughter stood, and stared hard into her still tear filled blue eyes. "I haven't said anything until now because I didn't want to frighten you," said her father almost sternly. "But the Russians suspect we might be onto something, and we've been concerned lately about the possibility of their having sent agents or spies to monitor our progress. You were fine until you took your nap this afternoon," he said seriously. "Did anyone approach you, talk to you?"

Lindsey took a deep breath before answering. Could this be the answer to her dilemma? Did she have what it took to look her father square in the eye and lie through her teeth, when she'd never lied to him in her entire life? "Yes, Daddy, there was a man that came to see me today."

"A man!" exclaimed her father; his eyebrows shooting up to nearly meet his hairline. "What kind of a man? What did he say?" Lowell took both his daughters' hands in his own, searching for the answer to his questions in own worried blue eyes.

Lindsey couldn't quite meet his eyes, "He had an accent Dad, but I couldn't quite place my finger on what nationality he was."

"An accent you say," exclaimed Lowell, the pain Lindsey had caused on his face was quickly giving way to a look of open shock. "What did he say to you Honey? It's important that you tell me."

Again searching her mind for an answer and finding herself severely lacking, Lindsey blurted out the first thing that came to mind, "He said he knew what we were looking for, and that if we didn't stop our search immediately, he'd do something bad to me."

"Lindsey!" her father fairly shouted, and then looking around the room as though the man in question might step out of the shadows, he lowered his voice to a near whisper. "That's why it took you so long to answer my link this morning isn't it? And why you looked like you'd been crying when you finally did answer." Lowell didn't give Lindsey the time to respond, as his face took on the expression of one who has just seen the proverbial light bulb of understanding click on.

Lindsey could do nothing but nod, the depth of her lies making her feel sick to her stomach, but the change in her father's demeanor at this startling new information made it all quite worth her discomfort. "I was afraid to tell you, Father," she continued in her best frightened–little–girl voice. "I know how much this discovery means to you, and I didn't want you to stop it on my account," the words were becoming easier now, the story more clear, even the phantom Russian spy began to take physical shape in her mind. "But when we got close to the Sphinx today, I started remembering what he said, and I guess I got cold feet."

"Cold feet indeed!" exclaimed her father, before remembering to resort to his low, conspiratorial voice. "The bastard threatened your life Lindsey, do you honestly think anything on this earth is more important to me than your life?" Lowell gave his daughter no time to respond, "We shall leave immediately. I'll link to the team this very moment and have someone sent to your room to pick up your belongings. I'm not letting you out of my sight for a moment."

Lindsey almost wanted to smile her delight. Her father was giving up the project out of fear; not the hurt caused by his daughter. There was no hurt look on his face now whatsoever, just intense worry, and that was so much better. Still, Lindsey knew she'd eventually forget all that had lead up to this point, forget Kevin, Glen, IBAT, all of it. She wondered as her father led her toward the door and out to the awaiting transport just how her new future would compare to the last one.

"I'll send word to the investors that the search brought no success and we are ending our quest," said Lowell, when he and his daughter were safely ensconced within the transport van and on their way back to Colorado. "It is a difficult thing to walk away from, Lindsey, but I could never jeopardize you, not for all the discoveries in the world. Besides," he added, "I hear their unearthing some really amazing mummies and artifacts in the Takla Makan Desert, of all places. Who knows," he concluded with a smile, as he sat comfortably next to his beloved daughter, "maybe you and I will make the discovery of a life–time there?"

"Maybe we will, Pop," replied Lindsey, feeling as though a thousand pounds had just been lifted from her tired shoulders. "Maybe we will."

Epilogue

June 7, 2250

"So what do you think?" asked Lindsey excitedly. "Why don't you two stay the night before heading back to Colorado, and we can make a night of it, have some drinks to celebrate?"

Lindsey's heart was light at the thought of the bright and exciting future that now lay before her. She still couldn't believe that a renowned institution such as IBAT would choose her, specifically, to assist in the study of the relics she and her father had unearthed in the Takla Makan Desert.

When the call had come from a Professor St. Germaine, offering Lindsey a position on the research team at IBAT, she had been beside herself with unparalleled joy. She was even further taken aback when the professor explained that two reclusive, yet very wealthy investors had taken an interest in the objects discovered by her and her father, and had requested that Lindsey, specifically, be called upon to assist in the research. Additional prompting on her part revealed that these investors were the same two, now quite famous men that had developed the plans for the underwater cities that were even now being constructed.

For over a period of eight years, they had discovered one ancient treasure after another, some of them miles apart, others side–by–side. It would be a true privilege indeed to assist some of the best scientists available attempt to fully validate the antiquities …especially the unexpected find of the Princess Ankhesenamun's mummy so incredibly far from where it should have been, not to mention the curious amulet buried with her.

"Well, I think that's a lovely idea," proclaimed Olivia. "We haven't gone out in ages on end, I'd love to go."

"And who knows," grinned Lowell, "maybe you'll meet a nice young doctor at IBAT, and we'll have even more to celebrate!"

"Oh Daddy," laughed Lindsey in return, "is that all you think about?"

"Well, your mother and I aren't getting any younger, Little

Miss Lindsey," replied her smiling father, placing an arm around his wife and hugging her to him. "We wouldn't mind the pitter–patter of little grandchild feet."

"Gosh, Dad," said Lindsey, giving her dad a playful poke in the stomach, "don't sugar coat it like that, just tell me right out how you really feel."

Lindsey supposed she did harbor a certain amount of guilt for not having settled into marriage and a family by now. But after so many exhausting years spent with her father, attempting to identify every piece he unearthed, and the intense campaigning she had done for President Emmett Hines, there hadn't been much time left over to search for 'Mr. Right.'

Now an 'old maid' of thirty–five, Lindsey had to admit that she truly was beginning to feel the urge toward motherhood, and though women had been giving birth and raising children as single parents for centuries, she had to admit even to herself, that she wanted the entire package.

Her work had been worth the sacrifice of a husband and family though. And while she couldn't explain to this day why she had felt the necessity of assisting in President Hines's campaign with such a passion, having never possessed a political bone in her body, she was glad she had done so. Hines was a fair and just president, and had certainly kept his campaign promises. All in all, it was time well spent.

The sky–cab had taken them directly to a lovely restaurant/lounge called 'Sal's,' with a quaint, yet fascinating display of Italian antiques and memorabilia. Lindsey had never been there in her life, had never even been in this city, yet Sal's seemed oddly familiar, as she and her parents entered the lounge area, and took three vacant stools at the bar. Had they not eaten before they'd left her new condo, Lindsey would have enjoyed sampling some of the fine Italian cuisine advertised out front, and made a mental note to do so sometime soon.

"We're going to miss you, Honey," said Lowell, sitting on his daughter's left, as he ordered their drinks. "We've been pretty much together for as long as I can remember. It'll be hard for your mom and I to go back to Colorado without you."

"I know, Pops," returned Lindsey, already missing her parents, but at the same time, looking forward to this new and exciting life that would undoubtedly come with the new and exciting job she would start first thing in the morning. "But you can link to me whenever you like, and I'll expect you to come and visit often."

"You'll be lucky if your father doesn't start shopping for a home here the first week we return to Colorado," chuckled Olivia. "I know your father, and he won't give you the opportunity to miss him for too long."

"Especially if there's any chance of pitter–patter's on the horizon," returned Lowell with a broad grin.

"You are incorrigible," laughed Lindsey, "just as incorrigible as they come."

"What can I get for you gentlemen?" asked the pretty, blond bartender.

No response. Kevin's head was turned slightly to the left and away from Glen...his eyes focused on something Glen could not see from his present position.

"Excuse me sir," the bartender said, attempting to get Kevin's attention.

"Uh, oh, I'm sorry, do forgive me, Pretty Lady. How about a couple of Lunar Lights to start us off?"

"Ah, I see what has you so captivated there Mister Kevin," laughed Glen. "She's a pretty one indeed. Maybe you should try talking to her, eh?"

Kevin glanced again to the beautiful brunette sitting a few stools away, between an older couple. The woman to her right was just blocking his view, so that he could only catch a glimpse of the brunette when the woman moved forward to sip her drink. For a moment, the usually confident Kevin Sanders faltered in indecision.

"Here are your drinks, Sir," said the smiling bartender, pushing her breasts forward a little more than necessary, as she took the proffered credit chip, and then frowning when Kevin failed to notice her overture.

"Ah, Lunar Lights, my favorite," sounded a soft, male voice from behind Glen.

Kevin looked up to see an olive-skinned, mustachioed gentlemen taking the vacant seat on Glen's right, "Raelene," he addressed the bartender by name, "would you mind bringing me one of these as well." The man nodded, indicating the drinks the young woman had just placed in front of Kevin and Glen.

"You got it, Sal," she smiled in return.

Kevin mouthed the name silently, "You wouldn't be the illusive Sal that owns this place, would you?"

"One in the same," replied the restaurateur.

It didn't take long for Kevin to realize that Glen was quite enamored of the charming Sal, and clearly, the feeling was mutual. Kevin took a long sip of his drink, and glanced over again at the woman to his left. The older woman sat forward at just that moment, and Lindsey looked up to meet Kevin's eyes briefly, before turning back to the man on her left and continuing their conversation.

'My God,' thought Kevin, 'she's got the most beautiful eyes I've ever seen on a woman in my life.' He simply had to talk to her, to at least get a closer look, but he knew in that instant, as though struck with an epiphany, that he would have to leave any arrogance or cockiness at the bar stool.

Glen and his newfound friend were deeply engaged in conversation, and from what Kevin could hear of it, had already scheduled a date. He was pleased to see his friend in such obvious good spirits, since he normally spent way too many hours involved in his work at the lab. At this moment, it didn't seem that Glen would miss him, were he to wander over and say hello to the brunette.

Lowell was the first to notice the tall, blond man that had just walked over and now stood a foot or so behind his daughter. Stopping the conversation mid-sentence, Lowell gently nudged his daughter.

"Uh," stammered Kevin, uncharacteristically nervous, "I'm sorry to interrupt your conversation, but I 'um" he suddenly felt like a high school boy on prom night. "I'm Kevin Sanders. Doctor Kevin Sanders," he added as though in afterthought. "I was wondering if I might buy this young lady a drink."

"A Doctor, you say?" questioned Lowell. "What a coincidence, our daughter Lindsey here is a doctor as well."

"Yes," interjected Olivia, "and she's going to start work here in town at IBAT tomorrow, are you familiar with the facility?"

Kevin's mood lightened incredibly, "Well, yes, as a matter of fact, I've worked there for some years now, and so does my friend, Glen," he included, with a nod toward the older man, who was at that moment laughing at some witticism with his new friend, Sal.

Lindsey turned fully around on her stool and smiled up at the incredibly handsome man, with the deep, green eyes standing before her. Somewhere from deep inside, she felt an odd, unexplained yearning welling up within her.

"Would you like to dance?" asked Kevin, almost holding his breath for her answer.

"I'd love to," replied Lindsey with a smile, as she rose from her chair and took the hand he offered, feeling a tingling in her fingers when her flesh touched his.

Lowell grinned broadly at his wife, as his daughter and the tall, clean-cut young doctor made their way toward the dance floor, "I can almost hear that pitter–patter now, Olivia."

His wife smiled back, suddenly feeling much better about losing her daughter to this new career move, and to whatever the future held. "You know what, Lowell?" she winked, "I can almost hear them too."